AN OCEAN OF STARS

IMOGEN MARTIN

Storm

PUBLISHING

Ebook ISBN: 978-1-80508-997-1
Paperback ISBN: 978-1-83700-000-5

Cover design: Emma Rogers
Cover images: Getty Images, Shutterstock

Published by Storm Publishing.
For further information, visit:
www.stormpublishing.co

ALSO BY IMOGEN MARTIN

Under a Gilded Sky
To the Wild Horizon
The Mountains Between Us

For my wonderful brother David—your unfailing optimism keeps our family together.

And to all the Edinburgh Martins, for the many years of festivals, birthday celebrations (mine!) and Hogmanays.

PART ONE

ONE

BOSTON, MASSACHUSETTS. MAY 1879

"Dr. McLennan? Would you be Dr. McLennan?"

Douglas halted and eased his leather cases onto the pier as he emerged from the customs house and into the early evening air. He scrutinized the elderly man who was dressed in black from his felt bowler hat to his shoes and wringing his liver-spotted hands.

"Aye," he replied. "That's me."

"At last. I must have enquired of half the men on your ship." The man seemed agitated.

Douglas wasn't sure why, but he felt an apology was required. "Immigration papers took some time to complete." He picked up a case in each hand. "And you are..."

"Merriman. Come to collect you on behalf of the Van Bergens." The man reached out his hand to take a piece of luggage.

As he did so, Douglas noticed a slight curvature of the spine and saw the old man grimace. "I can manage," he said with a firm nod, his fingers curling tighter round the handles.

Merriman gave a shrug. "As you wish. The carriage is on the street." He turned and set off down the pier.

"Wait." Douglas hesitated and a group of men pushed past him. He called louder over the clamor of ships' engines and sailors yelling at porters. "The rest of my luggage... I need to wait for it to be unloaded."

Merriman looked back. "One of our boys will collect it. Please hurry along, now, Dr. McLennan. My instructions are to get you to the hospital urgently." He started walking away once more.

Douglas dodged between men until he caught up. "The hospital? They cannae be expecting me *now*? I need to find my lodgings. Get some sleep."

"Can't be helped, Dr. McLennan. There's some sort of emergency."

Douglas liked sailing, but even so, he was worn out after the two-week Atlantic crossing and had been looking forward to Mrs. Angellotti's lodging house, which, the advertisement promised, had hot baths, homemade Italian food, and beds free of bugs. But it seemed it wasn't to be. He adjusted his hat and hurried after the man. Thankfully, one case held his medical equipment.

He was glad to find the carriage was comfortable. The black lacquered wood shone, the springs were generous and the leather seat upholstered. Merriman climbed up next to the coachman, leaving Douglas alone with his thoughts as the vehicle trundled its way from the harbor into the heart of Boston.

Was this how the Pilgrim Fathers felt, arriving in a new land? Aye, they were probably just as weary and hungry. Like them, New England was a chance for Douglas to make a new life, to put the mistakes of the past behind him.

He leaned back and smoothed his mustache as he looked out of the window. Dusk was falling, but he could see that the buildings looked fine in the lamplight. He'd lived in a number of cities: grown up in Dundee, studied in Edinburgh, worked in London. These American buildings were newer, taller, and more uniform than he was used to.

The carriage jolted to a stop and Douglas realized he'd fallen asleep. His bones ached as he climbed down to the sidewalk on a street of terraced buildings. He bristled at the high-handed behavior of the Van Bergens, expecting him to work when he had barely arrived. He hoped it wasn't a sign of difficult times ahead; he would need to put his foot down right at the beginning.

Merriman handed him his two bags and Douglas looked up at the building. In truth, it was much smaller than he had expected, given the enthusiastic recommendation from his old tutor Professor Moncrieff. Weren't the Van Bergens one of the richest families in the United States? This looked more like a domestic house: servants' quarters at street level, steep stone steps to the first floor and then three stories above. It was built of black brick with regular sash windows.

Douglas followed Merriman up the steps to the oak door, beside which was a small brass plate that read VAN BERGEN WOMEN'S HOSPITAL.

Merriman knocked and almost immediately the door was swung open by a short woman in an aproned uniform.

Merriman nodded towards him. "Dr. McLennan."

"Thank the Lord," the woman replied. "Come on in."

Douglas stepped into a lobby lit by two gas lamps. Merriman tapped his hat and hurried off into the dark.

The woman closed the door. "I'm Mrs. Hale, matron of the hospital. Follow me."

There was a strong noxious smell. Douglas tucked his medical bag under his arm so he could pull a handkerchief from his pocket to cover his mouth.

"The drains," Mrs. Hale said. "The building can't cope with the number of occupants: eighteen beds. Isn't usually this bad, though."

"Dinnae fash. I've known worse."

He followed her up the steep steps and around the landing, now sure the hospital was a converted home. Some doors were open to bedrooms and he could see bedsteads packed together. He heard a woman's moans emanating from behind one closed door and a male voice shouted out, "Mrs. Hale?"

"I'll be there in a moment," she called back.

Douglas hesitated at the door. "Look, is there something I could do to help that woman?"

The matron shook her head and hurried on. "I need you upstairs." They went up a further flight. "I've a woman who's just come in and I'm not sure what's wrong. Dr. Storer is finishing up with that patient who needed an operation. Dr. Minot is—well, who knows where Dr. Minot is. Probably at his club, halfway through a decanter of port. That's why we sent for you."

The matron pushed open the door to a small room at the back of the house. From the weak gas light, Douglas could see three bedsteads but only one was occupied. A woman lay on her side on the bed, curled up, writhing in pain, and groaning. She was muttering in a language he did not recognize.

There was another woman at the bedside, a white apron tied around her waist with a bow above the bustle, rather than the full apron the matron wore.

"Dr. McLennan," the matron announced.

The woman glanced up. "At last." She seemed to be trying to help the patient to drink.

Douglas stepped in and turned to the matron. "If you could—"

The matron was already at the top of the stairs. "I'm needed by Dr. Storer."

The situation was quite extraordinary. It was like being a student back in Edinburgh, being treated with so little respect.

Douglas gritted his teeth; no matter how exhausted he was, he had to put the patient's needs first. He placed his two bags beside the wall and dropped his hat onto a small chair in the corner.

"What's the diagnosis?" he asked the woman as he shrugged off his overcoat.

"I don't know. I don't even know who brought her here."

Her tone was brisk, and although American accents were new to him, he could tell she was frustrated. But, honestly, he expected more from a nurse. She must know *something*.

He pulled off his jacket, throwing it on the chair.

The patient groaned and curled tighter, away from the cup being offered.

"Has she said anything?" Douglas asked.

The nurse barely looked up. "She's said plenty. But do I look like I speak Hungarian?"

Douglas raised an eyebrow and stifled the urge to retort. But that would be wasting time. "Move aside while I examine her." He stepped forward.

The nurse put a hand up to halt him. "You haven't washed yet."

"Washed?"

She began removing the Hungarian woman's jacket. "We have a protocol here—"

"A protocol?"

"A system."

"Aye, I'm aware of the concept of a *protocol*." This time, he couldn't keep the distain from his voice.

She flashed him a look. "Everyone washes their hands before touching a patient. Dr. Wendell Holmes has established—"

Douglas didn't have time for this. "I'm familiar with Wendell Holmes. But I'm not performing an operation and I need to find out what's wrong *now*."

The woman stood up, as if trying to protect the patient. She was a little taller than most, with dark brown hair which earlier in the day might have been in a fashionable arrangement but was now untidy, with strands falling around her face. In the half-light, her eyes blazed with determination. "There's water in the pitcher. It won't take you a moment."

"Damnation, woman!"

The nurse's nostrils flared in response to his language, but she did not move.

Douglas tugged at his shirtsleeves to roll them up before pouring water in the bowl, wondering if he should tell her he was perfectly familiar with germ theory, having known Lister from the Edinburgh Infirmary. The water was icy cold. There was a nub of soap, and as he dried his hands on a linen towel, he doubted his ablutions had improved anything.

"I could do with more light in here," he grumbled as he approached the narrow bed.

The nurse stepped back to give him room.

He examined the patient's face: the woman's skin felt clammy and her eyes were bloodshot. He could smell something foul on her breath. "Has she vomited?"

"Not that I'm aware of."

"Get something because I think she's about to—"

"Sir, I'm not actually a—"

"Quickly!"

The nurse grabbed the bowl he had washed in, splashing water on the bed, and managed to thrust it in place just in time.

Bloody incompetent, as well as ill-mannered.

Douglas was familiar with the slightly sweet smell and had an idea of the diagnosis.

"I need to examine her. Help me remove her clothing."

It was clear from her garments that the patient was poor. Her woolen dress was worn thin, the edges of the sleeves and skirt were frayed. He couldn't help but contrast it with the nurse's dress, which, although a sober blue, was of a fashionable cut and made of expensive damask. She wore a jeweled brooch at the high neck. Even with the white apron tied around her waist, none of this was suitable for nursing.

The nurse removed the patient's dress and suppressed a gasp. The skirt of the underdress was stained with blood.

Douglas helped the patient to lie back on the bed.

"As I suspected. The smell is lead plaster. Apothecaries sell it to women who find themselves in this situation."

The nurse looked up at him, her mouth open. He couldn't help but roll his eyes. God save him from naïve, inexperienced nurses. Give him a working-class midwife any day, over a pretty wee thing like this. Was she going to faint on him with a fit of the vapors?

"It often goes wrong. Basically, she's swallowed poison. Never a smart idea." He was pressing his fingers on different parts of the belly, the patient groaning in response. "And if she was desperate enough to do that, then she probably..." He laid the woman's feet flat on the mattress. "I'll try to stop the bleeding. Nurse, I need you to help—"

"*My* help?" The sound was like a yelp.

"Aye—"

She fingered the broach. "But I'm trying to tell you, I'm not—"

He stood up straight, glaring down at her. "Just as I thought," he spat out in frustration. "One of those damn do-gooding rich women playacting being a nurse, thinking it romantic to waft around a hospital, plumping pillows and offering sips of water. As soon as you're faced with the reality, you're suddenly overcome." He returned to the Hungarian woman. "Get me more light, nurse. You can at least do that." He tossed his head at the lamp on the table as he maneuvered the patient in place.

The nurse fetched the oil lamp, her movements brisk and her expression stony. "How dare you—" she began to say but then thankfully gave up and lifted the lamp so he could see more easily.

Douglas finished examining the woman and shook his head. "She's already lost the bairn." He turned to the nurse. "Not much you can do at this stage except wait."

She glared at him, her breast rising and falling. "You're the doctor and she's your patient. *You* will do the waiting." She whipped off her white apron and dropped it on top of his jacket on the chair. "But I will inform the matron as I—what did you call it? —*waft* my way out." She sallied out of the room.

Douglas stared after her, speechless with anger. A nurse would never behave this way in Britain and he wondered whether all medical standards were as poor in this country.

Phoebe let out a deep sigh as she looked up at gas light shining in the windows of the tall redbrick townhouse in Beacon Hill. *Home at last.*

Even though it was a short walk from the unfashionable West End, she was so tired she could barely drag herself up the steps to the grand front door. It had been a dreadful day at the hospital, with more patients than they could manage. Yet again. And then that doctor they were planning to hire, newly arrived from Britain, and *so* highly recommended by her mentor, Professor Moncrieff... He was younger than she had expected, reminding her more of one of the outdoorsy college friends of her brothers. But despite that soft Scots accent, he'd turned out to be as disagreeable and condescending as all the other doctors she knew. What was it about medical training that turned an ordinary man into an arrogant curmudgeon?

She stretched each side of her neck and rolled her shoulders to steel herself for the battle that waited inside her home.

Merriman opened the door before she'd even reached the top of the steps. "They are still having coffee, Miss Van Bergen."

She gave him her hat and gloves, and a maid stepped forward to help remove her light summer coat.

"I'll have dinner brought through," Merriman said.

Phoebe gave him a grim smile: she knew he understood how the rest of the family regarded the hours she gave to the hospital, but he was far too discreet to ever say anything out loud. She went into the dining room.

Her mother glanced at her and rolled her eyes to heaven. "You know it is the height of rudeness to be late for dinner. I cannot *abide* bad manners."

Phoebe planted a kiss on her mother's brow. "I'm glad you decided not to wait."

Her brother Thaddeus breathed cigar smoke toward the crystal chandelier. Lateness was bad manners, but apparently smoking in the dining room was not. She knew her father would never have countenanced it.

"Getting to be quite a habit, Pheebs," he said lazily.

"I'm hoping the new doctor will make things more manageable." The words felt a little hollow, if this evening's encounter was anything to go by. Phoebe took her chair as the maid placed a meal before her: roast duck with buttered potatoes and steamed celery, all covered in the rich sauce their cook had learned in Paris. My, she was starving. Phoebe realized she hadn't eaten since midday.

Thaddeus's wife, Florence, tapped her porcelain cup to indicate to the maid that she wanted a fresh coffee. "Maybe, dear Phoebe, you should leave things to people who are qualified." She gave Phoebe a tight smile. "If you're struggling, I mean."

Phoebe tamped down the desire to blurt out exactly what she thought of Florence and her faux-concern.

Mrs. Van Bergen crinkled her nose. "What *is* that smell?"

Phoebe felt her cheeks redden. Oh goodness, had some of that vomit ended up on her dress? How could she have failed to check properly? She had washed her face and hands before she left the hospital, but she should have gone straight to her room to change, no matter how exhausted she was. "Sorry, Mother. I think that maybe... You see, a patient was—"

"A patient?" Her mother's voice rose an octave: "A patient! You are not supposed to be *treating* those women. Administrative work: that's what you said you were doing there..."

"Yes, but—"

Her mother was frowning, her voice stern. "Making sure the Van Bergen money is being spent appropriately. Nothing wasted."

Phoebe kept her eyes on the duck she was slicing. "That's still mostly what I do."

"Mostly?"

"But sometimes, when we're short-staffed..."

Thaddeus grunted. "I wouldn't worry too much, Mother. Hector will put a stop to this, once they're married."

Hector. She knew the conversation would come round to her fiancé soon enough.

"Ah, lovely Hector," said Florence, her eyes softly focused on the middle distance.

"I don't know what you're waiting for, Phoebe," said Mrs. Van Bergen, still frowning at her. "You were delighted to get engaged and seemed to be having fun, doing all the planning. He won't hang around forever. And at your age, an engagement this long is beginning to look unseemly."

Phoebe glanced at her brother and caught his smirk. Yes, some families were approaching the Van Bergen wealth as the economy boomed, but they didn't have her mother's pedigree, going back generations. Money *and* social cachet: two things Hector craved and would wait for, however much she procrastinated.

She shivered and reached for the salt cellar.

"What's that on your cuff?" Mrs. Van Bergen peered at the white linen at her wrist.

Phoebe glanced down at the reddish-brown mark and pulled her arm back.

"Is that... is that *blood*?"

Phoebe swallowed. "I think it might be."

Her mother threw her napkin onto her plate. "No, Phoebe, no! I draw a line. You are to leave your meal at once. Go and change. And wash thoroughly. How *dare* you sit at our dining table in that condition?"

Phoebe left her seat without a word and went upstairs, fighting back the tears. She was twenty-seven, for goodness' sake. A grown woman with her own mind. Would her mother ever stop treating her like a recalcitrant child? Phoebe had been the prime mover in establishing a hospital for women in Boston, something that filled her with pride. But her family dismissed her work. It was one thing to be a bountiful philanthropist. Something entirely different to actually get your hands dirty—literally, in Phoebe's case.

She reached her bedroom: a spacious sanctuary at the back of the house. Mrs. Farrell, her lady's maid, was already laying out an alternative dress for her to change into. Did the servants listen to every conversation and then race up the servant's stairs to anticipate what was needed?

She stood still as Farrell unhooked her clothing. Just at that moment, she longed to be alone.

No, not alone. She longed for Lex to be at home.

How could her twin brothers be so different from one another? Where Thaddeus was cruel, Lex was kind; where Thaddeus was disapproving, Lex would encourage her. Thaddeus would ignore her, but Lex would listen as she spoke of her hopes and dreams.

But Lex was far, far away in the Canadian Rockies, overseeing the construction of the Canadian Pacific Railway. Away with Ginny, his wife of two years, who had refused to leave his side, declaring that she knew about life in the open air and would be fine in Canada.

If Lex were here, he'd help her work out how to fix the problems at the hospital. He'd agree that it was crazy trying to run it in a rented house, even though it had seemed like a sensible first step four years ago.

She went to the washbasin and began cleaning her hands thoroughly. She had such ambitions: she wanted to create something special for the care of women. Deep down, she dreamed of building the best women's hospital on the Eastern Seaboard. If only she had more family support, maybe she could make it happen.

Phoebe glanced in the mirror and saw how tired she looked. She wished she could blame it all on work, but the truth was she couldn't. If Lex were here, he'd also help sort the godawful mess she'd got herself into with Hector.

TWO

Douglas paused in the entrance hall of the Van Bergen hospital to smooth back his hair and straighten the tie knot at his high, starched collar. He needed to make a good impression on the hospital Board of Trustees. His lodgings had been comfortable and Mrs. Angellotti's pasta had lived up to its billing, but he was still dog-tired by the Atlantic crossing and disorientated in the new city.

The door to the front parlor swung open and he was met by an elderly man with the air of a rural clergyman.

"Dr. McLennan. Welcome." The man put out his hand; the skin was papery and cool. "I'm Henry Haven. I have the privilege of being the President of the Board of Trustees for this hospital. Do come in."

"Thank you, sir."

The walls were paneled in wood and the window overlooked the street. Everything looked new, yet aped the baronial style of the rooms familiar to Douglas in Scotland. There were five chairs, roughly in a circle.

"Please, sit." Mr. Haven indicated to a wing-backed leather chair.

Two other men were sitting comfortably, and as Douglas took

his seat opposite the president, he saw to his surprise the fourth chair was occupied by the incompetent nurse from last night. Incompetent maybe, but in the morning light, her eyes shone even more brightly, the irises a delicate shade of gray. Her cheeks were slightly flushed and her lips were a rosy pink.

He swallowed, aware he was staring, and tried to recover his manners. "Good morning."

"Good morning, Dr. McLennan." Her American tone was firm, but her face revealed no emotion. She was at an advantage, as she'd been anticipating him.

The president raised his brows. "You've already met?"

"Indeed we have," said the nurse. "Last night. When the doctor arrived."

"Ah, good." The president rubbed his hands. "No need for further introductions then."

Heat prickled at Douglas's neck as he remembered their altercation the night before. He noticed she had a notebook and pen on her lap—she must be here to take notes. This was not good: he wanted to put his best foot forward this morning and forget about the unfortunate incident last night. Maybe he could find a way to remove her from the conversation?

He turned to the nurse. "Miss, might I trouble you for a cup of tea?"

Her mouth fell open. "Tea?"

"Aye, things have been a little rushed this morning, still getting my bearings, so..."

The president coughed and shuffled in his seat. "Maybe I could send—"

"No, no, Mr. President," said the nurse, getting up. Her voice was clipped and something else... Amused? "Let me go fetch a cup of tea for the eminent doctor."

She left the room and Douglas caught the anxious looks between the Board members. What sort of faux pas had he already committed? Was he, as a British man, not supposed to mention tea in Boston?

"Let me introduce the Board," said the president, "while we're waiting."

Phoebe hurried down the corridor to the matron's office. The man was no less insufferable this morning than he'd been last night. Still ordering her around.

She was relieved to find Adeline Hale behind her desk in the tiny space. Petite and pretty, the matron had the sort of fresh complexion found on a young woman who had worked in a dairy all her life, rather than an urban hospital.

"He wants tea," Phoebe said. "The new doctor."

"And he asked *you*—" Adeline raised a brow in surprise.

"Indeed. He doesn't know who I am."

Adeline's mouth dropped open. "Didn't you tell him last night?"

"Didn't get the chance."

She narrowed her eyes. "Miss Van Bergen, you're a cruel woman. You're deliberately not telling him now, aren't you?"

"Maybe." Phoebe lifted one side of her mouth and shrugged, making Adeline suppress a snorting laugh.

"So, tea," Adeline said, slapping her table and getting to her feet. "D'you think he means the whole service, with cakes and everything? I've heard the English..."

Phoebe hurried after her friend and colleague to the small kitchen at the back of the house. "No, that's afternoon tea. I think. This is just a cup."

"That's fine, then," said Adeline. "The kettle only recently boiled to make coffee for the Board. Won't take a moment."

Where would she be without the sensible help of her matron?

Phoebe reached up to take a china cup and saucer from the shelf.

"It'll be swell to have a younger doctor around," said Adeline as she put out the teapot. "How old d'you think he is?"

Phoebe leaned back against the table. "Early thirties?"

"He's gonna cause a stir among the nurses. And we could see a surge in the number of patients," she said with a wink.

"Do you think so?"

"Oh, come now, Miss Van Bergen. I know you're affianced, but you must have noticed how handsome he is."

"Can't say I did," Phoebe said, raising her chin.

Adeline smirked as she set out the sugar. "Really? That lovely sandy-colored hair. Those broad shoulders." She jokingly fanned her face. "I didn't see what color his eyes are, though."

"They're green."

Adeline and Phoebe exchanged a look and burst out laughing.

"No," said Adeline. "You never noticed *nothing*."

Phoebe dropped a couple of spoons of tea into the pot. "Being handsome doesn't make up for having a horrible disposition."

Adeline poured hot water into the pot and then fetched milk from the pantry and poured it into a jug, placing everything on a tray. She halted: "They take milk in their tea, don't they? The Brits."

Phoebe bit her lip, trying to remember. "I think so. Well, we shall soon find out." She picked up the tray.

Adeline put out her hand. "You shouldn't be taking that."

Phoebe gave a wry smile. "I'm happy to. I'm even slightly enjoying this."

Douglas tried to stop tapping his fingers on the arm of the chair. They had made the introductions and exchanged polite chat: why couldn't they get on with discussing terms? He'd only asked for tea as a way of removing that nurse. But, no, they were waiting for his refreshments to arrive. He should be grateful that at least the Board was being considerate. He could have done with a cup of tea last night, when he was exhausted and hungry.

The nurse breezed in with a tray. "Here we are," she said, as if it had taken her no time at all.

There was that same slightly throaty Boston accent he'd

noticed the night before. Again, she was dressed expensively: a frock made of high-quality linen, this time in florals, the bodice emphasizing her curves. Her hair was piled high, tidier than the night before, when wisps had escaped their pins. He was struck by how dark and glowing her hair was, and noticed the curve of her pale neck, set off by delicate drop earrings.

He sensed a flutter of awkwardness afflicting the trustees again. Douglas hoped it was because they agreed with him that her presence really wasn't needed. Maybe he could catch the eye of the president and hope he took the hint to ask her to leave.

She laid the tray on a nearby table and poured a cup from the teapot. "Milk?"

"Aye, a wee drop." Douglas breathed in and looked at the trustees. "So, gentlemen—"

"Sugar?"

"Nae. Thank you."

The president showed no inclination to pick up their conversation until this ceremony was over.

She handed him his cup and saucer. They were fine bone china with an elegant design and he couldn't imagine them surviving in the hospitals he was used to.

"I do hope that's good enough for you," she said sweetly. There was a look in those gray eyes he couldn't quite understand: a sparkle that could have been amusement or anger. Her mouth was slightly open and gave nothing away. She had a tiny notch in the middle of her upper lip and he glimpsed perfect white teeth. "I'm told the English are very particular about their tea."

"They may be," he replied evenly. "I'm Scottish."

"Is there a difference?" she asked, with a tilt of her head.

"All the difference in the world," he growled. Against his better judgment, he was allowing her to rile him, even though this might make a poor impression on the board.

She raised an eyebrow and turned to take her seat beside the trustees.

"Shall we get to know you then?" suggested the president, clapping his hands, clearly trying to jolly things along.

Douglas accepted defeat and realized the nurse was here to stay, but addressed the men as he ran through his career so far: he'd trained at the prestigious medical school in Edinburgh under the guidance of Professor Moncrieff, who, of course, the Van Bergen Hospital was familiar with from his time teaching in Boston, and who had personally recommended him for this position. He had worked for five years in the Edinburgh Infirmary, then at St. Thomas's in London. He had published research: *The Effects of the Antiseptic System of Treatment upon the Salubrity of a Surgical Hospital.*

The trustees made appreciative noises at all the right moments and Douglas began to relax.

"And do you have family?" asked a member of the board who was wearing a clerical dog collar.

"Aye, I do. My parents are still alive. And I have a sister."

"And what does your father do?" asked the president. "Is he also a medic?"

"No, he's an industrialist. Er, cloth manufacturing. But perhaps he influenced me in a love of the natural sciences."

"What I meant," the clergyman continued, "was, do you have family of your own? A wife, children."

Douglas clenched his jaw. "I'm a widower."

"I'm sorry to hear it," said the president.

"It was some time ago. Nearly eight years, now." His throat tightened: he hadn't expected this interview to touch on his personal life. They must do things differently here in the States. "And no. No bairns."

There was a pause in the questioning and Douglas prayed they would ask no more about his wife—or whether he intended to marry again.

"What made you want to be a doctor?" It was the nurse who broke the silence.

He turned sharply and frowned at her, uncertain why she had

intervened, and unsure how to answer the question. "I... I've always been interested in medicine," he replied cautiously. "I like to understand how things work."

"Not motivated by the alleviation of suffering, then?"

"Aye, of course." He flashed a look at the president who showed no surprise at the nurse's tone. "That goes without saying."

"Does it?" Her eyes were firmly on him and he felt strangely uncomfortable. Was she waiting for him to engage in debate?

He said nothing, and returned his attention to the president.

"And why women's medicine?" the woman interrupted again.

"I'm sorry?" He gripped the curved wood at the end of the armrest in an effort not to ask her to be quiet.

"Why specialize in women's health?" She put her head to one side, waiting for an answer.

By Jove, no, he wasn't about to reveal the long line of mistakes which had compelled him into this area of medicine, and had led to him sitting in a wood-paneled room in Boston. He felt an ache in his chest, as if this woman had inadvertently pressed on a bruise in his heart.

"Why not women's health?" he asked, trying to put on his most charming smile and suspecting he was failing.

She didn't look impressed. "Because it's not a prestigious area of medicine and you strike me as a man who enjoys prestige."

He glared at her. She didn't know the first thing about him. How dare she presume to think that she did.

"And why here?" she pressed on. "Why Boston?"

What was it with this damned woman? Did she expect him to tell her the truth? That he could no longer bear his life in Edinburgh, that every corner brought painful memories of all he had got so catastrophically wrong. That his attempts to start again in London had failed because it was still too near. That he wasn't sure if even crossing the ocean could take him far enough away from his past, or if a lifetime in medicine could atone for what he had done.

Instead, he turned to her again and forced a smile. "You must be aware of the attractions of the United States. Boston in particular. The innovations coming out of Harvard. Your *can-do* attitude, I think they call it."

The nurse looked no more convinced by this little speech than he was.

Douglas sipped his tea and found it was cold.

The president slapped his hands on the arms of his chair. "Well, I'm delighted you chose to come here. Professor Moncrieff is an old friend of the hospital. His recommendation carries considerable weight."

One of the other men leaned forward. "As treasurer, I detailed the terms of your engagement in my letter. I trust you received it and agree."

"Indeed," said Douglas. He was not going to reveal that the salary was three times what he was earning in London. Perhaps his father would finally approve of his career choice after all.

"In that case," said the president, "I think we can confirm—"

"One moment," said the nurse. "I'm not so sure."

The president turned to her and raised his bushy eyebrows.

"I'm not sure Dr. McLennan is a good"—she was searching for the word—"*fit* for our hospital."

Douglas's pulse rate increased. *A good fit?* What on earth was the woman talking about? And why was she being allowed to give an opinion anyway?

"We are trying to establish more of a collegiate environment here," she continued.

"Collegiate?" Douglas asked.

"Maybe that's not the right word. A place of mutual respect."

He loosened the knot at his neck just a fraction to let out some of the rising heat. His mind went to the night before: he knew he hadn't been entirely respectful to her. But, for goodness' sake, he'd just got off the ship and was shattered.

The nurse continued. "It's a women's hospital, so respect for women is important. And a willingness to follow the protocols we have established."

Was this the handwashing thing?

He looked meaningfully at the president expecting him to intervene and move the conversation back on track. Instead, he saw the old man shuffling uncomfortably.

The president turned to the woman. "And what do you suggest?"

"A six-month probationary period."

A probationer! Did she not understand how senior he was?

"During that time, we can see if Dr. McLennan is the right man for this hospital," she continued smoothly. "Whether to confirm his appointment."

He stared at the president in amazement. Was he going to let this woman prevent the confirmation of his appointment?

Instead, the president smiled. "That's a capital idea, Miss Van Bergen. Let's see how it goes for six months."

Miss Van Bergen.

Douglas's jaw clamped shut so tight it hurt, and he swallowed in an attempt to release it. Finally, the penny dropped.

THREE

How had he been so stupid? Douglas wiped a palm across his mouth, trying not to let the Board see his shock.

He glanced at Miss Van Bergen and saw a distinct look of triumph in those gray eyes. A smile played around the edge of her lips. She had set a bloody great bear trap for him. She *knew* he was unaware of her name. All that charade of making him tea—when she was the patron of the whole blasted hospital. Dammit, she was *enjoying* his discomfiture.

There was nothing he could do about it now. He had to accept the employment terms on offer. And somehow he needed to smooth things over with the hospital's young benefactor quickly, if he was going to plant roots in New England soil.

Phoebe hurried down the hall to her office.

"Miss Van Bergen?"

She paused. There was no mistaking that rich Scots voice. She turned and Dr. McLennan seemed to fill the space. The sun streamed through the fanlight above the main door behind him and brightened his thick, dark-blond hair.

"If I might have a word, Miss..."

She inclined her head, waiting for him to come to her. She was in no mood to discuss what had just happened.

He strode forward. "Obviously we were never introduced. Last night, I mean."

"Mm-hmm."

He stood with his legs apart and cleared his throat. "I... er... apologize if I was rude last night."

"*If?*"

He rubbed the back of his neck. "*That* I was rude to you. I shouldn't have spoken to you that way."

Well, this was a first: a doctor acknowledging he had made a mistake.

"If I'd known who you were, then I wouldnae..." He shrugged and tucked both hands behind him, under the tails of his jacket, the nonchalant stance filling his tweed vest.

Phoebe's heart sank. How disappointing: he was no different after all. Respect was for her surname, not for her.

"Would it have made a difference?" she asked.

He looked her in the eye. "Of course."

She took a long breath. "You see, that's why I know I'm right about your probation period. You're not the sort of doctor I want here." His eyes narrowed and she could see his jaw flex, but she pushed on. "I want doctors who respect *all* women, whether they be a patient, or a nurse, or a cleaning woman. Or, indeed, the benefactor."

He scowled. "You know nothing of my usual behavior, Miss Van Bergen. Last night, I was tired. Hungry. I'd been dragged straight from the harbor. Am I to be judged on just one night?"

His voice was firm but low. At least he was fighting back, rather than simpering before her. Or worse, trying to flirt with her.

"Not just one night. On the next six months: that is how we will judge you." She adjusted her cuffs. "Good day, Dr. McLennan. I have a busy day ahead of me. As, I am sure, have you."

She turned on her heel and strode to her office, where a mountain of paperwork awaited.

. . .

Phoebe rubbed her temples. She hadn't been able to concentrate all morning. The interview with McLennan had put her off her stride. This made her cross—she didn't have time to waste on recalcitrant medics.

There was a musical knock at the door, as if someone was tapping out a Souza march. The door opened and Hector put his head around, a broad smile on his boyish face. "How'ya doing, honeybee?"

He stepped inside her office and leaned his tall, athletic body against the closed door. His curly brown hair made him look younger than his thirty-five years.

She remembered how much she had once enjoyed threading her fingers through those curls, pulling them straight and watching them bounce back.

"I'm taking you for lunch."

She gestured to the papers on her desk. "I'd like to, Hector, but I have so much—"

"Not taking no for an answer." He took her summer dolman from where it was hanging on the stand. "Don't want my beautiful fiancée to lose her bloom."

She looked at the letter she was halfway through drafting. "If I could just finish—"

He shook out the garment for her. "I know what's best for you."

She sighed and got up from the chair. What was the point in resisting? She knew he had a way of getting what he wanted, and right now he wanted her. She hid her irritation as he helped put her arms through the loose sleeves and she adjusted the tassels hanging at the front. "Does the bank not need you?"

He waved his hand. "They're doing fine without me. Anyway, if I want to go out for lunch, that's what I'm darn well going to do."

She often wondered what Hector did at his father's bank; they seemed remarkably relaxed about the hours he kept. She picked up her hat and settled it at an angle on her chignon, skewering it with an ornate pin. She really must ask Adeline to sort out a looking glass for her office.

"Is that right?"

Hector looked her up and down and adjusted the curve of a feather. "That's better."

He led the way through the hall toward the entrance, striding ahead as if he owned the hospital, rather than the Van Bergens.

A door opened and Hector nearly bumped into the man emerging into the hall. Phoebe stifled a groan: was there no avoiding McLennan this morning?

Hector laughed. "Gee, old fella. Nearly knocked you over, there."

Phoebe glanced from one to the other. While Hector was slightly taller, McLennan had a pugilistic air about him: he was broad across the shoulders and didn't look like a man who would be easily knocked over.

McLennan ignored Hector and turned his attention to her. "Miss Van Bergen, I was coming to ask you—"

Hector raised a hand. "Whatever it is, it will have to wait. I'm taking her to lunch."

A flicker of frustration flashed across McLennan's face.

"This is Mr. Hector Gregson," Phoebe said. "My fiancé." She wasn't sure why she added that piece of information, but it somehow felt important the doctor knew.

Hector put out his hand.

McLennan shook it. "Douglas McLennan. Newly arrived doctor. Pleased to meet you."

"Likewise," said Hector, showing his perfect teeth. "Say, is that an English accent?"

"Scottish—"

"Scottish—"

Phoebe and McLennan spoke in unison. A look passed between them and he raised a brow in surprise.

"He only arrived last night," Phoebe continued.

Hector pulled a card from a pocket inside his coat. "Those are my details," he said, handing it to McLennan. "I'd be pleased to show you around. Introduce you to some of the guys at my club."

McLennan took the card and inclined his head. "Thank you. That's very considerate."

Hector put his hand on the small of Phoebe's back, just above the fabric of her bustle. "We must leave. Got a table waiting at Parker House."

They moved past McLennan, and as Phoebe fiddled with her parasol, she turned back and saw McLennan slipping the card into his vest pocket. Her shoulders slumped: she wasn't sure she wanted the new doctor pulled into Hector's orbit.

Phoebe was glad the waiter showed them to a quiet table by the window, where she had something to observe if the conversation flagged.

Hector ordered. "Beefsteak, cooked real long, with a pepper sauce. New potatoes but hold the vegetables."

The waiter turned to Phoebe.

"Oh, she'll have the same," said Hector, handing back his menu.

"Actually, I quite fancy—" Phoebe began, but as she looked up from her menu, she saw Hector's face drop. She gave waiter a polite smile and shrugged. "The same."

The man disappeared.

Once, at the beginning of their engagement, Phoebe had ordered exactly the same as Hector. She thought it a charming way of showing how right they were for each other. Guests at the table had found it adorable and Hector decided this was how it would always be. She'd tried to order food she would prefer on a number of occasions since, but Hector pretended not to hear, or would sulk. Phoebe learned it was easier to put up with eating the same food.

"How are things at the bank?" she asked and sat back to listen as Hector ran through his triumphs, trials and tribulations: how the board didn't listen to him enough, how he had spotted a new investment opportunity before anyone else.

Her attention drifted, but mention of her brother pulled her back.

"Thaddeus, you say?"

"Yeah, was in yesterday. Putting a deal together for a new railroad line."

Thaddeus never stopped working, and with his ambition that the railroad should span the continent, he was very much his father's son.

"I told him," Hector continued, "needs to get the Canadian Pacific finished first."

"I thought Lex had asked for more money for bridges and Thaddeus was raising investment for that." She had heard him talking about it at dinner.

Hector took a gulp of his wine. "Decided to invest in something new. Says he'll cable Alexander and tell him to make it work with what he's got."

Phoebe wanted to ask more. She dearly missed her brother Lex, and was interested in the extraordinary engineering feat he was undertaking. However, Lex seemed the only person in the world immune to Hector's charms. They had never liked each other, and she knew discussing Lex would put Hector in a bad mood—something she didn't have the time to manage today.

The food arrived and the conversation moved to Hector's club, his exploits on the rowing team, how a rival team had capsized on the Charles River and how funny it had been.

Phoebe suppressed a sigh. "Conversation" wasn't really the word; that implied some give-and-take between the parties. No, Phoebe was Hector's audience, ready to nod and smile at the right moments. He never enquired about her, never asked about the hospital, or her home life, or her interests. But at least he never pressed her to name the date for their wedding. That was something to be grateful for. Hector seemed as content as she to let this engagement drift on.

She allowed herself to float away and think about the designs for a new hospital sitting on her desk. She wanted to respond to the architect's latest questions, rather than be stuck here in Parker's listening to her fiancé's prattling. The wards would need to be large enough to serve the women settling in Boston from all parts of the world, and she wasn't sure how she would raise enough money.

Hector insisted on walking her back to the hospital. Two hours, that meal had taken, two hours she could not afford to lose. She urged him to leave her at the entrance. "Really, there's no need for you to see me to my office. And surely the bank wants you back."

"No trouble at all, my honeybee."

Phoebe swallowed and marched up the steps, her heels clicking on the stone.

Hector followed into her tiny office and closed the door, pulling her to him before she had the chance to remove her hat. He ran his thumb down her cheek and closed his mouth on hers, his tongue nudging between her lips.

There had been a time when she relished his kisses, when she had melted into him, feeling the same desire. But not now. Not anymore.

She pulled away. "I'm sorry, Hector. I really must get on with things."

He grinned and stepped closer.

She put up both hands to him, speaking more firmly. "No, really. I don't have time..."

He shrugged and lifted his hands in defeat, half-smiling down at her. "Until next time."

And he was gone.

Phoebe leaned her back against the closed door and shut her eyes before releasing a long sigh. She wiped her mouth with the back of her hand. What a fool she'd been, saying yes to this man. Lex had tried to warn her, but she hadn't listened. Now she had no choice but to live with a whole series of bad decisions she had made.

FOUR

Phoebe poured another cup of coffee for Mrs. Anthony as they sat in the parlor of the hospital. It was the only room elegant enough to receive the Boston ladies who made regular donations to the hospital.

She tried to keep her attention on Mrs. Anthony, but her eye was caught by McLennan outside, crossing the street, his head down and his hat low. He seemed in a hurry. Phoebe glanced at the wall clock. Ten o'clock. She thought he wasn't on duty until later in the day. He took the front stairs two at a time. That man always seemed in a rush. It was like having a tornado inside the hospital, going from room to room. Still, she had to admit he was getting things done and had already instigated useful changes. Doctors Storer and Minot bristled at the new ideas, but Adeline and the nurses clearly approved and had only good things to say about him. There had been no complaints from the patients either, and Adeline reported that his manner with them was distinctly less brusque and surly than Phoebe had experienced.

The door slammed and she returned her attention to Mrs. Anthony.

There was an almighty crash and what sounded like dozens of pieces of metal tumbling to the floor.

"Oh, my!" said Mrs. Anthony.

"What the devil is all this stuff doing here!"

The Scots accent was unmistakable.

"Would you excuse me?" Phoebe asked, smiling at Mrs. Anthony as if nothing had happened.

She hurried to the hall, where McLennan was standing, his legs wide and arms folded. At his feet were pieces of silver cutlery.

McLennan glared at Phoebe. "We can't have the hall used as a storage cupboard."

"Those boxes have only been there a minute," Phoebe retorted. "One of my ladies has donated them."

"What for?"

"What do you mean, what for? The patients have to eat."

"From silver cutlery?" He gestured to the mess at his feet.

Mrs. Anthony appeared at Phoebe's shoulder. "Good heavens!" she said.

McLennan dropped to his haunches to pick up some knives and forks and began placing them back in the box. "We've got plenty of cutlery."

Mrs. Anthony hurried forward. "But look at these darling little salt spoons." She picked one up. "I bet you haven't any of those."

"Indeed we haven't," said Phoebe, kneeling opposite McLennan to help pick up the cutlery.

He caught her eye and Phoebe widened hers, urging him to be polite. She hoped Mrs. Anthony hadn't noticed his tone.

"And this darling little mustard spoon. It has an ivory handle. See?"

"Beautiful, Mrs. Anthony," Phoebe said, giving her a reassuring smile.

McLennan dropped a pair of serving spoons in the box, making a racket. "But we don't *need* this stuff. It's just clutter."

Phoebe frowned at him hard enough to convey he wasn't to say another word and quickly finished picking up the cutlery. "There," she said, standing up and brushing dust from her skirt. "No harm done. Mrs. Anthony, this is Dr. McLennan. He's recently arrived from—"

Before she could introduce him, he had moved toward the stairs. "Sorry, already late."

Phoebe called after him. "But you're not supposed to be here until this afternoon, anyway."

"Didn't Matron Hale tell you? Dr. Minot is too unwell to come in again. I'm covering his shift."

Darn it! Phoebe knew exactly what "unwell" meant with Dr. Minot.

She spoke to the doctor's retreating back. "I want you to come and see me as soon as Mrs. Anthony has left."

He waved a hand and disappeared to the upper floor.

Phoebe blinked rapidly, embarrassed to have been treated this way in front of a guest. She forced a smile at Mrs. Anthony. "Shall we finish our coffee?" She led the way back into the parlor. "He's from Scotland. Maybe they do things differently there. Hasn't quite settled in here, yet."

An hour after Phoebe had smoothed things over with Mrs. Anthony and seen her off, McLennan had still not come to see her. She went in search, finding him on the third floor in a room which had once been a small single bedroom but now had four beds and a couple of cots crammed in. He was taking notes as he made observations of one of the patients. A nurse was scrubbing at a suspicious stain on a rug.

"Ah, Miss Van Bergen," he said, glancing up.

"I asked you to come and see me," she said sternly.

"I'll be there when I've got a moment." He calmly continued to press his fingertips on the woman's wrist. "What was it you wanted?"

Her hands closed into fists. "I wanted to impress upon you how important it is not to be rude to the benefactors."

He returned to taking notes. "I wasn't rude. I said nothing to her."

"You criticized her donation." Phoebe spoke slowly and clearly.

He shook his head. "Look, we don't need more teaspoons. Or wee salt spoons."

Phoebe put her hands on her hips. "I know, but we still need to be gracious."

He finally turned to give her his full attention. "What we *need*, Miss Van Bergen, is more catheters and syringes."

"Of course I know that, doctor, but it is highly unlikely Mrs. Anthony's mother-in-law left boxes with a dozen each of those, when she died."

"So, what's the point in taking donations we don't need?" he asked, frowning. "Can you sell it?"

"No, of course I can't sell it." She pushed her hand up her brow and breathed out through her nostrils. He really had no idea how the finances of this hospital worked.

"You're a dumping ground, Miss Van Bergen," he said, pointing at her with his pencil. "You need to be much clearer with these women about what you will and won't accept. I mean, look at this sheet someone's given." He shook out a sheet in a pile ready to make up the next bed. "Already worn to nothing."

"I'm trying to cultivate Mrs. Anthony so she will make a cash donation in the future," Phoebe said through gritted teeth.

McLennan snorted and refolded the sheet. "That'll be the day."

Phoebe was ready to explode. This man was so infuriating. Dr. Storer would never speak to her like this and he had been with the hospital since its opening four years earlier. "Dr. McLennan, you will come to the landing *now*."

She marched out, not sure what authority she had left if he failed to follow, but not wanting to have this conversation in front of the nurse and patients.

She turned to see him stepping out of the room and closing the door behind him. The two of them stood facing each other in the corridor beside the stairs. She was aware of how much taller and broader he was, but refused to be intimidated.

"How *dare* you criticize how I run this hospital, Dr. McLennan."

He shrugged. "I'm only a probationer trying to offer some wee observations."

"I've had about as much as I can take of your insolence!"

He leaned back against the wall and folded his arms. "Are you going to fire me?"

Phoebe's hand went to her throat, alarmed by how quickly things had escalated. All she wanted was for him to behave courteously.

He studied her, his head to one side. "You won't, will you. Because I've only been here a week, and we both know I'm a far better doctor than the two you've got here." He pushed himself up straight. "I've got work to do." He strolled back to the makeshift ward.

Phoebe put her palms to the top of her head and mouthed a silent scream. What did Matron Hale and the nurses see in him? He was one of the rudest, most conceited men she'd ever met. But the truth was, he was right: he was streets ahead of the other doctors. She badly needed him, particularly now Dr. Minot seemed to be barely in attendance. In the end, she had to put her patients above her own desire to send McLennan back across the Atlantic to Scotland.

Douglas paced the middle of the hospital parlor like a cat in a cage. Dr. Storer stood with one arm on the mantelpiece, flicking ash from his pipe into the fire. Miss Van Bergen was perched in a chair, her elbow on the arm, supporting her head and looking like she was in mild pain.

He felt a pang of guilt he wanted badly to shake off. He knew he had behaved abominably toward her over the past few weeks and couldn't remember ever being so ungracious to a woman. He didn't seem able to get beyond blaming her for putting him on a probationary period. He had trained at the best medical school in the world and was an experienced doctor; to be a probationer was humiliating. He really ought to be a bigger man than this, to accept the situation and show better manners.

But it wasn't just his personal situation that frustrated him. The hospital was far smaller than his old tutor Professor Moncrieff had implied. While the Board was supportive and the nurses hard-working, the facilities were lacking and his fellow doctors were more traditional than he expected in forward-looking United States. Miss Van Bergen seemed to hardly be present, instead she was out lunching with goodness knew who, or hidden away in her little office.

This morning was a typical example and he couldn't believe he was having this conversation *again*. "We need to isolate the mother and her child."

"And you're sure they both have scarlet fever?" Miss Van Bergen asked.

"Definitely. It's dangerous for her, so near her time of confinement."

Dr. Storer tapped his pipe. "I've only seen symptoms in the child. We need to send him home."

"She's unmarried," said Phoebe. "I'm not sure there is a home."

Douglas stopped in the middle of the carpet and turned to the other doctor. "We're a hospital, for God's sake. We're supposed to treat people when they're ill. Not send them packing."

Dr. Storer squared his shoulders. "Dr. McLennan, *you* said they need to be isolated."

"And there isn't anywhere we can do this, Dr. McLennan," said Miss Van Bergen, a frown appearing between her brows. "Every room is full."

Douglas pushed his hand through his hair. "That's why I keep saying you need to build an isolation room."

"Build another room!" scoffed Dr. Storer.

"There's space in the wee bit of garden out the back," said

Douglas. "You knock down that outhouse. Get a room big enough for a couple of beds. Could be done in a week."

Dr. Storer snorted. "So you're a builder now, are you? Is there no end to your skills?"

Miss Van Bergen rubbed at the side of her neck. "We're not spending money extending this place, Dr. McLennan. I thought I'd made that clear to you."

He lifted his hands in exasperation. "So, what do you suggest we do?"

Miss Van Bergen looked around. "We put them in here. The mother and son. Use this as the isolation room."

"But, Miss Van Bergen," said Dr. Storer, "if we lose the parlor, where are we going to—"

She put up a hand. "It's the only answer. We can't have infection spreading to the other women. The Trustees can meet in one of their houses. I'll receive benefactors in the public room of the hotel in the next street."

Finally, some sense! Douglas nodded. "That sounds a good solution to me."

Miss Van Bergen stood and straightened her frock. "Right. Dr. Storer, start making the arrangements." She turned to Douglas. "Dr. McLennan, come with me."

Douglas followed her down the corridor to the back of the house. He wondered if he had overstepped the mark one time too many and she really was going to fire him.

She opened the door to her office, and for the first time, he stepped inside. The desk filled most of the small space and had neat piles of papers. Around it were boxes of donated items piled on the floor, schedules pinned to the walls.

Miss Van Bergen stood tall and looked him directly in the face. "I know you are frustrated when I shoot down your suggestions for building improvements. So, I want to show you something."

She pointed to a framed sketch on the wall. Douglas leaned closer. It was a line drawing of a large building, with watercolored highlights.

"That's the first sketch of the hospital I'm going to build."

He glanced at her, taken aback by her words.

"This will mean we can care for the women of Boston and their families properly. *That's* where I'll build an isolation ward. Every dollar I spend here"—she waved a hand toward the window—"putting something in the yard, for example—takes me further from this goal."

He admired the sketch and whistled. "But this will take years to build."

She shook her head. "Not at all. I've been working on this for months. Nearly everything is in place. I've agreed a site in principle with the city fathers. The plans are complete. I know how much it will cost." She glanced directly up at him, her gray eyes shining.

He looked more closely at the other documents on her desk. There was page after page of architect's drawings of wards and treatment rooms, papers with long lists of items, each one of them costed. Professor Moncrieff had spoken of the ambitious woman behind the Women's Hospital. Now he recognized her for the first time. Miss Van Bergen hadn't been hiding away in her office; she had been working hard, planning something exceptional. He felt a hot wave of shame as he remembered how he'd scowled each time she dashed out for lunches in Boston hotels, or fancy events with Boston Brahmin families; all along she had been securing planning agreements and raising funds. The woman before him was like no other he had ever met, and that scared him a little.

"What I need, Dr. McLennan, is for you to concentrate on giving the patients the best possible care now. While I work on the best possible care in the future."

<h1 style="text-align:center">FIVE</h1>

Once the Van Bergen carriage had drawn to a halt, Phoebe was the last to climb out. Thaddeus helped their mother down the steps, then Florence. For a moment, Phoebe thought her brother was not going to bother to extend his arm to steady her. She would have preferred not to trouble him, but dressed up in all this finery, she needed a helping hand.

Looking up, she could only just see the golden dome of the Massachusetts State House, gleaming in the July evening sun. She would have been happy to walk the short distance from their townhouse in Beacon Hill, but her mother's joints were getting stiff and Florence wanted to make a show.

Phoebe walked beside Florence, as Thaddeus supported their mother up the gray steps to the high, redbrick arches below the Doric columns of the upper floor. There were three double doors and they headed for the set on the right: the center doors were only opened for presidential and state visits, or when the governor was leaving office. She could hear the hubbub of voices as they entered.

The cream of Boston was in the Doric Hall, with its high ceiling and white columns. They were dressed to impress and ready to raise plenty of money for a symphony orchestra. Washington might have politics, New York might have trade, but Boston, once the birthplace of the revolution, had culture and learning. Phoebe hoped as many people would turn out when she hosted her hospital fundraiser.

Hector had said he would be arriving later and she was determined to enjoy herself until then. Catching her reflection in one of the gilt-framed mirrors, she was glad she had made an effort tonight. For day wear, Phoebe favored the princess style, with its sleeker outline and less ornate bustle, but tonight she had decided on a golden dress of silk and satin, the top skirt drawn back with elaborate flounces below. The upper part of her arms was covered by pale lace and gauze, leaving the forearms bare. The front was scooped deep enough to be fashionable, but not so deep as to provoke her mother. Her maid had dressed her hair in a complicated arrangement, secured with ostrich feathers and silk flowers. She had chosen diamonds for her earrings and necklace, and a matching bracelet on her right arm.

Phoebe followed her family through the throng. No one knew how to circulate round a room better than her mother: she exchanged a few pleasantries with minor families before moving on alone to the important Bostonians.

A waiter brought drinks to her and Florence. Phoebe looked round, sipping from the crystal glass and hoping to spot some friends. Her eye fell on Dr. McLennan, looking remarkably spruce in a black suit, with the high collar of his white shirt emphasizing his jawline. He was standing near the back wall in conversation with a man and woman. She tutted in annoyance.

"What?" asked Florence.

"I wonder what he's doing here."

"Who?"

"One of the doctors from my hospital."

Florence moved to follow where Phoebe had been looking.

"Don't turn!" Phoebe didn't want the irritating man to know they were talking about him. She'd had plenty of opportunities over the past month to observe that his self-regard was big enough already.

"Oh, you mean Dr. McLennan?"

Phoebe's mouth fell open. "You know him?"

"I was introduced at a supper party last week. Mrs. McDonald has taken him under her wing. Sees it as her mission to make sure anyone with Scots heritage has a proper place in Boston society. And a newly arrived, handsome young Scot is a perfect project for her."

Phoebe took a sip of her wine and stepped closer to one of the columns. "What did you make of him?"

"A little reserved."

Phoebe grunted. "I'd say rude, rather than reserved."

Florence looked at her and raised an eyebrow. "You don't like him?"

"Rather too full of himself for my liking. Fortunately, I don't have to spend time with him now so much of my time is spent on arrangements for the new hospital."

At that moment, McLennan turned in their direction. Phoebe squirmed inside as he must have noticed she had been observing him. He inclined his head, acknowledging her.

"Come on," Phoebe hissed to Florence. "Let's move before he feels the obligation to speak to us."

"My!" said Florence. "You really don't like him, do you?"

The evening improved as she managed to chat with friends, urging them to consider what they might donate for the hospital. The musical entertainment was top quality, as expected, given the purpose of the fundraising ball. The organizers had commissioned a new piece from Brahms that was startling in its originality.

At the end of the music, two hands were suddenly placed over her eyes.

"Guess who?" a voice whispered into her ear.

There was only one man it could be, but she played along. "President Rutherford Hayes?"

"Nope."

"Thomas Edison?"

"Nope."

"Gee, I give in."

She felt a kiss on her bare shoulder and shivered, before Hector swung her round. She fixed a broad smile on her lips.

"Goodness gracious. I would never have guessed."

He threw his head back laughing, before pulling her close and kissing her on the brow. "Have you danced much yet?"

"Only once, with a friend of Thaddeus."

"Good, you'll have plenty of energy to dance with me now."

Hector took her hand and pulled her onto the area in the middle of the room dedicated to the dancers.

"Just one dance, though," she said. "I need to keep an eye on Mother."

When the dance was over, Phoebe was relieved to hear supper was being served from tables at the rear of the room. Maybe Hector would leave her to her own devices for a while.

She stayed close to her mother, trying to make sure no one was offended by her barbed comments, now she had drunk a few glasses of champagne. "Her eyesight's not what it was," Phoebe whispered to one middle-aged woman whose fashion sense her mother had condemned. "I think that color looks beautiful on you."

Phoebe wondered if her mother would want to leave early as she was getting tired, but Mrs. Van Bergen declared she was not so feeble that she couldn't last out a ball. Phoebe persuaded her to take a sofa next to one of her oldest friends in a quiet space off the main hall. She left the two of them gossiping and returned to the hall, where the dancing had started up again.

As she squeezed through the guests to Hector, Thaddeus, and Florence, she noticed too late that the man they were speaking to was McLennan.

Her brother waved her near. "Dr. McLennan has been telling me how things are going at the hospital."

McLennan turned and made a shallow bow. "Miss Van Bergen." His mouth remained a firm line.

"Dr. McLennan," she replied, trying to keep her voice light. "Delightful to see you here."

"How do we compare with London?" Hector asked.

"Some things are more advanced here."

Thaddeus stood taller. "Of course they are."

"But some things... well, they take a wee bit of getting used to."

The next dance was announced.

"Dr. McLennan," said Florence, "I don't believe you have danced yet."

"Very observant of you, Mrs. Van Bergen. I have not."

"But it's a ball, we can't allow that." Florence put her hand on Hector's arm. "Hector, darling, I'm sure you wouldn't mind lending Phoebe to Dr. McLennan for one dance."

Phoebe flashed a look at Florence. Her sister-in-law knew the last thing she wanted was to spend time in the doctor's company.

Hector squeezed Phoebe round the waist. "'Course not. Happy to share my beautiful fiancée."

Phoebe's cheeks began to burn with outrage at being passed around by Hector—and to McLennan of all people.

McLennan shook his head. "I'm sorry. I cannae dance."

Thank goodness. Phoebe's shoulders lowered; it seemed he was just as eager as she to avoid at least ten minutes together.

"Why would you come to a ball," Florence asked, "if you won't dance? That's hardly fair on the ladies." She tapped him playfully on the chest with her fan.

"It's not that I won't dance. I *can't* dance." He gave Florence a rueful smile. "Never grasped it. Two left feet."

There was a glint in Florence's eye. "I don't believe that for a moment, Dr. McLennan. You're being modest—"

He put up a hand in protest. "Nae, truly—"

Florence took the hand, reached for Phoebe's, and put it in his palm. Phoebe's eyes were wide with horror.

"I insist," said Florence.

The orchestra was playing the opening chords of the next dance to draw people to the dance area.

"Now, off you both go." Florence gave Phoebe a shove.

Phoebe opened her mouth to protest but realized she'd be

making a scene. McLennan might be an ill-mannered man, but she wasn't going to lower herself to his level. A glance at his face showed he felt equally trapped into seeing this through.

They took a place near the center of the room.

"What dance is this?" he asked.

"A waltz." Did he really not know?

"I warn you. I was not exaggerating. I'm very poor at dancing."

Phoebe saw a look of mild terror in his eyes and almost burst out laughing. "Let's just get through this with as little damage as possible. Then we *never* have to dance again."

His stiff arms kept her at a distance, but at least McLennan knew the correct ballroom pose. The strains began and his movements were more a sway, than the triplets the waltz required. He glanced round at other couples, trying to work out what to do. Phoebe attempted to subtly direct him, but he stepped forward when he should have stepped back and trod on her foot.

He looked mortified. "Miss Van Bergen. I dinnae ken what to say. I'm so sorry."

"Do they not dance in Edinburgh?" Surely the waltz was danced in Scotland's capital city.

"They do, and with great gusto. But I never went to lessons as a young man and saw no need later."

Phoebe glanced over to where her family had been standing. Thaddeus and Hector had already taken themselves off somewhere, probably to smoke cigars. Florence was watching, however, and Phoebe saw her nudge the lady next to her and whisper something behind her fan. The other lady looked their way and laughed outright.

Something snapped inside. Florence had deliberately set her up, knowing she would spend the whole dance in deep discomfort. Well, she would not be defeated by her sister-in-law.

Phoebe broke away. "Follow me, Dr. McLennan," she said firmly, ignoring the possibility of questioning looks as she made her way from the floor to the adjacent space where a staircase led upstairs.

He did as he was asked, following her up the wide steps to the next floor and into a large ornate room, with columns and a decorative ceiling. He stood for a moment, gazing around at the fine artwork and whistled his appreciation.

"This is where the legislators meet," she said.

"Are we allowed to be in here?"

"Probably not. But that means we shouldn't be disturbed. And you need the fastest ever lesson in how to waltz."

SIX

Phoebe almost snorted at the look of alarm on McLennan's face. "Now, I've seen enough of your work to know you are a clever man. And you can count to three, can't you? That's all there is to it."

He frowned down at her. "Count to three?"

"Forward-side-together. Back-side-together. Over and over. Like this." She stood beside, rather than in front of him, showing the man's steps and taking it slowly. He followed. "See? Forward-two-three, back-two-three. Say it out loud as you step."

He raised an eyebrow but did as she asked, whispering the numbers under his breath.

"Now," Phoebe continued, "let's speed it up a little."

"Aren't there other wee steps involved? Turns and the like?"

"No need for that now. Just keep doing that step. Picture a box shape on the floor."

He seemed to grasp that idea and laughed out loud. It was a warm, low chuckle that made Phoebe smile, and for a moment she wondered if they were actually enjoying themselves.

"So, now let's match it to the music. Can you hear the rhythm coming up through the floor?" She clapped so he could follow.

He nodded and matched his steps to her claps.

"Excellent! I'm going to take my place in front of you." She did so, but not near enough to hold arms yet. She lifted her skirts enough so he could see her shoes. "See how our feet match?"

"Aye," he said uncertainly.

"Look up at me now, though. Trust your feet to do the right thing."

He raised his head, but when their gaze met, he seemed alarmed to have all her attention on him, and lost the beat.

"Keep counting," Phoebe urged.

McLennan went back to chanting *forward-side-together*.

"Good." She stepped close enough to link arms, her hand on his shoulder, his in the middle of her back. She raised her right hand, lifting his and they began to dance in unison. "See? We're waltzing."

"And... that's all there is to it?"

"Essentially."

He grinned and she understood now why nurses would huddle to gossip about him. That smile was like sunshine breaking out after a rain shower.

Phoebe felt warm inside and couldn't help a smile creeping to her own lips. For the first time, they were on the same side. He might not know it, but they were in league against her sister-in-law.

"Now, Dr. McLennan, let's go back and teach Florence a lesson."

His eyebrows raised in surprise and he looked like he was going to ask a question, but she led him out of the room before he could speak.

Downstairs, the orchestra was tuning up with the opening bars of the next dance. Phoebe went first to the middle of the room, McLennan close behind. It would be harder for the judgmental eyes of the Boston harpies to notice how simple their steps were.

"Oh, lord," McLennan whispered. "This is the same dance, isn't it?"

She looked up at his worried frown and suppressed a giggle. "Yes, they announced two waltzes. Fortunately, this is the slower one."

The music started and he put out his arms for her.

"Try to be a little less stiff," she said.

"Easier said than done." He grimaced and lowered his arms fractionally.

"Never mind. We can work on that another time."

She blushed, realizing she had implied there would be further lessons. Which, of course, there would not. Never in a million years.

But she had to admit, she'd had fun teaching him the basics and McLennan was a quick learner.

"Now. One-two-three, one-two-three," she whispered. There was a line between his brows, he was concentrating so hard. "Try not to look at your feet."

He raised his head and studied her as they began to move in time with the music. A smile curled one side of his mouth, and in that moment she found him utterly charming. She blinked as she tried to dislodge this unexpected, but pleasurable feeling.

Once they had established a rhythm, she risked a glance toward her family. Hector was nowhere to be seen, clearly unconcerned that she was dancing with another man. She wondered if that showed his faith in her, or that he simply didn't care anymore, despite his flirtatious behavior in public. Thaddeus had returned and was deep in conservation with a man she knew he wanted to bring on as an investor. Florence, however, stood by a pillar, watching them, her mouth a thin, straight line.

McLennan followed her eyeline before returning his attention to her. "I wanted to ask about Mrs. Van Bergen." Suddenly, he stepped the wrong way, missing the beat. He tutted. "I'm a foutering numpty."

Phoebe burst out laughing. "Pardon me?"

There was a slight blush to his cheek. "A foutering numpty. An idiot. I can't count, move my feet, *and* converse at the same time."

She rolled in her lips to control her giggles. "Let's just concentrate on the dancing."

He mouthed *one-two-three, one-two-three* and, when he was confident, found the catch in the music and they set off.

"No conversation until the dance is over," Phoebe said.

"Agreed."

His confidence grew and they began to take larger steps. She was proud of herself: McLennan was one of the cleverest men she knew, even she had to admit that, so all it took to learn to waltz was an explanation and a little time.

The orchestra played a long chord to signal the end of the dance. McLennan bowed low to her as she dropped a curtsey. They exchanged a look and neither could stop themselves chuckling.

"I am enormously grateful to you, Miss Van Bergen."

"It was an unexpected pleasure."

"But tell me..." He put his hands on the tops of her arms to draw her closer, wanting to say something in her ear.

She winced at the touch of his fingers, pain shooting down her arms.

He caught her reaction and stood stock-still, all jollity draining from his face. "Miss Van Bergen?" The question was on his face as well as in his mouth.

She gave a tiny shake of the head. "It's nothing." She tried a smile. Nothing she wanted anyone to know about.

McLennan's frown was back, but deeper. In a swift movement, he brushed back the gauzy fabric covering the top of each arm.

She stepped back, horrified. "Dr. McLennan!" she hissed. Glancing round, nobody seemed to have noticed, not even Florence. "I told you. It's nothing."

She turned sharply and made her way to the side area where her mother was still sitting on her sofa, praying McLennan wouldn't follow.

Douglas stood in the middle of the room and watched Miss Van

Bergen weave her way through the couples and into the side corridor.

He stroked his hand through his hair while considering whether to follow her. The doctor in him wanted to ask questions.

He knew exactly what the series of small bruises encircling her arms meant. You couldn't specialize in women's health and not come across them frequently. That sort of bruising wasn't confined to lower-class women either, the sort of women who found themselves in a desperate situation with no way out.

But he was shocked to find them on Miss Van Bergen's arms. She was so much her own woman, so confident and sure of herself. Infuriatingly so, at times. He'd never met anyone quite like her.

His heart pounded as he made his way off the dance floor, all the unexpected feeling of frivolity from their waltz seeping away. He hadn't laughed in the company of a woman for a long time.

Douglas took a drink from a tray being held by a waiter and leaned on a pillar. He caught sight of the fiancé, making a group of women laugh. He had met Mr. Hector Gregson a couple of times at the hospital and he had struck Douglas as open and friendly, bursting with confidence. This evening, he had watched him playfully teasing Miss Van Bergen, and had noticed her shiver when he daringly placed a kiss on her bare shoulder. A perfect match for Miss Van Bergen: Gregson might smooth off her diamond-sharp edges. He watched Gregson more closely now, knowing a man who seems charming on the surface could hide a darker side.

Douglas shook his head. Miss Van Bergen wouldn't stand for that. Surely! She was a strong, independent-minded woman and she had plenty of money. If her fiancé had started being rough with her, she would have broken things off, wouldn't she?

He turned his attention to Thaddeus Van Bergen nearby, still flanked by his wife. He had liked Florence Van Bergen when they'd briefly met at Mrs. McDonald's soiree. Petite, with golden hair and a pale complexion, she was a contrast to her sister-in-law's dark hair, gray eyes, and sharp tongue. Florence was like a little bird, chirruping and hopping from branch to branch. He wanted to know what Miss Van Bergen had meant when she said they were teaching Florence a lesson. But, clearly, the moment to ask had passed.

Mr. Van Bergen, though? Douglas had heard much about him in the month since arriving in Boston. The Van Bergens hadn't become the foremost railroad family by chance. Thaddeus Van Bergen followed in his father's footsteps and was a ruthless businessman, ready to build alliances and break them at will. Douglas had been warned that Van Bergen was a man who gathered information on his friends and associates, as much as on his enemies and competitors, and didn't hesitate to use that information to his advantage.

Thaddeus Van Bergen was dark like his sister, but taller, and there was a fleshiness to his features, suggesting too many rich meals at his club, too many whiskeys with his partners. He had a strong physique at the moment, but Douglas's medical eye told him it would run to fat soon.

Douglas had heard there was another brother, Alexander, a twin, and that he was the more engaging of the two. This brother was in Canada, so perhaps the member of the family who actually oversaw the expansion of the railroad empire. Thaddeus was the businessman, the dealmaker.

Douglas studied Van Bergen, who was still in conversation. He'd been told the father had died some years before and Thaddeus was head of the household here in Boston. If anyone was grasping Miss Van Bergen until she was bruised, it was most likely her elder brother. And there was not a damn thing he could do about it. He knew from years of experience that confronting the abuser often led to worse treatment. Miss Van Bergen was engaged and hopefully would be out of his grip soon, both literally and metaphorically.

This charity ball had entirely lost its charm. Douglas pushed himself away from the pillar to say goodbye to Mrs. McDonald.

Boston might have a veneer of a gracious society, but after a month at the women's hospital, he knew it was no different from London, or Edinburgh, or his native Dundee. People were people and that was an end to it. Just now, he wanted time away from everyone.

SEVEN

Mrs. Van Bergen escaped to the summer residence in the middle of July and insisted Phoebe travel with her and make sure she was settled. Phoebe didn't need much persuading: only thirty miles north of Boston, the house was on a promontory near Manchester by the Sea and was a haven that she adored.

Phoebe and her mother traveled by train and then used a carriage for the short distance to the house. They were accompanied by ladies' maids, cooks, and butlers, but the house was run by servants hired locally.

Her father had built a cottage above Lobster Cove and called it the Lobster Pot. The area had become increasingly popular in the last few years, with more of the Boston elite buying land and building summer retreats. This meant Thaddeus was prepared to spend time there as he could cultivate business connections. One of the first things Thaddeus had done after their father's death in 1874 was to knock down the old house and commission Peabody & Stearns architects to build something grand enough for his ambitions.

The brand-new house was called Fairview and built to look like a French chateau, with circular towers topped with weathervanes, turrets, and arches. The walls were made of brick imported from France and resembled a burnt-sienna tapestry, contrasting with carved limestone from Indiana surrounding every door and window. The grounds were landscaped so the family could enjoy different views of the sea and islands, ancient trees having been dug up and others planted.

Phoebe sighed happily as she looked up at the house. She loved the sense of space, especially after their Beacon Hill townhouse and the intensity of city living. She stepped into the entrance hall, where the housekeeper was already helping Mrs. Van Bergen into the sitting room to rest in an armchair. Her mother scowled as no position brought her comfort. A maid appeared at her elbow proffering a cup of tea.

Phoebe saw she wasn't needed so went up one of the matching curved staircases to her room. She found Farrell unpacking her things. The light in the room made her smile—the wide windows flooded the room with sunshine, illuminating the floral wallpaper and reflecting off the white, painted furniture. She went to the French window and stepped out onto her own balcony to take a deep breath of sea air.

Today, the sea was blue, reflecting the cloudless sky. Seagulls cried above, flying in circles, catching the onshore breeze. She could hear the waves gently pushing against the beach below the outcrop the house was built on. Her father had chosen the perfect location, even if Thaddeus had pulled down his hideaway and erected this impressive edifice.

Phoebe closed her eyes. Bliss. Here she could escape the expectations of Boston life, and connect with the natural world. Tomorrow, she would get up early to see the sun rise over the Atlantic, walk down to Lobster Cove, and take off her shoes and stockings to bury her toes in the sand.

Thaddeus and Florence arrived the next day and gradually all the summerhouses in the area filled with wealthy families from Boston.

The round of social engagements began: picnics on the long private beach to the south of the house, tennis and croquet on the closely clipped lawn, sailing trips around the Manchester Sound. Phoebe enjoyed these carefree activities but would escape to Lobster Cove with a book when she needed some peace and quiet.

Hector arrived on the first Friday of August, raising the spirits of most of the occupants of Fairview.

"Come sit with me, my darling boy," commanded Mrs. Van Bergen. "You can tell me all the Boston gossip."

Hector willingly sat next to her, their heads close together, making her laugh with scandalous tales. Phoebe noticed how Hector could make her mother laugh in a way she and her brothers failed to do.

Naturally, Hector stayed for dinner, sitting next to Phoebe. She barely contributed to the conversation as Hector happily joked about his days at the bank, entertaining the whole family.

At the end of the evening, Thaddeus suggested Hector stay overnight. "You could use one of the guest rooms."

Phoebe swallowed, trying to suppress a jolt of alarm.

Mrs. Van Bergen was aghast. "Stay overnight? Phoebe's fiancé? Don't be a jackass, Thaddeus. You know reputation is everything. I can't allow even the appearance of improper behavior." She patted Hector's hand. "I'm sorry, my dear boy, no matter how late, and how dear you are to me, you need to go to your lodgings in the village."

"Of course, Mrs. Van Bergen. I didn't expect anything else." He gave a winning grin, which Phoebe returned with her own tight smile, feeling her pulse start to settle.

"But mind you come for breakfast and stay the day with us. We have a party invited for tomorrow."

It was Mrs. Van Bergen's habit to invite a large party for Saturday dinner and she wasn't going to let her ill health change things—although she left it to Florence to issue the invitations and undertake most of the hosting duties.

. . .

After a long day at the beach, Phoebe changed into evening dress. She paused at the double doors of their oversized drawing room. Hector was by the window, talking to two middle-aged women whose names she had forgotten. She fixed a smile and glided over to him. He gently kissed her cheek. "There you are, my honeybee."

"How are you, Miss Van Bergen?" asked one of the women.

Mrs. McDonald—that was it. She remembered now. "Well, thank you, Mrs. McDonald."

"This is my cousin, Mary McDonald. She is staying with me for the summer to see if the sea air will improve her health."

Phoebe smiled at the second lady. They looked remarkably alike: both with dark hair speckled with gray, both in blue dresses with tartan trims. Although Mrs. McDonald was a central member of the Boston set, she was large and robust in a way that made Phoebe think uncharitably that she must have been a dock worker in a previous life.

"Delighted to welcome you to our home," Phoebe said, putting out her hand.

"And you know my other house guest," Mrs. McDonald called over to a man who was deep in conversation with another guest. "Douglas, Douglas, I need you here."

Her mouth went dry: Dr. McLennan.

He turned and looked a little awkward, his eyes avoiding hers. He was less formally dressed than at the hospital, wearing a blue double-breasted reefer jacket and soft cravat. His hair was swept back and his mustache neatly trimmed.

Since the charity ball, they had been formal whenever they encountered each other at the hospital. Truth was, Phoebe avoided him when possible. Teaching him the rudiments of dance had been unexpected fun, but that had been shattered by the humiliation of him seeing her bruises. Her face burned as she remembered.

She noticed him swallow and clear his throat as he made his way to them. Perhaps he had been trying to avoid her too.

Hector eagerly put out his hand. "I remember you. From the hospital. Am I right?"

McLennan shook his hand. "Aye, good to meet you again, Mr. Gregson." He dipped his head toward Phoebe. "And you, Miss Van Bergen."

She nodded to him but was at a loss to think of small talk, so said nothing.

Mrs. McDonald patted Phoebe's arm. "Now, Miss Van Bergen, you mustn't be cross that I've taken him away from that hospital of yours."

She was sorry her silence had been misinterpreted. "I wasn't at all cross—"

"We both know how hard he works there."

"Indeed," Phoebe replied. "I was just surprised to see him here. At the coast, I mean." She dropped her eyes to the floor, aware that her words could be interpreted as implying he didn't belong in this summer playground for the gilded elite. Although, in truth, it didn't seem a natural place for a person of his taciturn nature.

"Dr. McLennan mentioned a love of sailing some weeks back," continued Mrs. McDonald, "so I promised to bring him here at my first opportunity."

"Sailing?" said Hector enthusiastically.

"Aye," McLennan replied. "I've enjoyed it since I was a wee boy."

"What do you sail? A dinghy? Scull?"

McLennan turned to him with a smile. "Anything I can get my hands on. I love going out solo, but nothing beats an afternoon with friends."

Hector put a hand on McLennan's shoulder. "D'you race?"

"Sometimes, if called upon."

"Excellent. Thads and I always race when we're here. We're planning to go out on Monday. You can join us. Add some excitement."

"I'd enjoy that, but I'm afraid I need to be back in Boston on Monday."

Hector patted McLennan's chest with the back of his hand. "I'm sure the hospital can manage without you for a few days."

Phoebe's mouth fell open. She was about to contradict her fiancé when McLennan gave a low chuckle.

"I'm not sure that would be a good idea. Particularly with my boss standing next to me."

Hector's curls bounced as he put his head back to laugh. "Pheebs. Your boss! Never thought of it that way." He put his arm round her waist and pulled her closer. "Well, that means the race will have to be tomorrow then."

McLennan frowned. "Tomorrow?"

"I'm sure Thads will be up for it. A circle round the Sound."

Phoebe put her hand to Hector's chest. "Come on, that's not fair. You and Thaddeus have been sailing here for years. Dr. McLennan has only just arrived. He won't know the tides and channels."

McLennan stared at her with those green eyes, the slight line returning between his brows. "Ocht, dinnae fash. If someone can lend me a boat, I'd be happy to give it a go."

Was everyone determined to misinterpret her this evening? She had tried to be kind to McLennan, but he seemed to have taken it as a challenge. Thankfully, the bell rang to announce supper.

"Good man. Look, I'll sort it out with Thads right now."

Hector skipped off to find Thaddeus, leaving McLennan to accompany Phoebe.

He put his hands behind his back as he walked slowly beside her. "I've been wanting to ask—that night, at the charity ball..."

Phoebe's chest constricted. Surely he was not going to ask about the bruises *here*.

He cleared his throat. "What did you mean when you said you would teach Florence a lesson."

Phoebe let out a gulping laugh in relief. "Oh, *that*. She was setting me up."

"Setting you up?"

"She knew that... I... well, I..." Goodness, this was awkward.

"Don't like me very much?" McLennan supplied the rest of her sentence.

There. He had said it, so she didn't have to.

She felt her cheeks get warm. "Well, no, I didn't say—"

"It's alright, Miss Van Bergen. We don't have to like everyone we meet. I'm not sure I like you very much either."

She stopped still and looked at him open-mouthed. What a thing to say out loud! Then he turned to her and she was sure there was a twinkle in his eye.

He continued across the hall. "I'm still making my mind up."

She fell in step. "Well, it was more about you having said you couldn't dance. That's what Florence was really up to. She knows how tedious it can be to stand up for a couple of dances with a poor dancer."

"Is it? Young women always look like they're having such braw time dancing, even when the partner is as poor as me."

"I assure you, a poor dancer can be agony. The humiliation of having your toes stepped on. Even by a handsome partner."

He paused at the door of the dining room and raised an eyebrow.

Phoebe dropped her gaze, her face warming. He couldn't be *unaware* of how handsome he was. And now she felt a little embarrassed she had said so out loud. She straightened her shoulders to pretend the moment had not happened. "We young ladies are very adept at painting on a smile."

"So your sister-in-law was punishing you with the humiliation of standing up with a poor dancer."

"Uh-huh."

"And you turned that round by teaching me the basic steps."

"I had to do something to get my own back."

He laughed. "Well, I promise you. I will never again allow myself to be forced into dancing with you. Indeed, it's quite likely I'll never dance again. Now I understand the full extent of the humiliation I bring."

Phoebe glanced up and this time was sure he was teasing her. He stroked his mustache to cover the fact he was grinning.

They reached the dining table and Phoebe let out a breath in relief as she saw her mother had placed them many seats apart. For the second time, she had come dangerously close to enjoying his company.

EIGHT

Douglas wasn't quite sure what sort of sailing race he had gotten himself into. Was this a serious race or some fun pootering around the buoys? He was relieved Thaddeus hadn't mentioned placing bets. Douglas was a confident sailor but wouldn't want to risk losing what could be—for him—a large amount of money. For Thaddeus and Hector, it would be small change.

He admired the dinghy a local sailor had loaned him, courtesy of Mrs. McDonald. It was good quality, sleek, with a jib and main sail that looked quite new. The sailor took him out before breakfast on Sunday morning, pointing out the currents and an area where a sandbar below the water slowed the channel. Part of the Sound was protected by the headland where the Van Bergens and other wealthy Bostonians had built their summer retreats. Beyond that, he was into the choppy Atlantic waters, where the wind whipped waves in a landscape of miniature mountains, each capped with snow.

Douglas soon learned how the boat handled and was pleased with it. Gratifyingly, the sailor complimented his technique and how fast he had understood the particularities of the bay.

The race was set for two p.m., so Douglas was waiting on the jetty at half past one. The Van Bergen dinghy was larger than the one on loan to Douglas. When Thaddeus arrived, Douglas commended him on the fine vessel, as a manservant made the final adjustments.

"Nothing but the best," Thaddeus said. "What my father always taught me."

Hector bounced toward them. "Ready for an afternoon's fun?" He was dressed in a white woolen top that hugged his torso, and white flannel pants. Douglas wore a navy-blue roll-neck sweater which had once belonged to Mrs. McDonald's husband. Even though it was August, Douglas knew the gusts off the Atlantic would be chilly once they were out in open sea.

The three men stood on the harbor as Thaddeus again went over the course.

"It's a triangular route. We start just beyond Bow Bell Ledge, in line with the oak tree on the promontory over there. Merriman will blow the hooter to set us off. Then, it's out to the buoy on Hunters Bar, across to the gybe mark at Sauli Rock."

Douglas shielded his eyes from the sunlight so he could look into the distance.

"Then back round and into the Sound. The finishing line is between Miriam's Rocks and Glass Head. The harbormaster will position himself in the correct place and his decision on the winner is final."

Thaddeus gave a stern look at Hector, who shrugged. Douglas suspected some debate about the winner in the past.

"Looks good to me," said Douglas.

"Right. Coin toss to decide positions." Thaddeus pulled a coin from his pants pocket.

The sailor had explained to Douglas that the boat on the left when they lined up was at an advantage. Hector punched the air when he won the position, with Thaddeus scowling that he had come off worst, with his boat furthest right. Douglas thought how different this was from the friendly races in Scotland, where a visitor would have been given the best position as a matter of course, to make up for his lack of local knowledge.

The three men clambered into each of their boats and hoisted sails, ready to depart. As they edged out into the Sound toward the starting line, Douglas saw a crowd had gathered on the promontory to watch. He spotted Mrs. McDonald wearing a tartan shawl. He was pretty sure she would have hoisted a saltire flag, if she'd had one.

The Van Bergen group were watching from the lawn of Fairview. The seated lady must be Mrs. Van Bergen with Miss Van Bergen standing close in a white dress. Florence Van Bergen stood near the steps that led down to a jetty by the rocks, holding a pale parasol.

They negotiated the tricky business of lining up as tides and winds were pulling them onwards. Then the hooter sounded and they were off.

Douglas had decided to enjoy the afternoon's sailing and not worry too much about the outcome, but he could soon see he was a better sailor than either of his competitors. He'd spent happy childhood holidays mastering the wild and challenging winds off the Scottish coast. He loved the freedom sailing brought, the feeling of being at one with the elements. The wind rushed through his hair and salt pricked his skin as water sprayed off the tops of waves. His boat sped through the slate-gray water, slicing the waves, sometimes bouncing when he tacked at the wrong moment.

Thaddeus was heavy-handed maneuvering his craft, not seeming to know how to take advantage of the wind. Hector, however, was a reckless sailor. He was ahead, taking advantage of the blanketing air disrupting the two dinghies behind. Douglas closed in on him by tacking on favorable shifts in the wind. Hector saw the reduced lengths between them as he reached the first buoy. He took the turn at an extreme angle, the boat heeling deep on its side. Douglas was fearful the boat was going over as Hector took his time shifting to the upper side to provide some ballast. As the dinghy settled, Hector whooped with delight.

As Douglas rounded the windward mark, he paid out the sheets so the sails were pregnant with the wind, then leaned far to the starboard to balance the craft while pulling on the tiller, thrilled to be picking up speed. He glanced back and saw Thaddeus was furious at still being in the rear. They were now in open water and waves were being fomented by the wind, although the sun was warm on Douglas's shoulders.

He looked at the coast to the north and south, the rocky promontories, the woodland growing close to the shore. The land beyond was flat. He saw a slither of white beach below the Fairview estate, and a line of low islands jutting into the sea. It must have been a sight like this that had greeted the Pilgrim Fathers more than two and a half centuries before. He wondered what their feelings would have been, arriving at a new continent. How many were trying to put bad things behind them and hoping for a fresh start, just as he was?

Douglas's superior sailing skills soon told in the open ocean. He slid ahead of Hector as they made their way to the gybe mark at Sauli Rock and the turn for home. Thaddeus had gained speed and was a close third. Douglas ducked under the boom as he rounded the buoy and the stern passed through the eye of the wind. He gybed back toward the harbor, the Van Bergen promontory now on his right. The crowd of spectators seemed to have grown at the edge of the Fairview lawn.

He could easily see the two boats close behind. Hector took Sauli Rock at a close angle, again recklessly pushing his luck, particularly when he was going to have the wind on his other side. A strong gust caught Hector's dinghy, but the sails had been sheeted too tightly and were making the boat unstable. The boom swung across the boat and the port side of the hull lifted out of the water as the boat heeled over, almost capsizing.

Douglas heard a yell, and the boat righted itself.

Hector was nowhere to be seen.

NINE

With one hand on the tiller and the other clutching the main sheet, Douglas looked back, his heart racing, searching for Hector in the waves. Maybe he was clinging to the gunwale of his dinghy?

Douglas let both the ropes pay out and pushed on the tiller so he could turn about. The wind filled his sail on the opposite side and he tacked back as fast as possible.

Suddenly, Douglas spotted Hector's head above the waves, his arms floundering, crying out and then bobbing under. The man was clearly not a strong swimmer and was panicking as he was swept away from his small craft.

Thankfully, Thaddeus was still sailing to the rock.

Douglas stood and shouted, "I've spotted him!"

"Hector?"

Who else would he damn well be talking about? "He's in the water. Struggling."

"But you've got him in your sights?"

"Aye!" Douglas kept his eye on Hector's head so he didn't lose him.

"Capital. I'll see you the other side of the finishing line then," yelled Thaddeus. He pulled at the tiller, and ducked under the boom, taking his sleek dinghy round the gybe mark.

"But—" Douglas's words were carried away on the wind as, incredulously, he watched Thaddeus sail home. He'd left his friend in the ocean!

Douglas brought his boat close to Hector as swiftly as he could. He tossed a line for the drowning man so Douglas could haul him in, but Hector was already too exhausted. There was terror in his eyes, as each time he went under could be his last.

Douglas pushed his deck shoes from his feet and dived into the water. It was freezing cold, but no worse than the North Sea of his youth. He swam to Hector with powerful strokes, grabbing the back of his neck as Hector slipped below the water again. He brought him, spluttering, into the air and supported his head above the waves.

"I've got you!" he shouted. "You're safe."

Hector's arms were flailing, making it harder for Douglas to support him.

"Try not to panic," Douglas said, as he sought to control Hector. At this rate, he'd have both of them drown.

Douglas held him firmly with one arm and swam with the other, back to his boat before it drifted away. At the hull, he urged Hector to reach up and put his hands on the gunwale. Dear God, he really could have done with Thaddeus's help. He took Hector's hips and lifted him up far enough for him to scramble over into the boat, sinking beneath the water himself as he did so before kicking to get his head above the surface. Douglas took a moment to catch his breath before reaching up for the gunwale.

The hull swayed toward the water, but righted itself as Douglas rolled into the boat. Hector lay on his back, his arms on his chest, taking deep breaths. Cold water pooled in the hull as it drained off them both.

Hector started to laugh. "I'm alive! Dear God. I'm alive."

Exhausted and spitting saltwater from his mouth, Douglas took the seat at the stern, grasped the tiller and set a course back home. Ahead of them, he could see Thaddeus crossing the line that had been designated as the finish. He sat open-mouthed as Thaddeus stood in his dinghy, his arms raised in triumph.

"My boat," groaned Hector. "Where's my boat?"

Douglas glanced over his shoulder. "I'm sure one of your lackeys will row out and fetch it."

Rather than return to the harbor, he gently brought his boat alongside the jetty that extended from the rocks below the Van Bergen's mansion, where a large party had gathered. Two manservants clambered in to help Hector, lifting him out, a man under each arm. Hector laughed again, as if the shock had made him drunk and he was delighted to find there was still a life ahead of him.

The owner of the dinghy put out a hand to help Douglas onto the jetty. "Good job you did there, sir. Diving in like that. We could see it all. Good job."

Douglas waved a hand. "Ocht, anyone would have done the same."

Thaddeus approached grinning, and Douglas's heart sank. Not everyone would have done the same.

Thaddeus embraced Hector at the end of the jetty and then put his hand out as Douglas joined them, shivering with cold and dripping from head to toe. "Hope you're not a sore loser, doctor."

Douglas was speechless as Thaddeus shook his hand. Was that all he was going to say? No apology?

They turned to make their way along the wooden jetty. Most of the women had rushed down to the rocks to greet them.

Florence Van Bergen stood on her toes to give her husband a kiss on the cheek. "Well done, Thaddy. Well done!"

Miss Van Bergen was behind, her face drained of color. It must be the shock of seeing her fiancé almost drown.

Mrs. McDonald offered to take Douglas home immediately to dry off and get warm.

"Heavens, no!" cried Hector. "McLennan is my savior. If I'm warming up at Fairview, I want him by my side." He glanced at Thaddeus, who shrugged his acquiescence. Hector clapped his hand on his wet shoulder as they turned toward the house. "Come on, Doug. Or Dougie?"

"Douglas," he replied firmly. Only his family called him anything more familiar.

Hector stumbled and a manservant helped him up the steep steps threaded through the rocks to the lawn.

As they neared the house, Douglas fell into step next to Thaddeus, unable to let the incident pass. "I was surprised you didn't come back."

"Come back?"

"To help. With Hector."

Thaddeus frowned. "Why would I have done that?"

Douglas blinked, amazed he had to explain things. "Well, I... I shouted... I said he was struggling."

"But you were there. You'd gone back to help the idiot who can't handle his own sailing dinghy."

Douglas stared at him.

Thaddeus tapped Douglas on the chest with his knuckle and winked. "And there was a race to win."

He stood motionless as he watched Thaddeus skip up the steps to the loggia and into the house.

Miss Van Bergen had been standing nearby and he was sure she had heard the exchange. The poor woman must be furious with her brother's heartless response.

"I'm sorry you had to hear that," Douglas muttered.

Miss Van Bergen paused and looked straight at him, her eyes bright with emotion. Then she turned and stepped toward the house.

"If it were me," she said in a low whisper, "I'd have left him to drown."

TEN

Phoebe hurried up the steps onto the stone loggia and into the drawing room. She put both hands to her lips as if in prayer, closed her eyes, and let out a long breath. Had she really said that out loud? How could she have let her guard down like that? And with McLennan of all people? She shook her head and hurried through the gloomy room, fearful the doctor would be close behind. Maybe he hadn't heard; that was the only thing she could hope for.

Reaching the hall, Phoebe found the place in uproar: servants rushing with towels and taking hot water to the bedroom upstairs.

The housekeeper, Mrs. O'Harvey, sought Phoebe out. "Mrs. Van Bergen is in the afternoon sitting room. She had a little turn when you were all down at the jetty."

"How is she?"

"We're making her comfortable."

A maid hurried past and up the stairs.

"And a bath is being filled," Mrs. O'Harvey continued. "I thought Mr. Gregson would want one. I've taken the liberty of finding him some dry clothes from Mr. Van Bergen's closet. Your father, I mean."

Phoebe stepped toward the sitting room. "And the doctor?"

"I've already sent a man to fetch one from town for your mother."

"I meant, we must look after Dr. McLennan. He's just as cold and tired as Mr. Gregson." And, after all, he was the one who had risked his life to save Hector.

Mrs. O'Harvey nodded. "I'll see to that next. But I wonder... Could *he* be asked to check Mrs. Van Bergen?"

Phoebe hesitated. Was it an imposition when they should be looking after him? But Mother's health came first. "Please would you do that."

In the sitting room, her mother was in an armchair angled to the window so she could see the garden. Phoebe walked round and knelt. Her mother's cheeks were pale, with dark areas around her eyes, and her breath was light and quick.

"Mother?" Phoebe touched her hand: the skin seemed thin, stretched over the knuckles, with veins standing out.

Mrs. Van Bergen half opened her eyes. They were watery with tears. "For a moment, I thought it was Thaddeus." Her voice was barely a whisper. "Tipping over his boat. I don't know what I would have done if he had—"

Phoebe patted her hand. "He's a good sailor, mother. Thaddeus was always safe." She huffed a breath: Thaddeus could be relied on to put his own needs first.

A smile fluttered on Mrs. Van Bergen's lips and she spoke more forcefully. "And he won the race, didn't he?"

Phoebe said nothing. Was she the only Van Bergen ashamed of her brother? Everyone had seen Hector flung into the ocean, and watched as Thaddeus sailed straight past. When he raised his arms in triumph, Florence had applauded his victory. Phoebe had felt sick in her stomach.

She heard someone at the door and looked up to see the housekeeper ushering in McLennan.

"Dr. McLennan said he was happy to look at you, ma'am, if that would help."

He stood there, his wet hair pushed back, the seawater making it darker than usual. A few drops were dripping from the bottom of his sweater and onto the Persian carpet. His pants clung to his legs and he had nothing on his feet. The poor man really needed to go and get warmed up and changed.

Phoebe tried to signal a look of gratitude for agreeing to look in on her mother, but he didn't meet her eye.

Mrs. Van Bergen scrunched her eyelids. "A lot of fuss and bother. And why can't I have my own doctor?"

Phoebe's skin prickled at her mother's rudeness. "It would take hours for him to travel from Boston. Aren't we lucky to have a doctor here, now?"

Mrs. Van Bergen grunted her acceptance.

Phoebe stood and glanced at McLennan, but his attention was fixed on her mother. Maybe he *had* heard what she said about Hector and was disgusted—avoiding even looking at her.

Phoebe coughed and straightened a crease from her skirt. "Perhaps it would be best if I left you to it," she said, hurrying out of the room. Much as he was a thorn in her side at the hospital, she found she couldn't bear him thinking the worst of her.

Douglas leaned back in the bath and slid down until he was underwater. At least his bones and muscles were warming up and he could soak away the smell of the ocean that had leached into his hair. He would like to stay in this enormous tub forever. He emerged, took a breath, and looked round. So, this was what American luxury looked like. In Scotland, wealthy families took pride in how old household items were, rather than how new.

The bathroom was huge and everything gleamed: the white roll-top bath, the brass faucet, the marble floor, the white tiles. Although the window was frosted, it was open a fraction and he could hear the sea. He could understand how attractive the location was for the Van Bergens to escape the busyness of Boston, even though his own time here had been anything but relaxing.

He had examined Mrs. Van Bergen as best he could in the

absence of his medical bag. Her pulse had been rapid and fluttering, her skin felt clammy. He suspected a weakness in the heart but could do little more than suggest she keep smelling salts close at hand and avoid too much excitement. He had heard of physicians in France and Italy using nitroglycerin for weak hearts and wondered about trying to get hold of some when he was back in Boston.

His thoughts wandered over the afternoon but kept snagging on Miss Van Bergen's words. Had he heard her right? He began to doubt himself. He had probably still been foggy from the sailing incident.

Douglas moved and realized the water had gone cold. He raised himself and climbed onto the wooden slatted mat where his feet left footprints. After he dried himself on the large towel left by a maid, he wrapped it round his waist, and went to the mirror to wipe a circle in the condensation. He pushed back his wet hair, noticing the blond streaks caused by the Massachusetts sun, then drew a hand over his jaw and mustache. He really wanted a shave, but his kit was at Mrs. McDonald's. He'd get rid of this stubble when he was back there and then be off on the train to Boston, first thing in the morning. He let out a long breath, looking forward to getting back to work and escaping the complex relationships in the Van Bergen family.

The private bathroom connected to a guest room. He went through and found dry clothing had been laid out on the bed. His own clothes had been spirited away and he imagined they were being laundered somewhere, at that very moment. He wondered whose clothing this was, knowing he was more muscular than Thaddeus. Maybe they belonged to the twin brother he had heard of: Alexander. Douglas dressed, finding the shirt a little tight across the chest and upper arms.

He suddenly felt weary—perhaps the shock of what had happened that afternoon was catching up with him. The sailing and swimming had been exhausting. He sat down heavily on the bed. The mattress was deep and firm, so he lay back and stretched out. Jings, the bed was comfortable. If he closed his eyes just for a minute, he would feel better.

Douglas's eyes flew open. The sun was casting shadows at a different angle and he wondered how long he'd been asleep.

He heard a voice, low but close, and guessed that was what had woken him. Disorientated, he raised his head. The voice was coming from the adjacent room, the other side of the wall the bed was against.

Douglas recognized the man's voice: Hector Gregson.

"Come on. No one will find us here."

There was a woman's voice, but he couldn't tell what she said.

"Have some mercy. I almost *died* today. Doesn't that make you want to grab everything you can?"

Douglas felt himself blushing to be overhearing the exchange: Hector was just the sort of man to take advantage of one of the young maids, even though he was engaged to be married.

"You liked it before. I don't understand what's changed."

The woman's voice replied but was indistinct.

"Come on, Pheebs. Stop holding out on me."

Douglas held his breath, still as a statue on a medieval tomb.

Pheebs.

Miss Van Bergen.

"No, Hector, please." Her voice was louder now, pleading. "Not here."

"Why not here?"

"Not with my mother downstairs."

Something fell over: perhaps an ornament, or a piece of furniture.

"I'll make it quick—"

"No, I don't want—"

Douglas sat up and moved his feet to the ground, feeling a wave of nausea, desperate to intervene. What could he do? Such a proud woman would be overcome with shame if she knew he could hear everything.

There was a movement in the adjacent room.

"No, no, no." Miss Van Bergen's voice was faint and quick, almost like a mantra. Douglas could sense she was on the edge of tears.

"Quiet, now." Hector's voice had lost its purring tone and was harsh.

Miss Van Bergen fell silent.

Douglas put his head in his hands and clenched his teeth. He didn't want to hear. Didn't want to be part of this through his own silence. He stood and quietly paced the room, every sense alert, fearing the worst.

There were muffled sounds and suppressed grunts, and then he heard Hector's laugh. "See? Told you I'd be quick. Now, you wait here for a few minutes while I go downstairs." There was a shuffling sound, footsteps on the creaking floorboards. "Although, I don't know why you keep making a fuss. We're going to be man and wife, after all."

The door clicked open and then closed.

Douglas stayed stock-still, his heart racing as he thought about his options. He wanted to dash down those stairs and punch Hector's self-satisfied face. He clenched his fists.

Maybe he should go and comfort Miss Van Bergen, see if he could be of assistance.

A ridiculous idea. He was the *last* person she would want to see now. She was so poised and self-assured—she wouldn't want a doctor at her hospital knowing she was being abused.

He should find her lady's maid, send her to help.

But how would he explain why a maid was needed, other than say he had been in the next room? Again, Miss Van Bergen would have the humiliation of realizing he knew everything.

He heard a movement, then some other sounds. Was she putting the room back in order? He listened carefully but could hear no tears or sobs. The catch on the doorknob clicked and then creaked shut; Miss Van Bergen had left the room as quietly as she could.

Douglas rested his brow on the wall and closed his eyes, coldness returning to his bones. He had been an utter coward; he'd done nothing. He pushed himself upright and crossed to the chair, where shoes and a pale linen jacket had been left for him.

He would speak to Thaddeus Van Bergen: that was his only choice. Much as he despised the man, he had to know what was happening to his sister, under their own roof; what had clearly been going on for some time.

He pushed his hands back over his hair. Now he understood those bruises. Now he understood those shocking words Miss Van Bergen had whispered to him that afternoon. What she was enduring. His heart broke for her.

ELEVEN

Phoebe walked along the corridor to her own bedroom, quietly closed the door, leaned against it and shut her eyes. She was not going to cry. She wasn't. She needed to be strong.

But she didn't feel strong; she felt pathetic, and small, and dirty. She collapsed onto her bed and lay on her side, her knees drawn up.

How had she let it come to this? Was there no way out for her? She couldn't keep putting off setting a date for their wedding. But marriage to Hector—a man she hated and despised—would be intolerable.

She thought back to when she had first met him at a theater performance. Thaddeus had introduced Hector as a friend from Harvard, although they had reconnected through business. How captivated she had been that night by his charm and wit. She was flattered that this man, who could hold a room full of people in the palm of his hand, had chosen her. Yes, she was a wealthy heiress, but Hector seemed to genuinely care for her.

And, ah, those first kisses in the darkness of a side room at a charity concert—they had been so thrilling. She had thrummed with desire for him. She remembered threading her fingers through his curls, studying every feature of his handsome, boyish face.

There was something almost elfin about his sharp, narrow nose, and those angular cheekbones. He'd pulled her close and whispered that he adored her, had never met anyone like her, that they were destined to be together.

She had been so happy when they got engaged. She had rejected a line of suitors in her early twenties and now, unlike some of her friends, she was going to marry for love. She was going to have everything she ever wanted: the work at the hospital, her own home full of children, a husband who made each day joyful.

When Hector had persuaded her to meet him at a hotel in South Boston, she had felt excited but nervous. She'd been so naïve; stupidly thrilled she was transgressing the rules of society. It had made her feel bold and independent. She had pretended to her mother she was meeting a friend for lunch in town, and had set off in a hat with a veil, in the shadow of her parasol.

She had crossed the bridge and found herself surrounded by Irish accents and the stink of the foundry. The small hotel was on a street off Broadway and she had thought it charmingly bohemian. Looking back now, she knew it was seedy and wondered how many other women he had taken there. The room had been small and threadbare, but that didn't matter: she only had eyes for Hector. Tremblingly, she had put her trust in him.

She had been uncertain what to expect, although the whispered tales of the young women at her finishing school told of pain and discomfort. Hector had been so loving and gentle. She had thought: if this is what married life would bring, it was one more thing to look forward to.

She had spoken to Hector about agreeing a date for their wedding, but he had been ambivalent. Aren't we enjoying being affianced, he'd asked. Wasn't it fun, being the center of attention? Soon they'd be just another married Boston couple. There was no rush.

He had persuaded her to meet at the hotel again. She'd not taken much persuasion, as she thought of that little room as a nest for the two of them. It had been different the second time, though:

Hector had not been attentive to her, instead thinking only of his own needs. The assignation was brief and uncomfortable. When he'd said he needed to return to the bank, Phoebe was confused but made excuses for him in her mind.

The time after that, everything changed. Phoebe shuddered at the memory, burying her face in the pillow.

She'd been to watch him rowing in a regatta on the Charles River and went with others to the clubhouse in Cambridge to congratulate him on his team's win. He had told her about the trophies he wanted to show her and she had willingly left her friends and let him lead her upstairs. He had pulled her into a tiny side room—she wasn't sure what it was—possibly a janitor's room. He began to kiss her and then his hands were on her skirts. Horrified, she had said no and pushed him back. He had grinned—surely she found the situation exciting, he said, with all their friends below. She had stared at him and said she was leaving the closet at once. He said that if she truly loved him, she'd let him do it. She remembered the hollow feeling inside, hearing those words. Was this love? Every fiber of her being said it wasn't.

Phoebe had pushed him aside and put her hand on the doorknob, but he had pulled her back. She saw a sudden change in his face, a coldness in his eyes, and it scared her. He had held her firmly until it hurt. She had wanted to cry out, but the only thing that could make this worse was other people knowing it was happening. She had screwed up her eyes and clamped her teeth shut, and held herself rigid during the short time Hector needed to satisfy himself.

Afterwards, he had grinned at her and kissed her on the end of her nose. "Let's go find everyone else, before they wonder what's happened to us."

She had been in a daze as he led her back down the clubhouse stairs to her friends, as if nothing had happened. She had stood wordlessly, barely hearing what was said to her, desperate for it to be time to go home.

A week later, they had sat next to each other on a bench in the park in the middle of Louisburg Square, in front of the Van Bergen townhouse. The light through the trees had dappled patterns around them. Her heart had raced like a steam train when preparing to speak, as she tried to push down her fear of him. She sternly told him nothing like that must ever happen again. She was prepared to overlook it once as a brief mistake. However, if he *ever* forced himself on her again, it would be over between them.

He had scoffed and then giggled. Yes, *giggled* at her. "What you going to do, honeybee? Tell everyone?"

She had stared at him, not quite understanding what he meant.

"Tell everyone that you frequent that hotel in South Boston?"

Her blood had turned to ice. He was right: she couldn't tell anyone. Not her friends, not Florence, and certainly not her mother.

She saw him properly for the first time then.

She had clenched her fingers into balls to stop herself from striking him, trying desperately to keep some dignity. "Our engagement is at an end, Hector. You are not the man I thought you were."

He had put his head back and laughed. "I'm the same man I've always been." He sat up and adjusted his position on the bench, drawing up one leg beneath him, until he was looking straight at her. Phoebe became aware of every sound and movement around them, her pulse thudding. "You're not going to tell anyone," he said. "But you break off this engagement, then I will."

She had stared at him, her mouth open and eyes wide.

"Everyone will know you're not the pure princess your mother would have them believe. Even the Van Bergen money won't protect you. The folks at that hotel, for starters, they'll remember you."

She had swallowed, but her mouth was dry. "You wouldn't," she whispered.

He had winked at her. "Wouldn't I?"

And, shockingly, she had known it was true. He would happily ruin her reputation with one indiscreet conversation. She would be ostracized. Any hope of marriage and a family of her own would be gone.

She had struggled to speak. "Was it always about the money?"

He had snorted. "Not *all* about the money. I'm very fond of you, Pheebs. And, God knows, you're a beautiful woman." He had put his hand over hers. "I think we're going to get along just fine."

From his point of view, they did get along fine. She became skilled at avoiding situations where they could find themselves alone, but she became more compliant, trying to keep him sweet as she searched for a way to escape him. As the weeks and months passed, she could find none, and began to shrivel deep inside, like a dry leaf in the fall.

There were occasions, like today, when she was trapped and she chided herself for not being more quick-footed. He knew she wouldn't make a fuss at Fairview, not with her family around, and so many servants.

There was a knock at the door and she was startled out of her thoughts as her maid entered: it was time to dress for dinner.

"Ah, Farrell." Phoebe swiftly pushed herself up and swung her legs over the edge of the bed.

Her lady's maid bobbed briefly. Farrell was a sturdy, middle-aged woman, born in Liverpool and had worked her way up to be a lady's maid. She kept Phoebe up-to-date with the most recent fashions and the latest hairstyles, particularly if they originated in her native country. Over recent months, Phoebe had begun to feel uncomfortable, knowing she must have seen the marks on her body. But never a word passed between them.

Phoebe allowed Farrell to unfasten her frock and replace it with an ornate evening dress. She sat at the mirror as her dark hair was brushed out, braided, and pinned into place. She looked at her face, proud to have fought back tears. There was no puffiness to pretend was hay fever, no pinkness on the nose to mask with powder. Instead, she trained herself to look blank, to conceal the emotions roiling inside.

. . .

Phoebe entered the dining room prepared to stoically endure the long meal. She had become adept at playing her part during formal dinners, pretending nothing was amiss between her and Hector. He was still there, of course, after the drama of the afternoon. Mrs. McDonald and her cousin remained, along with McLennan, who, goodness knew why, had been placed beside her at the table. Perhaps Florence still thought they were at daggers drawn and wanted to watch her unease, unaware there was a newer reason for Phoebe to be uncomfortable near the doctor.

Thaddeus was holding court about having won the afternoon's race. He couldn't draw attention away from Hector, though, who was the star of the evening's show. Diners asked again how the accident had happened, what it had felt to be out in the ocean swell, unable to reach his boat.

Hector was generous in his praise of McLennan. "I wouldn't be here without the good doctor," he said, raising his glass at McLennan, across the silverware and candles. "I'm going to take you under my wing, buddy, make sure you have the *best* time in Boston. My way of thanking you."

Phoebe slid her eyes to McLennan beside her and his head was lowered. She suspected he was embarrassed by the attention.

"That's very kind, Mr. Gregson," he said in that soft Scottish accent. "But I know how busy you must be."

"Nonsense. Plenty of time in the evenings." Hector dipped a spoon in his soup. "And it's Hector, not Mr. Gregson. We're going to be brothers now. Especially as it seems I can't rely on my old college friend to get me out of a pickle."

Hector punched Thaddeus's arm and Phoebe couldn't tell if it was serious or in jest.

The conversation moved on as the main course was set before them. Phoebe's cheeks burned at the memory of the words she had let slip to McLennan that afternoon. Now was her chance to cover them.

She spoke gently, as he was sitting so close. "I hope you weren't offended by my little joke this afternoon. What I meant was, I can't swim. So had *I* been out there, I would have left my fiancé to drown."

He cleared his throat. "Aye. Indeed. That was what I thought you meant."

They slipped into silence and she felt the need to lighten the conversation. She recognized he was wearing one of Lex's summer jackets. It was a little tight over the shoulders and she recalled the definition of his arms when he had stood in his wet sweater that afternoon. "But you, you're a strong swimmer. Where did you learn?"

"There was a loch on my family's land. I learned as a boy. And then I would swim in the Tay and the Firth of Forth, depending on where my family was living."

The unfamiliar place names sounded soft in his accent. "That must have been dreadfully cold."

He made a rueful smile. "Pfft. It was. But you get used to it and begin to enjoy the feeling afterward, when you warm up."

This was the most they had said to each other since the dance at the charity ball. He seemed to be making an effort to be amiable, which surprised Phoebe. He had always been so uncommunicative with her.

Phoebe leaned toward him so she could speak quietly. "I suspect if my brother had known what a strong sailor you are, he would never have agreed to the race."

He turned to her, his lips in a slight curl. She noticed the sun had brought out some freckles on his nose and turned strands of his hair golden. The stubble on his unshaved jaw gave him a roguish air.

"He still won, though."

"As he insists on telling everyone."

McLennan laughed and returned his attention to cutting his steak.

"I have to say, I feel quite ashamed," said Phoebe.

"Ashamed? Why is that?" He looked at her sharply.

"Of my brother's behavior."

"Oh." McLennan paused, holding his knife in the air. "You don't have to feel that, though. Shame. It's not your fault." He looked at her and held her gaze, the green of his irises flecked with bronze. She felt he was trying to communicate something more to her. "Men are responsible for what they do. Any shame is entirely on them. You do know that, don't you?"

She wasn't sure what to say in return. They seemed to have trespassed into a serious discourse; far too serious for the Van Bergen dinner table.

She heard Hector's voice and realized he was asking her something. She forced a smile. "I'm sorry, my dear. I didn't hear you."

"I was saying, you two seem to be plotting something."

Phoebe suspected he was unhappy to see her deep in conversation with McLennan, a man he had claimed as a bosom pal. She opened her mouth to reply, but McLennan spoke first.

"We were having a wee philosophical discussion about shame and responsibility," he said.

Hector sat back. "Jeez, that's heavy-going when we're trying to eat. Philosophy isn't really Phoebe's thing." He looked directly at her. "Is it, Pheebs?"

She felt silenced by him, and the truth was she didn't know how to talk philosophy. To her regret, she'd never had the chance to go to college, unlike her Harvard-educated brothers.

McLennan wiped his mouth with a napkin. "From what I've seen over recent months, I'd agree that Miss Van Bergen is a woman of action rather than words. The hospital, I mean. It really wouldn't run properly without her."

Thaddeus had been listening and grunted. "It wouldn't run properly without the Van Bergen money."

Phoebe's skin prickled as she feared the regular argument about her involvement in the hospital was about to spill out in public.

"The money is important, of course," said McLennan, seeming reluctant to let the subject drop. "But I've never known a successful establishment which didn't have someone of vision behind it. In this case, it is your sister who is that person."

Phoebe blinked quickly to hold back tears. When he had arrived, she had questioned McLennan's professionalism and deliberately put him on probation. And yet, here he was, standing up for her in front of her brother and fiancé. After the anguished day she'd had, it was a kindness that threatened to let loose the tears she had been so determined to hold back.

TWELVE

Back in Boston, Douglas was relieved to have left the hothouse atmosphere of Manchester by the Sea and threw himself into his work. He did everything he could to avoid meeting Miss Van Bergen, feeling embarrassed and humiliated by his lack of action in response to what he knew. Yet, he could not stop protective feelings rising in his chest, picturing himself calling out Hector Gregson, challenging him to a duel of some sort. Or writing to Thaddeus to alert him to the suffering of his sister. But every response would ultimately lead to more ignominy for the woman who was the victim.

He cried off the first invitation from Hector to join him at a performance of an operetta at the Gaiety Theater, but it would have been stretching propriety to refuse again, when a second invitation came. This time, it was for dinner at Hector's club—the Union Club.

The historic club was in a prime position, close to the State House and across the road from Boston Common. In the lobby, a man took Douglas's hat and coat and showed him to the dining room.

Hector spotted him and beckoned energetically. There were

two other men: someone he'd not met previously, and Thaddeus Van Bergen.

Douglas's heart sank further at the prospect of the evening ahead. He resolved to remain polite and make his apologies as early as possible.

"I'm sorry to be a wee bit late," he said on reaching the table. "An operation had some complications."

Thaddeus looked up briefly and nodded to him.

"Not at all, buddy," said Hector. "Come sit. This is Gerald Flagg, a colleague of mine from the bank."

Flagg was tall and thin, with a willowy quality. "Pleased to meet the man who pulled Hector from the waves."

Douglas felt the color rise in his cheeks. He glanced at Thaddeus, who rolled his eyes, as if he too was tired of hearing about the incident.

Douglas sat and scanned the menu.

"We've already ordered," said Hector.

Many of the items had names which were not familiar, so Douglas stuck with the chowder soup, followed by potted pigeon.

The conversation ranged over politics, business, and sport. Thaddeus expressed opinions in his forthright way, mostly berating politicians for not supporting the expansion of industry, as was their patriotic duty. The Thurman Act was going to harm existing railroad companies. Douglas was tempted to point out that the Van Bergens didn't seem to be doing too bad, but did not want to sour the conversation.

Flagg agreed with whoever was speaking, changing sides as easily as a chameleon if Thaddeus or Hector took opposing views.

Hector was as charming as ever. He took an interest in Douglas, asking about his family, his life in Edinburgh and London, his thoughts on Boston life. Douglas knew he would have been lured into a friendship, had he not been made so painfully aware of the brutish behavior hidden by that charm. The contrast appalled him.

"You're not married," Hector observed. "I'm surprised."

Douglas filled his water glass from the carafe on the table, feeling uncomfortable to be discussing marriage with such a man. "I was. I'm a widower."

"I'm sorry to hear that, my friend. Is that what made you leave Britain?"

"In a way. I lost my dear wife some eight years back."

"Aha!" Hector's eyes were bright. "You've come to the New World looking for a new wife?"

Douglas shook his head. "Nae. That's not for me."

Hector raised an eyebrow. "What? Not good enough for you? We've many beautiful and highly eligible ladies here. Haven't we, Thad?"

"Indeed," Thaddeus said without looking up. "Many rich young women."

"And beautiful," chipped in Flagg.

Douglas smiled ruefully. "That's as maybe, but not for me. After my wife died, I vowed never to take another."

Hector raised his glass. "Hmm. A romantic. Like a Trumpeter swan: mates once and then never leaves. Or so I'm told by a natural scientist of my acquaintance."

Douglas bit his lip and wished the conversation would change. Him? A romantic? His stomach clenched at the description. Aye, he had loved his wife, but that was not the reason for his vow.

It was guilt.

But he would never share the whole story with the three men at the table. Indeed, his true feelings were something he had only ever shared with one man: Professor Moncrieff. That was one reason the Professor had recommended him for the Van Bergen Women's Hospital, and had urged him to take a chance by crossing the Atlantic. So far, the gamble had paid off and his obsession with how his wife had died had loosened its grip. By working long hours in a new country, he had begun to become a different Dr. McLennan.

But he would *never* tell the truth to anyone here.

At the end of the dessert course, Hector made a proposal. "Say, Douglas, I hope you'll join us on the next part of our evening."

Douglas looked at him. "Which is?"

"Mrs. Lake's. Runs a great little place down on Endicott Street."

"I haven't heard of it."

Hector tapped the side of his nose. "You wouldn't. It's a discreet place. My, the women are something else."

"The women?"

Hector winked and briefly outlined a woman's shape with his hands.

Douglas stared at him, his jaw clenched.

Thaddeus leaned over and spoke in a low voice. "It's a whorehouse."

"Aye. I had worked out that much," he said through gritted teeth.

"But a good one. Hector would never be found in a less salubrious establishment."

Flagg snorted. "Or, not often." He laughed at his own joke.

Hector dropped his napkin on the tablecloth. "Come join us, Douglas. You're a widower, but I'm guessing you're not a monk."

"But... you are engaged." He turned to Thaddeus uncertainly. "To Thaddeus's sister."

Thaddeus shrugged and Douglas felt like striking the contemptible man.

Hector threw his head back and laughed. "A man has needs. Thaddeus knows that. Flagg's coming, ain't you, buddy." Flagg nodded enthusiastically as Hector put a hand on his shoulder. "And Flagg's married."

Douglas could not think of a worse way to spend his evening. He turned to Thaddeus and narrowed his eyes. "Are you going?"

Thaddeus gave a single shake of the head.

Hector chuckled. "My dear friend is too fastidious for such delights."

"I'll stay and have a nightcap in the smoking room," said Thaddeus.

"In that case, I'll join you," said Douglas. "If I may?"

Thaddeus shrugged and muttered, "Fine by me," although his face told a different story.

Douglas didn't look forward to more time in Thaddeus' company either, but it meant he avoided a trip to a brothel, and, even more importantly, he might find a way to raise two things with Thaddeus which were troubling: the serious ill-health of his mother and, even more delicate, the wellbeing of his sister.

The men all rose.

"I'm covering the bill, of course," said Hector. Douglas began to protest, but Hector put his hands up. "Already dealt with."

THIRTEEN

In the lobby, Douglas said farewell to Hector and Flagg before following Thaddeus down the corridor to the smoking room. The room had a faded charm despite the acrid smell. The decorative ceiling was high but dark with years of smoke. Douglas suspected the wallpaper had once been red, but had changed color over the years to a dingy brown. The wood furniture was substantial, the mahogany glowing in the lamplight.

A man poured two brandies and Thaddeus leaned back to light his cigar. Douglas declined to smoke but sipped at the glass; the brandy warm and silky in his mouth.

"I wanted to speak to you. About your mother," Douglas began, sensing this was the easier place to start. He needed to know doctors were taking Mrs. Van Bergen's weak heart seriously, but felt unable to raise this with Miss Van Bergen, not wanting to remind her of his presence in Manchester by the Sea.

Thaddeus paused his fiddling with his cigar and looked at him.

"Is she still at Fairview?"

Thaddeus shook his head. "No. Back at Louisburg Square now."

"And how is her health? Since I saw her, I mean."

Both corners of Thaddeus' mouth briefly turned downwards.

He made a clicking sound with his tongue. "Phoebe says she's slowed down a lot. Keeps to her room."

"Still getting up, though?" Douglas asked.

Thaddeus sighed. "Sometimes. When Pheebs can persuade her."

"Is your mother sleeping more?"

Thaddeus eyed Douglas with more attention. "Believe so, from what Pheebs says. Say, what's this about?"

Douglas edged forward. These were symptoms he expected for an elderly person with a weak heart. "You have a brother in Canada, I believe."

Thaddeus frowned. "Alexander. In the Rockies, overseeing construction of our railroad."

"It's a long way." Douglas leaned closer and laced his fingers on the table in front. "Look, I think it might be wise to telegram to your brother and ask him to return."

"He's doing important work out there."

"Aye. But even so..."

Thaddeus took a long pull on his cigar and opened his mouth to let the smoke out. It hung in a cloud above him. "You're saying my mother is dying, aren't you?"

Douglas sat back. "I'm saying your mother's heart is weak. Added to that, I noticed a slight cough, and at dinner she hardly ate anything."

Thaddeus shook his head. "You don't know my mother. Strong as an ox. Determined."

Douglas warmed his brandy glass in his palm. "Determined, no doubt. But strong?" He stroked his mustache and shook his head. "I don't think so. At the very least, your brother should be informed. Then he could make his own decision."

Thaddeus absorbed Douglas's words. "Very well. I'll cable him first thing." He swallowed a mouthful of the brandy. "Although I'm not sure what comfort it would bring. Mother and Alexander never saw eye to eye. And she hates his wife. A Midwest country girl."

Douglas had done his medical duty, although he was still

concerned that Thaddeus was not taking the situation seriously enough. He resolved to ask again in a few days to check the cable had been sent.

Now he needed to find a way to do his moral duty. Before he could think of a way to open the subject of his sister's engagement, Thaddeus spoke.

"So, how are you getting on at my family's hospital?"

"Well, I hope. There's always plenty of patients."

"Boston is growing every day. Women keep on getting sick and having babies." Thaddeus grunted.

"The plans for the new hospital are exciting." Although he had been avoiding Miss Van Bergen, Douglas had noticed the arrival of ambitious plans from the architect's draughtsmen.

"Hmm. I'm not sure it's needed. All that expense. If they used the rooms better... Surely more women could go into each room."

Douglas wondered if Thaddeus had ever actually visited. "Springfield Street is bursting at the seams. But more than that, Miss Van Bergen has ambitions to build a fine new hospital that will bear your name in perpetuity."

"Damn well ought to. The amount of money we're ploughing in. But... it's my sister's dream, I guess."

Douglas cleared his throat, taking this opening in the conversation. He would need to approach this circumspectly. "May I speak to you about your sister?"

Thaddeus frowned. "If it's hospital business—I stay well clear."

"No, no, it's not. It's... " Goodness, it was difficult to find the words. "Have you ever wondered if Mr. Gregson is right for your sister?"

Thaddeus puffed out a breath. "Right?"

"You know. Is he... good enough for her."

"I really don't know what you're getting at." The man looked genuinely perplexed.

"Well, take tonight. Going to... Was Mrs. Lake's the name?"

Thaddeus laughed. "Oh, that's just Hector being Hector. Man

of strong appetites, you could say. Always has been. Was even worse during his college days."

Douglas was dismayed by Thaddeus's acceptance of his friend's faults. He coughed to clear his throat, trying to work out how to pursue this. "I have a sister myself. I wouldnae want her to marry a man who behaved that way."

Thaddeus waved the hand holding his cigar. "My sister knows what she's getting herself into."

"Even if that's true, isn't it your role, as head of the family, to look out for her?"

Thaddeus's demeanor changed, like an animal in a cage being poked. "Are you saying I'm not doing my duty?"

"I'm just suggesting—" Douglas held up both his palms.

Thaddeus's face reddened. "Because who are *you* to come here and start throwing about advice? Barely been here five minutes."

"I just wonder if there might be a more suitable match for her if..."

"Say." Thaddeus pointed the cigar at Douglas and hot ash fell from the end. "You're not trying to make a play for her yourself?"

Douglas sat back in his chair as if Thaddeus had thrown iced water in his lap. "Don't be absurd!" The very idea. He wasn't sure he even *liked* Miss Van Bergen. What an infuriating man to turn things round in this way.

"All you can see is a rich heiress."

"That's not what I'm suggesting at all." Douglas felt the hair on the back of his neck rise, hating the whole discussion and longing to leave. Then he remembered those awful sounds from the room next to his at Fairview, and a pain throbbed in his temples. He had to try to do the right thing. "Look. What I'm saying is, if you asked Miss Van Bergen if she *truly* wants to marry him—"

Thaddeus's head flicked up. "Has she said something to you?"

"No! Not a word."

Thaddeus's brows lowered. "Because my sister knows she's got no choice but to go through with it. She was weak enough to get herself into this mess. Hector's got her over a barrel, so to speak. It's her own damned fault."

Douglas rubbed his temple. "I don't—"

"She was willing to..." He made a crude gesture with his fingers. "Gotta live with the consequences."

Douglas stared at him, aghast. He would never dream of speaking of his sister in this way.

Thaddeus pulled a thread of tobacco from between his teeth. "So, she decides he's not the Prince Charming she thought he was. Let's say she breaks off the engagement. That wouldn't reflect well on Hector, and he's clear what would happen next."

Douglas swallowed and waited, his heart beating hard. Thaddeus knew more than he had realized.

"He will sully her name and reputation up and down the Eastern Seaboard. I know him. He'd make her sound like one of those whores at Mrs. Lake's." He swallowed the rest of his brandy and signaled to the man to fill it up. "I'm afraid, for my dear, innocent-looking sister, unless she wants to die an old maid, it's Hector or nothing."

Douglas wanted to shout *nothing—nothing is a better choice than a man like that!* He took a deep breath and tried again. "But you could play him at his own game. Damage *his* reputation."

Thaddeus snorted. "You think a man's reputation is damaged by the Boston Brahmins finding out he's a rake?"

Douglas's shoulders sank as he recognized the truth of Thaddeus's words. Some in Boston society might regarded the behavior as natural for a young man.

"Couldn't you... I don't know... pay him off?"

"Tsk. He'd take every penny she's worth. And then what?"

Douglas tapped his fingers on the side of his glass as he considered Thaddeus's words. "Does Miss Van Bergen know that you know?"

He shook his head. "Not something one talks about. I got the picture direct from Hector."

A thought flashed through his mind: was this why Thaddeus had sailed past Hector in the ocean?

"Yet you're talking about it to me," Douglas said carefully.

"I am, indeed. Isn't that strange? Maybe it's your doctorly bearing. What do they call it? A bedside manner?" He paused. "Anyway, I know you're not going to tell anyone."

Douglas narrowed his eyes.

"Unlike Hector, I could ruin your reputation in a moment." Thaddeus leaned closer. "Just so we're clear, I wouldn't hesitate to get you fired from our hospital. Malpractice of some sort. You wouldn't get another position in the States." Thaddeus lounged back in his chair. "Anyway. Things will be better once she gets on and marries him. Once she's pushed out a son, he'll leave her alone."

Douglas tasted something bitter at the back of his throat and knew it was not the smoke hanging in the air of this shadowy room.

He wanted to escape. He put down his glass. "I have to be going. Early start." He stood. "Thank you for the evening's hospitality."

Thaddeus looked at him with hostility. He grunted but said nothing more.

Douglas gave a quick nod and strode out of the room, down the corridor to the lobby. Thaddeus knew everything, and yet did nothing to rescue his sister. It was abominable behavior, and left Miss Van Bergen with no choice but to spend her life with a violent brute for a husband.

He paced as a servant took some time to find his coat. Pulling it on, he missed the arm in his haste, the man stepping forward to help, before Douglas grabbed his hat, and headed out into the cool night air. He rushed over Park Street and spent a good half an hour striding the paths of Boston Common, waiting for his feelings of disgust and nausea to subside.

FOURTEEN

Phoebe took out the slim volume she had been reading while her mother slept in the bed the other side of the room. It was *Notes on Nursing* by Florence Nightingale, the British nurse who had set up a field hospital in the Crimea. There was much Phoebe was learning, even though this booklet was twenty years out of date. More than that, it kept her from the worries that circled her mind.

It was mid-September, and in the weeks since returning from Fairview, her mother had deteriorated at an alarming rate. Mrs. Van Bergen slept much of the day now, usually with gentle breathing, but sometimes dipping into something deeper, something closer to unconsciousness. In her waking hours, she was always uncomfortable. Too far down the bed, too far up the bed, food was too hot, food tasted strange. She railed against the indignity of being lifted onto her commode. Mrs. Van Bergen repeatedly asked Phoebe to get things right or to leave her alone.

Phoebe found it hard to bite her tongue. They had never had a good relationship: her mother disapproved of Phoebe's tendency to break the rules. Florence was the daughter she had really hoped for: someone who glided confidently through the Boston salons. Strange, but visits from Florence had all but dried up, now her mother-in-law was unable to gossip about the neighbors and pass judgment on the latest faux pas of a recent arrival in the city.

Phoebe had been listening for the sound of a carriage all day, and at last heard it drawing up outside the house. She set down the booklet on the table beside her and hurried to the bow window to look down at the man and woman descending from a carriage loaded with trunks.

Tiptoeing across the room and closing the bedroom door gently behind her, she flew down the stairs, arriving in the hall just as her brother came through the door being held open by Merriman.

"Lex!" She rushed to him, putting her arms around his waist and leaning her cheek on his chest. "I'm so glad you're here."

"How is she?"

"Sleeping at the moment. Sleeping most of the time." She looked up at him. Lex's dark hat and traveling coat were grimy and his face had a patina of dust, emphasizing the lines around his gray eyes. He looked a little older than his thirty-three years. He smiled, his face tanned and weathered from his outdoor life. Phoebe became aware of his wife, standing behind him at the threshold. She reached out. "Geneviève. Welcome."

"Come now, you know it's Ginny to you." Ginny took both hands and studied Phoebe's face. "How are *you* doing?"

"Me?"

"I hope you don't mind me saying, you look a little tired. It must be a burden, nursing your mother."

Phoebe was alarmed that Ginny thought her unwell, but tried a nonchalant shrug. "It's got to be done. And I have plenty of help."

"I'm sorry it's taken so long to get here," said Ginny. "It took a while for Thaddeus's message to reach us in the mountains. We set off as soon as we got it."

Phoebe was enchanted by that delicate lilt, a midwestern openness to her voice with an occasional hint of the south for some words. Phoebe remembered Ginny's deceased mother had been a wealthy Southern belle before eloping with her father.

"You're here now," said Phoebe. "That's all that matters."

Lex pulled off his outdoor clothes and handed them to Merriman. "I'd like to see her now, if you don't mind."

"I'll take you up."

Ginny put a hand on Lex's arm. "You should see her without me, first. I don't want to overwhelm her. I'll sort our things with your housekeeper."

Mrs. O'Harvey stepped forward. "If you would come through to the sitting room, Mrs. Van Bergen, I'll send in some coffee."

Phoebe led the way upstairs, Lex close behind. She put her palm on the door handle. "Remember, the decline in her health has been steep. She's barely eaten, so she's lost a lot of weight."

The curtains were partly drawn, leaving most of the room in deep shadow, but with sunlight making a stripe on the oak floorboards and the decorative rug. The bed dominated the room, with its ornate wooden head and footboard, and high mattress.

"You can go now," Phoebe said to the maid who had been keeping watch, who slipped out of the room, leaving just Phoebe and her brother.

Mrs. Van Bergen was asleep on her back, her mouth wide open, showing yellowing teeth. Her skin seemed stretched across her features.

"Mother?" Phoebe said in a soft voice.

A hand drifted up and then Mrs. Van Bergen opened her eyes.

"Alexander is here."

She looked confused for a moment.

Lex stepped forward and took her raised hand. "I'm here, Mother."

"Where have you been?"

"Canada, Mother."

"Tsch! Don't be so foolish. I only sent you to get some candy. What took you so long?"

Lex raised his eyes to Phoebe.

"She gets confused," Phoebe whispered. "Try again."

He kept hold of her hand and stepped closer. "I've been overseeing our railroad, Mother. The Canadian Pacific Railway."

She frowned. "You should be letting your father do that. He's the one who knows how to lay down a line."

Lex swallowed. "Father's dead, Mother. Died five years back."

"Died?" Her gaze drifted across the room, as if trying to anchor herself to the present. She blinked several times. "I remember. Of course I remember. Don't speak to me as if I'm stupid!" She looked at her son properly. "Come closer."

He sat on the quilt, making sure he wasn't touching her legs.

"You've lost weight," she said, raising her hand to his cheek. "At least you've still got your good looks. You got all the looks and kindness. Thaddeus got your father's business sense."

Phoebe balled her fists to stop herself butting in, wanting to remind her mother that Lex was the family member with the real brains. She suspected much of Thaddeus's success was from greasing the right palm.

"And that wife of yours. Is she here?"

"Sure."

"Geneviève. I bet she hated it in those mountains with you." There was a glint in the eye which made Phoebe suspect her mother hoped this was true.

"She's an outdoors kinda girl, Mother. You know she's used to the open air."

Mrs. Van Bergen tutted and turned her head away in disgust. "Missouri farm girl. Never thought we'd see *that* in the family."

Phoebe met Lex's eyes and they both knew it was better to say nothing, even though Phoebe was itching to leap to Ginny's defense.

"I daresay she'll want to go banging away on the pianoforte, now she's here."

Lex smiled, knowing how much Ginny loved the piano. "Daresay she will."

"Perhaps she could play something soothing for you," Phoebe suggested.

Mrs. Van Bergen harrumphed and tried to raise herself further up the bed. "Don't just stand there. Help me get comfortable."

Phoebe went the other side so they could each hook an arm below her armpit and ease her upwards. Phoebe slapped the pillows into shape.

"Fetch me a drink, Phoebe. Do something useful for once."

Phoebe bit her lip and went to the carafe on the dresser.

"Not water!"

"What would you like?"

"A sherry. That's what I want."

"I'll go fix something," Phoebe said, not sorry to be leaving the room. She let out a long breath, knowing that at last she would have an ally in dealing with her mother.

The atmosphere around the dining table was as tense as Phoebe could remember. Thaddeus sat at one end, where their father had always sat, Lex at the opposite end, in his mother's chair. Ginny was on his left, and Phoebe next to her. Florence sat opposite the two women.

No one was quite sure who should take precedence. Lex was the older twin, but those extra minutes on this earth meant little now. Phoebe had been mistress of this house, ever since her mother had taken to her bed, but Florence felt it was her place to decide meals and manage the staff, as wife of Thaddeus, who she saw as head of the family. Ginny sat politely, her brown eyes not missing a thing.

Thaddeus quizzed Lex about progress with the railroad.

"I've been looking at the costs," he said. "At this rate, there'll be hardly any profit in it."

"Not a lot we can do about that," said Lex. "You may recall, I argued that we should invest in steel. Then we'd have more control of prices."

"I'm sure you can engineer your way to something cheaper. I looked at the cost of the Ottawa River bridge. It was astronomical. What are you doing? Building it from gold?"

"Bridges are expensive," said Lex, calmly continuing with his dinner but flashing a look at Ginny.

"I bet I could find ways to make them cheaper." Thaddeus angrily shoved another piece of meat in his mouth.

"Not without compromising safety, dear brother. There's the rub."

Thaddeus rolled his eyes and muttered, "Safety. That's all I get from you. What about profits?"

"One accident and our reputation is done for, Thaddeus."

Ginny coughed. "Thaddeus, how is your mother this evening?"

Phoebe glanced at her, thankful for her efforts to move the conversation on.

Thaddeus spoke without lifting his eyes. "Not too well, truth to tell. Though she seems to have perked up, seeing Alexander today."

"What does the doctor say?" asked Lex.

Phoebe had barely touched her food and pushed it to one side of her plate with her knife. "Not much. He comes in, feels her pulse, recommends more little pills. Says she should be getting up and about."

Lex frowned. "Whose care is she under?"

"Dr. Aver," said Phoebe.

"Mm-hmm. I remember him from when I was a boy. Never thought much of him." Lex shook his head. "Why don't we get a second opinion?"

"How d'you mean?" asked Thaddeus.

"Another doctor. Just to be sure. I was thinking of one of the doctors at your hospital, Phoebe."

She looked up at Lex in surprise.

"It's a woman's hospital, after all," Lex continued as if it were the natural thing to propose.

"I guess. But for ordinary women, poorer women, not—"

"I don't mean she should *go* there. But I'm hoping you've engaged good men." Lex pointed his chin at Thaddeus. "You mentioned a guy in your cable to me, Thad."

"Dr. McLennan?" Thaddeus asked.

"That's the one. How about him, Phoebe?"

Phoebe hesitated. Although she knew McLennan was by far the best doctor at the hospital, she was nervous of inviting him here, although she couldn't put her finger on why.

No. She knew exactly why.

It was the look on his face when he'd seen those bruises on her arms. And then his words at dinner at Fairview, which seemed to have more behind them. McLennan might seem reserved, but she knew how sharp he was. If he spent time here, he might see the truth. Phoebe worked hard at the hospital to project an image of a confident woman. She couldn't bear the idea of McLennan finding out she was actually trapped and powerless.

"Well, I'm not sure—" She noticed Florence staring at her across the table, a half-smile curling her lip.

"Yes, Dr. McLennan," interrupted Florence. "He would be ideal. Mrs. McDonald can't recommend him too highly. He has been very attentive to her cousin."

"Sounds perfect," said Lex.

Florence lifted her wine glass. "I'll write to him this evening."

Phoebe blinked at her, feeling wrong-footed. "You know him well enough?"

"Sure. He's much in demand at evening soirées."

Phoebe couldn't imagine why: he'd never been one for small talk.

"One of the men should take my letter immediately," Florence said, putting her hand over Thaddeus's. "Anything to help your dear, dear mother."

FIFTEEN

Douglas had been puzzled to receive a letter from Mrs. Florence Van Bergen, delivered by hand late at night to his lodgings in Hanover Street. It asked him to attend her mother-in-law first thing in the morning. Surely Mrs. Van Bergen was under the care of the family doctor?

He paused by the railings round the park in the middle of Louisburg Square, the handle of his leather case of medical equipment in his right hand. It was mid-September so the elm trees were still in full leaf. Since that excruciating discussion with Thaddeus, he had no desire to get pulled into the private lives of his employers. But, equally, he could hardly say no to the request.

The Van Bergen house was made of Flemish-style redbrick with bow windows the full height of its five stories. The front door was wide, painted a silky black with an elegant fan window above. The house was narrow, but Douglas guessed it would extend back, with stables, a carriage house, and outbuildings at the rear.

He let out a breath, crossed the cobbled road, and mounted the steps. He had barely finished ringing the bell when the door opened, and Douglas was shown into a surprisingly bright drawing room with cream walls and a large white marble fireplace. Mrs.

Florence Van Bergen sat in an elegant chair opposite the sofa, with a man and a woman he hadn't met before.

Mrs. Van Bergen rose to greet him, putting out both hands and placing a gentle kiss on his cheek. "Ah, my dear friend, Dr. McLennan. Thank you for coming."

He tried to hide his surprise at her warmth, given he had barely spoken two words to her. Why hadn't Miss Van Bergen made contact? She was the one who knew of his medical competency. His heart sank with disappointment that perhaps she did not think him good enough to treat her mother. After all his efforts of recent months, did he still have to prove himself?

"This is my brother-in-law, Alexander Van Bergen."

Douglas could see the similarly with Phoebe: the dark hair, the intelligent gray eyes, the open demeanor.

Mr. Van Bergen moved toward him, his handshake firm but brief. "Pleased to meet you."

Douglas caught the Boston accent he was becoming familiar with, although it was softer than his brother Thaddeus's. There was something about it that reminded him of the English countryside.

"I'm sorry it could not be under happier circumstances," said Douglas.

"My wife, Mrs. Geneviève Van Bergen."

She stepped forward and warmly took his hand. "It's good of you to attend so quickly, when you must be a very busy man."

She was a real beauty, with thick chestnut hair escaping its arrangement, and dark brown eyes that looked up at him with openness. Unlike Florence's pale skin, Mrs. Geneviève Van Bergen's face had a healthy glow. That must be what the Canadian Rockies did for you.

"I hope I can be of help. Although"—he looked at Mr. Van Bergen—"I'm not sure why I'm here. Isn't Dr. Aver your family's physician?"

"I wanted a second opinion," said Alexander. "And I believe you saw my mother at Fairview?"

"May I call for some refreshments, Dr. McLennan?" asked Florence. "Coffee? Or perhaps you would prefer some English tea?"

He waved his hand. "Thank you, but I'd prefer to go straight to the patient."

Alexander nodded. "I'll take you there myself."

The rest of the house was as elegant and luxurious as he expected, with modern gas lighting and high ceilings. They went up a further flight of stairs to a room with the same bow window as the floor below. As he stepped inside, a huge array of bottles rattled on the chest of drawers: the pots and potions prescribed by Dr. Aver, he guessed.

Miss Phoebe Van Bergen stood and a book slipped to the floor. So this was why she had not greeted him downstairs: she had been keeping vigil.

"Dr. McLennan." Her voice was more tentative than usual.

He nodded to her. "Miss Van Bergen."

She picked up the book and held it to her chest, both arms crossed, as if defending herself.

"How is she?" he asked softly.

She seemed to be having difficulty meeting his eye. "Hard to say. She sleeps a lot of the time."

"Food?"

Finally, she looked at him properly. Although as handsome as ever, her face seemed drawn and he thought she had lost weight. They had barely crossed paths at the hospital recently; she had been there less in recent weeks and he was kept busy with patients. A memory of all she was dealing with flashed through his mind.

"Barely anything at all," she replied but remained at a distance.

He took a step closer, wanting to offer some comfort but knowing it would be deeply inappropriate. "What are you giving her?"

Her eyes drifted past him to her mother. "Cook has made chicken broth."

"And water?"

She nodded. "Yes. She still sips sweet drinks."

He set his case on a side table and opened it. There were bottles and tools, each in its own neat compartment. "If I could examine her now..."

Phoebe placed the book on an occasional table and moved to the window, where her brother joined her, and Douglas gave his attention to the frail lady on the bed.

Douglas had suggested they gather in the reception room. "Do you want to fetch your brother?" he asked Alexander.

"No. He told me he had meetings all day. We'll let him know your opinion."

"Very well." Douglas took a chair by the fireplace and invited the family to sit.

Alexander and his wife used the sofa on one side, with Miss Phoebe and Mrs. Florence opposite.

"It's quite simple, and I daresay expected. Your mother is reaching the end of her life. Her heart is very weak."

"But Dr. Aver thought that she would rally, given the right medicines," said Florence. "He said *aurum metallicum* and digitalis would revive her."

Douglas noticed the questioning glance from Miss Van Bergen toward Florence. He suspected she had a different opinion. "Miss Van Bergen?"

"At the beginning, maybe," she said carefully. "For a while, Mother responded to some of those pills. But I've seen a change over recent weeks."

"How so?" asked Alexander.

"A... weakness."

Alexander turned to Douglas. "What do you recommend?"

"As I say, it's simple. Make sure she's as comfortable as possible. Move her every two hours on the bed to help prevent ulcers. Give her a wee bit of soft food if she wants it. Drinks, of course. Laudanum if she seems in pain. And wait."

"Wait? That sounds like you're telling us to give up," said Florence.

"No. Not give up. It's a natural process. You make it as gentle as you can."

Miss Van Bergen looked at her brother, who nodded. Douglas sensed he was confirming what she had already told the family, but probably had not been listened to.

"How long?" Mrs. Geneviève Van Bergen asked.

Families always wanted an answer to this question. "A month, perhaps; maybe more. With her weak heart, it could be less. It could give out at any moment."

Alexander released a long breath.

Douglas got to his feet as there was nothing more for him to say or do. "I'll take my leave."

Alexander stood. "I'll show you out. We can discuss your fee on the way."

It was on the tip of Douglas's tongue to say there was no charge, that the visit hadn't taken long. He checked himself. He needed to keep his relationship with the powerful Van Bergens very clear: he was providing a service. He was not a friend of the family and he would present his bill, as he had for other rich Bostonians who had asked his opinion on medical matters over recent months.

He glanced back at Miss Van Bergen as he reached the door. Her eyes were on the carpet. She was not the fiery, energetic woman he had met four months before, the woman who had challenged him and held her own, or had laughed as she showed him how to dance. It was as if someone had knocked the stuffing out of her.

He had an impulse to go to her, to crouch on his haunches and take her hands in his, to tell her: things might be tough now, but they would not always be. Things could change, *would* change and get better.

Instead, he clenched his fist, knowing such a ridiculous display would humiliate them both. He dropped his head and followed Alexander into the lobby.

SIXTEEN

Florence stood and smoothed the creases from her skirt. "So. That's that then. I'll be off home now."

"As you're here, would you like to look in on Mother before you go?" asked Phoebe. She noted a shudder before Florence replied.

"I wouldn't want to disturb the dear lady." She picked up her reticule and left.

Ginny moved to Florence's place on the sofa and took Phoebe's hand. "Y'know what you need? Some fresh air. Why don't you join me for a turn round Boston Common?"

It was true: Phoebe had been confined to the sickroom for days and was in desperate need of respite. Within minutes, the pair were making their way down the steep sidewalk, each with light coats buttoned up and elegant hats fixed with long pins. Phoebe tucked a parasol under her arm, in case the September sun strengthened.

They crossed Beacon Street, picking their way between the carriages and taking care to avoid horse manure, before striking out toward the lake, where the leaves of the elm trees shimmered in the breeze. Ginny threaded her arm through Phoebe's as they walked, their skirts touching.

"So tell me truly, how are you, Phoebe?" Ginny asked.

"Me?"

"That must have been difficult news for you from Dr. McLennan this morning."

Phoebe was touched by Ginny's concern, which was such a contrast to Florence's indifference. "It was. But... not unexpected. For a couple of weeks I've thought Mother was near the end of her life. It was why I was surprised Dr. Aver kept prescribing so many pills."

"I'm sorry for you, though. Such a loss."

Phoebe had adored Ginny from the first time they met, delighted when her favorite brother had suddenly presented Ginny Snow as his prospective bride. There was a younger sister too, Marie-Louise, who Phoebe had met and liked, and who had also tried living in Boston after the wedding but hated it. Ginny had confided in Phoebe that she agonized over what to do. She wanted to join her beloved husband as he worked his way across Canada, but couldn't abandon Mary Lou to the snobbery and back-biting of Boston society.

The younger sister resolved things, forthrightly declaring she would go back to Missouri and live with her aunt in Jefferson City. From there, Mary Lou could keep an eye on the family farm. Phoebe had been impressed by the young woman: although still in her teens, she had been sure of what she wanted. Perhaps it showed the depth of her love for her older sister—enabling Ginny to travel with her husband without guilt.

Walking under the trees now, Phoebe felt that closeness to Ginny again. She was a kindred spirit, and they were united in their love of Lex. If there was any woman with whom she could confide her true feelings about her mother, it was Ginny. They sat on a bench beneath a tree and Phoebe tucked the parasol on her lap.

"Truth is, I've never got on with my mother. She's a smart woman and she was devoted to my father. But to me, she could be so cruel and cutting, even more so since Lex left."

"Oh, Phoebe! Didn't Thaddeus support you?"

"That's the thing: she behaved differently with him. Her favored son. If I said anything to Thaddeus, he'd laugh and tell me not to be silly." Phoebe absentmindedly stroked out the fabric portions of the closed parasol. "Her death will be a release for both her and me. Does that make me thoroughly wicked?"

"No." Ginny put her hand on Phoebe's forearm.

"I'm quite looking forward to having that house to myself. To peace and quiet."

Ginny nodded. "Freedom."

"Yes! Exactly. I'm looking forward to freedom."

Ginny frowned. "But you'll be married soon, won't you? What's his name? Henry?"

"Hector." Phoebe would never be free, married to Hector, but that fate was inevitable. She felt a cold shiver run through her and for a brief, mad moment she wondered if she could confide the truth about Hector to Ginny. But it was too unbearable, too shaming.

Ginny leaned closer and gently bumped her arm. "I could help you with your trousseau, if you like. Y'know, return the favor for my wedding. I couldn't have managed without you."

Phoebe rolled her shoulders as if they were stiff, and stood. The idea of preparing for her wedding filled her with dismay. Ginny joined her and they walked over an ornamental bridge, pausing to look at the lake below.

"Have you chosen your dress yet?" Ginny asked.

Phoebe swallowed. "No, not yet."

If she confessed how completely she was trapped by Hector, perhaps even Ginny would judge her. She had grown up with Southern sensibilities instilled by her own mother—in many ways so like the Boston ones: the importance of appearances in the eyes of your neighbor, the fragility of reputation.

Phoebe leaned on the balustrade and watched the water flowing below. She was too ashamed. And if she said anything to

Ginny, surely she would tell Lex. Phoebe knew there were no secrets between her brother and his wife.

There was a time when she had no secrets from Lex. But not anymore. Now her life was full of concealment and self-disgust.

"That's plenty about me," she said, pushing herself upright. "I want to hear about your life." They continued over the bridge and round the lake. "What's it like in the Rockies?"

"Oh, my! I never knew mountains could be so glorious. I love it. Every day, you go outside and beauty is all around you. It makes you feel small, but inspired as well."

"Where do you live? I'm picturing a hut somewhere."

Ginny laughed. "You're not far wrong. There are some townships where we rent a place. Once, we built something to live in from scratch, because Lex knew we'd be there months. But there's so many workmen: it's like a whole town creeping its way across the continent."

"I've never seen the mountains," Phoebe said, wistfully.

"Some places are flat, of course, like parts of the Midwest, and carry on as far as the eye can see, one wide horizon all around."

"D'you ever get lonely?" Phoebe had never had time alone and was curious.

"Sometimes Lex is away for a few weeks, when there's a tricky bit of construction to oversee. But there are plenty of women around. Some are wives of the workmen, making a living by cooking, cleaning, doing laundry."

Phoebe tried to picture Ginny's life. "And how do you spend your days?"

"Y'know, much the same. I'm not a clever cook like my sister, Mary Lou, but I get by. And there's always cleaning to do."

Phoebe stopped and looked at her in horror. "Does Lex know this? I mean, you're married to one of the richest men in the States."

Ginny laughed. "I've given a false impression. I've a housekeeper, a maid who does the laundry. It's just I don't like sitting round. Remember, I had to run my own farm for a few years after Papa died, just me and Mary Lou."

"Glory be! This isn't what I pictured at all."

Ginny giggled at Phoebe's reaction. "Lex is a darling and makes sure I have a piano. An upright one, nothing too fancy as it gets moved from place to place. And you know what he's like with books, so he's always getting new ones shipped out."

"Well, thank goodness for small mercies!" Phoebe was in awe of Ginny's willingness to uproot her life so she could be with her husband.

"Shall we sit again?"

Before Phoebe could reply, Ginny had gathered her skirts and lowered herself to the grass. She leaned her face back to enjoy the sun.

Phoebe copied her and chuckled: how her mother would scold her for sitting on the grass and risking a tan. But Mother's power was slipping away. "I imagine it's cold in the winter."

"Like you wouldn't believe! Even for you, with your long Boston winters. I would go round bundled up like a child's toy, so many layers I could barely move my arms. A liberty suit covered with a pair of pantaloons, below two skirts. Cotton chemise, woolen jackets. The locals have it all down, so I learned to dress like them: fur hat, fur coat, fur mittens. We'd have the stove on, night and day."

Phoebe's mouth fell open. "But, Ginny, you could come and stay here with us, at any moment."

Ginny laughed. "Away from Lex? No, thank you." Ginny took Phoebe's hand. "I know you'd welcome me here. But if I went anywhere, it would be Jefferson City with Mary Lou. I've thought about doing that." Ginny was pensive. "And winters turn to spring, then summer. And, my, the summers are hot. We were in a flat place last summer and it was like living inside a Dutch oven. And the insects! Would come up in great waves, like something biblical. Now, that was the only time I was tempted to abandon my husband!"

They both laughed.

A bell tolled somewhere, telling them time was passing. They stood and made their way back to Beacon Hill.

"You know I'm happy to sit with your mother," Ginny said, threading her hand through Phoebe's arm once more. "The hospital needs you. Make use of me so you can give it your attention."

Phoebe felt a wave of warmth toward her sister-in-law. Most people thought the hospital was a hobby, but it was *everything* to her. She had slowed her plans for it in recent weeks, when she so wanted to progress the new building, to show how a modern hospital could put women patients first.

"That doctor who visited," said Ginny, putting her head to one side.

"Dr. McLennan?"

"He's from your hospital, isn't he?"

"Sure."

"I liked him. Seemed to know what he was doing."

Phoebe nodded. "I appreciated him being straight with us."

It was true. Although she had been bothered by having McLennan call on the house and slip closer to her family, she had to admit he was the perfect doctor to call on. Probably the only one in Boston to tell the truth and not suggest an array of pointless interventions.

Ginny dodged one of the gas lamps on the sidewalk. "Daresay it's easier to take bad news delivered in that lovely Scots accent."

Phoebe chuckled. "Indeed. That voice is something else."

They began their way up the hill, Phoebe enjoying the sensation of her legs stretching, and thinking about McLennan.

"The truth is, I couldn't stand him to begin with," Phoebe confessed.

"Dr. McLennan?" Ginny raised both eyebrows.

"Arrogant. Rude. Self-opinionated. But then, that's no different from most doctors."

"Uh-huh." Ginny nodded. "They do seem a particular breed."

Phoebe snorted as she remembered. "He seemed to have a disdain for women. Made me wonder why he wanted to work in a women's hospital. I know many doctors see it as beneath them, that medicine for women isn't as important as for men. It's why I want to be careful about who we appoint for the new hospital."

"But... you didn't raise any objections when Florence suggested he examine your mother?"

"No." Phoebe took a few more steps. "I think I changed my mind after watching him at work. He's saved women other doctors would have given up on. His techniques are sometimes different, but they work. Adeline Hale, my matron, she *really* sings his praises."

"And tell me, how old is Adeline?" asked Ginny airily.

"Bit older than me. She'll be turning thirty soon. Why?" Phoebe paused at the corner of two roads and looked at her sister-in-law.

"Married?"

"Widowed."

Ginny scoffed.

"What *are* you trying to say, Geneviève?" said Phoebe in mock horror, a palm held to her breast.

"Oh, come on! Those broad shoulders. That blond hair. The voice. That jawline. *Of course* she's going to sing his praises."

Phoebe caught the twinkle in Ginny's eye, before they both burst out laughing.

"I'll have to keep an eye on Adeline," said Phoebe.

As they walked home, she thought further. Perhaps McLennan was a little lonely. He'd been a widower for, what—eight years, had he said? She wondered why he hadn't remarried. Adeline might be a good match. Even an austere man like McLennan deserved happiness.

By the time she reached the house, she already felt strangely uncomfortable about the idea of a union between her friend and the doctor. After all, she needed him herself, to make sure the new hospital ran smoothly.

SEVENTEEN

The card inviting Douglas to Mrs. Van Bergen's funeral had been embossed and had a black border. He wasn't sure why he'd received it: he wasn't family nor friend. He had visited her a couple more times in the month since his first attendance but had made it clear there was little to be done, other than keeping the matriarch comfortable. The dignified way Miss Van Bergen had accepted this reality added to his respect for her. Encouraging families to prepare for death was one of the most difficult parts of being a doctor.

Walking up the slope past monuments and mausoleums to the Bigelow Chapel in Mount Auburn cemetery, he saw that the death of a Van Bergen was a public affair. The winding path through the woods had a line of carriages of the great and the good. He was relieved he had purchased a black funeral tie for the occasion. Douglas would never have declined to attend the funeral, but he was mostly here out of consideration for Miss Van Bergen.

Inside, the chapel felt familiar, the gothic arches, thick pillars and stone floor reminding him of churches in Scotland. Familiar, but somehow new: everything was fresh and clean, rather than discolored by centuries of use.

The chapel was full so he stood in a side aisle, along with

others not important enough for a seat, watching shards of colored light fall from the stained-glass rose window.

The congregation hushed as the organ music changed. Everyone stood. The undertaker's men carried the ornate oak casket. Behind walked Thaddeus and Florence, then Alexander and Geneviève. Thaddeus had won that particular battle for supremacy.

Next came Miss Van Bergen and Hector Gregson, who gripped her arm and held her close. A bitter taste came to Douglas's mouth as he watched the man pass, and he found he had clenched his fists. He took a calming breath, telling himself he could do nothing about their relationship.

Phoebe was wearing a fine, black veil, so Douglas was unable to see her complexion. He was concerned about her: each time he had visited Louisburg Square, she had seemed paler and more preoccupied. He told himself it was not surprising, given her mother was close to the end.

But there was something else, something more that he couldn't put his finger on. She would not look at him during his visits. Douglas shrugged at the memories. Perhaps he was wrong, and deep down Miss Van Bergen was angry he had failed to extend the life of her mother. The animosity of their early days seemed to have returned. It was a shame, as he had begun to admire Miss Van Bergen and what she was trying to achieve in Boston, despite the difficulties of her personal life.

The eulogy was given by Thaddeus, but none of the rest of the family spoke. There were the traditional hymns and readings and soon the service was over, the undertakers carrying the casket outside, followed by the family and all the guests.

Douglas had never been to a burial ground like it: so different from the small cemeteries in Scotland, where gravestones jostled each other for space. Here, pathways undulated with memorials on either side. There were trees and birdsong and even a small lake.

The Van Bergen mausoleum was at the top of a hillock. Four neoclassical granite pillars supported a substantial roof over the structure where Mrs. Van Bergen would be laid next to her husband and, Douglas assumed, earlier members of the family. The area was surrounded by an ornate iron fence, keeping the riffraff at a distance. Douglas respectfully stood in the shade of a white pine tree and watched the interment.

With the ceremony over, Thaddeus and Alexander shook hands with various mourners, but not, Douglas noted, with each other. Miss Van Bergen kept her head tilted down so she didn't have to speak to anyone, sometimes putting her hand to her mouth and pausing to control her breathing. She stumbled slightly as she turned to leave, and Hector protectively took her arm once more. Douglas frowned in concern; was she unwell? And was that arm one of control, rather than support?

He had been told there was a wake at the Tremont House hotel back in Boston but couldn't face it. Mrs. McDonald offered him a place in her carriage, but he graciously declined. It would be a good hour's walk back through Cambridge to the hospital, but he longed for the fresh air to clear his feelings of unease at the funeral. He didn't belong with the Van Bergens and no doubt his absence wouldn't be noticed in the throng.

Phoebe sank into a chair in her father's study, her head throbbing and feeling nauseous. "Do we have to do this *now*? We've only just buried her."

More than anything, she wanted to curl up on the bed in her room, but even that was no longer possible. Thaddeus and Florence had moved into Louisburg Square the day after their mother died. Florence had moved Phoebe's things to the fourth floor so her bedroom could be used for guests.

Lex sat behind the desk. "Sorry, Phoebe, I can see you're exhausted, but Ginny and I leave for Jefferson City first thing in the morning. Once we've seen her sister, we're heading north back to Canada. I've been away too long already."

Thaddeus stomped in. "What's this about, Lex?"

"I need to get things in order before I leave."

"The business? If so, I don't see what Pheebs is doing here." Thaddeus dropped into a leather chair, frowning that Lex had taken the place behind their father's desk.

"It's about Phoebe. Her future," Lex said firmly.

"In that case, we need to haul Hector in here."

Lex put up his hand. "No. That's my point. I want to sort Phoebe's security, irrespective of a future husband."

Phoebe sat up a little, wondering what he meant. At the moment, she couldn't bear to think of a future with Hector. But he had left her with no choice.

Lex made sure both were attending before he began. "Father left fifty-one percent of the shares in Mother's hands and split the forty-nine percent between the three of us."

Phoebe's skin prickled as she remembered the fuss Thaddeus had made last time they had discussed this. Father had split the remaining portion twenty percent to each of the brothers and nine percent to her. Sometimes she wished she had been left with nothing. Maybe then she'd never have come to Hector Gregson's attention.

"I know," started Thaddeus, "but—"

"In her will, Mother split what she had: forty percent of her holding to me, forty to you, and twenty to Phoebe."

"And that twenty percent added to her existing holdings makes Pheebs a very wealthy woman, so I'm not sure what you're worried about," said Thaddeus.

"But not when she marries."

Thaddeus rolled his eyes.

Lex pushed on regardless. "When Phoebe marries, all that wealth will go straight to her husband."

Phoebe had been painfully aware of this as her relationship with Hector soured and she had discreetly tried to find out about her position. "Won't I be covered by the Married Women's Property Act?"

"I'm not so sure you will, Phoebe," said Lex carefully. "You can own and sell *property*, but it is not at all clear that includes investments." Lex lifted two sheets of paper from the desk. "So I asked Briggs to draw up this document. It transfers fourteen and a half percent—that's half of Phoebe's holding—into a trust fund. There's a copy for each of you."

"A trust fund?" asked Phoebe, taking her copy.

Thaddeus leaned forward to take the other document and sat back to scan it.

Lex steepled his fingers. "It will be held for you to draw down as and when you need it. It will not form any part of the wealth transferred to your husband on marriage."

"Who controls it? Me?" Phoebe asked, looking at Lex, her heart beating faster. *As and when she needed it.* Could she leave, take any children?

"It needs to be independent of you, and your husband. There are three trustees." Lex pointed at the relevant section. "Me, Thaddeus, and Briggs."

Phoebe frowned as she read, the brief moment of hope dashed.

"It means no matter what happens, you will always have some independent means," said Lex.

"Not that independent, if you two and Briggs are the trustees." She tried to keep the bitterness from her tone.

Lex shrugged. "Best I could do."

"Majority decision?" Thaddeus asked.

Lex nodded.

"So," said Phoebe with alarm, "Thaddeus and Briggs could overrule you. Give my money to someone else."

"No, that much is clear. You must be the beneficiary. And Phoebe, I trust Briggs."

Thaddeus snorted. "That sounds like you don't trust me."

Lex and Phoebe both turned to stare at him. Eventually he shrugged, silently acknowledging their skepticism.

"And if something happens to me," said Lex, "my position as a trustee passes to my wife's family."

That sounded safer than it reverting to Thaddeus.

"The terms Briggs has drafted are very clear. Funds are released specifically for the wellbeing of Phoebe and her descendants."

So any children would be protected.

"But not for my husband."

Lex nodded. "We all know that whoever you marry will become very rich under the law as it now stands."

There was a silence. Phoebe felt the weight of things unsaid but sat stock-still. She was paralyzed, unable to say more, but knowing things were worse than Lex feared. The throbbing headache returned.

Lex leaned back in his father's chair. "You should read the document more carefully. But if you're in agreement, you need to sign. Today. I want this sorted before I go back to the railroad."

"Do we need a witness?" Thaddeus asked.

"Briggs is waiting at his office for a message. He'll be straight over with a partner to witness everything."

Thaddeus sighed. "Let's get on with this then."

Phoebe looked at Lex, who gave a slight shrug and lifted his palms in response. He'd been against her engagement to Hector from the beginning, but now even Lex accepted the inevitable: she was to be shackled to a man who could not be trusted. And there was nothing she could do about it.

EIGHTEEN

Douglas groaned at the sound of Mrs. Angellotti knocking on his bedroom door. It was late and it had been a long day at the hospital. He'd already started to prepare for the night.

"A note, it arrive for you, Dottore McLennan."

He pulled his shirt back on and opened the door. "Grazie, Signora Angellotti."

Lighting a candle on the table, he snapped open the envelope. The message was brief but puzzling. Matron Hale was asking him —no, *begging* him—to come to her home immediately—and that he should say nothing to anyone about the request.

He pushed a hand through his hair. The handwriting was frantic and there was something desperate about the tone.

There was no question of his not attending, so he buttoned his shirt and tucked it into his pants before pulling up his suspenders. He sat to pull on his shoes, picked up his tie, but dropped it back on the chair. He didn't need to waste time on formal dress. He shrugged on his jacket and overcoat, made sure his medical case was fully stocked, and set off.

The matron's address was in the poorer West End, not far from the Van Bergen hospital and only a short walk from his lodgings in the Italian area. He arrived at a small, neat house, just as he expected of small, neat Mrs. Hale. An oil lamp burned in the front window, showing someone was still up. He knocked on the door, and when the door swung open, he saw relief flood over Mrs. Hale's face.

"Thank God, Dr. McLennan. You're here."

He stepped into the passageway beyond the front door. "I came as soon as I got your note."

Mrs. Hale stood in the half-light, unable to look him in the face. He frowned at her uniform and apron and wondered if she had only just got home from the hospital. But... that didn't make sense with the letter.

"What is it, Mrs. Hale? What's happened?"

"I'm going to take you upstairs." She spoke quickly, her voice strained. "But first you have to promise to never say a word about this. Ever."

"About what?"

She pushed away the hair falling over her brow, and there was blood on her hand.

"Look, Mrs. Hale. What's going on?"

"Promise me first. You won't tell a soul."

Douglas was mystified by this strange behavior. Mrs. Hale was usually so calm. "I am bound by my medical oath, as well you know, Mrs. Hale. I never discuss my patients."

"Good—"

"But if it's something illegal, then I can't promise—"

"No, no, nothing illegal. It's—" Mrs. Hale's chin wobbled as she tried to control herself. "I'll take you upstairs." She made her way up the narrow wooden stairs. "I didn't know what else to do. You were the only person I could think of."

Douglas followed her, each step getting darker as they reached the landing lit by a single candle. Mrs. Hale paused by the door of the room at the back of the house, and then opened it. The whole situation was an unpleasant echo of his first night in Boston. His mouth was dry, fearing what he would find.

The room was lit by two lamps. He recognized the sweet, tarry smell of phenol, which Mrs. Hale must have been using as a disinfectant. Furniture was sparse and the narrow bed took up most of the room. There was a figure on the bed, curled with her back to him. A pile of towels lay on the floor, bloodstained. A bowl of something that looked like porridge was on the tiny dresser, a spoon stuck in it, and a cup was lying on its side by the pitcher. Douglas raised an eyebrow at the disarray, so unexpected in Mrs. Hale's home.

The woman on the bed wore a white cotton nightgown and her hair was in a long, single dark braid, but with tresses broken free.

The window was open. Mrs. Hale saw him glance at it.

"She was hot, so I thought—"

The patient turned over, hearing Mrs. Hale's voice.

Douglas knew it would be a woman—a woman in trouble. But never for a moment did he think it would be Miss Phoebe Van Bergen.

His feet fixed rigidly to the floor and he was unable to speak. He was an experienced doctor, trained for emergencies, but his heart was pounding.

Miss Van Bergen's skin was pale and shiny, her eyes ranging over the room but not settling on anything. She turned and clenched her abdomen in pain, letting out a noise, like a wounded animal.

The cry broke the spell. Douglas stepped toward the chest of drawers, put his case down and threw off his overcoat and jacket, dumping his hat on a rickety chair. Rolling up his shirt sleeves, he moved to her bedside and put his hand to her brow. She was on fire. He lifted her arm and pushed back the cotton sleeve. The skin was mottled and there were red marks like pin pricks. She mumbled but didn't seem to know he was there.

"Water, so I can wash."

Mrs. Hale poured water into a bowl on the drawers and pushed a saucer with soap closer. He washed his hands in the cold water and dried them on the cleanest piece of linen he could find in his haste.

He took his trumpet and leaned over Miss Van Bergen to listen to her heart. It was rapid and light, just like her breathing. "Tell me everything."

Mrs. Hale rang her hands, tears glistening in her eyes. "She knocked on my door yesterday. Desperate. She had already started bleeding. I brought her up here and fetched linens."

"Had she induced it?"

Mrs. Hale stared at him, open-mouthed.

"Had she induced the miscarriage?" he repeated more forcefully.

Mrs. Hale's hand went to her throat. "No! Nothing like that."

"It is essential I know if there are any poisons that need purging."

"I am sure of it, sir. She said God had taken pity on her. Had delivered her from disaster."

Douglas put the back of his hand to her hot cheek. This didn't look like God's deliverance to him. "What next?"

Mrs. Hale hesitated.

"Look," Douglas said, "imagine you are matron on the ward. What would you be telling me there?"

This seemed to help Mrs. Hale get a grip of herself. "The fetus passed. I'd guess she was twelve weeks gone."

"And the placenta?"

"I made sure it had all come free."

He looked sternly at Mrs. Hale. "You're sure of that?"

She squared her shoulders. "I've managed this situation enough times at the hospital to know."

Douglas ran his hand through his hair. It was true: Mrs. Hale was the most competent of all the nurses at the Van Bergen hospital. She was an excellent midwife with skills superior to the male doctors.

Mrs. Hale picked up a towel from the floor and folded it. "I know, it shouldn't be like this. I tried to keep it as clean as possible, I brought carbolic acid back from the hospital, but..."

Her face told him they were thinking the same thing: puerperal fever.

"She was well to begin with. I said she should stay here a day or so and recover. She wrote a note which I sent to her home, saying she would be with a friend for a few days to recover after the funeral. And another to the hospital, saying the same thing."

He dipped a cloth in the water and smoothed it over Miss Van Bergen's face and down her arms. She seemed a little calmer than when he had first arrived, but not properly conscious. "When did she get sick?"

"I came back from the hospital this afternoon. She was breathless and speaking things that didn't make sense." Mrs. Hale swallowed. "I didn't know what to do, Dr. McLennan. She should be at home, or in the hospital, I know that, but... well, everyone would know why, or suspect at the very least. She would be ruined."

But she'd be safe, Douglas thought. "You haven't contacted her family?"

"Not yet. When she first came, she swore me to secrecy. Said no one should know, including her family."

Douglas clenched his jaw. With Alexander gone, he could understand why she would not want to reach out to her cold-hearted brother and his wife.

"I called you, Dr. McLennan, because... well, I had to do *something*. If she should die..." Although the last words were a whisper, they galvanized Douglas.

"We must not think like that. It's an infection. Serious, but the odds are with her. She's young and strong. Her natural defenses should protect her."

"Will you try to bleed her?" Mrs. Hale asked nervously. "Dr. Minot often does that."

Douglas shook his head. "I've seen no evidence it helps."

Mrs. Hale's shoulders dropped as she sighed. "Good. I think it does more harm than good."

Douglas went to his case and took out a small bottle. "I have some laudanum for the pain. Other than that, it's a waiting game.

Keep her cool when she seems too hot. Raise the covers when she's shivering." He stood and let out a breath. "Let's tidy the room. Are there any clean sheets or linens?"

"I've used all I've got."

"Here." He took some dollars from his coat pocket. "Gather these sheets and take them to the hospital laundry. Then bring back some clean sets of bedlinen. You are matron, no one will question you, I'm sure."

She left the room briefly and returned with a canvas sack. "I don't like to leave her, Doctor, even for a short while."

"Dinnae fash, Mrs. Hale. I'm not going anywhere. Has she eaten anything? Drunk?"

"Not for a while." Mrs. Hale glanced at the bowl of dried grits.

Douglas followed her eyes, thinking how unappetizing the grits looked. "Would you have any broth? Anything thin. You know, easy to swallow but nourishing."

"I have something in the cold pantry."

"Good. Bring that up, please, before you leave for the hospital."

With Mrs. Hale gone, he cleared the room, picking up blood-stained linens and pushing them into the sack. He set the cup upright, cleared some dishes, then pulled down the sash window until there was an inch or so at the bottom, and folded in one of the shutters.

Mrs. Hale arrived with a bowl of broth.

"Leave it on the dresser," he said. "I'll raise her up to administer the laudanum and maybe she can eat afterwards."

Mrs. Hale swung the sack onto her back and made for the door. "Thank you for coming, Dr. McLennan. You're a godsend. I don't know what I would have done." Her chin wobbled as she was on the edge of tears.

"Not at all," he replied softly.

"And you understand the secrecy? She'll be distraught when she finds out I called you."

"You did the right thing, Mrs. Hale. And you can both rely on my absolute discretion." He moved a chair adjacent to the bed.

"Mrs. Hale, before you go, tell me... were you surprised when she arrived?"

"That she came here?"

"No... I mean... were you surprised that she was in this condition?"

Mrs. Hale chewed her lip and glanced at Miss Van Bergen with compassion. "No, Dr. McLennan. Sadly no. I've never liked that fiancé of hers."

"No?"

"Truth is, I warn my nurses not to find themselves alone with Mr. Gregson. He may have a reputation as a fine fellow among you men. And those smart society ladies think he's most charming. But the women at the hospital? Well, we know when a man is to be avoided. It's a shame such a lovely lady got caught by him."

She shook her head and looked sadly at Miss Van Bergen, before closing the door quietly behind her.

Douglas sat in the chair and continued to cool her limbs. He was supposed to be in work in the morning but already knew he would send some excuse. He would not leave her side until he was sure she was out of danger.

NINETEEN

Adeline said Phoebe had spent three days in this small room, but she had only a hazy recollection of time passing. Her head throbbed and her limbs felt weak as a newborn foal, but she trusted Adeline's view that she'd come through the worst.

Phoebe and Adeline had always had a bond when working together, but the matron had turned out to be her greatest friend. If there was one thing Phoebe had got right, it was choosing Adeline's door to knock on. She wasn't sure she'd ever repay Adeline's mercy and goodness, but, God knew, she'd try.

Adeline set a tray of food before Phoebe, who shifted her legs so she could sit on the bed. Phoebe made a start on a slice of buttered toast. The bread tasted chalky—probably all Adeline could afford on her wages.

"D'you feel well enough to get up?" Adeline asked.

Phoebe bit her lower lip. "I guess I have to try."

"Thing is, it's getting hard to conceal where you are. That story we made up about you going to a friend's house in Cambridge to rest after the funeral? It's starting to unravel. People asking questions." Adeline picked at a thread on the coverlet. "And I can't look after you like you need. I've hated leaving you when I've had to show my face at the hospital."

Phoebe felt bad at the complications she had caused for Adeline and the burden she was creating.

"I need to get you back home to Louisburg Square. You'll get far better care there than I can give now. You need to take your time convalescing. Resting."

"It's not my home anymore," Phoebe said quietly.

"No? I thought—"

"It's where my things are. But Thaddeus and Florence moved in straight after Mother died. Florence is mistress of that house now, even though she says it's too small and wants to sell up. She wanted my bedroom as a guest room and has moved me further up."

Adeline stroked the back of Phoebe's hand. "That must have been tough."

"I put up a fight. A polite one, you understand. She said she wanted to get on with renovations, get it ready to sell. And I'd be moving out, soon as I married."

Adeline lowered her head. "Do you *have* to marry him? I can't see much happiness for you on that path."

Phoebe put her head back on the wooden headboard. She'd always pictured herself with her own home, filled with children. Was she willing to let that dream go? "He was already threatening my reputation to force me to keep quiet about what he was doing. Look at what's just happened to me. If anyone ever finds out, I'm ruined. No one else would marry me." Phoebe's chin wobbled as she held back tears. "I'd lose the hospital too. All that work for nothing... Florence is right: I have to get on and marry him, fast as I can."

The look of pity on Adeline's face made her feel even more ashamed.

Adeline sighed out a long breath. "I'll get you back to Beacon Hill and tell people you collapsed from exhaustion. Long hours at the hospital and then losing your mother. I promise, not a soul will suspect anything else."

Phoebe closed her eyes. Adeline was right. She needed to get back. "Very well."

Adeline put the tray on the drawers. "Let's get you up."

She pulled back the coverlet and sheets. Phoebe shuffled her legs over the side of the bed. She'd helped many a patient do this, never dreaming one day it would be her. She was dizzy and took a moment to catch her breath. Adeline put her arm round her back and helped rock her forward onto her feet.

She was standing. Phoebe leaned her arms against the chest of drawers opposite to get her balance and felt nausea rise. Breathing carefully, the feeling subsided, like a wave rolling back into the sea.

"I'm fine," she whispered. "Completely fine."

But she wasn't. Without Adeline's help, she couldn't take a step.

"How am I going to do this?" She looked at Adeline's kind face, terrified she'd never be able to walk by herself again.

"That's a grand start," said Adeline. "Let's sit you on the bed again. I'm going to send a note to sort out the cab to drive you home. Then I'll bring your clothes to get you dressed."

Once Adeline left, Phoebe sat on the edge of the bed, looking at her bare toes. She pulled up the cotton nightdress to examine her legs. Even after only three days, she had lost weight. She circled her feet one way, then the other. She longed to lie back down, to slip into the luxury of sleep, where the wreckage of her life couldn't reach her.

The last few weeks had been agony, at first thinking her weariness and general feeling of being unwell was from the strain of caring for her mother. She didn't want to acknowledge the truth to begin with, but gradually knew she had fallen pregnant. She had berated herself for blindly hoping the inevitable wouldn't happen to her, as it did to so many of the women who turned up at the doorstep of the Van Bergen Women's Hospital.

She had never felt so lonely. There was not a soul she could talk to about the disaster. The sensible part of her knew the only option was to tell Hector and to marry as fast as possible. She wouldn't be the first Boston society lady to have a baby surprisingly early in her marriage, and wouldn't be the last.

The fact that she kept putting off this action told her how much she hated the idea of a life with Hector. Every time someone commented on how pale she looked, or how little she was eating, she would ask what else they expected, with the imminent passing of her mother.

The only thing that had kept her going over the past weeks was her vision of a new hospital. It gave her something, a way to keep busy, an excuse for leaving the house, and hope for the future.

She had been promenading alone by the Charles River the day after the funeral and heartbroken to have said goodbye to Lex and Ginny that morning. Suddenly, she had felt a sharp pain in her abdomen and thighs and soon realized she was bleeding. She had sat on a bench, frantically trying to work out what to do. Then she had remembered Adeline lived close by. It was the only option: confess everything to Adeline and throw herself on her mercy. At least she could be sure Adeline would know how to help medically.

The kindness and compassion she had received from Adeline had restored her faith in humanity. She understood now how ill she had been over recent days and was in awe of the care Adeline must have given and wondered how much time she had taken away from her hospital duties. She would be a burden no longer.

Phoebe let out a long growl; she must keep moving. Adeline had miraculously managed to keep everything a secret so far, but she had to go home. She reached for another piece of toast. It was brittle and the butter had congealed, but she needed something in her stomach.

Adeline slipped back into the room, her arms full of Phoebe's clothes. "That's everything sorted. A cab will be here in half an hour. Plenty of time to get you dressed."

Phoebe recognized her dress but not the foundation garments. "These look new."

"I had to throw away your undergarments," said Adeline, her cheeks a little pink. "You understand."

Phoebe nodded.

"I bought these new."

"Thank you," Phoebe whispered. "I'll pay you, of course."

"Don't worry about that now." Adeline went to the dresser and dipped a flannel in the water before ringing it out. She handed it to Phoebe, who washed herself under the nightdress.

Phoebe started to dress, her arms feeling as if there were bracelets of lead fixed around her wrists. Every movement was slow and labored, and without Adeline's help it would have been impossible. She put on the uniform of a rich Boston woman: the whalebone corset, the elaborate bustle, the skirt and bodice fitted to look like one dress. Adeline fastened the lines of fiddly buttons, knelt to slip her feet into smart shoes with a low heel.

Phoebe ran her fingers through the long single braid to separate it into three strands and brushed her hair before Adeline looped it back into place and secured it with pins.

"Your hat and jacket are downstairs," Adeline said. Phoebe had a vague recollection of wearing the hat with a veil—being in mourning meant she had been able to conceal her face. "And someone is here to help."

Phoebe jumped at a knock on the bedroom door.

"I left the door on the latch," said Adeline, avoiding Phoebe's eyes, "and told him to come up."

"The cab driver?" Phoebe swallowed, unready to face the world and fearful the driver might recognize her.

The door opened and McLennan stood at the threshold. All strength flowed from her legs and she stumbled back to sit on the bed, staring up at him. Of all the men to be standing there...

"You said..." Her voice was a croak. She turned sharply to Adeline. "You said no one knew. No one would *ever* know." Her skin felt hot with betrayal, thinking Adeline had been the only person she could trust.

Adeline tried to take her hand. "I couldn't do it by myself. I'm sorry, dearest Phoebe. You were so *very* ill, I was afraid. I *had* to call someone."

"But McLennan. Dr. McLennan. Why *him*?"

He remained in the doorway. He removed his hat and threaded its rim through his fingers, looking like he wished he were anywhere but here.

"Because he's the best, simple as that," said Adeline, raising and dropping her shoulders. "You've said so yourself. And I trust him. Of all the doctors I know, I trust him."

Phoebe's hands were clammy as she stared at the man before her. Notions dashed through her mind. Maybe he thought she had been taken ill with—oh, who knew what. Fever? An infection?

She pulled Adeline close. "Does he know...?" she whispered.

Adeline glanced at McLennan, whose face revealed nothing. "He knows everything. He had to."

Phoebe screwed her eyes shut and pushed her palms against them. McLennan was friends with Hector and her brother, for God's sake. This was the *worst* possible man to have called. The nausea returned as humiliation swept over her.

But it was true she had confided in Adeline that McLennan was a far better doctor than the others at the hospital. He might have infuriated her when he had first arrived, but over the months she had grown to grudgingly admire his skills and noticed he was gentler with the sick women than she had originally given him credit for. Despite what she had experienced on that very first night, he gave even the poorest of women respect they did not receive from Dr. Storer and Dr. Minot. Nevertheless, she'd been too proud to admit to anyone but Adeline that she had been wrong.

McLennan came into the room and dropped to his haunches so his face was level as she sat on the bed. His eyes locked on hers. "Miss Van Bergen, I treated you as a patient, like anyone else. But Mrs. Hale is an excellent practitioner. There was little I did other than give advice."

She dropped her head. This was a crumb of comfort.

He lifted her chin with his palm with unexpected gentleness. "I promise you, until my dying day, I will never speak of this. You have nothing to fear from me."

She pushed her lips together and sniffed; she was not going to cry in front of him, not show yet more weakness.

"So, Miss Van Bergen, let's get you into the cab that's waiting. Mrs. Hale doesnae think you're mauchty enough for the stairs."

"I'm sure I'm fine." She anchored her fists into the mattress and pushed herself upright. "See?"

Using the dresser to steady herself, she put an arm to the open door. It was like crossing a harbor footbridge where the slats were moving and she had to cling to handrails for safety. At the top of the stairs, she swayed, all blood having rushed from her head. Maybe this was not such a good idea. Her legs began to buckle.

Before she knew it, McLennan's arm was round her back and he bobbed down to pass the other one below her knees, before standing upright, holding her secure against his chest. She had no choice but to put her arms around his neck, feeling pathetic and powerless.

"We'll take this slowly," he said, his voice close and low.

The stairs were narrow and poorly lit. He had to go sideways and took one step at a time, then along the landing, with Adeline following.

"Just one more flight."

Phoebe sought a quip to make light of the situation, but she could think of nothing. Her mind was too full of the mortification of the undignified situation.

They reached the hall and McLennan set her down, keeping an arm around her back to steady her. He was close enough for her to smell his musky aftershave—a more subtle scent than the Morgan's pomade Hector used to control his curls. He was breathing deeply but did not seem out of breath. She should say something to thank him, but her throat was dry.

Adeline hurried forward with the fur-trimmed princess-style jacket and black hat with a single feather, which Adeline pinned through Phoebe's thick hair.

"Mrs. Hale is traveling with you to Louisburg Square," McLennan said. "She has sent a note and they are expecting you."

Phoebe swallowed. "Thank you," she finally whispered. She coughed to clear her throat and spoke more clearly. "Thank you for…" But she trailed off. Words were inadequate for the mix of emotions she felt, the circumstances they found themselves in.

He took her hand and squeezed it. "You're going to be fine, Miss Van Bergen." His voice was gentle by her ear. "It will take a wee while, but one day, all this will be in your past. The future"—he frowned and bit his lip as if working out what to say—"the future is in your hands. That's not true for most women. You are an exceptional woman. And you are brave. I've seen that. Hold on to that bravery."

She looked up at him and held his gaze as he studied her. His green eyes were flecked with bronze. She paused and fought the desire to lift her hand to his cheek, to touch the fair stubble on his jaw, the thick mustache on his lip.

Adeline opened the front door and the hall flooded with October light. Sunshine made his blond hair glow.

His mouth curved in a slight smile. "Ready?"

She pulled down the veil and stepped onto the sidewalk, Adeline supporting her, as McLennan opened the cab door. Adeline helped her climb into the back and then got in the other side, holding the small reticule Phoebe had brought three days before.

The cab driver shut the door and climbed up behind the single black horse, flicking his whip so the cab jerked forward.

The cheap cab was without glazed windows, so Phoebe leaned out and looked back as they set off. McLennan was already hurrying away down the street.

Phoebe felt a pang of regret that he didn't look back.

TWENTY

Douglas put his head down and strode away from Mrs. Hale's house, toward the hospital. Walking swiftly had always cleared his mind, and he was desperate for clarity now. A delivery boy made his way along the sidewalk, a wide tray of bread held at his shoulder, so Douglas sidestepped him.

His probationary period would be complete in a month. In the beginning, he had been so resentful of this condition to his employment. A trial period, and all because one bossy woman had caught him off-guard on the night of his arrival in Boston. But now he was relieved, because it gave an easy way out. He wouldn't have to make up excuses or explanations for his departure.

Thank goodness he had put out feelers for positions elsewhere when the Van Bergen hospital had failed to confirm him in a permanent post. He had some connections through his training in Edinburgh and work in London. A week ago, a letter had arrived offering him a position at Mount Sinai Hospital in New York. He had failed to reply—uncharacteristic behavior—not because it was a general hospital and he had hoped to find one where his particular skills would be of use, but because part of him wanted to stay in Boston. He had come to like the city, its compact size, its sense of revolutionary history, its culture of enquiry driven by the academics of Harvard. Most of all, the plans for the new purpose-built hospital were exciting. Miss Van Bergen had spoken inspiringly about building the most progressive women's hospital on the Eastern Seaboard. He wanted to be part of that—more, he wanted to *shape* it. After years of drifting after the death of his wife, he had something that gave him purpose and a worthwhile future.

But not any longer. He needed to escape Miss Van Bergen's orbit as quickly as possible.

Over the months, his admiration of her passion for women's health had overcome his original dislike of her. How mistaken he had been, thinking she was a rich, bored young woman trying to relieve the tedium in her life by playing at nurses.

Then, at Fairview, he had discovered a different story. She was just as trapped as the working-class women he treated day after day. He wanted to help her and was frustrated he could think of nothing he could do—or nothing that wouldn't make things worse in the end.

When he had walked into Mrs. Hale's bedroom three days ago, he had been thoroughly shocked. But then a wave of compassion had flooded over him, threatening to knock him off his feet. This strong, clever, generous woman had been broken by the abuse of her hateful fiancé.

This morning, he had felt something far stronger than compassion. When he had lifted her up and held her close, he wanted nothing more on earth than to protect her from everything. Something electric had shot through him. Every nerve was alive to her. Her scent had filled his nostrils, he had felt the softness of her hair, a stray strand tickling his ear, felt her breath on his cheek, sensed the rise and fall of her chest against him.

They were sensations he was entirely unprepared for.

When he had set her down, he had felt like a young man who had never been close to a woman before. There was a wee notch in the line of her upper lip which meant they didn't quite meet in a line. He had noticed this unusual feature early on, but now he found it captivating. She had been on the edge of saying something, but words were trapped inside her, in just the same way they were for him.

She seemed so alone, and he wanted to give her some hope, to remind her of her strength. Life had taught him that dreadful things happen, things you thought would destroy you. Yet the sun still rose, the day was still waiting to be lived. Maybe not the life you had planned—but something. He hoped his words reminding her of her bravery had touched her, because words were all he could give. He hoped she would find a new path.

As he approached the hospital, his shoulders slumped as he realized how unlikely that was. Miss Van Bergen's future was locked with Hector Gregson's. She was the only daughter in a wealthy family—a family led by Thaddeus Van Bergen, who knew all about Hector but didn't care. In all likelihood, Hector would curtail her leadership of the hospital, controlling her emotionally and physically.

McLennan couldn't bear to stay in Boston and watch it happen.

The only thing for him now was to take the position in New York. In time, his burning attraction to Miss Phoebe would pass. Nothing had happened. He hadn't succumbed to the urge to find out how sweet those lips were. No one need ever know how deeply she had touched him.

Douglas reached the hospital steps and opened the heavy door. He had made a decision: the first chance he had, he would write to New York and say he was immediately available. As soon as that was confirmed, he would send a letter of resignation to the Van Bergen Women's Hospital board and leave Boston forever.

Phoebe went back to the hospital after three weeks. A box of navel oranges had been delivered by a benefactor with an estate in Florida, saying they were from the first November harvest of the year. Phoebe took the fruit room to room, giving one to each patient.

Some were skeptical, but others plunged in, stripping back the peel.

There were still far too many women in the small rooms, the beds almost touching each other. Whiffs of carbolic acid masked even more unpleasant smells. She had always pictured her hospital being an oasis of calm, like those lithographs of Florence Nightingale as the Lady with the Lamp. This hospital was filled with the noise of many accents arguing with each other, of hawing coughs, of babies crying and small children refusing to sit still. Dr. Minot still had a long list of questions, and reasons why he couldn't do the work required of him.

Phoebe retreated to her office downstairs. Adeline had done a good job keeping things in order. Letters were in a neat pile on the right and the latest pamphlets on the left; she decided to take those home to read in the evenings.

Even with the noise and demands, she was glad to be here, despite a heaviness inside. She recalled Hector's first visit once she felt strong enough to receive visitors at Louisburg Square. She had felt physically sick when he had walked into the drawing room, and her hand had trembled as she raised it to her mouth to calm the biliousness. He had been his usual charming self, all smiles and attention. He had not seemed to notice she'd been away, but feigned concern for her health now. Did he suspect? Perhaps. But it was easier for him to put her ill health down to grief after the passing of her mother—a fiction she was prepared to maintain.

Phoebe picked up a golden envelope opener shaped like a dagger, and started on the letters.

There was a knock at the door and Adeline stepped in.

"Good to see you back, Miss Van Bergen."

Phoebe shook her head. "I think we're well past that formality. Please call me Phoebe in private. Unless that makes you feel uncomfortable."

"Happy to... er... Phoebe." Adeline put a thin sheaf of papers on the desk. "These are the things addressed to the president of the

Board that I think you need to see." Adeline tapped a letter at the top. "Beginning with this."

Phoebe picked up the opened envelope, and noted with surprise that Adeline took a seat, despite having so much to do.

The hand was familiar but she couldn't place it. Taking out the single sheet, she glanced at the name at the bottom.

"Dr. McLennan?"

Adeline nodded and a crease appeared in her brow.

Phoebe read swiftly. She took a sharp intake of breath. "He's leaving!"

"Indeed."

"He's taking a post in New York. But why?" She dropped the letter onto her desk as if it were poisoned, and rested her head in her hands. "This is my fault. He can't bear to work with me anymore."

"I don't think that's true—"

"Of course he wouldn't want to be associated with a hospital with Van Bergen on the nameplate. Not when he knows I—"

"Truly, that isn't the case—"

"You've spoken to him?" Phoebe looked up at Adeline.

Adeline swallowed. "I did. Briefly. When the rumor had gone round that he was to leave."

"What did he say?"

Adeline waggled her head left and right. "He was stiff to begin with. Formal."

Just as Phoebe expected.

"I tried to ask... you know... in a roundabout way. I felt bad. If I hadn't asked him to visit my house, then he wouldn't have got involved and..."

"And?"

"He said it was nothing to do with that. He said he'd always wanted to go to New York. That, having traveled this far, he wanted to know what other places had to offer."

She supposed it could be true. But he'd never mentioned it before.

Adeline shrugged. "I said it seemed kinda sudden, but he said he'd made approaches early on. You know, with the six-month probation period an' all..."

Phoebe closed her eyes and groaned. Another of her mistakes. At the time, she had truly doubted he would fit in here. That first evening of his arrival, his behavior had been so rude and dismissive. She should have trusted her old friend Professor Moncrieff's letter of commendation. Everything the Professor had said about McLennan had turned out to be true: an innovative doctor with new ideas, conscientious, reliable. It had taken her a while to see it.

She curled her hands into fists and tapped them against her lips as she recognized that, over recent months, many of her plans for the new hospital had been built around him—that he would make the ideal director, would attract excellence from Europe, insist on the high standards she knew, deep inside, they were failing to meet with the current leadership of unadventurous medics and a part-time Board of trustees. Not that she had said anything out loud, of course, and she certainly hadn't suggested anything to McLennan himself. She had been more interested in keeping him at a distance after he had noticed those bruises on her arms and heard her unguarded comment at Fairview. But even after the calamity of him knowing everything about her miscarriage, she still hadn't pictured a Boston without him.

She pushed back her chair and stood up. "I have to speak to him. Immediately. Persuade him to stay."

Adeline screwed up her face. "Sorry, Phoebe. It's too late."

"Too late?"

"He's gone—"

"He can't—"

"He already has. He left Boston yesterday."

"Yesterday!" She turned to the wall, controlling her breathing. "Why didn't anyone tell me?"

Adeline picked up the letter and fiddled with it. "The President instructed me not to bother you, when you'd been unwell."

Phoebe sank back into her chair. He hadn't even said farewell.

She shuffled through the remaining letters on her desk, looking for his handwriting, hoping he might have left a note.

There was nothing.

She growled as she realized she was the *last* woman he wanted to see. He must think her a dreadful hypocrite, trying to do something for the needy women of Boston, when, in reality, she was a fallen woman. She thought she had seen compassion in his eyes that day he had helped her at Adeline's house, but perhaps it had been pity. Clearly, over the past three weeks, that pity had turned to disgust. He wanted nothing to do with her.

Not even to say goodbye.

TWENTY-ONE

Although she had only been there a few hours, Phoebe couldn't face remaining at the hospital any longer. She was on the verge of tears and kept pausing to force them back.

Phoebe arrived home in time for a stilted lunch sitting opposite Florence, who informed her Hector would be joining them for dinner and, yet again, told Phoebe she really needed to get a move on and set a date for the wedding. People were beginning to raise eyebrows at the length of their engagement and it would soon turn to malicious gossip.

Phoebe wondered what Florence suspected, and whether she'd be leading the gossip, but said nothing.

She went to the garden room at the back of the house and asked for tea to be brought there. It had been a favorite room of her mother's, with glazed doors looking onto their landscaped yard. Most of the leaves had fallen now, and the wind lifted them into eddies before settling into bronze and yellow piles.

She picked up a novel, opening it where she had left the bookmark. She couldn't remember reading that far.

A maid set the tea tray on the occasional table. "A letter has arrived for you, miss." She bobbed and left.

More correspondence. Would it never stop?

Phoebe looked at the envelope and saw the edges were frayed and it was well-traveled with numerous postmarks. The paper was thick but the writing a scrawl. No wonder they hadn't been able to find the right address at first.

She pulled out the letter and her heart leaped when she saw it was from Professor Moncrieff. She had been thinking about him, only that morning. Perhaps her old mentor and friend would lift her spirits.

He began by politely enquiring after her health and that of the family. Then he asked how her plans for the new hospital were going. Her stomach tightened when he asked whether Dr. McLennan had lived up to the personal recommendation he had given.

"And now to the meat of this correspondence," Moncrieff wrote. He was inviting her to a symposium he was arranging at the famous medical school in Edinburgh. It was to be the first international symposium to consider women's health. Some of his colleagues were skeptical, but he knew Phoebe would understand the importance of the gathering. He had invited Miss Florence Nightingale to give an address. She could not be there in person; indeed, she rarely left her house, but had promised to write a paper that could be read out loud.

Might Phoebe be the person to present it?

He wrote of the importance of learning from all parts of the world, and how they would benefit enormously from hearing her plans for a new hospital in Boston.

Phoebe's pulse beat faster as she searched for the date. The letter had been written on the first of September, almost three months ago. Even with crossing the Atlantic, that had meant a delay in reaching her.

She turned to a second page: the symposium was to last three days, just before Christmas, because, with students gone, Moncrieff had access to public spaces.

She dropped the letter onto her lap and thumped the arm of her chair. The dates simply didn't work. She would have to leave immediately to cross the ocean to England and travel north to Scotland in time. It was a ridiculous idea.

And yet, a bubble of excitement was brewing inside. She stood to stretch her legs and took the letter to the door to the garden. A cloud must have moved because she felt a shaft of weak sunlight on her face. Her mind wrestled back and forth. It would be crazy to suddenly take off for Edinburgh. She was afraid of the sea journey, for a start. She knew it took around two weeks, even with the most modern steamers, and the Atlantic could be wild and stormy at this time of year. So many people had taken that dangerous journey from Europe to the New World over the past two centuries. Very few crossed back. What had William Penn said? *Death is but crossing the world, as friends do the seas; they live in one another still.*

McLennan's words came back to her, the ones he had said as they stood at Adeline's door. He had told her she was brave. She wasn't sure if it was true. Was she going to let fear of the journey stop her? A journey her Van Bergen ancestors had taken, when they left Amsterdam, a century before? She put her brow to the cold windowpane. No, she would live up to whatever it was McLennan had seen in her, and face the challenge.

She turned and strode across the room as she thought. She couldn't travel alone, of course. That was unthinkable. Who could go with her? Hector? Her stomach clenched at the very idea. Would Florence want to join her adventure? Phoebe laughed out loud. Florence would never leave Boston in a thousand years, and a month or more in each other's company would be agony for both. She thought about her mother's friends: was there a respectable widow? She shook her head: they were too old and stuffy.

Her thoughts alighted on Adeline. Why not? She was a widow: that made her a suitable chaperone. The more Phoebe thought about it, the cleverer the idea seemed. Adeline would learn as much from the symposium as she would. Indeed, Adeline would be able to contribute her knowledge as matron. Phoebe was sure she could persuade her.

She bit her lip as she thought further. Who would make sure the hospital was being run properly if they were away? With neither Phoebe nor Adeline there, those fossils on the Board of trustees would have full control. There wasn't even McLennan to keep things going in the right direction.

Phoebe sighed. Maybe it was a stupid dream. Her duty was to remain here and marry Hector. She had lost so much already; going to Edinburgh for more than a month, she could lose everything.

She sat back in her chair and re-read the enthusiastic words of the professor, the man who had fired her imagination when she had met him almost a decade ago. He had been giving a lecture at Faneuil Hall in the center of the city about the lack of facilities for women's health. Phoebe had been eighteen and gone by chance. That night changed her life. He had ignited her with a vision of what the world could be. At last, she had a purpose in this world. Her father and brothers laid railroads; she could build something special as well.

She had sought out the elderly professor after the lecture, encouraged her mother to invite him to dinner, where they instantly became friends. They had corresponded immediately, and he sent her pamphlets and answered her many questions. He said he saw something special in her—no one had ever particularly taken notice of her before, except for Lex.

When the professor had returned to Britain, they had continued to exchange long letters. He encouraged her to volunteer with existing medical establishments and, as her confidence grew, to open a clinic in the Van Bergen name. From this had grown the women's hospital, proceeding in fits and starts, but gradually becoming established, taking over the house in the West End where so many of the women she wanted to help lived.

A robin alighted on the lawn outside the French window. Phoebe watched it busily pecking away at the soil. She moved slightly and the bird cocked its head, fixing its brown-button eye on her. It darted away over the wall.

Phoebe turned back to the room. The professor had changed her life once. Maybe Providence was using him to do so a second time. She was struck by the serendipity that his letter should arrive *now*, when she was at her lowest ebb. She had been drowning and opened her hand to grasp something—and the professor had reached out to save her. This was not coincidence: this was her destiny. It meant all barriers, all her fears would be overcome, somehow.

Phoebe said little over dinner that evening. She had a fizzing sensation inside but knew she needed to reveal her plans at the right moment and in the right way. Most of the conversation was between Hector and Thaddeus. She was not expected to contribute and that suited her just fine.

At the end of the meal, she turned to Hector. "Dear, I wonder if we might go up to the drawing room. There are things we need to discuss."

TWENTY-TWO

Phoebe caught the look between Florence and Thaddeus and knew what they were thinking: *At last, troublesome Pheebs is going to set a date.*

"Of course, honeybee," said Hector, rising. He stood behind Phoebe's chair to move it back.

She led the way across the black and white hall tiles and up the staircase to the next floor. Her mother used this rather grand drawing room overlooking the square when she had guests.

As soon as they entered, Hector stepped close behind, running his fingers down her spine. Phoebe hastened her steps and sat in the rococo armchair near the fire. She nodded to the sofa opposite and Hector took his place, flapping the long tails of his dress-coat so he didn't crease them. He extended his arm along the back of the sofa and folded one leg over the other. A slight smile curled his lips as he fixed his eyes on her.

"So, Pheebs, we setting a date?"

"We are. March."

His eyebrow raised. "March? That's another four months."

"It is. Just before Easter should be pleasant."

He sniffed. "Thing is, that doesn't work for me. I need it to be sooner."

"Well, Hector, I can't marry you sooner because I'm going away."

Hector's eyes narrowed. "Away?"

"I'm going to Edinburgh."

Hector said nothing, his expression stony.

"It's in Scotland."

"Yes, I damn well know where Edinburgh is. What nonsense is this?"

Phoebe took a breath. "I received a letter from Professor Moncrieff today inviting me to an international symposium."

Lines appeared around Hector's eyes and he moved his hand in front of his mouth to hide a smile.

Phoebe pushed on. "It's a medical conference on women's health."

"You!" Now Hector laughed outright. "You think you're traveling across the ocean, to Edinburgh, to talk about—what did you say? Women's health?"

"I plan to take Mrs. Hale as my chaperone. She is the matron at the hospital. She will be ideal."

Hector tutted and shook his head, as if amused by the antics of a child.

Phoebe ignored him. "The symposium is from December tenth to the twelfth. That means I need to leave immediately. I will enquire about ships tomorrow. I plan to stay in Great Britain for a few weeks afterwards and maybe travel across to France or Germany. I recently read an article about a hospital in Paris which is exploring neurological conditions. I plan to visit."

Hector put up a hand, the palm facing her. "Whoa! Let's stop this right here. You are not going to Scotland. And you are most definitely not going to Paris."

Phoebe pushed on as if she hadn't heard him. "I will be back in Boston by the beginning of February. That will give us a month or so before the wedding."

"Not happening. Thing is, Pheebs, I was going to broach this myself this evening, so I am grateful for this timely conversation. I need to marry before the end of the year."

Phoebe frowned. "*Need?*"

Hector sat back in the sofa again. "One of the good things about us is that we've always been honest with each other. Truth is, I'm in a spot of bother. Made a couple of investments that haven't worked out. Got some payments due by the end of December." He plucked the crease in the fabric on his thigh and straightened it. "So, you can see, honey..." He left the sentence hanging.

"You need my money to pay off your debts." She failed to keep the distain from her voice. Nothing Hector said surprised her any more.

"Hey, honeybee, that's not a kind way to put it. Remember, once we're married, what's mine is yours, what's yours is mine. We're a team."

Phoebe knew their marriage would never be a team. Paying off his debts. How humiliating for both of them. This would just be the start. Once they were married, he would bleed her dry, exactly as Lex had feared, leaving only the money he had set up in trust for her and any children.

Douglas's deep Scots voice came to her mind once more. He had said everything she had endured was in her past and her future was in her hands.

Phoebe took a long breath through her nose. "Well, Hector. The thing is, I am determined to go to this symposium. You will have to solve your money problem some other way."

He whipped his head to her, the smile gone. "I don't care how determined you are. You're not going."

Phoebe swallowed. "I *am* going. And you can't stop me."

Hector unfolded his legs and calmly stood. He prowled the few steps to her chair and leaned forward, a hand on each of the arms, trapping her like a caged bird. His face was inches from hers. "You'll do as I damn well say, or this engagement is over. And you know what that means."

Phoebe's heart was beating fast, but she held his gaze.

He spoke slowly and carefully. "I won't hesitate to let it be known what you're really like. How eager you were to open your legs to me. Everyone will know you're a woman with loose morals. Of easy virtue. You'll never be able to enter a quality drawing room in Boston again. You'll never be able to walk down Mount Vernon Street without wondering if those catcalls are about you. And all that fundraising for the hospital?" He clicked his teeth like he was geeing a horse. "Gone."

Hector stroked her cheek with the back of his hand. Her heart was pounding and she had to steel herself not to flinch.

"Now," he said quietly, "tell me you understand, and we'll pretend this conversation never happened. We'll go downstairs and tell your brother that we've decided on a Christmas wedding."

Phoebe leaned as far back in the seat as she could. Brave. She had to be brave. She slipped the ring from her finger, put it on her right palm and lifted it to him in the narrow space between them. "Yours, I believe."

He glanced at it and frowned. "Think about this very carefully, Pheebs."

"Oh, I have. I know *exactly* what I'm doing."

Hector stood and snatched the ring from where her palm was still raised.

"I *will* be going to Scotland," she said, as steadily as she could. "And this engagement is at an end."

"You know what this means—"

He straightened as she forced herself to her feet, still inches between them. "It means I don't have to put up with you a moment longer." She pushed him hard enough for him to take a step back.

"It means everything is over for you." The suave tone had gone, replaced by a sneer.

"No, Hector. It means everything is just beginning." She stepped past him and stood by the sofa, one hand on its back to steady herself. "Do your worst. Say whatever you wish about me. But remember that cuts both ways. I know things about you. I can make your position at the bank very precarious. No one will ever loan you money again."

She walked to the door and put her hand on the knob. "But I'm willing to take the chance that yours are idle threats. I should have seen this months ago. Are you really going to make an enemy of the Van Bergen family? You're a bully, Hector. You've probably had exactly what you wanted ever since you were a boy. Well, you won't have me. And you won't have my money. If you say a single word about me, I'll make sure you won't have a chance of marrying some other rich young woman. Which, after all, is the only way you'll make your way in the world: through marrying money. You're too idle and stupid to make it yourself."

He stood there, bewildered by what she was doing, but now his brow lowered. His lip curled and he made a sound like a snarl. He took a step closer, but she was quicker, flinging the door open and stepping out.

"Phoebe!" Hector roared behind her.

This was the advantage of a house full of servants: Merriman was waiting outside.

"Mr. Gregson is leaving now," she said, trying to keep her voice even. "Merriman, please see him out."

Merriman inclined his head. "It will be a pleasure, Miss Phoebe."

She caught his eye. Suddenly, she understood he was a silent observer of all that took place in this house. He had probably heard every word, and her chest filled with relief, knowing Merriman was on her side.

She picked up her skirts and ran up the next flight of stairs without a backward glance. Reaching her small room at the back of the house, she closed the door and leaned against it. She took a number of steadying breaths and then a laugh bubbled from her. This feeling wasn't fear; it was triumph.

What McLennan had said was true: the future was in her hands. She was free. And this was just the beginning.

PART TWO

TWENTY-THREE

Phoebe threaded her arm through Adeline's, trying to contain the mix of excitement and trepidation in her chest. Her enquiries had revealed that there were no transatlantic crossings from Boston for a week, other than cargo ships with no provision for respectable female passengers. So now they stood on the dock in New York, looking at the liner that was going to take them to Britain. It was bigger than any ship she'd seen before: long and sleek, with four masts, as well as funnels for the steam engines. She had been assured the SS *Arizona* was one of the fastest liners to cross the Atlantic—which was exactly what she needed.

Phoebe had faced down her brother and Florence. They were horrified the engagement had been broken off and Thaddeus had set about trying to restore relations with Hector. Surprisingly, support of sorts came from Florence, who declared that if there was a scandal brewing, the best thing was for Phoebe to be out of the country. That way, gossip might blow itself out by the time she returned.

It had taken very little to persuade Adeline to come as her chaperone. She had an adventurous spirit and a desire to learn more about nursing. Phoebe's biggest concern was how the hospital would run with neither of them there. She had paid handsomely to secure the temporary services of Miss Emma Whidden, formerly head nurse at Boston Lying-in Hospital, who was willing to cover Adeline's absence. She convinced herself that they would learn so much in Europe, the hospital would be better in the long run.

Phoebe had dashed around Boston, making sure she had everything for the trip. She was uncertain about the climate in Scotland. She had the impression from McLennan it could be chilly, but surely it couldn't be as cold as Boston in December, where snow was already thick on the ground?

Merriman traveled with them by train from Boston and supervised the transfer of their trunks from train, to cart, to dockside, and now into the hold. They were taking just one maid on the journey: her lady's maid, Mrs. Farrell. Florence said Louisburg Square could not spare any more. Farrell was perfect, though, as she was a native of Liverpool and had crossed the Atlantic several times since first emigrating to the States, accompanying various employers over the years.

The dock was heaving as almost a thousand people were traveling on this new liner. Most were in steerage and Phoebe wondered what exactly that meant. Thaddeus had grudgingly secured her a cabin appropriate to a Van Bergen, with Adeline in the neighboring cabin and Farrell in an inboard cabin across the corridor.

Phoebe stepped onto the gangplank and up the steep steps to the deck. A smartly dressed sailor greeted her, and Merriman went in search of the purser to make sure everything was in order for the ladies. A steward showed the way to the rooms where things needed for the next two weeks had already been delivered.

The cabin was considerably smaller than she expected. In fact, it was probably the smallest space Phoebe had slept in since she was a girl. Two bunks on the left faced a sofa on the right with a porthole above. A sink stood between and there were various neat closets and drawers. A small stove stood close to the door. The room was faced in wood and had a carpet.

Phoebe put her head round the door of Adeline's cabin and

found it was much the same. The real luxury was that they hadn't had to share. Apparently, there was less demand for berths on the New York to Liverpool route, particularly at this time of the year.

"I'll get your things unpacked in a jiffy," said Farrell. "It will take about an hour before everything is ready to depart. Why don't you ladies have a lie-down?"

"And miss all this excitement?" said Phoebe. "Not on your life."

Adeline laughed. "Well, if you don't mind, I'm going to have a rest before we leave."

Phoebe had to keep from hugging herself as she explored the ship. She felt like a child on her birthday, sure something special was about to happen. She loved the noise and busyness, the shouts of the sailors, the porters hurrying past with baggage.

The SS *Arizona* had been launched that year and carried little freight: its important cargo was people. Phoebe went upstairs to the saloon on deck level, where she put her head back to admire the domed skylight casting light on the polished wood. She ran her fingertips through plants placed on pillars. The saloon extended the entire width of the ship. She sat at one of six long tables and was delighted that the back of the bench flipped so people could sit either side. Such ingenuity. But who decided which way a whole bench of people would sit?

Unable to stay for long with so much to experience for the first time, Phoebe rose and opened double doors onto the deck and was blasted by the noise and bustle. The air was perishingly cold, so she pulled her muffler further up her face. She was startled by a crashing sound and leaned over the barrier to see coal tumbling into the bunkers in the hull.

She ambled to the port side and looked down at the pier, hearing someone shout "All ashore!"

"Miss Van Bergen!" Merriman hurried to her, red-faced and breathing heavily. "There you are, Miss. I've made sure the purser knows who you are and will see to anything you need. He will ensure you are taken care of in Liverpool. I must bid you farewell and wish you fair winds and a following sea. Wouldn't do for me to become a stowaway."

Phoebe took his hands and he stepped back in surprise. "Thank you for everything you've done for me, Merriman. And don't worry: I can look after myself."

"True enough. You've been doing that since you were a little girl." Merriman bowed and hurried away.

Phoebe looked over the rail and soon saw him taking careful steps down the gangplank, along with others who must have been saying their farewells.

The buildings in front were even taller than the ones in Boston. She admired the ambition of this city, the enormous towers of the Brooklyn Bridge which soon would span the river, the forest of masts crowding every pier. She wondered how the cities in Europe would compare.

There had been a constant low growl, but now it became louder and moved up a note, making her feet vibrate. They must be firing up the engines. The gangplanks rattled as they were pulled onboard. Sailors moved briskly, each with his own task. Despite the cold, more people joined her at the guardrail as excitement gathered. A man and woman stood to her right, both bundled up.

"I thought they would have unfurled the sails by now," Phoebe said.

"Not until they reach open sea," the man replied. "They'll move away from Manhattan under steam with the guidance of the pilot."

The ship shuddered and there were more shouts as the dockers uncurled thick ropes from bollards and flung them onto the deck below where Phoebe was standing. The hull moved fractionally and parted company with the city. As they slid away, Phoebe could see straight down the regimented avenues of New York. She fizzed inside and felt the urge to clap her gloved hands.

With a few other intrepid souls, Phoebe watched the city recede as they moved into New York Bay, flat land fading into the distance. She knew they had reached the ocean when the swaying of the deck changed to something more pronounced. She felt thrilled to be properly underway. A gust threw fine rain against her face and she turned to make her way back to the warmth of the saloon.

As she reached the double doors, a passenger held the door open for the muffled couple to step inside, and she followed them. Glancing up at the passenger, she froze.

Dr. McLennan's mouth fell open in equal surprise. "Miss Van Bergen!" The familiar Scottish voice vibrated through her.

"I... Yes..." Her mind went blank, so she dropped her head and hurried inside, her heart thundering so hard it hurt.

Of all the men in the world to be trapped on a ship with, why did it have to be him?

TWENTY-FOUR

Letting the door bang behind him, Douglas stepped inside the saloon. Clearly, she had been as shocked as he was. What on earth was she doing on this ship? He removed his hat and pushed his fingers through his hair. Miss Van Bergen must have swiftly married and this was her honeymoon trip. Perhaps they were doing the grand tour of Europe. He clenched his teeth: he couldn't think of anything worse than a transatlantic voyage with Hector Gregson displaying his latest acquisition—his beautiful and wealthy wife.

He could see her near the door at the other end of the saloon, waiting in a crowd of people to leave the busy space. She was wearing a smart, brown, military-style coat, edged with fur and a matching hat. He steadied his breathing. The best thing would be to follow her and acknowledge each other properly, and then he would keep out of her way for the rest of the journey.

Douglas strode across the saloon. "Mrs. Gregson?"

She did not respond.

He raised his voice. "Mrs. Gregson?"

There was a ripple across her shoulders and she turned. She looked puzzled, but her eyes were shining as if on the verge of tears. And, oh God, what beautiful eyes.

"Why did you call me that?" she said so quietly he could barely hear her in the press of people.

"Well... I... I assume that—"

Her mouth became a tight line and her nostrils flared.

More people gathered at the doorway and they were crushed closer together.

"Look, might we... perhaps have a wee word?"

She made a noncommittal sound which he didn't know how to interpret.

He gestured toward the window. She nodded and he cleared a way for her.

"Would you prefer to sit?" There were upholstered chairs nearby.

"I'm fine as I am."

He swallowed. "Well, this is unexpected—"

"I thought you'd taken a position in New York—"

She spoke over him, her words coming in a rush, as if she were accusing him of something.

Douglas smoothed his mustache with one hand. "Aye, I had. I have. But I found it wasn't quite as... well, not the position I'd been hoping for."

"So you're going back home? Leaving the States?"

Her tone made him feel as if he were running away with his tail between his legs. "Only temporarily. I'm going to a medical symposium in Edinburgh."

"Ahh." She nodded slowly.

"Something Professor Moncrieff invited me to, months ago. He asked me to present a paper."

"Months back? You didn't say anything—"

"I turned him down at first. Thought I needed to establish myself with..." He trailed off. Everything led to a sensitive area when talking to her. "But when New York didn't turn out as I expected... I thought, well, why not? It should be valuable. And I'll enjoy seeing my family again."

She closed her eyes for a moment. "That explains it. This absurd coincidence."

He shook his head ruefully. "Aye, it is quite a chance, us both being here."

"The professor invited me too."

Douglas took a step back. "Moncrieff? To the symposium?"

"In Edinburgh. Yes."

He stared out of the window, absorbing the news. The sky was pale above the gunmetal gray of the ocean.

"I can see you don't think I deserve to be there, either," she said.

He thought there was bitterness in her voice. "Not at all! It makes perfect sense, when you think about it. But... well, you didn't mention it to me."

"I only got the letter recently. It was mislaid in transit."

She turned to look out of the window and they stood shoulder to shoulder. The ship rose and fell as it nosed its way through the growing waves as they made their way into open sea.

Douglas ran a hand over the back of his neck as he thought about the uncomfortable implications. Not only were they on this liner together, they would all be traveling onward to Edinburgh, spending time in that city. If only he had made up his blasted mind earlier: he would have been on a different ship, maybe even be on British soil by now.

"And Mr. Gregson," he said, "I haven't seen him yet."

"He's not here."

"Still below deck? I guess he thinks it generous of him to include a medical symposium on his honeymoon."

Now it was him sounding bitter, but her gentle laugh made him turn toward her again. She looked so different from when he'd last seen her, when he'd carried her weak body to that carriage and realized he had developed deep feelings for her. Now her skin glowed, her hair was glossy, pinned in thick folds and secured with a fashionable fur-lined hat, pinned at a jaunty angle. For a woman interested in things more important than couture, she really could carry off today's fashions with style.

"Hector gave me an ultimatum. Stay in Boston and marry him. Or go to the symposium." She glanced at him. "And here I am."

It took him a moment to process this information. "So... you're no longer engaged."

She pulled off her glove, lifted her left hand, and spread her fingers as confirmation.

Douglas could not help but let out a long breath. "I'm glad."

She arched an eyebrow.

"I'm sorry if I'm supposed to be offering condolences, but I never liked the man. He may have been charming on the surface, but underneath he was a brute."

Her mouth fell open.

Dear God, he'd been far too candid with his response, but he couldn't stop himself.

"I wish I'd had your insight into his character earlier." Her tone was surprisingly playful. "Shame my brother didn't have the measure of Hector too."

"Oh, I think your brother knew. The shameful thing was that he said and did nothing."

She dropped her eyes and seemed to withdraw. "We both know the shame was mine," she whispered.

He flexed his jaw, wanting to cry *no!* Instead, he cleared his throat. "You are free now. You can marry whoever you want. Remember, whoever *you* want."

She scoffed.

They had stepped into dangerous territory yet again. He searched for something else to say. "So. Who are you traveling with?"

"Mrs. Hale."

He glanced at her in surprise. "Oh, I'm glad."

"I thought she could learn as much as me at the symposium."

Douglas snorted. "I think she could teach them a thing or two as well." He leaned against the window. "So, it's just the two of you?"

"Other than my maid, Farrell, yes, just the two of us."

He felt a warmth inside: this was more like the bold woman he had first met. "If I can be of any assistance, I am, of course, at your service."

She smiled graciously and her eyes seemed to sparkle. "Thank you, Dr. McLennan. I'm sure we'll do just fine, though."

She put out her hand to indicate the conversation was over. He shook it briefly and remained by the window as she turned to leave. She reached the door between the saloon and the main corridor, and glanced back over her shoulder. He nodded, and was rewarded with the briefest of smiles before she swept away.

TWENTY-FIVE

Phoebe hurried along the corridor, edging round passengers trying to keep their balance with the movement of the ship. She skipped down the staircase and threaded her way to her cabin, where she found Adeline reclining on the sofa.

"There you are," said Adeline, putting down a copy of *Harper's Bazaar*. "Farrell is in her cabin, making a repair she found on a dress. Shall I call her to help you change?"

Phoebe shook her head and threw her gloves on the top bunk before unpinning her hat.

Adeline frowned. "You feeling well?"

Phoebe stabbed her a look. "What makes you ask?"

Adeline shrugged. "I don't know. It's just... something..."

Phoebe started unbuttoning her coat.

"Say, why don't I help you with that?" Adeline got up and helped remove the shapely woolen coat, stroking the fur at the collar and wrists.

Phoebe dropped heavily onto the bottom bunk. "It's McLennan. Dr. McLennan."

"What is?" asked Adeline.

"He's here. On the ship."

Adeline's mouth fell open. "He can't be!"

"He is. I've just spoken to him."

"Why would he—?"

Phoebe explained that McLennan was attending the conference too.

When she finished, Adeline looked pensive for a moment. Then she leaned forward. "You have nothing to fear." She took Phoebe's hand and looked in her eyes. "I know what you're thinking, but Dr. McLennan would never—*never*—refer to the miscarriage."

She knew Adeline was right. There had been an awkwardness with McLennan, but things had remained unspoken.

"Maybe it will be a good thing," said Adeline.

Phoebe looked up. "How so?"

"Maybe he can help us—get from Liverpool to Edinburgh, I mean."

"But that's all arranged."

"I guess. He could show us round the city."

"I'm sure he'll be far too busy to play guide to us. And if not, he'll be with his family." Phoebe stared at the little circle of gray through the porthole. Meeting McLennan had disorientated her far more than the motion of the sea. When she had pictured her time in Edinburgh, it had most definitely not been with a man so thoroughly connected with Boston.

Adeline shrugged. "I just thought..."

Phoebe looked at her and bit her lip. She remembered musing about Adeline making a good match for the lonely widower. Adeline certainly admired him; she often joked about his golden hair, his alluring Scottish accent. "Well, maybe. We'll see."

Farrell opened the cabin door, a dress over her arm. "Ah, Miss Phoebe. You're back. Won't take me a moment to put this in your closet."

Farrell carefully hung the dress and smoothed the creases.

"Your things are unpacked and shipshape—so to speak. I wondered, Miss..." Farrell's hand covered her mouth.

"Yes?"

"If I might lie down in my room. I'm not feeling so clever."

Phoebe looked more closely: Farrell was a little green. "Of course. I daresay it will take us all a few days to get our sea legs."

Farrell disappeared to her room across the corridor.

Adeline took a long breath. "I'm feeling much the same, truth to tell. D'you mind if I go for a nap?"

"Sure. You must do whatever you see fit, Adeline. You are here as my companion, not my maid."

Adeline gathered her things and closed the door behind her, leaving Phoebe to consider the journey ahead. She made a fist and tapped the mattress. Of all the darn bad luck. To take this first step into her future and have this anchor dragging her back, reminding her of the worst few days of her life. She resolved to avoid McLennan as much as possible over the coming ten days. She'd stay in her cabin, she'd read. Not the Atlantic crossing she had pictured, but needs must.

Phoebe's resolve was short-lived. By early evening she was hungry, and why should the unfortunate presence of McLennan prevent her from fully experiencing her first ocean voyage? She decided to go in search of the dining room.

The ship was increasingly unsteady, so she kept a hand out to the wood surfaces as she made her way around her cabin. She buttoned up her shoes and fixed her hat but decided on a shawl, rather than her coat.

Leaving the room, she raised her hand to knock at Adeline's door but thought better of it: it was kinder to let her rest. She set off down the labyrinth of corridors.

Arriving in the saloon-class dining room, Phoebe was surprised by how few people were there. A steward showed her to a table for two. Her stomach clenched when she spotted McLennan on the far side of the room. He glanced up and made a slight bow of his head in acknowledgment but returned to his meal. Maybe he had decided to avoid her. Her shoulders dropped. Well, that would make everything much easier.

Phoebe slept surprisingly well that night, finding the rocking of the ship a comfort. She woke once in the early hours and gazed out through her porthole at the multitude of stars. Adeline slept less well: her seasickness got worse and she failed to emerge from her room in the morning. Farrell managed to help her dress, but Phoebe took pity and said she could go back to her room. Farrell said she thought a turn around the deck would do her more good.

Phoebe again entered the dining room alone and found even fewer people had arrived for breakfast. She drank coffee and nibbled at a piece of toast, thinking it unwise to eat much more. Again, McLennan nodded to her, before returning to his breakfast. Phoebe noted his plate was full of sausages and eggs. That man seemed to have a cast-iron constitution.

She completely abandoned the idea of hiding away in her cabin for the journey. The new Phoebe didn't hide away. Although fortunate her seasickness was slight compared with most passengers, Farrell's idea of a turn around the deck was exactly what she needed, so she returned to her cabin to put on her thick coat. She chose a more old-fashioned winter bonnet, which she could tie in place, and pulled on fur-lined gloves.

The wind slapped her cheeks the moment she stepped onto the deck. Looking out at the sea, she couldn't believe the size of the waves with their giant peaks and troughs. She was exhilarated by the feeling of cold on her face, the salty taste on her lips, the sense of the elements being in control.

She made her way to the leeward side, staying close to the wall. A few hardy souls were promenading and an elderly couple were wrapped in blankets in their chairs. She would have to remember that trick next time.

"May I?" She indicated to an empty chair.

The elderly man inclined his head.

She settled and looked across the rails to the monotone environment: the white and gray clouds scudding, the waves of slate gray. Even the squawking gulls were white and black and gray. She leaned back and listened to the rhythmical whoosh and whisper as the liner cut its way through the waves.

After half an hour, she was too cold to stay any longer and went back inside. The warmth enveloped her like a shawl. She knew there was a reading room at the aft of the ship and decided to go in search of it.

She found the door with LIBRARY engraved on a brass nameplate. Inside, her mouth opened at the opulent room, with yet more polished wood, and books behind glazed doors. There was little natural light; instead, golden gas lights made a welcoming cocoon.

Phoebe could see only two people in the room, both reading yesterday's newspaper. As she stepped onto the oriental carpet, one of them lowered his paper. It would have to be McLennan. She hesitated.

He folded his paper. "I can leave."

She put up her hand. "Not on my account."

"Very well." He shook his copy of the *New York Times* open again.

"After all, we'll both be reading."

"Exactly. No need for conversation." His head bowed as he continued to read.

Phoebe opened the glazed door of a bookcase, chose a book at random, and took a seat near a table with a lamp. It bothered her that relations had returned to the frostiness of their early days. She suspected this was her fault and resolved to be more polite. She looked at the cover of her book.

"Have you read any Gibbons?" she asked.

The other person in the library tutted and shushed her.

They both glanced at the man and then back at each other. A smile passed between them and she shrugged her shoulders, as if she were a small child accepting admonishment.

McLennan looked at the book. "Yes," he mouthed.

She opened the first chapter. Sometime later, she had barely taken a word in. Her eyes drifted toward McLennan. He was leaning back, one leg over the other, completely absorbed in his newspaper. He smoothed his mustache and pressed his lips with the first and second fingers of his hand and she remembered seeing him do this before when he had been concentrating. She found the unconscious gesture endearing.

Once again, she returned to her history book, but the words swam in front of her. Why had she chosen the most boring book in Christendom? She wanted to put it back and find the latest Wilkie Collins novel, which she hoped would be there. But she feared appearing stupid in front of McLennan. Surely he was the sort of man who would disapprove of sensational novels? She turned another page, releasing a sigh.

McLennan folded his paper and hung it on its rail. He came close and leaned down to put his mouth near her ear. "I *have* read Gibbons. But found it one of the most tedious books I ever endured."

She looked up and felt a tingle deep inside as she caught the twinkle in his eye, the smile curving his lip.

He stood and strode out. She suppressed a giggle and got up to return *Decline and Fall* to its gap on the shelf before searching for Mr. Collins's *A Rogue's Life*.

TWENTY-SIX

The dining room was all but deserted as Douglas sat down to eat at one p.m. He knew the first couple of days at sea were the worst for most people and a winter Atlantic crossing was likely to be a challenge, but he was grateful seasickness had never afflicted him. Maybe it was all that time messing about in boats and swimming in the loch as a boy. He anticipated eating alone for most of the voyage.

He glanced up and couldn't help but smile when Miss Van Bergen entered, once again standing out from all the other upper-class ladies, even if this time it was for her resistance to nausea.

She returned his smile and made her way to her usual table. But it wasn't just her physical resilience he admired. She had managed to escape from Hector just as he had hoped and was doing something bold and independent. Any other woman would have been broken by what she had gone through.

He tutted to himself. They were behaving like a couple of wee dafties. Before the dreadful time at Mrs. Hale's house, they'd worked together, even danced together—they couldn't keep avoiding each other now.

He stood before he could change his mind. "Miss Van Bergen. Would you care to join me?"

She hesitated.

"And bring Mrs. Hale, of course," he added.

"She's not well enough to eat."

"Ah." It would be rude to withdraw the invitation now. "Hopefully there's no harm in it being the two of us?"

"No harm at all." She lifted her chin and arranged her bustle before sitting opposite him. "Have you ordered?" she asked.

"Not yet."

She picked up the menu card.

A steward approached and she chose escalope with new potatoes and green beans, and he the halibut with poached celery hearts.

"Wine?" Douglas asked.

She shook her head. "Sarsaparilla would be better."

He asked the steward to bring two glasses.

Douglas sat back in his chair. "So."

"So." She put her hands in her lap.

He looked around the room, searching for a subject to discuss. "You seem to have found your sea legs," he observed.

"I've been fortunate. Mrs. Hale and Farrell less so."

"I was talking to the captain. He's very proud of the SS *Arizona*. Proud of its speed. But, er, he admitted the design had sacrificed comfort."

She raised her eyebrows. "I am amazed by how comfortable it is. These public areas, I mean. I hadn't expected it."

"I think he meant comfort in how the ship handles. How much it rolls."

"Oh, I see."

"It's why there are so few of us in the dining room." He nodded to the empty tables.

"And why there are so many of us on the deck."

Douglas chuckled. "Aye. Best place when you're feeling ill."

"But cold."

"Aye. Cold."

The conversation ground to a halt. It didn't used to be this difficult to speak to her. But then, his pulse rate didn't used to increase as if he had a fever when she sat opposite him.

"Are we likely to meet your family in Edinburgh?" Miss Van Bergen asked.

He glanced up. "My family? Unlikely."

"Do they not live there?"

He shook his head. "No. Dundee."

"Ah. Is that far?"

"Not really. Not now they have a railway."

She laughed. "Railroads. We get everywhere, don't we?"

"A good thing. For the future."

They paused while the steward set a glass in front of each of them.

Miss Van Bergen put her fingers around the stem, perhaps worried it might slip off the table. "So, Dr. McLennan. You know all about my family; I'd like to know about yours. What does your family do in Dundee?"

Douglas was never comfortable talking about himself, but at least this seemed a safe subject for conversation.

"Textiles. My father produces textiles. Jute, mostly."

"What's jute?"

"It's a fiber, a plant. Like cotton from the South. It's grown in India and shipped to Dundee. One of those lucky coincidences. Dundee has lots of whalers too. Turns out whale oil is perfect to soften the fibers." He glanced up briefly, worried he was boring her, but she seemed attentive.

"Doesn't it smell?"

"Aye, but the fabric is thick. Tough enough to be used for sails and the like."

"And your father makes this?"

"Aye. Well, his factories. They're huge, with all the latest machinery running on steam. Dozens of people."

She put her head to one side. "Not what I pictured at all."

"No? What did you picture?"

"Something more like a Walter Scott novel. You know, rugged mountains, wild landscapes."

He glanced at her face and caught the wistful look, before his eyes settled on the notch in her upper lip. He forced himself to look away. "Aye, we have those too. The family has a long history back in the Highlands. Father is proud of our heritage. But that's no' where the money is."

Miss Van Bergen leaned slightly closer. "Do you have brothers?"

"Just a sister. Why do you ask?"

"Because you went into medicine. Didn't your father want you to follow him in the business?"

The steward set down their meals. He flapped open a napkin, spreading it across Miss Van Bergen's lap, before doing the same for Douglas. He was relieved to have a distraction: she had pressed on a tender spot.

They ate a few mouthfuls.

"So, you haven't told me how you became a doctor."

Douglas took a breath. "You are right: my father did want to train me to take over the factory one day. There was quite a tussle." He paused, remembering those family arguments. "But I had always wanted to be a doctor, even as a lad. I would spend time on my grandfather's estate. There was a wee lamb with a twisted leg which I tried to straighten. It survived."

"How wonderful."

He shook his head. "I'm not sure. It spent its life limping, relying on farm workers to feed it. Might have been better to let nature take its course."

She took a sip of her drink. "But you wanted to mend it."

"I guess so. Anyway..." Douglas shrugged. "Not even my father's disapproval could stop me applying for medical school in Edinburgh."

"It must have been hard, without his approval."

"Aye. But I have a cousin who's more suited to running factories. The business is in better hands with him."

He parted a section of the flesh of his fish from the bone.

"You said you have a sister?" Miss Van Bergen asked.

"Aye. Isla."

She looked at him, waiting for him to say more. His skin prickled under her gaze.

"A few years younger than me. She'll turn thirty next year." He paused and bit his lip. Wasn't there some sensitivity about revealing a woman's age? Particularly as his sister was unmarried. "Lives in Edinburgh with my aunt. My mother's sister."

"Oh? Not with your parents?"

"Prefers the grandeur of the capital city."

Miss Van Bergen sat back in her seat and clicked her tongue approvingly. "Sounds like a woman who knows her own mind."

He scoffed. "Ocht, she does that."

The steward took their empty plates and asked if they would like desserts, or perhaps cheese and nuts.

"No, thank you," said Miss Van Bergen. "That was plenty."

"Would you, er, care to join me for coffee?" Douglas asked, trying to think of a way to keep her there longer. For once, he wished he had the smooth charm of the Hectors of this world, that he could be witty and amusing in the presence of a captivating woman.

She shook her head. "I need to check on Adeline and Farrell."

He jumped to his feet to help draw back her chair. She began to leave, but hesitated and looked back.

"But perhaps we could take a turn around the deck during the afternoon? Or play a hand of cards? If the weather is foul."

He struggled to stop himself from grinning. "I'll meet you in the saloon at three?"

She nodded and left.

Douglas sat down, wondering what on earth he was doing. There could never be anything between him and Miss Van Bergen. Why was he deliberately putting himself in this situation, when her presence made him behave like a lad who had only just discovered womankind? This was a crush brought on by circumstances, by the experience of carrying her down the stairs at Mrs. Hale's. Before that, he had admired her beauty and been impressed by her strength of character, but hadn't felt this heat whenever she was near.

Eventually, he convinced himself it would be like an inoculation. By increasing his exposure to her company, he would gradually become immune to her charms. Familiarity would lead to a simple friendship, he was almost sure of it.

TWENTY-SEVEN

Phoebe hesitated at the door of the saloon. She had spent most of the previous hour wondering why she had impulsively suggested they meet. It didn't matter what the other passengers thought; she was unlikely to meet them again. But she worried McLennan might think her unladylike. A crazy thing to fear, given what he knew about her relationship with Hector. He might be cross with her for putting him in an awkward position, unable to say no to her invitation.

The truth was, she had enjoyed their lunch and was intrigued to find out more. She had longed to ask McLennan about his wife, but something had prevented her. He had mentioned being a widower in that infamous interview when he had first arrived in Boston, but had clearly been uncomfortable talking about it. He had never spoken of his marriage since and she felt it would be intrusive to ask. She didn't even know the wife's name. But there was a mystery, and she thought it would be the key to understanding him. He was a handsome, fascinating man and had showed many times there was kindness underneath the dour exterior. Surely there was a line of women eager to catch his eye. His dedication to the memory of his wife was another indication of how badly she had misjudged him in those early weeks.

Phoebe checked on Adeline and Farrell and was relieved stewards had brought small plates of food. She encouraged each to drink some distilled water. When three o'clock came round, she didn't tell either of them where she was going. There was something exciting about meeting McLennan and she liked the idea of a little secret between the two of them.

The saloon was busier than the previous day. She spotted McLennan in a dark overcoat, leaning against the wall close to the far door. He turned and raised a gloved hand, and when a smile broke over his face, her skin tingled. She looked forward to spending the next hour with him, but also felt inexplicably shy.

He strode toward her. "Inside or out?"

"Is it raining?"

"Not at the moment."

"Outside then. Some fresh air."

He took her coat from her arms and shook it out before standing behind to help slide it on. She wrapped her shawl over her bonnet and around her neck, suspecting she looked like a peasant, then secured the ends inside the coat and pulled on the fur gloves.

McLennan was equally armed against the cold with a hat and muffler.

"Ready?" he asked.

"Ready."

He held the door for her. The cold sea air made her eyes water. The wind blew among the rigging, making a discordant melody of metal tapping on metal. The sails were at full extent as the captain was determined to cross the Atlantic as swiftly as possible. All four masts were laden with sails, bulging like a parade of fat old men.

They set off toward the bow. The smooth wood deck was slippery, so McLennan put out his elbow and she threaded her arm through, possibly holding him closer than was necessary.

"Thank you, Dr. McLennan." There was a rasp in her voice that betrayed her emotions.

"Do you think... do you think you might drop the title and surname?"

She glanced up at him in surprise, but he was determinedly facing ahead.

"I mean... we know each other quite well. I hope we may even think of each other as friends." Now he looked down at her. He had pulled his hat low, but she could see a softness in his eyes, under the brim.

"Friends. Yes." Her mind went back to that time in Fairview when he said he wasn't sure he even liked her.

There was the slightest curl at one side of his lips. "My friends call me Douglas."

She looked away over her shoulder to hide her confusion. Part of her wanted to be a modern, carefree woman, but another part still hesitated. "I could call you that here, now. The two of us. But it may be difficult to change my habit when we're in company. And people may make assumptions."

He nodded his head in thought. "Perhaps you could call me McLennan, when we're in company. Always calling me 'doctor'... It feels so formal."

"Very well. I'll try." They took a few steps as the plunging motion of the ship pushed them closer. "And as we are friends, you may call me Phoebe. When we are not in company, I mean." Goodness knew what her mother would have thought of this breach of Boston's high society rules. Mrs. Van Bergen had regarded friendship between a man and woman with suspicion.

"Thank you. That is generous."

They continued walking in silence as she sank into the warm feeling inside at becoming friends. She looked out at the sea to hide her smile. Maybe this was the moment to try to find out about the real Douglas McLennan, the one he kept hidden.

"If it is true, that we are friends, there are still many things I do not know about you."

He paused and when she looked at him, his face was serious, as if he were preparing himself for a difficult task. "What would you like to know?"

"Well..." Phoebe swallowed and plunged in. "You have been married. I'd like to know about your wife."

A shadow seemed to cross his face and she feared she'd stepped too far. She could have kicked herself.

"I'm sorry. Maybe that's—"

"No, I said we are friends. It's understandable you..." He took a deep breath. "My wife's name was Joan. We met when she was not yet twenty and I'd been a student a couple of years."

They walked on, Phoebe careful to keep her tone light. "How did you meet?"

"Through my sister. They were friends."

"What did she look like?"

She saw a movement in his jaw as he studied the distance. "Ocht, so bonnie. She had flaming red hair, pale skin like milk. And a smile... Oh, she was so quick to smile." He paused as if picturing her.

Phoebe watched him and thought this might finally be the secret. He was still desperately in love with his wife, despite the passing years. She felt something inside that she didn't quite understand: a heaviness of regret perhaps, that she had never been loved in this way. She left his side and went toward a bench against the body of the ship.

"Here," he said, following her. "Let me..." He pushed water droplets from the seat and wiped it down with his gloved hand. Phoebe almost told him of the benefits of wearing so many layers of skirt, but stopped herself, not wanting to seem flippant.

He sat beside her.

"And so you married?" she asked softly, still wanting to know more.

A line appeared between his brows. "To be honest, we didnae have her parents' blessing, nor mine. They felt we were too young. My father said he would not support us financially if we married with so little time courting. Her father questioned if I had the money to support her, as I was still a medical student. She was from a well-to-do family. And he had a point. But... we were young and in love and thought that was all we needed." He let out a long breath. "The arrogance of youth. Turns out you can't live on love alone."

It was on the tip of her tongue to say that she had learned you can't live without love, either. She glanced at him and wondered if the water in his eyes was from the cold air or emotion.

"And in a matter of months, I lost her. She died..."

"So soon?" Phoebe had pictured them together far longer.

He sniffed. "When I buried her, I swore never to marry again."

Phoebe dropped her head. "I'm sorry. I shouldn't have asked."

"It was eight years ago. I really should be able to speak of it. To a... friend, I mean."

She wanted to take his hand, to comfort him. But she held back. "I'm sorry if my questions have caused you pain."

He leaned back and studied the rigging. "People are too afraid or too embarrassed to ask me about Joan and that makes it as if she never existed. Which is even worse. So... thank you for being kind enough to ask, Phoebe."

She felt uncomfortable he had thought it kindness, when she simply wanted to make him less of a mystery. Even now, she was sure there was more he was not yet ready to tell her. She shivered. "The cold is making its way into my bones. Let's go back inside."

Douglas stood and put out his hand to help her up. Again, they walked in step to manage the movement of the ship. Phoebe wondered what the Boston ladies would say if they saw her so close with an unmarried man. She decided she didn't care. She was going to a different continent and she intended to be a different woman there. She had managed to break free of Hector, and now she would see how many other chains could be broken.

Douglas put his hand to the saloon doorknob. "How about that game of cards you mentioned?"

She glanced at him and her chest tightened. "I'd be delighted."

The truth was, she was dreadful at cards, but she could hardly tell him that she desperately wanted any excuse to spend longer in his company.

"There's plenty I want to know about *you*, mind," he warned. "So maybe I'll be asking the questions."

He pushed open the door and she dropped her head to conceal the blush she could feel growing.

TWENTY-EIGHT

He watched Phoebe find her way to a table by the window. A steward was at her side almost immediately. Douglas couldn't help clenching his hands, wishing it was him gently helping with her coat.

"Are you warm enough?" Douglas asked.

"Quite warm, thank you." The saloon was well supplied with coal-burning stoves.

Douglas turned to the steward. "Could you bring a blanket, just in case. And a set of playing cards."

She settled down and watched him remove his hat and muffler, followed by his leather gloves and finally his coat.

The steward brought two packs of cards, a cribbage board, and a backgammon set. "I thought I'd bring a selection."

"How thoughtful," Phoebe said with a smile.

"Would you like a drink, Miss Van Bergen?" Douglas asked, careful to use her surname in front of the steward.

"D'you know, a hot chocolate would be mighty fine."

He asked for two, then rubbed his palms to warm them. "What shall we play?"

"Do you know piquet?"

"Aye, I do." He picked up the deck and discarded cards below seven. They cut the remainder. Phoebe had the queen so she began dealing.

"Your turn to ask the questions," she said.

He glanced at her and half smiled as he picked up his cards. "Is this so you can put me off my game?"

"I'm sure you're smart enough to converse at the same time as selecting cards to exchange, Douglas."

He felt a warm buzzing deep inside, realizing she had used his name for the first time. "Now, that really *will* put me off my game: hearing my name in that lovely Boston accent."

She put her head to one side and raised an eyebrow. "Douglas," she murmured teasingly, "you have the elder hand."

He studied his cards, shaking his head to dislodge the laughter that threatened. He placed his unwanted cards on the table and picked up alternatives. She kept her eyes on his face, no doubt to see if his reaction would tell her about his hand. He was determined not to reveal anything, even though he feared his skin was coloring under the intensity of her gaze.

She exchanged her own cards and failed to suppress a frustrated sigh.

"Tell me about your father," he said as play began.

"My father? Where do I start? He died five years ago, after several years of illness. But he kept his hands on the reins of the business until the very end. Much to Thaddeus's frustration." She laid her last card, having lost the hand.

Douglas scooped up the cards and it was his turn to deal.

"He could see railroads were the future. Got in right at the beginning." Phoebe picked up her cards and smiled as she exchanged a better hand. Douglas bit down on his lip to stop himself smiling at how transparent she was.

They paused as they bid and then she continued with the story of her father. Douglas was fascinated to learn the truth of Mr. Van Bergen Senior, a man he had heard so much about in Boston.

"The Civil War made his fortune. I feel bad saying that, but it's true. Government wanted trains to transport troops and equipment and was willing to pay for it. Not that it *all* went his way. There were lean years. Or so I'm told." She gave a slight shrug. "I was too young to know."

They played out their cards and again she lost. Douglas began to feel bad that he was winning every hand. It was her turn to gather the cards on the table, shuffle, and deal.

Douglas looked at his cards. "If you want to tell me more later, and concentrate on the cards now, that's fine."

She glanced up and snorted. "Thing is: I know *how* to play cards. Didn't say I was any good at it."

He grinned. "I noticed. May I give you a tip?"

"All advice welcome."

Leaning forward, he spoke in a whisper. "Try not to sigh when you pick up a poor hand."

Her eyes opened wide. "I do that?"

"Uh-huh. Every time."

"Let's push on to the sixth hand and see if I can improve."

She went to pick up her cards, but he swiftly his put his hand over hers. "Wait a moment."

Her eyes snapped to his, the black pupils dilated. He feared he had overstepped the mark, but was too far in now to pull back his hand.

"Compose your features."

She kept her warm hand beneath his and swallowed, then let her shoulders drop and blinked twice. He was relieved she was playing along.

"*Now* look at them," he instructed, releasing her hand so she could lift the cards.

He could see she was trying her hardest to keep her mouth still, but was on the verge of giggling.

"See?" he said with a wink. "I can't tell if that means you've got a very good hand or the worst one possible."

She exchanged cards and they made their bids. This time, he made sure the trick laying went her way and she won.

"There, now," he said, covering his mouth to suppress a chuckle.

"Douglas. I am under no illusions: you let me win that hand."

They carried on, but Phoebe's playing continued to be atrocious. Douglas tried to hide his amusement, but gradually her poor decision-making got the better of him and he snorted with laughter. By the end of play, they were both helplessly giggling.

"Why on earth did you propose cards?" he asked, drying his eyes.

"Well, I..." She shrugged and their eyes met. This time, he held her gaze and wondered if she had wanted an excuse to spend time with him. His heart beat faster with the possibility.

The steward appeared with their hot chocolates. "Sorry for the delay, ma'am. Sir."

Douglas was frustrated the man had broken their shared moment. "I thought you'd forgotten us."

The steward left and Douglas swept up the cards to stack them to slip back into their box, trying to think of a way to put their conversation back on track. "And your mother? Was she always a formidable person?"

Phoebe bit down on her lower lip, her white teeth making the flesh go pale. "Formidable. That's one way of describing her."

"What word would you use?"

She thought for a moment. "A snob."

"Oh?" That hadn't been the word he expected.

"She comes from a very old Boston family. The sort who can trace their ancestors back to the Pilgrim Fathers. And thought that made her better than others. Take my darling sister-in-law Ginny. Her mother came from a wealthy Southern family with links back to France in the last century. But her father had fallen on hard times. Mother treated her dreadfully when she first came to Boston and there is not a kinder or more cultured person alive."

She leaned back and took a sip of the chocolate. He echoed her movement, the taste bitter and sweet at the same time.

"And you?" Douglas continued. "What made you start the hospital?"

"Hmph, that could take a while."

He kept his eyes on her face. "We have plenty of time," he said softly.

He thought he could see a slight flush on her cheeks.

"Part of the story goes back to the fire."

Douglas raised his eyebrows.

"You've not heard of the Great Boston Fire?" she asked.

Her surprise made him feel a wee bit foolish.

"It was November, 1872. Broke out one Saturday night and raged for more than twelve hours. Afterwards"—she shook her head with the memory—"the devastation... But we took to rebuilding pretty darn fast."

"And how did this lead to the hospital?"

"I guess the fire made me face how safe my life was, hidden away on Beacon Hill. All those people who lost their homes. Lost everything. By chance, I went to a lecture by Professor Moncrieff and decided I wanted to do something to make a difference." She gave him an apologetic smile. "I went to Father and said I wanted to set up the Boston Women's Hospital. He insisted I go away and research it first. So, I did. Professor Moncrieff sent pamphlets from Scotland. I tried to meet with physicians, but that didn't work. They either turned me down, saying they didn't want to waste their time. Or they met and tried to court me."

Douglas noticed her shudder at the memory.

"Mother recruited the Board to make sure I wasn't exposing myself or the family to ridicule. You can't do anything in Boston without a board of the great and the good."

"Seems like that the world over, Phoebe," he said with a laugh.

"I took a lease on the house, but, as you know so well, it's not really fit to be a hospital. That's why it's become my dream to build something new. Something perfect."

He put his head to one side to look at her. "Oh, Phoebe, if you want perfect, you're always going to be disappointed."

"But you have to shoot for it. Don't you?" She looked up, a slight frown between her brows, but her gray eyes shining.

Before he could stop himself, he reached out and put his palm to her face. "Yes, you have to shoot for it," he whispered.

He pulled his hand back, heat rising at his neck.

Her cheeks blushed as she picked up her cup but found it was empty. "I should be getting back to Mrs. Hale and Farrell. See how they're getting on."

He sat back and feared his impulsive gesture had spoiled things. "You always seem to be caring for someone else."

"You say that like it's a criticism."

He shook his head. "Phoebe, I wouldn't dream of criticizing you. I just mean... sometimes you might take time for yourself."

She stood and gathered her things. "Oh, I promise you, Douglas. There are people I'm through caring for. I mean, why d'you think I'm on this boat and headed for Scotland, if it weren't for taking time for myself?"

TWENTY-NINE

Adeline was feeling better by the end of the day. Douglas had told Phoebe seasickness often improved in a day or two—as long as the ship didn't run into any violent storms. Farrell remained unable to keep much food down.

"I'm sorry, Miss Van Bergen," she cried, "it's never taken me this bad before. An' I've crossed the Atlantic loads."

Phoebe assured her there was nothing to worry about, that Adeline and she could help with each other's toilette, that there were plenty of stewards who would come rushing at a ring of the electric bell they had all marveled at when they first arrived.

With Adeline feeling better, there were fewer opportunities to talk to Douglas, and Phoebe found she regretted this. She missed having him to herself. He was surprisingly good company. An excellent listener, and despite knowing her failings—that she was what her mother would call in hushed tones a fallen woman—he never seemed to judge her, and for that she was grateful.

Nearly every single man she met, whether a youth barely shaving or an elderly gap-toothed politician, looked her up and down when they first met, as if appraising her market value. *Just how big a dowry would the only Van Bergen female be worth? How much of the fabled wealth had she inherited?*

Douglas McLennan would never look at her that way. His expressive green eyes regarded her with kindness, despite knowing the very worst about her. She suspected he knew the child's conception was not a piece of dreadful bad luck after a single, foolish coupling. Instead, she had willingly succumbed to Hector the first couple of times, and, after that, had learned it was safer to accept his demands when she was stupid enough to fail to avoid being alone with him. She shivered at the memory.

Whenever Douglas was near, she felt a little fizzing energy inside, like the tiny bubbles in a glass of champagne. It was a completely unfamiliar sensation. Knowing nothing would ever come of it gave her unexpected freedom: freedom to watch how the wind ruffled his blond hair, freedom to study his hands as he laid his cards or ate his food, freedom to appreciate the way lines gathered around his eyes when he laughed. She was disconcerted by the flip of excitement when she realized it was him behind a newspaper in the library, or hidden by his hat and muffler, leaning out over the railings on the deck.

With Adeline in better health, the rest of the journey was often spent the three of them together. They would dine at breakfast and in the evening—although at the main midday meal, Phoebe found she was expected to join the tables of more well-to-do passengers who were emerging, bleary-eyed, from their cabins. She took her turn at the captain's table, making the polite conversation expected of her. Each time, her senses were aware of where Douglas was sitting and she struggled to stop herself from looking over too often.

During the day, the trio would promenade the deck, or play quoits and skittles until the cold defeated them and they retreated inside. They played cards in the evening, with Adeline trying to teach her which card to lay. In the end, Phoebe gave up and threw her cards on the table.

"Look, Adeline. It would be much better if you played with Douglas. Then he'd have a decent opponent."

Adeline took her place and Phoebe fetched her Wilkie Collins novel. She watched the pair, each intent on their cards, and sharing rueful laughter when one or other won the round. She was disconcerted to find herself experiencing jealousy for perhaps the first time in her life. She had toyed with the idea that Adeline could make an ideal partner for Douglas. She didn't find the idea entertaining any more.

On the morning of the tenth day, a pilot ship met the liner to guide it through Liverpool Bay. The Atlantic crossing had taken longer than the ambitious captain had hoped and Phoebe spent the last couple of days between Ireland and England fretting about whether they would make it to Edinburgh in time.

Phoebe went on deck to watch the ship pull into the Mersey River. On her right, tall cranes swung cargo into the ships waiting in the Birkenhead docks, while the SS *Arizona* pulled to the Liverpool side of the river, sliding toward the magnificent waterfront of stately edifices and storage buildings with stone walls as thick as the castles she had imagined from books. Sailing ships and steamboats jostled for space at the docks. Squawking seagulls circled above and men shouted at each other as they teemed along the pier. The ship pulled into Princes Basin and sailors threw ropes to the shore.

The ship's purser personally accompanied her to the gangway, where the captain was saying farewell to the saloon passengers. As so often, she was aware of the protection the Van Bergen name brought. A thought struck her that it was unlikely to carry the same cachet in Britain.

Phoebe carefully followed Adeline down the gangplank and onto terra firma, a New World woman returning to the Old World, taking the first step on an adventure. She made her way along the dock, Adeline close at her side, experiencing a strange sensation that the pier was not quite still. She looked around for Douglas and her heart rose as she saw him striding toward her, his heavy overcoat unbuttoned. Goodness, that man could take her breath away.

He took off his hat, the onshore breeze rippling his hair. A small line appeared between his brows. "Now, you're sure you have everything you need?"

"Quite sure."

"You go straight to the Custom House to complete your paperwork." He pointed to the magnificent building with a row of columns holding a long pediment, and a dome above that reminded Phoebe of the Massachusetts State House.

Phoebe exchanged a look with Adeline. "As everyone said, you can't miss it."

He threaded the rim of his hat through his fingers. "I would be happier if I ken you were settled. I can wait for a later train."

She raised her chin. "I wouldn't hear of it. You want to see your family as soon as possible. I understand that."

He leaned closer. "Another day won't—"

For a moment, Phoebe fought her own desire not to say goodbye, but stood firm. "Once we're through customs, Adeline and I will be staying at the Adelphi Hotel. Farrell is waiting here to make sure our luggage is unloaded from the hold and sent to the hotel. She will spend the night at her sister's before joining Adeline and myself first thing. Tomorrow, I will return to the Bank of Liverpool on Water Street to confirm my finances are in order. And then, off to Lime Street for the first steam train to Edinburgh we can find. See? Everything arranged."

Douglas was still frowning. "It's just, well, three ladies, together..."

"Are you telling me Liverpool is more dangerous than Boston?" she asked, raising an eyebrow.

"Well, no..."

She smiled. "We've managed there very well. And I'm sure we'll manage here."

"Of course." He straightened up. "I look forward to seeing you all in Edinburgh."

He took her gloved hand and bowed over it. It was a sadly formal gesture after the intimacy they had known on the ship.

"I look forward to it too," she replied softly.

He put on his hat and made a brief nod to Adeline before turning on his heel. Part of her now regretted being so eager to show her independence. She had to admit she liked the sensation of Douglas fretting about her wellbeing. As he disappeared into the crowds, she knew there was nothing she'd enjoy more than a long train journey in his company.

THIRTY

Phoebe and Adeline joined the stream of people walking to the Custom House. Truth was, Phoebe felt considerable anxiety about what was ahead of them, but she wasn't going to show that to Douglas, or anyone else. She had lain in her bunk, running through what ifs. What if the bank hadn't transferred her money? What if there weren't any trains and they didn't get to Edinburgh in time? What if someone stole all their luggage?

But she was also excited that she was responsible for overcoming any disasters herself. There was no one here to take over, treating her like a child.

An hour later, they emerged from the Custom House. Phoebe had been assured passports were not needed for entry, but the various documents from Thaddeus, their family lawyer, and the letter of invitation from Professor Moncrieff, all helped smooth their path.

The cab driver helped the women into the back and flicked his whip. The horse set off at a clip, up the slight incline toward the center of the city.

Phoebe kept her nose to the window, looking up at the grand buildings, some new, others blackened by soot. The streets were wide but full of horse-drawn vehicles, with men and women hurrying along the sidewalk, their heads down, faces determined. Phoebe nodded: things were just the same as in Boston.

They reached the Adelphi Hotel, a fine building which took up the whole of one block. Phoebe led the way up the steps to the lobby and asked at the reception for two rooms, close to each other. One of her what ifs had been the hotel would be full, but Farrell had assured her there were three hundred rooms. All Phoebe and Adeline had with them was the hand luggage that had been in their cabins. They would have to wait for their trunks to be delivered under Farrell's direction.

The bellboy took them to their rooms. Phoebe was pleased with hers. A double door insulated the suite from the corridor. There was a wood-paneled sitting room, a bedroom with ornate wallpaper and a four-poster bed, and her own white and black tiled bathroom. After her tiny cabin, it felt palatial. Yes, this would do her very well. Very well indeed.

They ate in the high-ceilinged dining room, ordering the fresh turtle soup the hotel was famed for, and then retired for the night. She slept well until awoken by a knock on the door.

"Morning, Miss Van Bergen," Farrell said. "I'm here to help you dress."

Phoebe stretched and sat up. She noticed Farrell's eyes were pink and puffy, and her nose was red.

"Mrs. Farrell. What is it?"

Farrell sniffed. "Nothing, ma'am."

"Nonsense," Phoebe said, padding to the bathroom. "Something has happened."

Farrell followed and filled the basin, sniffing every few seconds. "It's my sister. She's sick. Dreadful sick." Tears began to fall. "I don't know how long it will be before she..."

Phoebe took Farrell's hands. "My goodness, I'm so sorry. Come, let's sit." She led her to the sofa in the sitting room.

"She's got eight little nippers, Miss. Eight." Farrell pulled out a handkerchief that was already sodden.

"Here," said Phoebe, fetching a fresh one from her reticule. "Use mine."

"What will become of 'em? The youngest is only a babe in arms."

"How old is the eldest?"

"Only twelve. She could get work, but not enough to..." Farrell sobbed again. "And who will look after the rest?"

Phoebe touched Farrell's arm. "What about their father?"

Farrell waved a hand. "At sea. Not expected back for months."

"That is unfortunate. Is there anyone else?"

"We have brothers and sisters, but not here. They've gone to Manchester for work." Farrell blew her nose. "It will be the poorhouse for them. All those kiddies."

Phoebe stood and paced the room in her slippers, thinking through the possibilities. "You have to stay here with them. That's clear."

Farrell shook her head. "What would we live off? At least now I can send through my wages. Maybe... maybe I can hire someone to look after them."

Phoebe pulled at her lip as she paced. "It is perfectly obvious I need to keep paying your wages and you stay here to look after your sister and the children."

Farrell looked up at her, confusion on her face. "But you need a lady's maid."

"Do I, though? Really? Adeline manages without one. I'm sure the two of us can help each other dress. I can pack my own bags. We're staying at hotels and they will see to laundry." Phoebe stopped and rested her hands on the back of a chair. "I've decided. You stay here. Adeline and I will go to Edinburgh. When we return to Liverpool in a few weeks, you'll have had time to settle things with your family and come back to Boston. While I'm away, you will draw your wages. I insist."

She swept into the bathroom to indicate the discussion was at an end.

. . .

Phoebe and Adeline discussed Farrell's difficulty over breakfast. While Adeline agreed Farrell's first duty was to her sister, nieces and nephews, she thought they should try to engage a new maid.

"In one day? And a Sunday at that. We don't know anyone here," replied Phoebe. "We can't take up references, and I never engage staff without a personal recommendation." Phoebe saw doubt pass over Adeline's face. "*You* manage without a lady's maid," she said firmly.

"I'm not one of the richest women in the United States."

"Please, Adeline." Phoebe poured more hot water into the silver teapot. "We can help each other, like we did on the *Arizona*."

Adeline pulled a face. "Just so you know, I'm very poor with hair. I won't be fixing those fancy styles Farrell does." She circled her fork in the direction of Phoebe's hair. "All those braids and curls."

Phoebe put her hand to her breast in mock sacrifice. "I look forward to simpler coiffure while we are here, then."

Adeline cast a skeptical look down Phoebe's frock. "And all those fancy buttons and bows..."

"As long as nothing's going to fall apart and expose me, I'm happy," said Phoebe, gently slapping Adeline's arm.

They both burst out giggling.

"Come on," said Phoebe, leaning close. "It will be an adventure. Just the two of us."

THIRTY-ONE

The young clerk ushered them into the head financier's office on the second floor of the Bank of Liverpool's offices. "Here we are, Mrs. Hale and Miss Van Bergen." He pulled out a chair for Adeline, and then one for Phoebe. "You are rather early, but Mr. Collet will be here any moment, Mrs. Hale."

Phoebe glanced at Adeline, who shrugged. Adeline carried the higher status as a married woman, and the Van Bergen name was meaningless to this Liverpool clerk.

Phoebe drummed a rhythm on the arm of the chair as they waited. It was first thing Monday morning and they were booked on the ten a.m. train to Edinburgh. Frustratingly, they had kicked their heels the day before as the bank did not open on a Sunday and now they were cutting things very fine.

"I am so sorry to have kept you waiting," said the banker as he rushed in.

Phoebe stood and put out her hand. "I am Miss Van Bergen. This is my companion, Mrs. Hale."

Mr. Collet shook her hand. "Delighted to meet you in person. I have all the paperwork ready for you. Your brother has authorized the drawings."

Phoebe suppressed a sigh. With her growing independence,

she was getting increasingly irritated that she needed a man's permission to withdraw her own money.

They swiftly went through the financial arrangements of her trip, Phoebe signing document after document.

"One last thing," Phoebe said. "I want arrangements made for this lady to draw ten shillings each week until I return to Liverpool." Phoebe slid over Farrell's details.

"And this is her address?"

"Yes, Empress Road. Here in Liverpool."

Mr. Collet's eyebrows raised.

"She has been a valued lady's maid," Phoebe said, although not sure why she should be providing any sort of explanation. She felt intimidated by the surroundings and fearful the bank would suddenly say all the arrangements were a mistake.

"Of course," said Mr. Collet and handed the note to the young clerk. "We can set that up for you today."

With business complete, Phoebe and Adeline dashed to Lime Street Station by cab, where their luggage had already been taken. Inside was alive with people: passengers, porters, railroad staff in uniform.

Phoebe paused to take in the enormous curved roof, made of a crisscross of iron girders and glass. The butler at the Adelphi had proudly told her it was the largest free-standing structure in the world, and she could well believe it. Her breath was taken away. She made a mental note to tell her brothers about it when she got home.

They made their way to the platform, a porter behind pulling a trolley with their trunks, and a steward leading the way.

Boarding the train, Phoebe and Adeline stood and slowly turned round. It was completely different to the long carriages they were used to on the Van Bergen railroads, where they could walk the length. Here, it was exactly as if a series of horse-drawn carriages and been pushed together, with a wall separating them from the next little compartment, which was entered through its own door. Their compartment had two upholstered benches, where a pair of passengers already sat, facing each other. There were blinds over the windows, which they would be able to pull down, and nets for their bags above the seats.

Phoebe and Adeline settled by the windows at the far side as four more passengers entered, filling the carriage. The passengers nodded to each other and said *good morning* but avoided conversation. The compartment was cold and nobody removed their winter coats.

Phoebe grabbed the fabric strap as the train shunted and set off, pulling out between the high, stone rock of the cutting, sliding under a bridge, and then out onto the main line, chugging between the tightly packed terraces of Liverpool. Phoebe wondered which of them was now home to Farrell. She laid her cheek against the window and was overcome with weariness. She'd close her eyes, just for a moment to rest.

Phoebe woke with a start and watched the countryside through half-closed eyes. She was struck by how swiftly the landscape changed from flat fields, to rolling hills, to mountains in the distance. Her experience of travel back home was that you could journey for the best part of a day and the view from the window would barely change.

She drifted off again, jerking awake to find Adeline gently patting her arm.

"Phoebe," Adeline hissed. "We're approaching Carlisle. People are saying there is enough time to buy something to eat on the platform restaurant, and use the public lavatories."

Later, a passenger told her they were traveling through Scotland. As they passed snow-topped hills with dark conifers on their lower slopes, and valleys of ferns and heather, dotted with sheep, Phoebe thought of Douglas. So, this was his land, the landscape he had grown up in. There was a wildness that suited him and she could picture him energetically striking out across the fields.

The sun dropped behind the hills and by late afternoon it was dark outside. Someone had lit the oil lamps, which made Phoebe's eyes water with the smoke, but gave puddles of light and a hint of warmth.

The steam train rolled into Edinburgh at six. In the darkness, she was sorry not to see the fabled castle sitting on its high rock. She felt a shiver of excitement, proud they had arrived in time for the symposium. Indeed, they had crossed the Atlantic and made their way up through Britain with a day to spare.

The train slowed, metal screeching against metal as the brakes drew it to a stop. Phoebe and Adeline descended to the platform at Waverley Station. She wrapped her furs closer around her neck against the cold. The station was grand, but different from Lime Street. Here, the roof was of intricate ironwork, the stone walls heavy and solid.

They proceeded to the first-class room to wait for their luggage to be unloaded. Phoebe stamped her feet to stay warm. A porter arrived, pulling a trolley with their trunks.

"We are booked into the Old Waverley Hotel," Phoebe said. "Could you find us a cab?"

The man scrunched his features. "Have ye lassies lost the use of your legs?"

"Pardon me?"

"It's not far to walk. I can bring your luggage for a pound."

Phoebe hesitated. She knew that was a ridiculous amount of money. "I'll give you a crown."

The man pulled a face again and muttered something about needing to feed his family before sighing, "Follow me, ladies."

He took off with their luggage and they hurried to follow him up the sidewalk beside a long ramp to a narrow road where a line of horse-drawn cabs was waiting. The porter pushed on up the road to the wide street at the top.

"This is Princes Street," he said. "And there, opposite the Scott Monument, is your hotel. So, lassies, walk? Or cab?"

It was barely a block away. "Walk. Thank you."

Again, they scurried to keep up. Even though it was dark,

Phoebe wanted to stop and stare at the buildings around her, but instead kept her eyes on the cobbles, dodging the horse muck and making sure her heel didn't get lodged in a tram line. They stopped at an elegant, seven-story building opposite the monument the porter had pointed to.

Hotel staff jumped to attention, bringing in the trunks. Phoebe drew a coin from her purse and put it in the porter's hand.

He grimaced. "Ocht. That's an English crown."

Phoebe blinked at him, confused by the objection. "Will it do?"

"I suppose it will have to." He slipped it into his pocket and hurried away.

They stood in the lobby and were met by Mr. Robert Cranston, the owner of the hotel.

"Mrs. Hale. Miss Van Bergen. We are delighted to welcome you to the Old Waverley Hotel."

Phoebe was relieved the telegram making arrangements for their stay had arrived. Another what-if to tick off her mental list.

"We are, of course, the first temperance hotel in this city," he continued. "I daresay that was why two respectable American ladies chose us."

Phoebe was about to say she had simply followed the recommendation of Professor Moncrieff, but sensed the hotelier's pride would be dented.

When they were shown to their adjoining rooms, Adeline helped Phoebe undress, in the absence of Farrell, before retiring herself. Phoebe was so exhausted, she didn't bother to braid her hair. She wanted to sink into the bed and sleep for at least a week.

THIRTY-TWO

The housemaid drew back the window drapes, the rings clattering and forcing Phoebe to put her forearm over her eyes to protect them from the watery light.

"What time is it?"

"Your companion said we should let you sleep in, ma'am," said the young maid in a crisp Edinburgh accent. "It's eight o'clock."

Phoebe groaned inwardly. Did Edinburgh operate on a different time system, where eight was considered a lie-in?

"I've brought breakfast."

Phoebe hoisted herself up and shoved the large white pillows behind her back.

The maid placed a tray with short legs over her lap. "There we are, my wee lassie."

Phoebe peered at the pale mush in the bowl. "What is it?"

"Porridge. Freshly made."

"Porridge?"

"Aye. There's a wee drop of milk if you'd like it. And salt. I put honey in this bowl for you. I'm told Americans prefer it with honey."

The look on the maid's face told Phoebe it was a sinful weakness of her countryfolk to prefer something sweet.

"Any chance of coffee?" Phoebe said, trying to put her most appealing look on her face.

"I'll bring a pot of breakfast tea."

Once the maid had bustled out, Phoebe pressed the spoon into the beige sludge and took a mouthful, grimacing at the oaty taste. She looked at the salt and honey and decided on sweetness, pouring a copious amount over the porridge. Her next mouthful wasn't much better—she'd simply ruined the taste of perfectly good honey. Maybe she should have opted for the salt.

She pushed on, mouthful after mouthful, wanting to make a stand for her fellow Americans.

The maid returned with a tea tray, which she left on a table. She looked at the bed and beamed. "I see you enjoyed your porridge. I'll bring a larger bowl tomorrow." She lifted the little table from the bed and left.

Phoebe pushed back the bedclothes and got up, edging her feet into her rabbit-fur-lined slippers and wrapping her velvet dressing gown around her. The room had a slight chill, despite the fire in the grate—the maid must have lit it while she was asleep.

She stirred the tea leaves in the pot and put the metal strainer over her teacup before beginning to pour. Wasn't there some British thing about whether the milk should come first or after? She was damned if she could remember which way round it was.

She took the cup to the glazed alcove in the corner of the room and looked out of the window. My, what a view! First, there was the Scott Monument directly opposite: a multi-layered steeple reaching high into the sky, with buttresses and spires. At the base was a huge statue that she knew was Sir Walter Scott, looking thoughtful while the ornate stonework protected him from the elements. She was impressed a nation could build such an elaborate monument to a man who was, in the end, simply a storyteller.

Below her window, Princes Street was alive with people and traffic. A dray horse pulled a wagon laden with barrels. A horse-drawn tram clattered past, packed full of people.

The sight that excited her most, though, was the castle perched on the top of a huge rocky outcrop, stark against clouds heavy with rain. It wasn't a single structure; rather a gathering of robust stone buildings surrounded by high walls. The cliff face made it impregnable. She could see why the ancient Scots had chosen this place.

Phoebe sipped her tea, taking in the panorama before her. This was the city where Douglas had been a student, where he had lived with his wife, before she had died only months into their marriage. He was out there now, somewhere; perhaps with his family, telling them about his time in America. She wondered—she hoped—the friendship they had forged on the Atlantic crossing had survived his return to his native land.

Although the symposium was not due to start until the next day, they decided to take a cab to the Royal Infirmary on Drummond Street, where Phoebe hoped to meet her old friend Professor Moncrieff.

The weather had improved, with a blue sky and crisp air. As they trundled across the bridge that joined Princes Street to the steep road up to the Old Town, Phoebe could not take her eyes off her surroundings. She had never experienced a place like it. Tall buildings of different shapes and sizes balanced on what seemed to be the side of a cliff. There were turrets and steeples, grand buildings and what looked like apartment blocks, all pushed together on whatever land they could cling to.

She paid the driver and they stood at the ornate gates in front of the Infirmary. The building was similar to many in this part of the city: solid-looking, made from heavy, dark stone. Although it looked a little shabby, the Infirmary was a proud building, adorned with columns and speaking of the importance of its purpose. Phoebe thought back to the makeshift nature of her own hospital, how she had tried to adapt a leased house to her purposes. Yes, she was right to insist on a new building, providing her patients exactly what they needed.

Phoebe's shoes echoed on the stone slabs of the impressive

entrance hall. She explained to the porter they wanted to meet Professor Moncrieff, and gave her name.

After a short wait, the wooden door to the main area opened and an elderly man burst through. "Miss Van Bergen! You are here. I cannae say how *delighted* I am to see you again."

He rapidly shook her hand.

"Likewise, Professor. I'm honored you invited me." She turned to Adeline. "This is Mrs. Hale, my companion, and more importantly, matron of the Van Bergen Women's Hospital."

"Pleasure to meet you, Mrs. Hale. We hope to learn from your experiences in New England."

Adeline looked a little overwhelmed but took the hand that was offered. "I think I am far more likely to learn from folks here at the symposium."

"Well, that's what I'm hoping. All learning from each other." Moncrieff led the way, speaking as he went. They followed him up a flight of steps to his rooms. "I didnae think you were going to get here on time." His black teaching gown flew out behind him. He was long-legged and wiry, taking the steps two at a time. His vigor belied his years, although his white hair and lined face gave a closer indication of his age. He opened the door to his study, which was packed full of books and cabinets. He cleared piles of pamphlets from two chairs. "Sit, sit. Can I get you something to drink?"

"Just water, thank you," said Phoebe.

"The same," chimed Adeline.

"Aye, I thought I was going to have to ask someone else to deliver Miss Nightingale's address tomorrow."

"I didn't mean to put you out..."

He waved a hand. "Nae bother. You're here now. That's the important thing." He gave them a glass each and tipped more coal on the fire before settling into a wing-backed chair. "Now, tell me all about developments in Boston."

Phoebe described the architectural plans for the new hospital, a subject she could happily talk about for hours, inviting Adeline to contribute too. Moncrieff showed her the floor plans of the extensive new infirmary which had just opened on land overlooking what he called the Meadows.

"And my Dr. McLennan?" Moncrieff asked. "How's he getting along? I know he's here for the symposium, but he hasn't dropped in to see me yet. Most unlike him." He frowned briefly, but then raised his head with a grin. "I daresay you've kept him busy."

Heat spread up Phoebe's throat for so many reasons. "He... Dr. McLennan is an excellent surgeon and physician. Thank you for sending him to us."

"Delighted to hear it."

She couldn't leave this false impression, though. "Regrettably, he has decided to take a position in New York."

Moncrieff raised his bushy eyebrows. "New York! I *am* surprised. I thought he would take to Boston. And, I have to say, dear Miss Van Bergen, I thought he would have innovative ideas you could make use of."

What could she say? That they had butted heads when they first met, and then she had insulted him by insisting on a trial period, during which time he had—naturally—looked for a position elsewhere?

She swallowed and looked at the ground. This was only part of the truth. She could never tell Moncrieff what else had happened: that Douglas had been called to a shameful and humiliating emergency with the hospital's principal benefactor. And after, he had decided he wanted nothing more to do with the Van Bergen hospital.

Adeline came to her rescue. "We were disappointed also. The New York position must have been very attractive."

"Hmm. He'll be here for the opening address tomorrow. I'll get to the bottom of it."

Phoebe's mouth went dry. She knew they would face each other again soon—after all, Douglas was expressly here for the symposium. But she was already nervous about giving the address, and knowing he was going to be in the audience made her jitters worse. She didn't want to look foolish in front of him.

"Speaking of which"—Moncrieff sprang to his feet—"here's Miss Nightingale's address. I have had it set out and printed for you."

Phoebe took the small pamphlet. "Such a shame Miss Nightingale could not deliver it herself. I would have been thrilled to meet her."

"Indeed, that would have been quite a coup for our inaugural symposium. Sadly, she barely leaves her bed these days."

"She's sick?"

"It seems so. Yet her mind is as sharp as ever. She is still seeing things the rest of us miss."

After they returned to their hotel for lunch, Phoebe retired to her room to read and re-read the address. She practiced speaking it out loud, striding around the room, eager to give weight to every word written by the great woman.

THIRTY-THREE

Douglas enjoyed a sense of calm as he walked through Stockbridge, an area with the air of a village, even though it bordered Edinburgh's New Town. The weather had turned cold and damp, as Decembers were wont to do, but it felt like home. More than the house in Dundee, this was where he had spent his formative years —in the handsome house on Belgrave Crescent, opposite private gardens and overlooking the ravine of the Water of Leith. His maternal grandfather had bought the honey-colored house at a time when the north side of Edinburgh was being rebuilt with elegant terraces and well-tended gardens in the middle of circuses.

He had spent most of his twenties in this city—admittedly much of it on the south side in cheaper, cramped tenements, much to the horror of his parents. The Edinburgh medical system was three years studying every facet of medicine, before specializing for a further two years in order to matriculate. It was the system which made Edinburgh the best medical school in the world—an accolade even the Americans acknowledged.

Edinburgh was where he had known joy and deep sorrow. Even now, every turn brought memories of his wife which pressed heavily on his shoulders. But he acknowledged it was not the black cloud of despair that had enveloped him in the early years after his wife's death. Perhaps time was a healer after all—as everyone had been so eager to assure him.

He was returning from visiting Dean Cemetery. After Joan died, his mother had softened her hostile stance and insisted Douglas's wife be laid among their ancestors. The cemetery was full of substantial monuments and statues, a place where you could flaunt your wealth and importance from beyond the grave. Joan's headstone was modest, close to a yew tree. This morning, he had traced his fingers over the inscription: JOAN McLENNAN, 1852–1871, BELOVED WIFE AND DAUGHTER. He had dropped his chin to his chest, wishing he had insisted on 'mother' being included. He had stood quietly for some time at the graveside, remembering. He was pleased the grave was well-tended and wondered who had done this. Perhaps his sister, Isla, had visited.

Now he was putting that behind him and was on his way to the Royal Infirmary. He walked briskly to Queen Street gardens, over the brow of the first hill, and down to Princes Street. The sight of the looming castle gave him a patriotic thrill. How many generations of Scots had defended this city?

He strode across the dip of the Mound and up the steep hill to the Royal Mile before turning east and making his way to the Infirmary. His heart pumped hard from the exertion, but it was not just the exercise. Soon he would see her again.

Miss Van Bergen. Phoebe.

He knew it was reckless to let his feelings for her range in this way, because nothing would make him break his vow never to remarry. But he longed to see her again, and had missed her company in the few days since leaving Liverpool. She made him laugh, she gave him hope. He would find himself thinking of things he wanted to share with her, sights he wanted her to notice. He would read a column in the paper and wonder what she would think of it.

He swiftly took the steps to the Infirmary door, as if making sure he wouldn't falter at the last moment.

Inside was packed with people. There were plenty of men,

some of whom he knew, but what made this unusual was to see so many women. By their dress, he guessed some had traveled from Europe, or perhaps even further afield. He recognized Miss Sophia Jex-Blake. He didn't know her personally but knew her reputation as the first woman to matriculate in medicine from Edinburgh. There was a coterie of women around her and he wondered if some were the Edinburgh Seven. He knew the story: the medical school had denied Miss Jex-Blake entry, saying they could not admit a sole woman. She had advertised in the paper and six other women came forward, eager to gain medical training, leaving the school with no choice but to accept them.

As he made his way through the throng, he was stopped by a colleague who had been a student with him. Douglas gave him a hearty welcome, but was in no mood to stop and chat, or to précis his career since they had last met.

He scanned the crowd, knowing there was only one person he was looking for, but she was nowhere to be seen. His heart sank. It looked like she had not reached Edinburgh on time, after all.

He swallowed. Perhaps something had happened to her. God, he *knew* he should have waited another day and insisted on traveling with her from Liverpool. All manner of things might have befallen her.

With a sick feeling in his stomach, he hurried to the lecture hall and took the printed sheet being handed out by a steward. He scanned it: the usual list of welcoming speeches, then the opening address written by Miss Florence Nightingale herself. And there it was: *Presented by Miss P. Van Bergen, of Van Bergen Women's Hospital, Boston, Massachusetts.*

"Have there been any changes to the speakers?" he asked the steward.

"I don't think so."

Douglas was hesitating to speak her name. *Stop being such a damn fool.* "Miss Van Bergen, I mean. Is she still presenting the address?"

"As far as I know."

His shoulders dropped with relief as he slipped inside the semicircular lecture theater where the benches were already filling, and moved along the back row to a space near the next aisle. The windows were high and light brightened parts of the space, but where he sat was in shadow.

Douglas removed his hat and overcoat, rolling them together to tuck under his bench. He took a leather-bound notebook from his inner pocket and a sharpened pencil. The excitement in the room was audible with so many women's voices.

He scanned the delegates already seated near the front. There —at last—was Mrs. Hale. He wondered if he should make his way down the steps to greet her. But no, the narrow aisle was filled with men and women finding their places. He had missed his moment. And Phoebe was not beside her anyway.

People settled and there was an expectant hush. A door opened on the right of the stage and Professor Moncrieff strode in, rubbing his hands together. He was followed by a man Douglas knew to be dean of the medical faculty. How had Moncrieff persuaded him to be here? He was a well-known skeptic of the role of women in medicine. Then Sir Thomas Boyd, the Lord Provost, chains around his shoulders, wearing ornate robes.

At last, Phoebe. His chest tightened. She was walking tall, as always, her dark hair pinned simply behind, a small hat fixed at an angle. She was wearing the smart, midnight-blue dress he had seen before, the height of ladies' fashion.

He now wished he had sat closer to the stage so he could see her face better. There was something slightly hesitant about her. Was she overawed by the occasion?

The audience applauded as they each took a chair, Phoebe sitting neatly, adjusting her dress. She kept her eyes on the professor, ignoring the packed hall.

Moncrieff went to the lectern and leaned on it. "Welcome, welcome, ladies"—he paused to let that word sink in—"and gentlemen. I haven't been able to make *that* greeting here before."

The audience laughed.

"Welcome to the inaugural International Symposium of Women's Health, hosted by the University of Edinburgh's School of Medicine. This day will go down in medical history as the beginning of a new medical age. An age where all people, whether man or woman, are treated according to their needs."

There was a round of applause.

The professor introduced the dean, who made some anodyne remarks which Douglas suspected had been written for him by the professor. Then the Lord Provost spoke about the new hospital he had done so much to promote. Douglas barely heard a word: all his attention was captured by Phoebe.

As she seemed to relax, her eyes drifted over the faces in the audience. Her features remained steady until she spotted Mrs. Hale in the front row. A brief smile lit up her face before she returned to watch the city father who was speaking at some length about the history of the "Athens of the North." Had she been looking for him? Douglas wondered. He tutted at himself for being so self-regarding.

At last, Professor Moncrieff stood again. "And now, we are privileged to hear an address written by Miss Florence Nightingale. I am deeply grateful for her patronage of this symposium. Although, sadly, she is unable to be here in person, I am thrilled the address will be read for us by Miss Van Bergen, who has traveled across the Atlantic to be with us. For those who do not know, she has established a women's hospital in her home city of Boston, which I have no doubt will become a beacon for the world. With her vision and drive, a new hospital will make women's lives better."

Phoebe's eyes fell to her lap and he sensed she was blushing. She rose and took the few steps to the center of the stage, placing the pamphlet on the lectern.

Phoebe paused and took in the audience. "I'm feeling slightly embarrassed by that introduction, knowing how many brave women there are in this room. But... too late now."

There was a ripple of laughter. Douglas's chest filled as he watched her. He knew she was as brave and progressive as any woman in this room.

"I cannot begin to express the honor I feel to be reading the address from Miss Nightingale. Her lamp shines as a beacon to us, still today."

She began the first sentence, but a frog in her throat revealed nervousness below her confident exterior. She coughed and took a sip of water.

"Please excuse me. I'll try that again."

His heart went out to her, but this time, her voice came loud and clear, the rich American accent giving Miss Nightingale's words a modern air. Phoebe read at the perfect pace: not so slow the address dragged, but not so fast it was hard to follow. Miss Nightingale had written about her favorite subject: the training of nurses.

Douglas leaned back and a warm feeling swept over him. He couldn't concentrate on the words; he just wanted to hear Phoebe's voice, to watch her slightest gesture. He luxuriated in being able to sit and stare without anyone considering it rude, because every other face was enraptured by her too.

Phoebe reached the end and there was applause. She smiled apologetically, knowing this was for Miss Nightingale, not for her. She allowed herself a moment to look at the audience, raising her chin to the back of the hall.

And then her gaze stopped, right in his direction. She had seen him, surely she had. His heart raced so hard, he feared his neighbors could hear it. She gave a slight nod before turning and shaking hands with the professor and returning to her seat.

The International Symposium had begun. The room was full of fascinating people.

But there was only one person Douglas wanted to speak to, only one person who fascinated him as no one ever had before.

THIRTY-FOUR

Phoebe sipped a glass of sherry in the reception room where the great and the good had gathered and felt heady with the success of her address. She had lived up to the honor of reading the great woman's words. She smiled and chatted as people congratulated her and asked about the hospital in Boston.

She glanced at the wall clock; she wanted to attend the lecture on *The Use of Chloroform for Pain Relief in Childbirth* and waited until she felt it would be polite to slip out.

Phoebe made her way down the corridor. Mid-afternoon in December in Edinburgh meant the light was already failing and lights had been lit at intervals.

She stopped when she saw him leaning in a leisurely way against the wall in a pool of light, one foot raised against the stone, his attention on a book in his hand. Her stomach did an excited little flip at the sight of him. She thought it had been Douglas at the back of the lecture hall, but had not been sure.

She swallowed and continued down the corridor. The elation and nervousness she had experienced when spending time together on the ship came flooding back.

He looked up from his book and put his head to one side, his hair falling over his brow. He gave a shy smile. "I was hoping to catch you. If I waited long enough."

"Well. Here I am."

He pushed himself away from the wall. "Here you are."

She was uncertain how to greet him. They had become friends on the liner, but here, among the august buildings of Edinburgh and the atmosphere of an international symposium, she felt shy.

She put out her hand. "Dr. McLennan."

He shook it. "I thought we'd agreed on Douglas, when others weren't around. Or at the least, McLennan."

It had only been a few days, but she had missed that soft Scots accent.

She cleared her throat. "Douglas."

"Phoebe." He held her hand.

She looked up and saw those intense green eyes studying her face. Her mouth went dry.

She dropped her hand and turned to continue in the direction she had been walking. "Shall we?"

He nodded and fell into step beside her. "You were excellent, by the way."

"Was I?" She wasn't fishing for compliments: she had been fearful of not doing justice to the words. "Was that you at the back? Could you hear?"

"Every word. Clear as a bell."

"Despite my odd Boston accent."

"Nothing odd about it at all. I've come to like it."

That fluttering feeling returned, but she tried to ignore it.

They reached the main area which was almost deserted.

"I had hoped to go to the chloroform talk," she said.

"Aye. That looked interesting."

"It will be halfway through now. I wouldn't want to interrupt."

Douglas put a hand to the back of his neck. "I... er... know Dr. James Duncan who is delivering the talk."

"You do?"

"I could introduce you afterwards."

Phoebe waved a hand dismissively. "Oh, I wouldn't want to take up his time."

Douglas smiled at her. "I'm sure he'd be delighted to speak to you. The symposium is only three days. You need to make the most of it."

"Well, thank you, Douglas. That would be kind." She fingered the brooch at her throat, wanting to stay in his company and searching for something to say.

He spoke first. "Where are you staying? With the professor?"

"No. The Old Waverley Hotel."

Douglas seemed enthusiastic. "Ah, I ken it. On Princes Street."

"That's it."

"A wee bit noisy, I imagine."

She huffed a laugh. "Not compared with Boston."

"But beautiful views. If they have given you rooms at the front, that is."

"They have. And they are. Beautiful, I mean. The Old Town and the castle." She waved in the general direction she thought was the castle, but realizing she had no idea where it was, changed the movement to patting the hair at the back of her neck. "And you, are you with your parents in Dundee?"

He scoffed. "Ocht, no. That would be too far to be traveling in each day. Even with the new ferry and train line."

She dropped her gaze, feeling a little foolish to have not worked out the distances in Scotland.

"I'm staying at my aunt's house," Douglas said. "My sister's there as well. Between Stockbridge and Dean Village."

"And that's... close?"

He coughed to clear his throat. "It's just beyond the New Town. To the north."

He looked round and she sensed an awkwardness between them. It was strange and disappointing that their conversation was so stilted after their easy familiarity on the ship.

"Are you staying on after the symposium?" he asked. "You and Mrs. Hale, I mean."

"Yes. I want to see everything I can. While I'm here. The professor has organized visits to various institutions."

"Good."

"Calling in favors so we get private tours, I sense."

"Has he mentioned the Botanics?"

She glanced at him. "I don't think so. What are they?"

"The Botanical Gardens. They have a long history. Perhaps... perhaps I could take you there. For a walk. They are a favorite place of mine."

Phoebe felt warmth rising in her cheeks. He wanted to show her a special place. "That sounds delightful."

"And Mrs. Hale."

"Of course." She hoped her disappointment wasn't evident in her tone.

A clock chimed somewhere, ringing out the hour. A door opened and the lobby filled with people leaving the lecture.

Phoebe spotted Adeline and waved. "Look who I found," she called.

Adeline hurried over and greeted them. "My! That was such a useful talk. I have taken *so* many notes."

Much as she'd like to, Phoebe knew they could not stand there all afternoon. "Well... Douglas..."

"How are you getting back to the Old Waverley?" he quickly asked.

"Cab. The professor has organized it."

"Ah, yes. The professor." He nodded and looked toward the door.

She didn't want the conversation to end with this disjointed feeling between them. "But I hope... we'll see you tomorrow?"

"Aye. I'll be here." He gave a self-deprecating smile. "I have a paper to deliver."

"Of course you have."

"Until tomorrow." He nodded briefly to each of them and left.

Phoebe let out a breath. He had seemed tense, as if he wanted to be somewhere else, but something was keeping him fixed to the spot. Even though he had been waiting for her, and offered a tour of the Botanical Gardens, she feared he'd talked to her out of politeness and this made her unexpectedly crestfallen.

For the rest of the symposium, Phoebe packed her days with every talk and lecture she could manage. She filled her notebook, gathered pamphlets and books. Her mother had taught her that a lady carried nothing larger than a purse, and that only a working woman had need of a capacious bag or basket. Well, she was a working woman now. She wrote down names and addresses to correspond when she returned home; she exchanged ideas and knowledge.

This was exactly what she needed: a renewed purpose. If marriage and children were not her destiny, then this was something to pass on to the future. When she'd first written to Professor Moncrieff saying she wanted to build the finest women's hospital on the Eastern Seaboard, she'd wondered if she was being naïve and foolish. Now she had a fire in her belly. Why shouldn't she be ambitious? She had been blessed with wealth through no merit of her own; the least she could do was turn it into something for the benefit of all.

Her days were so busy, she barely said a word to Douglas. Perhaps it was for the best. He remained the one thing that could distract her, at a time when she was trying to concentrate on all the new information flooding her way.

But there could be no denying that what she was feeling for Douglas was something far more than friendship. If he were a friend, she would feel relaxed in his company, whereas she felt every nerve was on full alert. She had a sixth sense of where he was, knowing he was in a room even before she saw him. Her eyes would be drawn so many times, she would blush if he glanced over and caught her staring. She had become familiar with his smell, the particular brand of cologne he wore. Memories of times they had touched would come unbidden to her mind: on the SS *Arizona* when he had put his hand over hers when playing cards, or when they had danced at the State House in Boston.

But nothing could ever come of this growing attraction. He had vowed never to marry again, and even if he had not, she was the last person he would be interested in, knowing her history. Her skin prickled with shame as she tried to close her mind to memories of the bedroom at Adeline's.

She could not resist going to his presentation, though. It was called *The Treatment of Puerperal Eclampsia by Chloral* and, the truth was, she found it difficult to follow. He talked of the chemical structure of chloral hydrate and investigation methodologies. But more than the science, she struggled to keep up because she spent too much time gazing at him, studying the way his hands moved as he spoke, listening to the soft burr of his accent, rather than the words. Occasionally, he would glance in her direction; she would drop her head and scribble some notes.

On the second evening, Phoebe was thrilled that she and Adeline were invited to a supper party with Sophia Jex-Blake and her cohort. The meal was in the upper room of a hotel in Grassmarket. Miss Jex-Blake entertained everyone with stories of the ways men had tried to keep her from matriculating, even releasing a sheep into the hall as she went to sit her exams. Adeline fell deep in conversation with Miss Angélique Pringle, matron of the Royal Infirmary, who was a close associate of Florence Nightingale. They talked at length about the trials of keeping a ward in order and challenging the orthodoxy of male doctors.

Traveling back to her hotel, Phoebe thought about the male doctors who were attending the symposium. Yes, many still had the air that they knew more than the women, and there could be condescending phrases. But they were here: they were making a start.

The symposium ended with a ceremony similar to the opening. Again, everyone crowded into the lecture theater. Again, Professor Moncrieff took to the stage.

Phoebe sat in the audience, next to Adeline. She noticed

Douglas was in the back row. They nodded, but she kept her place near the front, determined to keep her growing admiration in check. She barely heard a word of Moncrieff's speech as it suddenly struck her that after the proposed visit to the Botanical Gardens, there was no reason for her to meet Douglas again. The very thought brought a hollowness to her stomach. She closed her hands into fists: this was why it was so foolish of her to let her heart govern her head.

THIRTY-FIVE

That evening, Adeline and Phoebe dined at the hotel. Phoebe felt deflated after the stimulation of the symposium and the realization that her time with Douglas was fast coming to a close. Adeline reminded her of all the activity the professor had arranged for them over the coming week, and then it would be Christmas. This would be the first time Phoebe had been away from her family for Christmas and she wondered if spending it the other side of the Atlantic would make her homesick.

The next morning, an invitation arrived for her and Adeline to spend Christmas Eve and Christmas Day with the professor. *I know you Americans enjoy your yuletide holiday*, he wrote.

They spent a week of fascinating, if cold, sightseeing, and each day Phoebe wondered if she would hear from Douglas about the Botanical Gardens. She kicked herself for not making a definite arrangement.

On Christmas Eve, they arrived with light luggage at the grand terraced house on Ainsley Place where Professor Moncrieff lived alone, having lost his wife many years before. It brought thoughts of home as many features were familiar: the uneven cobbled street, the little park opposite enclosed by an ornate metal fence, the high flight of steps leading up from the sidewalk to the front door, the servant quarters tucked into the basement below.

Over dinner, Professor Moncrieff explained that the Scots did not particularly mark Christmas. Yes, Prince Albert had tried to introduce some German traditions and in the almost twenty years since his death, some had taken root. Moncrieff particularly enjoyed decorating an impressive spruce tree he had brought into his entrance hall.

"It's all about Hogmanay, for us Scots," Moncrieff explained.

"Hogmanay?"

"New Year. That's when the Scots really get together and have a hoolie."

Over dessert, Phoebe asked about the attractive part of Edinburgh they were in.

"Aye, the New Town. A much healthier part of the city to live in."

"Is it close to Stockbridge?" she asked.

He raised his brow. "This almost is Stockbridge."

"Oh? Isn't that where Dr. McLennan lives?"

"It's where he stays over. His sister lives on Belgrave Crescent, just over Dean Bridge, but the house is owned by his mother's sister."

She wanted to ask more but felt tongue-tied. Now she was close by, it would be an ideal time for Douglas to show her the Botanical Gardens, but he didn't know she was here, and she had no way to contact him.

Her shoulders slumped and she blinked back tears: it had been more than a week and she feared he had changed his mind about seeing her. Once again, she wondered if this was for the best.

At ten the next morning, Phoebe was alone in the drawing room when she heard the butler admitting someone to the house. Maybe they had Christmas Day visitors after all? The morning so far had been strangely anticlimactic, with none of the extravagant present giving of a Van Bergen Christmas in Boston. Moments later, the butler showed the visitor into the room.

Phoebe jumped up, unable to suppress her surprise and delight. "Douglas! Good morning. Merry Christmas."

He looked relaxed in a way he hadn't during the symposium, as if he was now on home ground. She smoothed her dress and wished she had made more effort with her hair.

"Merry Christmas to you, Miss Van—Phoebe. I hope I'm not disturbing you."

She swallowed and gestured to the writing paper on the table. "I was working on correspondence. Keeping in contact with all the interesting people I have met here."

He took off his hat but remained standing, looking more handsome than ever as he ran his fingers through his hair.

Phoebe was not sure if she had the authority to invite him to sit, in someone else's home. "You are calling on the professor? I'm sure he'll be here in a moment. I daresay it's a surprise to see me here. He generously invited Adeline and me to stay for Christmas."

"Aye. Well, no. I wanted to call on you and Mrs. Hale. I went to the Waverley Hotel and they said you were here."

Phoebe blinked. He had made the effort to go all the way into town and back. "Sorry to have put you to trouble."

"It's no trouble at all."

He really couldn't continue standing for the whole visit, so she gestured he should sit.

Douglas put his hat on the table and eased into the chair near the fire, stretching out his legs. He looked comfortable and Phoebe guessed he'd been in this room many times, hammering out new ideas with the professor.

"The morning walk did me good."

She sat opposite. "You walked? In this weather?"

"Edinburgh folk tend to walk within the city."

"I had noticed. I also noticed that every journey seems to be uphill. How can that be?"

Douglas chuckled. "True, it certainly feels that way."

She felt pleased he had laughed at her observation, but before she could say more, Professor Moncrieff entered, as energetic as ever, followed by Adeline.

"McLennan! Good to see you. Merry Christmas."

Douglas leaped to his feet and shook Moncrieff's hand before noticing Adeline and making a slight bow. "Mrs. Hale. Good to see you."

"And you, Dr. McLennan," she said, taking her place next to Phoebe on the sofa.

"You get back to your favorite armchair," said the professor to Douglas before glancing at the ladies. "I've asked the housekeeper to bring some Linzer biscuits and a pot of tea."

Moncrieff settled into his old chair, its back to the window. The conversation immediately turned to the success of the symposium. Moncrieff was already planning another in a year's time.

"I know there was some criticism in the press about the dangers of encouraging women doctors, but we have to keep going."

The housekeeper brought tea and biscuits.

"Mmm. What are these cookies?" Phoebe asked.

"Two rounds of shortbread," the housekeeper replied, "made only with butter. Held together with jam. And they are *biscuits*."

Phoebe took another, which crumbled in her mouth in the most delicious way. "Biscuits are something very different where we come from."

"So I've heard," said the housekeeper with a sniff, and left the room.

"Are you staying here through to Hogmanay?" asked Douglas.

Phoebe shook her head. "We return to our hotel tomorrow."

"I have prior obligations," said Moncrieff, with a significant look at Douglas. "My family in Ullapool."

"Of course, I recall now," said Douglas, and Phoebe sensed a hidden story. "You go there for the holiday. It's a long way to travel."

"The professor has told us how beautiful the north-west coast is, though."

Moncrieff poured a second cup. "Sadly, it means the ladies will be spending Hogmanay at the temperance hotel."

"I'm sure they will have something special laid on," said Adeline.

"Aye, maybe they will," said Moncrieff, "but it's no' the same as being with a Scots family. It's a shame, with you lassies traveling all this way from America. Doesnae feel like we're being properly hospitable."

"They could come to my family," said Douglas with a shrug. He turned to Phoebe. "If that would be acceptable. Isla, my sister, is there already, with my aunt. There's always a big gathering."

"That sounds capital," said the professor, slapping the arm of his chair. "Hogmanay in Dundee with the McLennans. That's settled then."

Phoebe's mouth opened, bewildered by how swiftly this plan had come about.

Douglas glanced at her, a line appearing between his brows. "Well, it's only settled if that's what the ladies want. They may prefer to stay in Edinburgh."

Phoebe looked at Adeline, who opened her eyes wide.

"We wouldn't want to be an imposition," Phoebe said carefully. Part of her was dying to see where Douglas came from, to understand him better. But she could imagine what his mother might feel. "And if you already have a houseful, there may not be room for two more."

Moncrieff snorted. "I've been to the McLennan family home. I assure you, there'll be no problem fitting you in."

Phoebe stole a look at Douglas, who shuffled in his seat. "You'll be telling me you live in a castle next."

"Nae, it's not a castle. But..."

"But?" Phoebe smirked. "But it's *like* a castle?"

"It's big. And it's old. But I assure you, it is not a castle."

Phoebe raised an eyebrow. Douglas had always given the impression he came from a modest background. Now she was even more intrigued to see where he had grown up.

"If your mother is truly agreeable to have two American house-guests she has never met, and at such short notice, then we'd be delighted to visit. Wouldn't we, Adeline?"

"You bet. I mean, staying in a castle—"

"Honestly, it's *not* a castle—" Douglas raised his hands in protest.

Moncrieff laughed and kicked Douglas's foot. "The lassies, they're only teasing you."

"I'll write to my mother today. I'm sure she'll be fascinated to have Americans staying."

Moncrieff took another Linzer biscuit. "The McLennans always do Hogmanay right. First footing—"

"What's that?"

The professor waved a hand. "A midnight tradition. You'll see. And a big ceilidh."

"I've heard of that," said Adeline. "A folk dance, right?"

"Sort of," said Douglas. "There'll be a band and lots of set dances."

Phoebe scoffed. "*You* don't dance, surely?"

Douglas looked straight at her and grinned. "Not if I can avoid it. But sometimes they're short of partners. Even ones who are poor dancers."

Phoebe felt warmth spinning up her body as she remembered the ball in Boston. That was when her feelings toward him began to thaw. How different things were, now she had come to know and admire him.

The clock on the mantelpiece chimed eleven o'clock.

Douglas sat forward. "I must be on my way. But I haven't fulfilled the purpose of my visit. I promised to show you the Botanical Gardens. They are nearby. I wondered if you ladies would like to take a turn there, this afternoon."

Phoebe took a breath, thrilled that he had remembered the suggestion. "Are they open? I mean, it's Christmas day."

"Well, no. But I know the Regius Keeper. He has a house within the gardens and has agreed to open a gate."

Phoebe glanced at Adeline, who nodded. "We'd be delighted."

"Excellent." He got to his feet. "Please don't get up. I'll return at one o'clock. And I suggest you wear sturdy shoes. It can be uneven underfoot."

Phoebe made a mock salute. "We'll be ready for anything."

THIRTY-SIX

Douglas waited in the professor's lobby for the ladies, walking back and forth in the narrow space, passing the brim of his hat through his fingers. How on earth had he ended up inviting them to Dundee? It had been a moment's reaction and he wasn't used to impulsive behavior.

His thoughts were interrupted by a rustling on the staircase. Phoebe walked down, one hand on the balustrade, looking as lovely as ever. Clearly his plan of inoculating himself by exposure to her was not working. What was he thinking, putting his emotions through the wringer?

He was thinking she was a friend, he sternly told himself. Perhaps even a good friend.

She wore a dark green outfit—a skirt with layers, a long shapely jacket over it, edged with white fur at the high neck and forming a line down the front. The hat was larger than her usual choice, tied with a green silk bow. She was wearing her fur-lined gloves.

She reached the hall and lifted her skirts an inch to show her black leather boots. "There, Douglas. Sturdy enough?"

He couldn't help but grin. "They look grand. And Mrs. Hale?"

She passed her tongue over her lower lip. "She's decided not to come."

"Uh-huh?" He had not prepared for this eventuality.

"Thought the weather looked bad." She glanced down and then back at him, a question hanging between them.

There was a momentary tremor through his hand as he picked up the black umbrella he had brought, in case the rain returned. He swallowed to get a grip of his responses. An afternoon walk with a friend, that was all.

"She may be right." He glanced at her. "You're sure you want to come?"

Phoebe stepped forward. "I can manage bad weather."

"What I mean is, just the two of us. In public."

She shrugged. "No one knows me in Edinburgh. You're the one who is known here." She arched an eyebrow at him. "Will your reputation withstand a walk with a mysterious woman?"

He grunted. "Not sure I've got any reputation to protect."

The butler opened the door and Douglas gave her his arm for the steps to the street.

He took her along the smart streets toward Stockbridge, proud that the tall, elegant terraces in pale, gray stone could match the smart residences of Beacon Hill and Back Bay. The pavements were wide with even stones, the roads well maintained. They walked through Stockbridge village, past the butchers, a hardware store, a public house with ornate windows.

They reached the gate to the Botanics, where he was relieved to see his elderly friend waiting. The Keeper winked at him as they slipped in and muttered something about leaving them to it.

Douglas enjoyed sharing the Garden's history, how the first physic gardens in Edinburgh had been planted elsewhere and been moved here fifty years before. As they wandered along the paths, he showed the wide range of plants, many of which helped with medicine, pointing to sage, chamomile, and juniper.

Phoebe admired the varied trees. Even in winter, there was plenty of color, with the range of evergreens the gardeners had planted over the decades.

"And it's a royal garden. Does that mean we might meet Queen Victoria promenading?"

Douglas scoffed. "I don't think it works like that. There must have been some sort of patronage back in the mists of time."

"Back before my country even existed."

"Come, now, Phoebe. Most things in Scotland are from before your country existed. I have a dinner set older than your country."

She burst out laughing and he stopped in wonderment at the sound. He knew he was not good around women; he didn't have smooth charm. His sister had often chided him for being dour and solemn. The strange thing with Phoebe was all the seesawing between formality and intimacy. When crossing the Atlantic, he had felt comfortable in her company, yet in Edinburgh he had struggled to find the right thing to say. At last, they were connecting again.

"Come. I want to show you something special."

She walked by his side, step by step, along the wide path. They turned a corner and she stopped short at the sight of an elegant building of cream stonework columns supporting tall narrow windows, each with a fanned semicircle at the top. Above was a curved glazed roof of two levels, as delicate as spun sugar.

"The Palm House," Douglas said, delighted by the look of awe on her face.

"I've never seen anything quite like it," she said, hurrying forward. "Can we go in?"

He tried the door and it was unlocked. "Don't see why not."

The sound inside was muffled, almost hushed. Water dripped somewhere. The change in temperature was unsettling—sudden warmth after the December chill. They wandered between lush vegetation, admiring palms that reached upwards to the glazed roof.

They walked in a circle, back to the entrance. Stepping outside, the air was sharp and cold.

Phoebe shivered.

"Are you warm enough?" Douglas asked. "Do you want to go back to the professor's?"

"Not yet. A brisk walk should warm me up."

He led her back to the Garden's side door and they wandered the familiar streets of stylish terraced homes. Passing Belgrave Crescent, he pointed out his aunt's substantial home. He reached high railings and a pair of iron gates between sandstone pillars. He couldn't explain why his feet had led him here and his teeth chattered before he could set his jaw and take control.

"What's this?" Phoebe asked, pushing open the gate. "Oh, it's a graveyard." She stepped inside. "It's beautiful. I mean... I know it's a graveyard, but... look at these statues."

She took off along the path before he could stop her. This was a bad idea.

He watched her run gloved fingers over an inscription. "It feels like you get a whole family history from these stones. You know... parents outliving their children. Or a wife who lived for years after losing her husband." She moved on. "Oh, look. *McLennan.*" Slowly, she turned to him. "Is this your family?"

Douglas was unable to answer. He was fixed to the spot by the sight of a woman standing near Joan's grave beneath a yew tree. She was dressed in black. A chill ran down his back as he realized he had made a huge mistake.

The woman heard a noise and turned to face them, her face painfully familiar. He witnessed on her pale features the same shock he was experiencing. Still he could not move.

The woman raised her chin. "What are ye doing here?"

Douglas swallowed, unable to speak.

"Ye have no right to be here."

"You have been tending her grave?" His voice was hoarse.

"Someone has to care for her. Even if you never did."

"Douglas?"

The American voice cut through the air and he remembered Phoebe was next to him. He glanced at her questioning face.

The woman took a step closer, scowling at him. "Have ye no shame? Bringing your new wife here."

Phoebe shook her head. "You are mistaken, madam. We are not married."

The woman cackled. "His fancy woman, then."

"Maud, please..."

She turned to Phoebe. "Has he told you about her? About Joan? His wife?"

Phoebe's chin trembled slightly and she glanced at Douglas before answering. "A little."

Maud tossed her head and scoffed. "Bet he didn't tell you the truth."

Douglas stepped toward her, a hand outstretched, hoping to calm her. "Please, Maud. I'm sorry—"

"You're *sorry*!" she cried. She drew back her arm and slapped him across the cheek.

He staggered back, one hand to his face. He was shocked by the strike, but the truth was, he deserved it.

She lunged forward, her hands in fists, and struck him on the chest. There was not much force, but she drummed against him, over and over. All he could do was stand and soak up the poor woman's despair.

He could hear Phoebe's calls, trying to tell the woman to stop. Gently, he took hold of Maud's wrists and gradually she came to a halt.

Maud roared like a wounded animal. "You killed her. You're the devil and you *killed* her."

With that, the fury seemed to have leached out of her. She panted, her hands against her legs, getting her breath back.

He glanced at Phoebe; the color had drained from her face. What on earth must she be thinking?

Maud stood and stepped away from him. She turned fully to Phoebe, and Douglas stood ready, in case she attacked again.

"Did he tell you that?" she yelled. "Did he tell you he killed his own *wife?*" She turned and spat at him, the spittle landing on his chest. "If I had my way, you'd have *hung* for what you did."

Maud gathered her skirts and ran to the iron gate, disappearing into the late-afternoon gloom.

Douglas stared after her. He wondered if he should follow, make sure she was safe. He shook his head; he was the last person on earth she would accept help from.

He felt a hand on his arm.

"Douglas?"

He turned to Phoebe and saw questions in her eyes. The prickle of humiliation spread over him as he thought of what had happened. Oh God, why had he come to this place? Why had he arrived as Maud was tending the grave? What devilish fate had taken pleasure in seeing things fall out so?

Douglas swallowed but could find no words to explain. He took out a handkerchief to clear the spittle from his jacket, then picked up the hat and umbrella that had been scattered.

Phoebe moved toward the grave Maud had been tending. "Joan McLennan," she read from the headstone.

"I'm so sorry. I can't... That was... my wife's sister."

Phoebe stared at him and then crouched to tidy the flowers Maud had dropped. Douglas felt the first drops of rain.

"We had better be getting back," Phoebe said, rising.

"Aye." Although her voice was soft, he suspected she was desperate to leave.

Trembling slightly, he opened the umbrella and gave it to her. She took it and made her way to the street.

The rain fell harder. She waited for him. "We'd better share this umbrella. Otherwise, you'll be soaked."

He took the handle and put out his elbow for her to lean on. There was no alternative but to walk closely, even though what she had just witnessed must surely make her want to stay away from him. The rain drummed on the taut black fabric.

She did not say a word, did not ask one question about what

had happened. For that, he was grateful, although the silence showed how he had ruined everything.

At Moncrieff's house on Ainslie Place, he knew he must speak.

"After what you heard, I would understand if you did not want to take up the invitation."

"The invitation?" she said, frowning.

"To Dundee. Hogmanay."

She faced him. "Would you rather we didn't come?"

"The offer still stands. It's just—"

"If you are happy for us to be there, we're happy to come." She took the steps to the door and knocked, before turning back to face him. "The words of a poor, grief-stricken sister are not going to change my good opinion of you, Douglas."

The black door opened and she slipped inside. Douglas stood, staring at the closed door. Such generosity of spirit toward the sister, such faith in his integrity. Were the gods mocking him by showing him a woman of perfection?

Because her faith in him was entirely misplaced. The problem was the grief-stricken sister was right.

He was responsible for his wife's death.

THIRTY-SEVEN

Phoebe was quiet over dinner with the professor and Adeline, their last meal together before he set off north in the morning and she and Adeline would return to the Old Waverley Hotel.

"Did you enjoy the Botanics?" Moncrieff asked as they neared the end of the meat course.

"Indeed. Beautiful. I'm sorry you missed it, Adeline."

"You should see them in the spring," Moncrieff continued, "when everything is bursting into life. I expect McLennan was good company. He knows a lot about healing plants."

Phoebe took a sip of her wine. The incident at the cemetery had circled her thoughts ever since her return and she could not resist trying to find out more. "Tell me: Dr. McLennan—he was married, I believe?" She caught Adeline's look, but if Moncrieff was likewise surprised by the turn in the conversation, he hid it.

"Aye, he was," said Moncrieff slowly. "As a younger man."

"Did you know him then?"

"He was one of my students."

"And... did you ever meet her?"

"The wife?" Moncrieff paused and put his knife and fork on the plate, lined against each other. He looked at Phoebe with kind eyes. "No, I can't say I did. I believe she was from a leading Edinburgh family."

"From around here?"

"Aye, I believe so."

The maid cleared their plates and the housekeeper put glasses of cranachan in front of them.

"Gee, that looks delicious," said Adeline, pushing in her spoon.

Phoebe was not ready to let the subject drop, though. While she could not believe the sister's accusations, she needed to know more. "Do you know what happened to her? Dr. McLennan's wife."

Moncrieff nodded. "She died not long after they were wed."

"Do you know how?"

He shook his head. "I'm afraid, Miss Phoebe, I never felt it my place to delve into my students' lives. A failing of mine, no doubt. But I know it hit McLennan hard. I remember having to speak to him forcefully about completing his studies." Moncrieff poured more wine. "What brings on these questions, my dear?"

She had gone too deep and needed to retreat. "Nothing in particular." She laughed lightly. "My mother always said I was too inquisitive for polite society."

She turned her attention to her dessert and resolved to try to follow Moncrieff's example and not delve further into Douglas's past.

Early the following morning, Phoebe and Adeline thanked Moncrieff for his hospitality. Just before climbing into the cab, Phoebe hugged the old gentleman, bringing tears to his eyes. They both knew they were unlikely to see each other again.

"My, all those questions. Did something happen?" Adeline asked as the cab swayed side to side on its way to Princes Street. "With McLennan."

Phoebe grasped the strap to steady herself as the carriage rocked. "How d'you mean?"

"When you returned from the walk yesterday, you seemed quiet. I thought something must have happened."

"No, nothing."

Adeline tutted and looked out of the window. "I've known you some years now, Phoebe. I can tell when you're concealing something."

"Like what?"

"Like maybe he kissed you—"

"Kissed me!" Blood rushed to her cheeks.

Adeline turned back to look at Phoebe, one corner of her mouth lifted. "See? You're blushing."

"He did *not* kiss me. I don't know why you would *think* such a thing."

"Because the two of you clearly have... There is *something* between you."

"Adeline!"

"Been there right from the start. Plain to see," Adeline blurted.

Phoebe opened her mouth. "Do you mean people in Boston were gossiping..."

"Well, plain for *me* to see, anyway. Can't say anyone else noticed."

Phoebe's toes curled inside her boots. She had to put Adeline right. "He did *not* try to kiss me. And given he knows the shameful truth of... about me and Hector, he is likely to be the last man on earth who would *want* to kiss me." Adeline opened her mouth to speak, but Phoebe pushed on. "We visited his wife's grave. That's why I was asking about her."

It was enough of the truth to keep Adeline satisfied. Phoebe longed to tell her friend all that had happened at the graveyard, about the attack from the sister-in-law—but it was Douglas's private business. She would not breach his confidence by sharing the whole story, even though she itched to discuss it and work out what it meant. She didn't believe a word about Douglas killing his wife, but something dreadful had happened and it was still casting a shadow over his life.

. . .

Unfortunately, Adeline began to show symptoms of a cold that Boxing Day evening. Phoebe tended to her, asking the hotel for drinks of hot lemon juice, but was denied the splash of whiskey. For the first time, she thoroughly missed having Farrell with them.

The next day, Adeline's coughing grew worse. Mr. Cranston called a doctor, who declared it a heavy cold but no more. It seemed the doctor was right, because by the evening Adeline was sitting up in bed, drinking bone broth.

"You don't look well enough to travel," said Phoebe.

Adeline blew her nose. "I'm sorry, but I'm not."

"I'll send a message to McLennan and tell him we can't go to Dundee after all."

Adeline waved her handkerchief. "I shan't hear of it. You can still go."

"Me? By myself?"

"Why not?"

Phoebe stared at Adeline, her mouth open. "You know why not! I can't travel alone with McLennan."

Adeline rolled her eyes.

Phoebe briskly straightened the bed cover. "It's one thing to promenade with a man for an afternoon. It's something else entirely to pack a travel bag and board a train with him."

Adeline closed her eyes briefly. "Tch. Who'll know? Seriously. No one. Will. *Ever*. Know." She drummed each word out with her finger on the coverlet. "Who is it you think is going to judge you? Your mother's dead, Phoebe. She can't criticize you anymore."

Phoebe sat up with a start. Adeline had an extraordinary ability to pinpoint what was happening under the surface. She had guessed the truth of Hector; now she understood Phoebe's relationship with her mother.

Phoebe opened her mouth to object, but Adeline jumped in.

"And all those women in Boston?" Adeline waved her soup spoon. "I think you lost *their* good opinion when you broke off your engagement to one of their own and ran off to Europe with just me and a lady's maid."

Phoebe thought about it and realized everything Adeline said was true. She had promised herself to be a different woman on this side of the Atlantic. A brave, independent woman. Maybe she *could* still go to Dundee.

But it wasn't that easy.

She sighed. "What will McLennan think? If I turn up at the station in the morning and it's just me?"

"I know he can seem all buttoned-up, but I don't think he's going to judge you either. I think he'll want you to go."

Phoebe took the empty soup bowl. Adeline's assessment of Douglas was pretty accurate too. She studied her friend. "But I can't leave you. Not when you're unwell."

Adeline wiped her hands on the napkin Phoebe handed over. "I feel rotten, but I'm not at death's door. And anyway, Phoebe, you've *got* to go. You've got to find out if McLennan lives in a castle and was just pretending to be an ordinary man."

Phoebe laughed. Whatever the truth, Douglas had never struck her as ordinary.

"So you better start packing," said Adeline. "Or I'll have to drag myself from this bed and do it for you."

THIRTY-EIGHT

Douglas ran down the slope to Waverley Station. *Damn it.* He was never late. And yet, this morning, trivia had prevented him leaving on time. His sister had written to ask him to bring a favorite scarf she had left behind and he couldn't find it anywhere; the housekeeper had fussed about locking the house properly as it would be empty while she was at church. She had made it very clear she disapproved of him traveling on the Sabbath.

Thank God he had collected the tickets the day before and reserved four seats in a first-class compartment.

He rushed to the platform where the steam train bound for Aberdeen was waiting to depart. They would reach Dundee by seven.

He recognized Phoebe immediately, even with her back to him. She stood tall, a number of cases around the hem of her dress. He hurried toward her. "Miss Van Bergen."

She turned, and raised a gloved hand in greeting. Again, there was that moment when he thought his breathing had stopped as he saw her face: the delicate pink of her skin, her expressive gray eyes half shaded by her hat. Would that happen every time they met? It was damned inconvenient.

"I'm an idiot for being late."

"I was beginning to wonder if you'd changed your mind." She fiddled with an earring and he regretted making her worry.

He called a porter. "Could you take care of this luggage? We are getting off at Dundee." He pulled the booking paper from his pocket. "We're in compartment four."

She picked up a small leather bag to keep with her in the carriage and followed him.

He stretched up to open the carriage door. "Are Mrs. Hale and Mrs. Farrell still in the waiting room?"

"They're not here," she said, stepping up past him and into the compartment.

"I'll go fetch them. We're cutting it fine."

She turned her head. "Sorry, Douglas. It's just me."

He paused, one foot on the step and the other on the platform. He must have misheard her. "Where are they?"

Now she turned completely to him. "Adeline is too ill to come but insisted I join your family anyway. Mrs. Farrell is still in Liverpool—"

"Liverpool!"

"It's a long story, I'll tell you on the way." She looked down and met his eyes. "I realize this is unconventional. If it bothers you, I can stay here in Edinburgh."

Douglas hesitated at the door, taking in the implications. The mix of feelings was dizzying: he was delighted to grasp time alone with her, but troubled by the impropriety. A porter handed him two huge tartan blankets and pushed a brass foot warmer across the floor. The idea of leaving her behind in Edinburgh was unthinkable.

"Nae. I dinnae mind. I'm just... surprised." He climbed the steps and into the compartment. The porter slammed the door behind him. Surprised? He was astonished.

Phoebe sat by the window, beside the door, placing her bag on the upholstered bench beside her. He spread the blanket over her. It seemed an extravagance to have just two of them in the compartment for eight. Would it have been worse or better to have fellow passengers?

He pulled off his hat and gloves, but it was too cold to remove his coat. He pushed the warmer toward her so she could rest her feet on it, then took the seat opposite and wrapped a blanket around himself.

A whistle blew and the carriage jolted, followed by a steady pull as the train edged forward.

"We only just made it," he said, trying to make light of the delicate situation.

"Back home, they'd hold the train until we arrived. An advantage of owning the line."

He laughed and then glanced over to find her looking at him with a raised eyebrow. "Oh God, you're serious, aren't you?"

She smiled, showing her neat, white teeth. "Well, just the once. And it was Mother who was late."

He shook his head. What must it be like to be so wealthy the trains waited for you?

Phoebe laid one gloved hand over the other. "As I said, Mrs. Hale sends her apologies. She has a heavy cold."

"I'm sorry to hear it. And Mrs. Farrell? You said there is a story to tell."

"We arrived in Liverpool and she discovered her sister is sick. Did I mention she's a native of Liverpool?"

Douglas smoothed his mustache. "I'm Scottish. I knew where she was from as soon as she spoke."

"There are children to be looked after, so I insisted she stay. We'll collect her on our voyage home."

"So, does that mean you and Mrs. Hale have been traveling alone ever since?" He frowned, feeling anew the pang of guilt at not having stayed another day in Liverpool to accompany them north.

"It does."

"That's very..." He wasn't sure what word to use. He did not want to seem judgmental. "Bold."

"Bold?" Her eyebrow raised once more and she pursed her lips.

He held her gaze. "Other words come to mind. Brave, modern. Reckless."

"Scandalous?"

"Only if the gossips find out," he answered.

"Precisely. And no one here knows who I am. So it hardly matters."

He stared at her reflection in the window, her face calm and unreadable, as they traveled east and then north through the tunnels under Edinburgh. He hoped his parents would be broad-minded enough not to object to her coming to stay alone. How would he feel if his sister behaved like this? He pushed his hand through his hair. He couldn't imagine her taking the risk. He couldn't imagine *any* woman of his acquaintance doing this. And certainly not one of the richest women in the world, traveling without a chaperone or a protector. He wasn't sure if he was flattered she trusted him, or horrified by the gamble.

His skin tingled as he realized he was her guardian once more. He experienced the same flood of protective feelings he had felt when carrying her down the stairs at Mrs. Hale's house and acknowledged he liked this feeling.

They reached Granton on the Firth of Forth—the wide expanse of water to the north of Edinburgh, too narrow to be a sea, too wide to be a river. The weather was worsening as the winds grew stronger.

"Look outside," Douglas said. "I'm sure you'll want to tell your brothers about this. The world's first train ferry."

He was delighted by how interested she was, watching the engine and carriages roll down the tracks and straight onto a huge paddle steamer.

"You didn't warn me about this," she said, her eyes bright.

"I wasn't sure you'd come, if you knew more water was involved, after ten days on the Atlantic."

The train was secured and the boat paddles turned as the ferry worked its way into the foaming water. Phoebe was sitting with her back to the engine so could watch Edinburgh disappearing behind them. Horizontal rain drummed against the carriage windows.

"I assume we stay inside."

"Indeed. There are no facilities on this ferry. It's purely for the train, and usually takes cargo, not passengers."

Douglas watched their progress and rubbed at his temple. He tried not to reveal his unease about the worsening weather and how hard the paddle steamer was having to work to cross the gray expanse. It took longer than the usual half-hour to reach Burnt Island.

As the ferry was secured in the harbor and the train engine started up, Phoebe let out a deep breath.

"What a crossing. To be honest, Douglas, I'm glad that's over."

He leaned forward. "No more ferries, I promise you. The Tay is spanned by a new bridge."

The train picked up speed, following the coast before turning north and inland. As they passed towns and stations familiar to him, he told her of local traditions or battles fought on this land.

Outside, it turned dark as evening fell. The wind and rain buffeted the carriage and the two weak gaslights in their section flickered. There was a kind of magic to being contained with her in this dimly lit carriage, the weather wild outside, utterly alone and able to talk freely.

"Are you warm enough?" he asked.

She grimaced. "I can't lie, it's cold in here. But I've known worse."

He took his own blanket and tucked it around her before sitting back opposite again. "Not much longer. We'll be at the Tay Bridge soon. And then it's Dundee."

His chest filled as he looked forward to introducing her to his family. His parents had been against him moving to Boston, believing the New World a place where civilization had not fully taken root. Edinburgh was at the heart of the Enlightenment, of new ideas about the world. Why would anyone go anywhere else?

Well, Miss Phoebe Van Bergen would show them how wrong

they were. She'd show America was a place of fresh ideas and attitudes, a place to match their beloved Scotland.

She had closed her eyes and was in a light sleep. He looked at her dark lashes on her cheeks, the slight pink of her nose in the cold of their carriage, and his eyes wandered to the notch in her upper lip. He clenched his fists inside his coat pockets. He'd been a damn fool thinking he could *ever* inoculate himself against his feelings for the beautiful and fascinating woman opposite him. And now he was going to spend the next few days struggling to hide the fact.

THIRTY-NINE

Something jolted Phoebe back into consciousness. Her eyes sprang open and she looked across at Douglas.

"The bridge woke you," he said, his expression gentle and his voice reassuring. "The wheels sound different on this piece of track."

The pale light inside their compartment made it impossible to see anything through the window other than her own reflection. The carriage swayed back and forth rhythmically and Phoebe could feel the power of wind, which was so strong there were sparks as the wheels scraped against the rails.

"Not long now, Phoebe. We're nearly in Dundee."

On the last word, the whole carriage began to shake.

She clutched the armrests. "What's happening?"

Douglas grimaced. "I don't know." His voice was low.

Metal squealed and groaned, as if being twisted. Something heavy crashed, then slowly the carriage tipped forward, forcing Phoebe's back against the seat. The movement continued, with a ripping sound. Douglas slid forward out of his seat and was forced onto the bench beside her.

She looked at him, terrified. "The bridge. It's... it's collapsing!"

The noise was deafening as iron wrenched away from iron.

"Hold on!" he cried, reaching his arms around her.

He held her tight as the whole carriage sank downwards. Though her head was tucked low, she saw a flash of light from the corner of her eye. Was it the engine?

There was a roar as parts of the bridge and train hit the water. Phoebe's back jolted and she felt a stab of pain. She was alarmed by the screams from people in the other carriages but clutched Douglas's arms, too frightened to make a sound.

The light in their compartment spluttered and died, and her eyes adjusted to the darkness. She could hear rushing water.

"We're in the river," she gasped. Fear gripped her. "We're going to sink. Oh, God, we're going to drown!"

Douglas's face was almost touching hers. "No. No, we're not," he said, his voice firm and gruff. "We're going to survive this. I promise."

The carriage lurched to the left and water began to seep around the carriage door. Looking out of the opposite door, Phoebe could see a mass of twisted metal girders emerging from the black, flowing river. She jammed her feet against the opposite bench to stop herself slipping toward the deepening water in the carriage and grasped her leather bag with one arm. Douglas reached up and grabbed the bars holding the netting above the seats. Every minute, the water got deeper.

"We... we need to get out and climb on top of the carriage," he said.

"Wouldn't we be safer in here?" Outside was wind and rain and rushing water that terrified her.

He shook his head. "The carriage will float."

"For how long?" Her voice was little more than a squeak.

"I dinnae ken. But help will be on its way."

Phoebe screamed as the carriage lurched and the water poured in more quickly.

Douglas took her face in his hands and spoke firmly. "We have to take action so we survive until help gets here."

The benches were at an angle now. Douglas climbed onto the

padded seat and stepped over her, then up and across, so he could push at the carriage door, taking all his strength to force it open. He gripped the frame and pulled himself out, then lay down so he could reach back in for her.

Phoebe shoved the blankets away, braced her boots against the armrests and pushed forward. She tossed her overnight bag up to where Douglas was leaning in. He pushed it behind him onto the carriage roof. She reached up one hand which Douglas grabbed and she used the other to pull up to the door frame, the muscles of her arms aching with her weight. As she got closer to him, Douglas's free arm reached around her waist, pulling her through the gap and into the freezing air.

They climbed onto the sloping top of the carriage, and wedged their feet against a vent on the roof, to stop themselves slipping over the edge.

The wind whipped salty splashes from the Tay into her face. Again, she heard yells and cries, but in the darkness could see no other passengers escaping their compartments.

"Has anyone else has climbed out?" Phoebe shouted above the wind.

"Doesn't look like it." Douglas looked around to check she was secure. "I must see if anyone needs help. You hold tight to this vent. Do not let go."

He edged his way on his hands and knees along the roof to see if he could reach other carriages. Phoebe gripped the vent and watched, praying he wouldn't fall. The train hadn't been carrying many passengers, as it was the Sunday before Hogmanay, and she thought they were the only ones in first class.

The carriage lunged downward once more. Phoebe's leather bag slid away from her and she sprang to grab it, but it slipped over the edge. She grasped the vent more tightly, and looking up almost cried with relief to see Douglas edging back toward her.

"It's the engine," Douglas shouted above the noise as he reached her and wrapped one arm around her, holding the vent with his other hand. "It's so heavy, it's pulling the rest of the train down with it."

Phoebe was shivering with terror. "What are we going to do?"

Douglas looked around. "The piers. The things that were supporting the bridge."

Despite the darkness, Phoebe could see huge stone and iron structures rising out of the river, lapped by waves.

"If we could get to the closest one, we can stay there until rescue."

"But how will we get there?" Phoebe asked, trying to keep a sob from her voice.

"We get as close as we can on the iron bridge remains. Then I'll take you across the water."

It looked a foolhardy plan. Surely they were better staying where they were?

Phoebe screamed as again the carriage slipped closer to the rushing river.

"No time to lose," Douglas said, holding her tighter and meeting her terrified gaze.

She had to trust him. "You lead. I'll be right behind."

He climbed the wide gap between the carriage roof and the nearest girder, where he stood and turned to help her cross. The girder was a few feet wide and the raised rivets made it more secure underfoot than the smooth carriage roof. She reached out to the crossgirders for balance, her gloves sodden and the metal freezing to the touch.

They inched forward to the pier, stepping from one tangled piece of metal strut to the next. As they came close, Phoebe could see the whole upright structure had been wrenched from the pillars supporting the bridge from the water. It was like the trunk of a tree had been ripped in half, leaving only the stump behind.

"There's a ladder," Douglas called. "We can climb that, then rest on the top."

But between the iron girder and the ladder up the pier was the flowing Tay river.

She shook her head. "I can't swim."

Douglas took her shoulders and faced her. "I promised you we'd survive this."

Phoebe swallowed, nearly in tears with fear. She followed him along the girder, a little distance beyond the pier. She could see what Douglas was thinking: the tide would pull them down to the pier, rather than swimming across to it.

He lowered himself into the water and grasped the edge of the girder. "You have to climb in," he shouted. "I'll hold you."

She sat on the iron and was about to move when something swept by. At first, she thought it was a piece of luggage or something wrapped in dark canvas. With horror, she saw it was a body, face down and lifeless, being swept away by the current.

She couldn't do it, she couldn't. But Douglas was already in the water. She looked at his determined features, his strong shoulders above the water. He was her only hope: she had to trust him with her life.

With an anguished cry, she slid into the icy water, into his arms. Her body was in the river, up to her shoulders, and the cold took her breath away. It was like being stabbed, everywhere at once.

"I'll need you on my back so I can swim. You have to hold on to me."

Phoebe nodded, although she was shaking so severely, she hoped he could tell.

He maneuvered himself round until she was tight against his back, both arms round his neck, trying not to strangle him in her panic.

Douglas pushed off hard into the flowing water and took the few strokes to propel them across the gap. They were swept toward the ladder. Douglas reached out. Dear God, if he missed it, they would be away downriver and out to sea, just like that body she had seen.

She saw his fist close around the lowest rung, then the other hand grabbed it and he pulled them both close to the ladder.

"You must go first," he yelled.

Somehow she found the courage to loosen her grip on his shoulders and reach up to take hold of the ladder. It was like holding a block of ice. He moved her around in front of him, holding onto the side of the ladder.

"Feel there," he said. "With your feet, where the ladder is below the water."

It was true. She put her foot against the rung.

"Now. Step by step. I'll be right behind you."

She part pushed, part pulled, so her shoulders were out of the water. Then the next step. Her waist, her skirt. As she rose from the river, her waterlogged dress felt like it was made of lead, pulling her back down.

She *had* to do this. She glanced up. There seemed such a distance to go. She gritted her teeth and heaved herself up, then she reached up to the next iron bar, waited until her foot was secure and pushed again. Slowly, slowly she made her way up the pier.

At the top, she pulled herself onto what remained of the structure that had once supported part of the bridge, panting from exhaustion. It was wet from the rain, but was flat, and there was no danger of it sinking below the waves. She crouched on her hands and knees, sobbing with relief, praying Douglas was close behind.

She looked back at the immense tangle of wreckage. There was another roaring sound as the engine and its tender holding all the coal sank further underwater. Phoebe watched in horror as the carriage they had been sitting in minutes before plunged beneath the waves, parts of the metal trusses of the bridge folding in on top of it. The other carriages were nowhere to be seen as the whole train sank into the black water.

She took a deep breath. She had not heard any screams or shouts from the other passengers for some time.

No one else had emerged alive.

· · ·

Douglas dragged his foot to the final step of the ladder and hauled himself onto what was left of the wide pillar that had once proudly held up the new railway bridge. The vertical metal struts had sheared away like broken branches on a tree after a storm.

He lay on his back, his chest heaving as he got his breath back. Every muscle in his body screamed in pain.

Pulling himself to sitting, he turned toward Phoebe. In the half-light, her skin was white, her eyes wide circles. Her chin was quivering from cold and fear. She reached for him and he took her hands, shuffling close and pulling her shuddering body to him. He had promised they would survive, but the truth was their ordeal was nowhere near over. The wind was blowing fiercely, and if they were not rescued soon, they would die of cold.

FORTY

Douglas held Phoebe close, putting his back against the wind and trying to give her some shelter. She curled into his chest and he could hear her teeth chattering.

"We'll be rescued soon," he murmured. "Someone will come."

She said nothing in reply and he wondered if it were true.

Sitting in the cold and dark, knowing death was near, he feared it was meaningless. His life had been meaningless. He had been a poor son, ignoring the wishes of his parents, and a disastrous husband. Were it not for his arrogance and mistakes, Joan would be alive. A lifetime of service as a doctor would not atone for his hubris. How much of his career was vanity? He had deluded himself that each life saved would go into the balance against all the ill he had done.

He pulled Phoebe nearer and stroked her hair. Holding her tight, he knew her life meant more to him than his own. She was a force for good in the world, whereas he only caused damage. He scrunched his eyes to hold back tears of regret. It was his fault she was here. If he hadn't given in to that impulse and invited her to his home... Now there was every chance she would not survive.

The very thought caused a pain worse than the cold seeping

into his bones. This strong, brave woman with a vision of the future, a *better* future. Despite suffering terrible abuse by her fiancé, she had held on to that belief. He found himself silently praying in his head, trying to bargain with God. *Take me. Take me, but leave her. Please, God, leave her.*

A light caught his attention and snapped him out of his thoughts. It flashed and disappeared, only to return a moment later. It had to be the running light on a boat, dipping behind the waves, but coming closer. A boat! Someone had seen what had happened. Someone was brave enough to launch into the River Tay on this godforsaken night.

The light came closer and he could hear the rumble and chug of a steam engine. He remembered that many of the local fishing boats now had an engine as well as sails.

He made sure Phoebe was safe before standing and waving his arms. He yelled until his throat was hoarse.

Phoebe struggled to her feet and joined him, screaming at the boat.

A fisherman near the bow gestured to them and hurried back to the enginehouse.

"They've seen us!" Douglas cried.

The boat changed direction, coming toward the pier.

Douglas gestured to the metal ladder and the skipper seemed to understand, guiding the vessel nearer.

"Dear God, it can't come too close," Phoebe said. "The boat will be smashed."

Douglas pointed to the fisherman at the bow. "He'll throw us a rope."

Douglas scrambled down a few steps of the ladder and reached out. The fisherman threw the rope and Douglas caught it. He climbed back up to Phoebe.

"These men have been handling boats, man and boy. They'll bring it near." He looped the rope around her waist and secured the knot. "This will keep you safe, no matter what."

Her breathing was ragged, but she gave a small nod. His heart clenched in awe of her determination to overcome her fears.

She climbed back down the steps, her voluminous skirt making it difficult to see where the rungs were. The edge of the boat was close, two men reaching out their arms. She hesitated, shaking her head back and forth, clutching the metal bar in her fist.

"You have to trust them," Douglas yelled. "Jump!"

She glanced up and locked her eyes on him, before turning and leaping to the boat. One man caught her arm, then the other fisherman leaned out and hauled her over the gunwale. They untied the rope and tossed it to Douglas. He tried to work quickly, though he could no longer fully feel his hands, knowing every minute in this cold would bring death closer.

He leaped to the safety of the fishing boat.

"Are there others?" the fisherman asked, his accent thick Dundonian.

Douglas shook his head. "I havenae seen anyone else. Not for a while. Not living, anyway." He didn't want to think of the body of a woman he had seen trapped within a carriage, or the man swept away downstream.

The skipper nodded. "We need to get you to the harbor." He adjusted the engine and the rudder until the boat swept round, pointing its bow toward Dundee. A sailor pulled a blanket around Phoebe and found a tarpaulin for Douglas. It didn't keep him warm, but it stopped him getting any colder. His body shook with shivering, just as Phoebe's had.

The river was choppy as they made their way to the Dundee harbor. The fender pushed against the stone pier extending into the estuary and a wall rose high above them.

"Just one more ladder," he said softly to Phoebe. "Then we'll be safe."

A crew member went first, securing the boat at a bollard. Then Phoebe, climbing slowly. Her dress was sodden and heavy with water and he could hear her labored breathing.

He followed and finally was on firm land. But every fisherman in Dundee knew the risk of being soaked through in this icy water, with a biting wind. He had to get her to the warmth and safety of the McLennan family home as fast as he could.

The skipper had flagged down a carriage, begging for help. Douglas sat in the back, pulling Phoebe close. He had struggled to give the name of his home clearly, but now the kindly driver was urging his horse through the dark streets of Dundee, and out to Taybrae Hall, the McLennan residence on the edge of the city.

Phoebe's shivering had become more severe and he felt his own body shake uncontrollably. Her eyes were fixed on something he could not see and he was concerned she had not spoken for a long time.

The carriage sped through the two stone columns at the entrance to the Hall and the wheels crunched on the gravel. The driver pulled the horse to a halt and leaped down from his bench to bang on the old oak door, sheltered by a porch of two pillars. Douglas helped Phoebe climb out of the carriage. She could barely stand, but he was too weak to carry her.

The door of the Hall creaked open. The butler he had known as a boy stood there, looking none too pleased to have been summoned so late in the evening.

"Paterson!" Douglas shouted. "I need help."

The old man lifted his oil lamp to peer out, "Dr. McLennan? We expected you some hours back. Assumed you'd decided against traveling on a Sunday."

The coachman took part of Phoebe's weight and the three of them stepped to the door. They struggled past Paterson and into the candlelit hallway of the ancient building; Douglas's father had resisted installing gas light.

The space filled with people and voices. His mind was sluggish and he was having difficulty making sense of the sounds.

"Douglas—"

"What on earth?—"

"Son, what's happened?—"

His father was there, looking severe, his gray eyebrows lowered, and his mother with softer concern, wringing her hands.

Isla ran down the ornate wooden staircase. Thank goodness. He could trust her to look after Phoebe.

"Isla," he gasped, "this is Miss Van Bergen."

"Miss—"

"She's—Ocht, it doesnae matter. I can explain later."

Isla came close. "Dear God, you're both wet through and freezing."

"You need to do as I say. Take her to the warmest room in the house. Remove every stitch of wet clothes, wrap her in warm blankets, and lie her down."

Isla glanced at her mother. "The parlor is warmest."

"Fast," said Douglas. "Quick as you can."

Isla put Phoebe's left arm over her shoulder and threaded her right arm round her back. The housekeeper took the other side, all but carrying Phoebe away.

"A hot bath?" asked the housekeeper, over her shoulder. "Would that help?"

"Get the servants to start warming water. But not too hot. And make sure Miss Van Bergen has begun to warm before you put her in."

The door closed behind them.

His mother stepped forward. "Dear boy, you are in as much need."

Douglas knew it was true. He had spent enough time as a youth swimming in the freezing rivers and lochs to know he was in danger of collapse.

"I had already warmed your room in readiness for your arrival."

He nodded and began to climb the staircase. He stumbled.

Paterson was at his side. "Steady as you go, young Douglas. I'm with you."

His room was deliciously familiar, and warmer than he remembered from childhood. He pulled at his overcoat, but his fingers couldn't feel the buttons. Paterson undid them, then removed every garment until they lay in a sodden heap.

"Take these away," Paterson told a manservant, "before we have half the Tay soaking into the floor."

Douglas was vaguely aware of busyness around him: a servant banking up the fire with coal, a thin blanket wrapped close around him, and then a larger, coarser one dropped over his shoulders. Someone helped him to a chair close to the fire and Paterson rubbed his hair with a cloth. His shivering began to subside.

The whole house was in uproar. He could hear voices, wooden floors creaking, footsteps on stone in the hall. He recognized the creak of the front door being opened, and heard the hubbub of more voices.

His father was by his side. "I've brought a wee dram of whiskey. It might be the Sabbath, but I'm making an exception. This will warm you from the inside, laddie."

He took the glass gratefully.

"The bridge," his father said, looking at Douglas gravely. "We've just had news. The bridge has collapsed."

Douglas closed his eyes. "Aye, and a whole train with it."

Mr. McLennan sank into the armchair opposite. "How can that be? They've only just built it. How did you survive?"

Douglas pushed his fingers through his wet hair and Paterson gave him a dry cloth. He sighed, not wanting to think about the terrifying experiences of the night. He had expected to die. Feared Phoebe would die. It was too heavy for him to contemplate. All he wanted was sleep and rest.

He pushed himself up from the chair but was unsteady on his feet.

"Son, sit longer."

"Bed. I need my bed."

Paterson helped him across the room, pulled back the blankets and sheet, then slid out the warming pan. Thanking God one of the servants had warmed his bed, he prayed someone had done the same for Phoebe. Surely Isla could be relied upon—

Paterson pulled the sheet over him, then blankets and a quilt. The heaviness was a comfort.

"I'll keep the fire lit," he heard Paterson mutter, before he slipped into sleep.

FORTY-ONE

Phoebe half opened her eyes and panicked, taking quick breaths: she was on her back and a heavy weight held her in place so she couldn't move. Was it a girder? The weight of water? She moved her head back and forth, trying to release her arms.

"There, there, lassie." It was a woman's voice. "Dinnae fash. You're safe."

Phoebe opened her eyes fully, taking in the shadowy room, realizing she was tucked tightly in bed, but goodness knew where.

"I can't... I can't." There were no words to express what she wanted, she felt so exhausted.

"I'll move this," said the woman. "Maybe I overdid the furs and blankets."

Some of the weight lifted as an enormous fur coat was pulled off, but Phoebe was still pinned to the mattress.

The woman opened a drape and light seeped into the room. She came close and loosened the remaining blankets, before sitting on the edge of the bed.

"I'm Isla McLennan. You're safe in our home."

Phoebe could see echoes of Douglas's features in her face: the same green eyes and fair hair, although the woman's tended to auburn, rather than Douglas's gold. Relief began to warm her from inside.

"What time is it?"

"It's midday. Can I get you something to eat?"

Phoebe's throat was dry. "A drink, please."

"How about some milk?"

Milk? That wasn't what she had in mind, but she shrugged her acceptance.

Isla whispered to someone outside the door, before returning and tending to the fire. "My brother said you were American. I love that accent."

A memory floated through her mind of Douglas saying he liked her accent and being distracted when she whispered his name when playing cards.

"I'll put some more logs on; keep this room toasty," Isla said. "I was worried for you last night. Thought you'd never warm through."

Last night. The memories began to intrude: the sensation of falling, the cold. Yes, biting cold. This house...

She looked round the room more carefully. Wood paneling on the walls, leaded windows divided by a mullion of carved stone, the smell of woodsmoke. The mattress was wide but high and lumpy.

"You're in one of our guest rooms," said Isla.

Phoebe levered herself upright and Isla helped. "In Dr. McLennan's castle."

Isla laughed. "Did he tell you it was a castle?"

"No. He was at pains to insist it wasn't a castle. But it was fun teasing him."

Isla adjusted the pillows behind. "Not many people are inclined to tease Dougie."

"I'm sorry, I didn't mean any disrespect—"

"Nae, it's exactly what he needs. Can be rather too full of himself," she added with a wink.

Phoebe ran her hand over the complex weave of the top blanket. *Rather too full of himself.* This was the man who had saved her life. Without him, she would undoubtedly be trapped in that sunken train, like all those other poor passengers. He might have infuriated her when they first met—but now? She couldn't think too highly of Douglas.

Phoebe heard a knock at the door. Isla stepped aside as Douglas entered, holding a tray.

"I met Mary on the stair," he said, "and took the liberty of taking this tray from her. I hope you don't mind."

He paused, seeming uncertain, looking nothing like the smart doctor she had known in Boston. His hair was disheveled, he had stubble across his chin. He was wearing a dark, woolen shirt tucked into tweed pants.

"I don't mind at all," she replied.

Their eyes met and she could barely breathe. Last night, he had promised she would live. And he had kept his word. Her chin trembled as she realized she couldn't remember a man ever keeping a promise to her before. Douglas meant *everything* to her, and she fought the impulse to leap from the bed, to beg him to hold her tight, as he had on the bridge pier.

Isla was by the door and Phoebe felt her cheeks redden in her presence, fearing her longing would be visible to anyone watching. She pulled the blanket up to below her armpits.

Isla cleared her throat. "I'm, er, I'm going to check how the laundress is getting on with your clothes."

The door closed softly behind her.

Douglas put the tray on an ancient chest of drawers by the door. "You asked for milk?"

"Isla suggested it."

Douglas poured some from the jug into an earthenware cup. "Sounds like an Isla suggestion." He brought it to her.

His sister was right: it was exactly what she needed—slightly sweet, thick yet refreshing. She gulped it down.

"More?" Douglas asked, taking the cup. "There are oatcakes too."

"Oatcakes?"

He brought a plate of beige crackers.

"Cookies?"

He smiled. "Not quite. They're savory."

She bit one and found she was ravenous.

Douglas sat on the ladder-back chair in the shadows by the window and watched her.

"Why don't you come where I can see you properly?" She tentatively patted the bed, wondering how he would respond.

He slowly rose and settled where Isla had sat just minutes before, facing her. She could see lines around his eyes.

She had clung to him last night, her life dependent on his strength. Now they sat at a tentative distance.

"I'm so sorry, Phoebe." His voice was soft and his eyes remained on her hand.

"*You're* sorry?"

"I put you in that situation. If I hadn't invited you here—"

"Pfft! Don't be absurd. Are you suggesting you had some fore-knowledge that the bridge would fail?" She folded her arms. "I've noticed men with medical training tend to believe they are omniscient. *I* made the decision to come here for Hogmanay. What happened was pure chance."

He gazed at her, a smile curling one side of his lips. "I like it when you get angry. Shows spirit."

She reached for his hand and threaded her fingers through his, noticing the hairs on the back of his hand were fair.

He let out a long, slow breath and stroked her hand with his thumb. "Father says there are mutterings about the accident being a punishment from God. A lot of folk believe it's wicked to travel by train on a Sunday."

Phoebe wondered what the pious people would say if they knew she had been traveling unchaperoned with Douglas. Maybe they'd think that was reason enough for Divine retribution.

"Do *you* believe that?" she asked.

"Ocht, no. I don't believe in a cruel God. I mean, why would

God send all those men and women to their deaths, and only save us?"

She thought about his words. "It was *you* who saved us."

He shook his head and his eyes slipped beyond her to a tapestry on the wall.

She thought he seemed embarrassed. "You got us out of the carriage. You got us onto that pier."

"I didn't send for the boat—"

"You gave me faith we would be rescued," she whispered. "And that's what I needed. Otherwise, I might have thrown myself into the freezing water."

In a swift movement, he lifted her hand to his lips and kissed her palm, breathing deeply.

Leaning forward so she could place her other hand on his face, she ran her fingers over the rough stubble on his jaw. She placed her palm behind his neck and pulled him to her. Nothing else mattered but to feel his arms around her as she had last night, to feel safe and protected. She yearned to kiss him, to let her lips convey the passion she felt.

She closed her eyes and placed her lips on his in a strangely chaste gesture. His lips were rough and warm. He barely responded. Then she heard a sigh that seemed to come from deep inside him.

He dropped her hand and wrapped each arm around her, moving closer on the bed. The slowness of the kiss changed, becoming more intense. A fizzing began in her stomach and ran all the way to her toes and back. One of his hands massaged her spine, moving over the thick cotton nightgown Isla had dressed her in last night.

She sank back onto the pillow and his body came with her, his lips not leaving hers. He moved until he was lying full length alongside her, the blankets forming a barrier from her breasts downwards.

He paused, so she opened her eyes and found him looking intently at her face, his pupils dark and the golden flecks lighting his green eyes in a way she'd not seen before. He was breathing quickly, about to say something, but gave a single shake of the head and lowered his mouth to kiss her forehead, her nose, each cheek. Her body tingled and she closed her eyes, consumed by emotion. He pushed his nose to her neck, just below her ear and let out a low grumbling sound which vibrated through her.

"You have the most captivating neck," he whispered, placing light kisses down it.

She wanted to laugh. Of all the parts of her body...

He pushed the white fabric to one side. "And this is the suprasternal notch. Did you know that?"

She could hear teasing in his voice. "No, doctor. Women aren't allowed in anatomy lessons."

He grinned up at her. "Sometimes called the Plender Gap." He placed a kiss in the notch between her collarbones. "It's a shame yours is so often covered, when it's so beautiful. And the clavicle..." He kissed along her collarbone to her shoulder before looking at her face again. No one had ever looked at her like this before—a mix of desire and tenderness—and it kindled a warmth deep inside.

"The philtrum." He ran his thumb over the groove above her top lip. "And you have a most beautiful mouth. I've been fascinated by it since we first met."

She covered her lip with her fingers, aware of what she had always thought was a defect. "That's from a childhood accident."

Douglas removed her hand from her face, leaned forward, and placed his mouth over hers once more. She threaded her fingers through this hair, feeling the knots and salty thickness from being in the Tay River. She moaned and longed for the anatomy lesson to go further.

His left hand slipped below the blanket and his palm enveloped her breast, as he kissed her with a deep passion which made every nerve ending ripple. She moved her fingertips down his neck to his shoulders, feeling the muscles which had moved so powerfully through the river last night. She felt the weight of his leg over her hips as their bodies pressed to each other.

He groaned again and pulled his mouth from hers, then rolled onto his back, one arm bent behind his head, as the hand closest felt for hers. They lay side by side, each breathing heavily. She wished she were not protected by the blanket, wished she could entwine her legs in his.

"This is not a good idea," he whispered.

"No," she replied softly.

"I mean... nothing can come of it."

"I know. Nothing." Her words felt hollow.

"I don't want to... well..." His voice faded away.

She let go of his hand and scrunched her eyes so he would not know tears were threatening.

He moved to the side of the bed and sat, elbows resting on his wide thighs and his head in his hands. He took a deep breath before standing, his back still to her.

She had to find a way to release him. "It's fine, Douglas. You don't have to say anything. I understand. We both got caught up by the emotion, after what we went through last night."

He let out a sigh. "You are kinder than I deserve," he said, his voice gravelly and thick as he strode from the room, closing the door behind him.

Phoebe clutched her hands into fists and pressed them to her eyes, her breath coming swift and shallow. Thank goodness he was not here to see how painful his rejection was. She mouthed his words, trying to accept them. *Nothing can come of this.* He couldn't be clearer.

It was a disaster: she had fallen for him. This man who had once exasperated her, who had been reserved to the point of rudeness—he was now all she wanted in the world.

Phoebe knew this wasn't some temporary reaction to the danger they had come through together. She had told him that because she couldn't bear to hear him reject her further. The kiss had been extraordinary, but she knew deep down she had desired him for a long time. Perhaps her feelings had begun to melt when he had laughed as he tried to learn to dance at the ball. Crossing the Atlantic together she got to know the real Douglas and feel a closeness never experienced with a man before, even if she tried desperately to pretend it was just friendship.

But between those two fixed points—the ball and the ocean crossing—was the experience that would define her life: the devastating consequences of succumbing to Hector.

I don't want to... Douglas's voice rang in her ears. Of course he wouldn't want Hector's cast-offs. Being wealthy did not erase moral failure in the eyes of an upright man like Douglas.

Her heart broke at the irony: the only man she had ever loved was also the only man in the world who knew she was a fallen woman. She could not hide her past from him. And so they could have no future either.

FORTY-TWO

Douglas hurried from the bedroom. *Bloody fool. Bloody, bloody fool!* What was he thinking? That was the problem: he *wasn't* thinking. All good sense abandoned him when he came close to her; his brain froze and his passion took over. Well, he would not let it happen again. He would apologize. Profusely. Just as soon as—

He was at the door of his father's study. Mr. McLennan had not asked questions last night, but that could not last. Douglas knocked and waited until he heard his father giving permission to enter.

"Son." Mr. McLennan sat at his desk with neat piles of ledgers.

"Sir."

Everything about this room reminded him of his boyhood: his father always working, the smell of pipe smoke and candlewax, the tap of his own feet on the flagstone floor.

"Sit." His father nodded to a chair in front of the desk, put down his pen and folded his hands.

Douglas swallowed. "I've come to ask a favor."

His father raised an eyebrow but stayed silent.

"News will soon travel of the disaster last night. We will have newspapermen coming to sniff out a story."

"We already have," his father replied. "A journalist from *The Courier* came knocking this morning."

Douglas froze, fearful he had left this too late.

"I sent him away, making it clear the McLennan household had nothing to say."

"Thank God. We need to keep Miss Van Bergen's name out of the papers." He shifted in his seat, uncomfortable under his father's stare. "The newspapers must say there were no survivors."

"And how do you propose we make them do that?"

"Your influence. You are good friends with the proprietor. You have considerable influence in this city."

Mr. McLennan waved a hand. "And the fishing boat that rescued you? The coachman who brought you here last night?"

"I will go to the harbor now and seek them out. Beg them not to say anything."

Mr. McLennan snorted.

Douglas ran his hand over his face. "And, in all likelihood, offer money. I have savings, but I hope you might assist. I will pay you back in time."

His father unlocked his fingers and leaned forward. "So, you would have me use my influence to see an untruth published. And then throw money around so the lie sticks? And for what? To keep your mistress's name out of the papers?"

Douglas felt a heat in his cheeks as if he'd been slapped. "She's not my mistress."

"What is she then?"

"She's..." He struggled to find the right word. "She's my friend and I want to protect her."

Mr. McLennan shook his head. "Is there a Mr. Van Bergen who'll be on the warpath? Who is this husband you want me to help you deceive?"

"There is no husband. She is unmarried, I assure you. But, well, her family is well-known in America."

Mr. McLennan put his head to one side. "Son, are you engaged to her?"

Douglas sat back. "No, sir. You know I've sworn never to take another wife."

"Ocht! That foolish promise of yours. I hoped for a moment you had come to your senses."

"You'd have me break a vow?"

"Aye, when the vow made no sense in the first place," his father snapped back.

Douglas took a long breath. This wasn't what he wanted to discuss.

"So, this Miss Van Bergen," his father continued. "She's an unmarried woman prepared to travel in an enclosed carriage with an unmarried man."

"I'm a widower."

"It is unseemly, no matter what."

"She has been traveling with a companion. It's pure chance her companion was too ill to make the journey." Douglas could sense his father's disdain and knew he was losing the argument. "Please, sir. I beg of you. How many times have I asked a favor of you?"

"Maybe if you had asked for my help in the past, things wouldn't have ended as they did."

Douglas rubbed at his temples, knowing his father was referring to his student days. Was he never going to escape those memories? "I admit I was young. I was headstrong."

"Stupid—"

"Aye, stupid." Douglas looked directly at his father once more. "What I care about is *now*. Please, for the sake of an honorable young woman. Miss Van Bergen has done so much good in the world. She is the most generous person I have ever known, dedicating her life to the wellbeing of others. She has plans which could truly help so many lives. It would be... a better world if her name were not forever connected with the Tay Bridge. Protected from exactly the assumptions you have made."

Mr. McLennan clicked his tongue and rubbed his beard with his hand. "Do you have feelings for her?"

"Feelings?"

"Don't be obtuse, Douglas. Do you have feelings for this woman?"

Douglas didn't know what to say. He couldn't tell his father the truth: that he had suspected for some time, and known for certain last night, that he adored Phoebe. He couldn't say that the only sound he wanted to hear was her throaty, Boston laugh; that the only thing he wanted to see was her beautiful face. He couldn't tell his father that he longed to take Phoebe to bed, to touch every part of her, to feel her soft skin, untangle her hair.

Douglas ran a finger around the collar of his shirt and cleared his throat. "As you know, it is irrelevant whether I have feelings for her. I will never marry again."

His father leaned back and spread his fingers on the desk, looking at his son with piercing eyes. "You are just as foolish as when you were young. Just as obstinate." He sighed deeply. "I'll see what I can do. It's not as if I want the McLennan name in the papers, either."

He got up, took a key from his vest pocket, and opened a wooden box on the dresser, pulling out some notes. "You'd better go in search of the fishing-boat crew as quick as you can. This should be enough to keep them quiet."

Douglas stood and his father handed over the money. He felt able to breathe again. "Thank you, sir."

His father grunted and waved his hand to dismiss him. Douglas couldn't get out of the study too quickly.

Phoebe stayed in bed for the rest of the day and the following one. She was exhausted, and dreading seeing Douglas again. She wasn't ready for the humiliation just yet.

The third day, however, she sensed excitement in the air when she woke. The maid hummed as she set down her tray of porridge and steaming tea.

Isla soon followed, carrying a pile of clothing. "I'm thinking you'll be wanting to rise today."

Phoebe's cheeks heated as it was clear she was being a poor guest, hiding away in her room.

"Sure, Isla. I've been lain in this room long enough."

"It would be a shame for you to miss Hogmanay this evening. The public festivities have been canceled in respect for the disaster. But Father has agreed to a quiet celebration here as he says the McLennans have things to be thankful for."

"The survival of his son."

"Indeed."

Thoughts of a similar vein had swirled round Phoebe's mind over the previous day. So many had died. Why should there be just two survivors? And why would she be one of them?

"I have brought you a dress and undergarments. They are mine but should come near to fitting you. Your frock has been ruined, I'm afraid. The laundress did what she could, but there was tar or oil on it. And rips around the bodice. Your smalls weren't much better."

"Smalls?"

Isla nodded to the linen undergarments. "Such a beautiful dress as well. Fine fabric. I'm afraid my frock is rather old and dowdy in comparison."

"I am grateful for your generosity."

"My lady's maid will help you dress."

Phoebe pushed her legs out from under the warm covers and placed her feet on the wooden floor. Isla left and the maid was with her in minutes.

The shift was of thicker wool than she was used to, but everything was good quality. The maid helped with old-fashioned stays. Isla was right: they were of a similar size. The dress was of a dark tweed and Phoebe smiled at the tartan trimmings. The shape was some years out-of-date and Phoebe quite enjoyed the more relaxed outline and lack of a bustle over her derrière.

Phoebe sat at the dressing table and the maid brushed her hair. She could not hold back a sob as it struck her: she had nothing. All her personal items had been lost in the disaster. Not just her clothing, but her hairbrushes, her jewelry, her favorite pots of face cream. There was the unique perfume she had made up by a perfumer in Boston—it was a mixture of vanilla and chocolate and came in the prettiest glass vial with a pale blue puff-atomizer.

Her private journal was gone, where she had carefully recorded her thoughts each evening of the trip. There was the book of poetry she had been reading and marking up favorite passages.

Her sobs came thicker as she remembered the necklace her mother had worn, a silver pen her father had given on her eighteenth birthday. All lost. All gone forever.

She leaned her head on the dresser, her brow on the back of her hands, and cried. The maid hurried from the room.

Isla was back at her side, a hand rubbing in circles between her shoulder blades, making clucking sounds.

"It's gone," gasped Phoebe. "Everything's gone."

Isla crouched and held her close until the sobs subsided, then whispered, "It can be replaced."

Phoebe shook her head. "Not my journal. Not the gift from my father."

"Ocht," Isla said, and stroked her arm. "'Tis true. But you have your memories. And you are here. It seems to me, that is something of a miracle."

Once she had recovered and was properly dressed, Phoebe took up Isla's suggestion that fresh air would do her good.

"Why don't we take a turn around the garden?" Isla proposed.

Isla made sure Phoebe was protected against the elements, with a fur coat and a shawl over a fur hat. The gloves were too large, but the boots fitted well.

Phoebe made her way through the McLennan house, along dark corridors, down the wide staircase into the huge hall that formed the heart of the home. She stood open-mouthed as she studied the deer heads mounted above the doors, the arrangement of swords above the fireplace, which was tall enough to stand in.

Isla caught her staring. "A lot of that is very old," she said. "Brought with us when Father moved down from the Highlands."

Outside, the air was sharp and a dusting of snow crunched under her boots. Phoebe stopped to look back at the house. Douglas had insisted it was not a castle, but he would not be able to deny there were castle-like elements: the stepped stonework at the gables, the little turrets topped with a cone of gray slate.

"Douglas—Dr. McLennan—he implied he came from much more modest origins."

"I only know him as Dougie, so you can use Douglas with me. And he likes to play this down." Isla waved her hand at the building. "'*A classic of the Scots Baronial style.*' That's how an expert described it, anyway. The house is not old, though. Only, what, thirty years? My father had it built as the business began to grow."

"Ah, yes. Textiles. I remember."

"Aye. We have a number of factories in the city."

"Will Douglas inherit all this?" Phoebe had not thought of him living in this grand style. She dropped her eyes to the path. "Not that it's any of my business, of course."

"Our cousin works with our father in running the factories and I daresay will take over when Father can no longer do so. It would seem fair that the cousin takes this also."

They continued around the large garden overlooking the river before returning to the house. Isla was a good conversationalist, but Phoebe could not shift her embarrassment that Isla might suspect her of investigating her brother's worth and prospects, when nothing could be further from the truth.

FORTY-THREE

There was a gentle knock at Phoebe's bedroom door.

Isla entered. "Ready?"

"I am."

Isla led the way along the corridor. "I should explain that the understanding in the city is that there were no survivors of the disaster. No one knows you were there. I hope that is acceptable. Dougie seemed very keen your name should be kept out of the papers."

Phoebe felt a wave of gratitude toward Douglas. It was typical of his quiet way of looking after people. She would not have to spend her future explaining her presence on the train with the doctor and enduring disparaging looks.

Pausing at the top of the stairs, she looked at the hall decorated with fir branches and ivy, a fire burning fiercely in the inglenook. There were perhaps twenty people stood in groups, most of whom turned to look up at her, and she had the sense they had been waiting.

She followed Isla down the stairs to a trio near the fire.

"You may remember my father and mother from when you got here?"

"Thank you for your hospitality," said Phoebe with a swift

curtsey. In truth, her memories of her arrival at Taybrae Hall were hazy.

"Miss Van Bergen," said Mr. McLennan. His accent was stronger than his son's.

"It's good to meet you properly," said Mrs. McLennan. "This is my sister, Mrs. Ross. My children live with her, when they are in Edinburgh."

Douglas strode over and Phoebe tried hard not to stare. Although all the men were in Highland dress, he looked particularly magnificent with his kilt, jacket, and sporran. He was cleanly shaved and his hair was brushed back. Phoebe felt her cheeks redden: they had not encountered each other since their passionate kiss and she was not sure how to behave around him. He had made it clear the moment had been a dreadful mistake. She felt even more humiliated realizing she would like nothing more than to be firmly in his arms again.

He brought a couple with him, who he introduced as cousin Archie and his wife, all the while managing somehow to avoid looking at her.

Isla took control of the explanations. "Miss Van Bergen is staying with us. She has been in Edinburgh for a visit. She's an American."

"An American!" said the cousin. "That is a long way to have traveled."

Douglas leaned a forearm on the mantelpiece, his eyes steadily on the fire, clearly reluctant to speak. It was the frustrating pattern of their relationship: easy warmth followed by awkward distance.

Phoebe turned at the sound of nasal droning and a door opened to reveal a piper, also in Highland dress. Three pipes were angled over the man's shoulder and his fingers ran over a flute-like pipe extending downward. The man led the way to double doors the other side of the hall, the tartan cloth swaying.

Phoebe swallowed hard as Douglas finally came to her side so they could join the guests following the piper into the dining room, where a long table was set for supper.

"I've sent a telegram to Mrs. Hale," he whispered close to her ear. "To let her know we are both well."

Phoebe shook her head, ashamed she had not thought of this herself. News of the failure of the bridge would have reached Edinburgh and Adeline would have been fearful they had perished. Thank God Douglas had taken the initiative.

She was seated near Isla and cousin Archie, her back to the fire, with Douglas at the other end of the table. She could hear nothing of his conversation, but, glancing more frequently than was wise, she observed him deep in conversation with his neighbors. At one point, he looked her way and Phoebe gave a brief smile, met with the slightest nod from him.

The experience on the train had left her uncharacteristically tentative. She felt nervous around so many new people and had difficulty understanding what was being said, sometimes not noticing she was being addressed. Isla intervened when needed, translating words she didn't know.

Her appetite was affected too. She forced herself to finish the game soup but had difficulty picking her way through the plateful of strongly spiced haggis, surrounded by potatoes, turnips, and carrots. She worried how many more courses there were, not wanting to look even more ungrateful if she were unable to eat.

The diners took their time between courses. Phoebe knew the festivities would last at least until midnight when they would greet the new decade. Voices grew louder as more wine and ale was drunk. After a desert of trifle and slices of Dundee cake, the old whiskey was brought out. Phoebe wondered if the women would go to a different room, but no, they remained at the table, also drinking the amber liquid. Phoebe took only the slightest drop for form's sake.

A grandfather clock chimed half past ten and the double doors reopened. Mr. and Mrs. McLennan led the way back to the hall, where a small band had set up. Chairs scraped as all the other guests rose and followed them.

"Now for the dancing," said Isla with a wink.

Phoebe sat in an armchair as far from the band as she could manage, and watched. Fortunately, no one asked her to join in.

Four couples took to the floor. Phoebe sat up straighter and blinked as Douglas partnered with his cousin's wife in the set. She knew how much he disliked dancing, but his face revealed nothing: neither pleasure nor discomfort. The dance began: a simple reel involving moves similar to folk dancing the world over. Everyone knew the steps effortlessly and Phoebe smiled to see Douglas was competent, if not enthusiastic.

As the band played the long final note, and the dancers bowed to each other, Douglas made his way to Phoebe. He smiled and she felt like a ray of sunshine had fallen on her. "That's my duty done for the moment. They can't press-gang me into standing up for at least three dances."

"I thought you acquitted yourself splendidly."

"You mean, I didnae tread on anyone's toes."

"As far as I could see. I haven't interrogated your partner, though."

He laughed. "These dances are drilled into us from childhood. Even I learned how to get through them."

She rolled her lips inwards to stifle a laugh as he took the seat beside her. That old feeling of fear and excitement flooded back at having him so close.

"You look very dashing in your kilt, by the way."

"Thank you for the compliment. Father likes to see the traditions maintained at Hogmanay."

"I feel fortunate to be a witness."

Music started again and made conversation impossible. Instead, they sat close and watched the couples. Phoebe steeled herself not to look at him but could not help relishing being near him, breathing in the scent of his familiar cologne. At the end, Isla joined them, flushed with the dance and fanning her face.

"Sister, take my seat," Douglas said, "and may I fetch you both something to drink?"

"Simple water will be enough for me," said Isla.

"The same," said Phoebe. "I've had quite enough alcohol for the evening."

Isla settled in the space Douglas left.

"I didn't expect to see your brother dance," said Phoebe.

Isla tutted. "He knows it's expected of him. He hates it, though. Will only do the simpler dances." She turned to Phoebe with an eyebrow raised. "You know of his aversion?"

"He attended a fundraising ball. In Massachusetts State House."

"Ocht. He must have been there under duress. Sounds like torture for him."

Phoebe laughed gently at the memory. "He knew what duty expected of him in Boston, just as he does here."

Douglas was right that by the fourth dance, he was cajoled into making up a pair again. This time, he danced with his sister and seemed more relaxed. Phoebe watched the affection between the siblings and thought of the different relationships she had with her two brothers. She recalled the uncomfortable New Year's Eves when Thaddeus and Lex were together.

The vigorous dance ended and the band started a gentle waltz in contrast. Mr. and Mrs. McLennan took to the floor first, everyone watching them spin slowly round the space. Mrs. McLennan looked up at her husband's face with a sparkle in her eye. They moved easily together, comfortable and at one, before other couples gradually joined them.

Douglas stared at Phoebe for a moment and then briskly approached her, his hands tucked behind his back.

"I wondered if you'd care to dance?"

"I'm..." Phoebe was amazed and wasn't sure what to say. Part of her *did* want to be moving after all that time hidden in her room. More than that, part of her longed to be close to him. But she hated the feeling he was asking her out of duty.

"It seems a shame for you to be seated all evening." Douglas put out his hand.

"That is kind. But I know there is nothing you would want to avoid more."

He grinned. "Are you afraid I'll trample your feet again? At least let me try to make up for last time?"

Phoebe was unable to resist his charm. She took his hand, and let him lead her to the dance. He put his right hand firmly in the small of her back and extended his left hand, holding hers. There were inches between them, but it was as if electricity flowed in the gap. He set off at the right moment in the tune.

She swallowed, amazed by the change: he led with confidence, guiding her in slow triplets around the room. She glanced at his face, and could see a line between his brow.

"Goodness, this is transformational," she said.

The line grew deeper. "Don't speak. I'm afraid I cannot concentrate on more than one thing. Oh, darn!"

He missed the beat of the music. They paused, while he composed himself. She saw him counting the rhythm and they set off again. She had to stifle the laughter bubbling up inside.

"Would you like me to count out loud?" she teased.

"Stop it," he said through his teeth. "I need to get this right."

By the end of the dance, he had even made a couple of daring turns before he led her back to the corner she had commandeered. Her thoughts were a jumble. Was this his way of trying to restore their friendship, even if they could never be anything more?

Isla applauded her brother. "When did you learn to waltz? Is this the effect of traveling to the New World?"

He looked at his feet, a slight blush on his face. "Well, I had to do something about my shortcomings."

Isla patted his arm. "Have you taken up lessons?" She turned to Phoebe, who was enjoying the exchange. "My brother cannot abide to have anything he's not expert in."

"That's not true," said Douglas. "I was quite content to be an utter failure at dancing. And it's plain that I'm still very much a novice."

"What changed?" Isla asked.

He put a hand to the back of his neck. "It came to my attention that my dancing was so bad, it could be used as a weapon to humiliate my partner. Whilst I was prepared to accept my shortcomings, it did not seem fair on the lassie who had been forced to stand up with me."

Isla spluttered with laughter. "So you *have* taken dancing lessons!"

"Indeed I have." The music started up again. "I should make it clear though—I have only learned the waltz as yet. So, Isla dear, do not expect anything more from me."

Phoebe stared at him, unable to tear her attention away. She tried to steady her breathing, telling herself he had not necessarily been thinking of *her* when he had taken the lessons. It could have been for any young woman. But Phoebe didn't believe that. He had done it for her. She breathed so deeply the bodice of her dress felt tight.

And then another thought struck, and inside she wilted. No doubt Douglas had taken lessons soon after the charity ball at the State house, when he still thought her decent and respectable. Before he knew the truth. She sank in the chair and sadness flowed over her.

The hall was filling with servants. She glanced at the grandfather clock—midnight was approaching.

Isla took her hand and helped her up. "Everyone has to join in."

Douglas had melted away and was beside his mother. Everyone formed a circle holding hands before Mr. McLennan put his finger up for hush as they listened for the clock. It began to chime, people counting each ring until it reached twelve, and then they cheered. The band struck up and everyone sang "Auld Lang Syne." She was the only one not to know all the words. With the second verse, the dancing became more vigorous. Mrs. McLennan held her son's arm close, clearly delighted to have him home and safe.

As the laughter subsided, there was a knock at the door.

Everyone stood expectantly as a boy was sent to open it and a man entered.

"That's Scobie," whispered Isla beside her. "One of the footmen. Tallest and darkest man here."

Phoebe blinked at her.

"First Footing. It's traditional."

Scobie went to Mr. and Mrs. McLennan and gave them some objects.

"That's a piece of coal for warmth, bread for sustenance, and a penny for prosperity," Isla explained.

Mr. McLennan made sure everyone had a glass, even the young ones, and raised his own. "To the new decade. May we experience the joy of having family close and safe at this time. With the disaster just three days ago, we feel keenly how fragile and precious each life is, and how important for us to *carpe diem*—to seize the day."

Mr. McLennan's words made the gathering more somber and reflective. Everyone drank and cried, "Carpe diem."

Phoebe looked at Douglas and their eyes locked as each stood still for a moment, before Douglas raised his glass to salute her.

FORTY-FOUR

Although it was morning, it was still dark. Light snow was falling, the flakes melting as they touched the ground. Douglas paced the gravel in front of the house.

His mother had produced an old valise and filled it with things Phoebe might need for the journey to the Old Waverley, to replace her lost belongings. He had secured the case behind the enclosed compartment of the McLennan family carriage. A stable-lad, looking worse for wear after last night, struggled to harness the pair of horses. Douglas suspected most of the household had not bothered to go to bed at all.

There were minutes of her company left and then she would be gone. Out of his life forever.

Maybe it was for the best.

He had run through in his head how to say goodbye. There was so much he wanted to say, yet little that could be uttered out loud. And even less he could say in front of family and servants. Perhaps he should have knocked on her door this morning; they could have had a few private moments together.

He clenched his fist and then shook it open. Another darn stupid idea. Who knew where that might have led? Feeling as he did, he no longer trusted himself to be alone with her.

Douglas heard voices at the door and turned to see his sister leading the way outside, followed by Phoebe, then his parents.

The young women were wrapped in furs and shawls. It had been decided that Isla would accompany Phoebe to Edinburgh and then stay a few days in Stockbridge. The family carriage-driver would make sure they arrived safely.

Douglas strode over to Phoebe and all those prepared words vanished. Her eyes looked larger and darker under the fur-lined hat. Her skin was pale and he longed to take her cold cheeks in his warm palms. He could not help his eyes drifting to her mouth, pink in the cold, remembering what it had felt like to kiss those lips.

She looked up and her mouth parted a little; he wondered if she was remembering the same moment.

"So, this is farewell." It was the best he could manage.

She swallowed. "It is." She took her hand out of the fur muff and extended it. He was surprised to find it gloveless and he took it between both of his. Her hand was cold and fragile, and he wanted to tuck it into his jacket, to warm it against his heart.

"Thank you for..." Her voice was soft. "Well... everything."

"There is nothing to thank me for."

"Oh, but there is," she whispered. She glanced back at his parents and cleared her throat. "You know there is a place for you. In Boston. A place where you could really make your mark."

This was such exquisite torture. He wanted to cry, *Yes! Wait! I'll travel with you. Right now.*

Instead, he clicked his jaw and stared down at her. "That would not be wise. I think we both know that. Too many shadows from the past."

She dropped her gaze. "Of course. The past." She took a breath. "I understand. Farewell, Dr. McLennan."

She turned and hurried into the carriage. He closed the door, but she did not look at him again. She stared straight ahead, her gray eyes glistening. Were they tears? He certainly felt like crying.

The whip cracked and the carriage moved forward, the wheels

crushing the gravel as the vehicle swung away from Taybrae Hall and off to the turnpike toward Edinburgh, leaving him bereft.

Phoebe folded her fingers into her palms. Maybe, if she clenched them real tight, she'd be able to stop those tears from falling. She was never going to see Douglas again. Ever. There would be an ocean between them.

Who was she kidding?

There already was an ocean between them. He could never unlearn what he knew about her.

A moment ago, she'd abandoned what remained of her dignity to push the door open, just as far as she could, to suggest maybe, perhaps he could come back to Boston. And he'd slammed that door back in her face.

It wouldn't be wise, he'd said. *There were too many shadows in her past.* She was destined for a life alone.

Douglas turned to find his parents still standing in the stone porch, watching him closely. They parted for him to enter the Hall.

His mother put her hand on his arm as he passed. "Douglas," she said gently.

He shook his head. He was working so hard to keep his emotions in check, he didn't trust himself to speak.

Douglas took the stairs to his room two at a time. He was right to say goodbye, he was sure of it. He'd promised never to wed again. After all, if you loved someone, why would you put them in danger? He saw it every day in his work, saw how many women failed to survive childbirth. For God's sake, Phoebe had nearly died herself. Thankfully, he'd managed to save her. But the memory of his wife's death still haunted him.

He closed the bedroom door behind him and kicked off his boots. He had never expected to fall in love again. He'd worked so hard to build a wall around his heart, to pluck out any growing affection and throw it away like a weed.

He'd get over her. In time. Isn't that what everyone said?

And it was true. While he never forgot his responsibility for Joan's death, the agony had diminished with time. The numbness of the early years had melted, like a patient emerging from a coma.

This would be something similar. He would just have to endure the early days and months when she would fill his thoughts, remembering the softness of her mouth, the shape of her chin, the smell of her dark hair. In time, he would forget her American accent, forget how he would look up whenever he heard her near. In time, he would remember how to breathe in a room where she hadn't taken up the oxygen.

He picked up a book and threw it across the room. What a ridiculous idea! He would never forget her, even if he lived to be a wizened old man.

All he could do was work hard, here in Scotland. The scar was red and raw at the moment but would eventually fade to a pale line. He had observed this with injuries many times.

He lay on his back on the bed. The scar would never disappear.

The grandfather clock chimed the hour. Time. In time, this pain would not be so sharp. But for now, he was going to wallow in it. He was going to lie there and remember every last thing he could about her.

FORTY-FIVE

Phoebe patted around her and found the ancient reticule Mrs. McLennan had given. Unclipping the fastener, she rummaged for a handkerchief but found nothing.

"Do you need something?" asked Isla.

Phoebe sniffed. "Yes, a—"

Isla held out a square of white cotton. "Keep it."

Phoebe blew her nose and tucked it into the bag, wishing she could be more in control of her emotions in front of Douglas's sister. "It's mighty kind of you to accompany me."

"It's nae bother at all."

"How long will the journey take?"

"All day, I'm afraid. We go west until we can cross the Tay at Perth. Then down to Stirling, then swing back east to head for Edinburgh."

All day. A whole day in a cold carriage feeling desolate, trying to make conversation with the sister of the man she had fallen for. Fallen so hard it had knocked all the air from her until she felt like she was on her knees.

"We'll stop on the way, but I've brought food as well. And a couple of books. And knitting."

"Knitting?"

"It helps pass the time," Isla replied with a shrug.

"But how do you manage with all the ruts in the road?"

"Not a special piece of knitting. I can always unpick it." Isla pulled something brown and shapeless from her bag, with big wooden needles.

Phoebe stared out of the window. The dawn sky was beginning to lighten and the snow had stopped. Pale hills emerged from the gloom. She thought back over the past month and knew this was her only chance to find out what had really happened to Douglas. She had respected his privacy so far. But now? To hell with it. She would never see him again, so it didn't matter if Isla told him she'd pried and he thought her ill-mannered.

Phoebe cleared her throat. "There was a woman. At the cemetery we visited."

The needles paused.

"Your brother and I."

Isla started knitting again. "Which cemetery?"

"The one in Edinburgh. Dean's Village."

"Hmm. That's where his wife is buried."

"I know. But the woman. She attacked him. Struck him."

Finally, Isla looked up, her mouth open.

Phoebe had started, so she might as well push on. "She said he'd killed her. That Douglas had killed his wife."

Isla shook her head sadly. "That sounds like Maud."

"Yes, Maud. That was her name. Said she was Joan's sister."

Isla sighed. "And what did Douglas say about it?"

"Nothing. And I didn't want to ask. I don't believe it for a moment, of course. But now... I find myself needing to know what actually happened. I'm sorry, Isla, but if I don't ask you now, I'll never get the chance. And it's eating me up."

Isla placed her knitting beside her. "It's a long tale."

"We've a long journey."

Isla sat back and took a long breath. "Joan, his wife, had been a friend of mine from a smart ladies' academy in New Town. That's how they met—through me. I wish they'd never set eyes on each other. But there's no changing the past. She was from a rather grand family. I think they might have accepted Douglas if he had been following my father's footsteps. But a student doctor? Oh, no, that was somewhat suspect. Both families tried to keep them apart. Or, at the very least, get them to wait. With two stubborn people, that was a red rag to a bull."

"Yes, Douglas can be stubborn at times," Phoebe said.

Isla grunted. "They went off and had an 'irregular' marriage. You can do that in Scotland. No need for banns or a minister. Legal, but it's frowned upon. Father was so angry, he cut off Douglas's allowance. Much the same for Joan, I believe. So, they set up home in one of those dingy tenements to the south of the Old Town."

Phoebe nodded. She'd driven past the high sandstone buildings packed close together.

Isla picked up her knitting and talked as she kept her eyes on the needles. "I stayed in contact, unbeknownst to our parents. He's my only brother, for goodness' sake, and I love him. And she was my friend. They pretended they were happy in that pokey little place." Isla shrugged. "Maybe they were. To begin with. Love's young dream."

"Young love can make you blind to many faults," said Phoebe.

"But Joan was not used to shifting for herself. Douglas was spending long hours studying. And, naturally, she found herself with child." Isla stretched the yarn from her ball of wool. "Douglas was over the moon. So proud. He always said a marriage without bairns is like an apple tree without fruit. All he wanted was a family. He ran himself ragged, trying to train, to look after her, working so he could pay the bills."

Phoebe was moved by this different picture of the man she knew. He'd never spoken of wanting children and she had assumed he was happy without them, as he had never remarried. With a sinking feeling, she feared whatever tragedy had befallen them, it had included a child. "And his wife?"

"Joan? Aye, she was happy enough. Hoped a babby would heal the breach with her family."

Isla paused and stared out of the window before turning back to Phoebe, the needles resting on her fingers.

"The last part of the story I only know what Dougie told me. Joan's time came early, perhaps a few weeks? I'm not sure. He couldnae ken if laboring had properly begun and he thought of calling the howdie, but Joan said no, not yet."

"The howdie?"

"A midwife. That night, she was in more pain. But Dougie, he'd been to a class on this, studied and thought things were progressing as described in his textbooks. They agreed they would seek out the howdie first light."

Isla sighed before she continued her tale.

"But in the wee small hours, Dougie could tell things were not as they should be. He had a friend, a medical student who lived down the street. He tore down there and begged his friend to fetch help at the medical school. To knock up the professors if need be. He ran back to Joan, but found her time was close." Isla looked up at Phoebe and lowered her voice. "He whispered these things to me in the days after, when he was half-mad with grief. Are you sure you want to hear?"

Phoebe nodded in response. Her mouth was dry. She was finally going to learn the truth.

"Joan was in agony and Dougie thought he couldnae wait for help so prepared to deliver his bairn himself. He tried, he did what he had learned in university..."

Phoebe put her hand to her lips, picturing the small room and Douglas's desperation. "Isla, I can see this is painful for you. If you'd rather not—"

Isla shook her head. "You might as well know it all." She swallowed. "The babby wouldnae come and Joan began to weaken from hemorrhaging. Dougie thought he would lose them both. He managed to deliver the bairn, but..." Isla paused and sniffed hard. "The wee thing was already with the angels."

Isla produced another handkerchief to dry her tears. "The student friend arrived as it was getting light and managed to drag a professor with him. I spoke to the student at Joan's burial. He still seemed shocked, days later. He told me he'd never seen so much blood. And Joan, lying there in the middle of the red sheets, already dead. Dougie sitting on a stool beside the bed, sobbing. He'd wrapped the infant boy in a cloth and laid it next to its mother."

Phoebe couldn't speak, her throat aching and a heaviness in her chest.

Isla let out a long breath. "Things crashed down around Dougie's head after that. Joan's family blamed him for everything. Our father pretty much did also. The university wasn't best pleased either; the wife of a promising medical student dying in such circumstances."

"Maud—the sister. She accused him of killing her."

"Aye. Sadly, deep down, Dougie believes Maud is right. He did kill Joan."

Phoebe had a sudden picture in her mind of Douglas remaining with women in labor at the Van Bergen hospital, after others had given up on them, sometimes pulling them through. The nurses talked of him having a miracle touch. When all else failed, you called for Dr. McLennan.

Nevertheless, he could not save them all. "Women die in childbirth. Sometimes it just..."

"Happens."

"Yes."

Isla shook her head. "But Dougie doesn't see it that way. If only he'd known how to deliver the bairn. If only he'd got help earlier. If only he'd not got her with child in the first place. And all the way back, step by step: if only they'd waited like everyone said. If only they never met."

"But that's crazy," said Phoebe, shaking her head.

Isla clicked her tongue with the memory. "He fell apart for a while. A month later, he dragged me to Dean Cemetery. Her stone had only just been erected and I remember the ground was muddy. It was just the two of us and he said he wanted me to be his witness. He put his hand on the stone and vowed never to marry again, never to be the cause of a child dying, and its mother after. And that's how he's been, ever since."

FORTY-SIX

The two women fell into silence. There was nothing more to say. Isla picked up her knitting and Phoebe turned to stare out of the window at the hills and trees, swaying to the movement of the carriage.

This all made sense of the man she loved and her heart broke for him. His whole career was a form of penance, trying to atone for the death of his wife and son. This explained why he had specialized in the less prestigious and financially rewarding area of women's health. Maybe, if he saved enough women's lives, it would make things right.

But she recognized that streak of arrogance in the tale: even as a student without experience, he thought he *should* have been able to deliver a baby, know how to stop the bleeding. Yes, this was also the man she knew.

They stopped at a hostelry for lunch, Isla ordering food when Phoebe struggled to understand the accent. They changed horses at Dunblane and pushed onwards, not fast, but steady. Darkness fell early on the first day of the year and they wanted to reach Edinburgh before night.

Phoebe saw the city in the distance, the castle on its craggy outcrop, and felt a tremble inside. She'd grown fond of this city of hills and stone, even in the short period she'd been here.

Isla studied her closely. "What will you do now?" she asked.

"Hopefully Mrs. Hale will have recovered enough to travel. Then it will be south as soon as we can. I had toyed with the idea of going to Paris, but I've changed my mind. We'll get the first steamer across the Atlantic. My lady's maid is in Liverpool and she may be able to return with me."

"You must be looking forward to being home."

Phoebe paused for a moment. Was she? "In some ways. I have a notebook full of ideas for my hospital and can't wait to get started."

"And you'll be pleased to see your family."

Phoebe shrugged. The truth was, she disliked the company of Thaddeus and Florence. If only Lex and Ginny were not so far away. It could take years to complete the Canadian Pacific railroad.

Maybe she should move out of the family home. She knew it would kick up an almighty fuss because an eligible heiress should not keep a house independently. Increasingly, she didn't really care what people said about her. Since her mother's death, she didn't even have to play the game of maintaining acquaintances in order to raise funds for the hospital.

"You say 'my hospital.' Dougie said you fund it. Is that true?"

"It is."

"You must be very rich."

Phoebe raised a corner of her mouth in a wry smile. "I am. Indeed, I am."

Isla frowned. "Is that why you won't have my brother? My family's not rich enough for you."

Phoebe stared at her open-mouthed. There were so many things to rebut in that sentence, she didn't know where to start. "First of all, your family lives in a castle. I know Douglas keeps saying it isn't. But to someone from New England, it sure looks like a castle."

Isla chuckled. "Maybe, but the McLennans haven't the spare money to build a whole new hospital."

The carriage lurched as it went over a rock in the road. Phoebe grasped the cloth handle hanging from roof.

"And what makes you think it's me who won't have your brother?" Phoebe asked.

Isla curled her lips in, looking like she was struggling with the words. "Look. You've said you're traveling south, but I might as well say it. My brother is in love with you."

It was like Isla had slammed open the carriage door for a gust of cold air to fly in. Phoebe's heart beat painfully fast. "What on earth makes you say that?"

Isla scoffed. "He's been dour for years, but watching him the last couple of days... It's like an oil lamp has been lit inside him. Light shines from his eyes. And he laughed at my jokes. He hasn't done that in years."

Phoebe reached out her hand. Isla clearly cared deeply for her brother. "Isla, my dear. Your brother has been through a terrible accident. Honestly. Our lives hung by a thread on Sunday night. I think something like that can affect people differently. Like your father said: carpe diem."

Isla shook her head. "Nae, I noticed it before, when we were staying at my aunt's during your symposium. I knew something had shifted inside him. And then, when I met you, I thought, *Well, that's the reason.* Seeing you together, it's clear he adores you. You might not know the signs, but I do. That is Dougie in love."

Phoebe put her hand over her mouth to conceal a smile. It was such a glorious idea: the kiss had shown that Douglas desired her... but that he *loved* her!

She closed her eyes and deliberately calmed her breathing. This was foolishness and she needed to put a stop to it now.

"I'm sorry to disappoint you, Isla. But me and your brother? We're never going to be anything other than friends. And it's nothing to do with how much money either of us has."

"It's because of his damn stupid promise," Isla said, her eyes flashing. "But remember, I was there when he made it. He wasn't himself. He was a young man trying to make a deal with God, that somehow if he promised never to marry again, it would bring a balance back to the world." Isla sat forward on her bench and took both Phoebe's hands. "Because, Phoebe, I'm sure if you loved him, I could talk to him, explain to him. Mother and Father both despair of him putting aside that promise. Everyone who knows and cares about him wants Dougie to have a full life, to stop living in the past."

Phoebe felt the world was holding its breath and had gone silent. She was jerked back to reality by a different sound in the carriage. They were running over close-paved cobbles rather than open road.

She kept hold of Isla's hands and tried to keep her voice steady. "I want him to have a full life too. But I'm sorry, it will never be with me."

"Why not? I mean... Oh, goodness, does this mean Father was right and you *are* married after all?"

Phoebe snapped back, blinking rapidly. "You have a very low opinion of me. First, you think I would reject someone because they weren't rich enough. Now you think I'm conducting an affair." She sniffed and looked out of the window. They were nearing the center of town.

"I apologize, Miss Van Bergen. Truly I do. Dougie always said I open my mouth and put my boot right in. It's just, I don't understand... I thought I saw signs of affection from you."

Phoebe turned back to her. "Like what?"

"Well, the way your eyes would go to him, whenever he entered the room. The way your breathing changes when he's near."

"My. You do observe closely." Had her behavior been so obvious? Her cheeks burned.

Isla was not to be deflected. "You seem so well matched. I thought... well, I thought you loved him."

Phoebe glanced out of the window to give herself time to think how to respond. They were approaching Princes Street and the castle loomed nearby. Isla had been kind enough to tell the whole story of what had happened with Douglas's wife. She deserved an honest response from Phoebe now.

"I do," she said softly. "I do love him. You are right." She looked back at Isla. It was painful to see Douglas's features in her face. "The thing is, he'll never marry me. Even as I got into this carriage, he said there are too many shadows from the past."

Isla went to speak, but Phoebe shushed her. "It is a horribly ironic situation. I am completely, *utterly* in love with your brother." The carriage drew to a stop. "But the thing is, there is something I've done. Something only two people in the world know about. My companion Mrs. Hale, and your brother. And knowing what I've done—it means Douglas is the one man in the world who would never dream of asking me to marry him."

FORTY-SEVEN

Adeline dashed down the hotel stairs as soon as a maid told her Miss Van Bergen had returned.

"Phoebe! Oh, Phoebe." She hugged her tightly, ignoring propriety. "I got McLennan's telegram but couldn't quite believe it. The papers have been full of it. How—?"

"Shh," warned Phoebe. "I'll tell you everything privately."

The hotelier, Mr. Cranston, appeared. "Would you like some tea in the drawing room while we take your bags upstairs? Dinner will be served in half an hour."

Phoebe looked at the lone travel case. "That's all there is." A youth took it upstairs. "A gift from Mrs. McLennan," she explained quietly to Adeline. "All my things were lost."

Adeline's mouth fell open and she was about to start asking questions again.

"Mr. Cranston," Phoebe called. "I will take that tea, thank you."

They sat by the window, overlooking Princes Street, now lit with gas lights.

Adeline ran a hand over the tartan tweed of Phoebe's dress. "Another gift from Mrs. McLennan?"

"This is from Isla, Douglas's sister." Phoebe shivered from the memory of Isla's dismayed face when she left the carriage.

Adeline leaned forward, too eager for news to wait for tea to be served. "How did you and McLennan survive the disaster?"

Phoebe told her the bare bones of the story.

Adeline let out a whistle. "So, he saved your life. Gee, he really is something else."

Phoebe didn't trust herself to respond. She paused as the teapot was set down with cups and saucers, sugar cubes and milk.

"I don't understand, though," whispered Adeline, when the waiter was out of earshot. "The papers said everyone died."

"Mr. McLennan is a man of influence in Dundee. Isla says her brother begged him to keep our survival out of the newspaper. Douglas tracked down the fishermen." She leaned closer. "I daresay money was exchanged."

Adeline put her palms to her cheeks. "Thank goodness, though! Otherwise, you'd forever be the railroad heiress who survived a railroad disaster."

Phoebe sipped her tea. "And let's face it: my name would be connected with his. There would always be eyebrows raised about why I was on that train with Douglas. Gossip behind my back."

Adeline shook her head and dropped a sugar lump into her tea. "So, tell me, was it a castle?" She winked at Phoebe.

"Yep. A castle."

"I knew it!"

"I mean, he still kept trying to say no, it was just a big old house, and it hadn't been in the family long. But, Adeline, there were turrets. The walls were three foot thick. The stones around the roof had those up and down bits—"

"Crenelations—"

"Oooh, look at you!"

"I've been researching. Y'know. In case I encountered my own Scottish laird."

Phoebe burst out laughing. How she'd missed her friend's company. "To think when Douglas first came to Fairview, he was so polite, nodding and pretending interest as my mother proudly showed him all the features Thaddeus had designed into the house. The damn place was brand-new but *pretending* to be a hundred years old. And French! He must have thought us so gauche."

Adeline laughed. "I could never be quite sure what McLennan was thinking. He got that unreadable face thing down to a fine art."

Phoebe looked out of the window, but all she could see was her own reflection. "Anyway. We won't need to worry about trying to work out what he's thinking."

"No?"

She turned back to Adeline and swallowed. "No. He's staying here. For good."

Adeline opened her mouth to reply, then shut it again. She knew Phoebe well enough not to ask more questions, well enough to know how low she was feeling.

Suddenly, Phoebe longed to be in Boston. Now she understood what homesickness was: a mild ache somewhere in the stomach when she looked at unfamiliar architecture and wanted to be surrounded by the tall redbrick rows and narrow tree-lined streets of Beacon Hill.

They started packing the next day. Thankfully, lots of Phoebe's clothes and personal belongings had remained in Edinburgh. She spent an hour in Jenners department store buying a new brush and comb, a gilded hand mirror, some cold cream and powder.

She vacillated about how to return to Liverpool. She was scared of using the train, knowing she would be terrified with every bridge they crossed, but the coach journey would take days, cheek by jowl with people they didn't know. At least on the train they would travel first class and have a compartment to themselves.

In the end, she decided on the quickest route. She was a Van Bergen, for heaven's sake. The daughter of the most famous railroad man couldn't go through the rest of her life avoiding trains.

She would have to overcome her fear at some point—it might as well be here with only Adeline to witness her terror.

They left the following morning on the first steam train headed south, Mr. Cranston having made arrangements for them. Phoebe clutched the armrests as the train pulled out of Waverley Station and crawled beside the massive cliffs of the castle mound. As they gained speed and left the city, she closed her eyes, chanting prayers she had learned as a child.

The rocking movement had never affected her before. She put a gloved hand to her mouth. "Oh, Adeline, I think I'm—"

Adeline sprung open the carpet bag beside her and produced a metal bowl. Phoebe grabbed it and vomited her breakfast. Adeline took the seat beside her, and handed a cloth for Phoebe to wipe her mouth.

Phoebe kept her head over the bowl. "How did you know?"

"I've been a nurse ten years, Phoebe. I'm always prepared for these things. Better now?"

Phoebe nodded. Yes, she felt much better, like she had purged her fear as well as her stomach.

Adeline took the bowl and stood to release the catch on the window.

"You're not..." Phoebe asked, her eyes wide.

"Don't see what else to do with it," Adeline replied, before leaning right out and flinging the contents into the Scottish countryside.

They pulled into Lime Street Station in Liverpool on schedule. Adeline had telegraphed ahead to Mrs. Farrell. It was close enough to walk to the Adelphi Hotel, where Phoebe longed for a long sleep in a soft bed and to try to put Douglas from her mind.

"I can tell..." said Phoebe, sitting on the bed to unlace her boots.

Farrell was unpacking the cases. "Ma'am?"

"You've got something to tell me."

Farrell put things away a little faster.

Phoebe let her boot drop onto the floor. "Might as well get it over with."

Farrell turned and held her hands in front of her bodice. "I've got to stay, Miss Van Bergen. Stay here in Liverpool. My sister, she's still not better, you see, and her little 'uns need me."

Phoebe sighed. "Family comes first, Mrs. Farrell."

"I've found three young women for you to interview, Miss, all with excellent references."

"Thank you, Farrell. I'll do that."

By the next morning, Phoebe had all but decided not to take another maid.

"Do you think I'm foolish?" she asked Adeline over the breakfast table in the dining room.

"Not foolish, exactly."

"We'll be home in less than a fortnight. Do I really want to spend time on the ship with a lady's maid I don't know? We've managed well enough recently."

"Sure have."

"I've learned how to dress myself—Goodness, doesn't that sound an infantile thing to say?"

"Our clothing isn't designed for a lone woman."

"I can manage my stays, now I've learned to leave the laces as they are and simply hook up the busk at the front. I know my hair isn't coiffured as fashionably, but, honestly, who's taking notice of me?"

Adeline buttered another piece of toast. "Nobody's taking notice here. But I'm warning you, as soon as we're in New England, that attention will be back. People here might not have heard the Van Bergen name, but we both know it's not the same in Boston."

"And why should it matter? Matter there, I mean."

Adeline gave her a stern look. "You know perfectly well why it matters. If you want public support for the hospital, they won't give it if they think the woman in charge is eccentric."

Phoebe growled. "You know there's no one else who would say that to me?"

"You know there's no one else as good a friend as I am."

Phoebe sighed. Adeline was right, she would have to put the freedom she had enjoyed in Britain behind her. Another treasured thing she was leaving on this side of the Atlantic.

They hurried to the shipping clerk's office and discovered there was a ship leaving for Boston in two days. Phoebe couldn't believe her luck. The clerk reluctantly explained there were no saloon-class cabins available. She and Adeline would have to share a second-class cabin.

"That will be no problem at all," said Phoebe, the desire to be home growing stronger each day.

Back at the hotel, she explained to Farrell she would not be interviewing for a lady's maid. She would manage for herself for the sea voyage and appoint someone in Boston.

Farrell's face fell and Phoebe asked what the difficulty was.

"For one of those girls, ma'am, this would have been a big opportunity. A step up."

Phoebe's shoulders dropped. She hadn't seen it from the maid's point of view. But she remained firm: finding the right lady's maid would take time, and she wanted a woman who knew Boston. Nevertheless, she took care to write a fulsome reference for Farrell, should she need it for future work.

Two days later, Phoebe stood alone at night wrapped in her furs on the deck of the SS *Bothnia*. Run by the Cunard line and direct to Boston, with a fair wind she would be home in little more than a week.

The wind whistled through the huge sails and the steam

engines churned as they made their way into the Atlantic Ocean. The sea was black and the sky a velvety indigo blue. More stars appeared the longer she looked, until she was aware of a sparkling host spreading from one horizon to the other.

She thought how different she was from the woman who had sailed in the opposite direction just a month before. She had almost lost her life. It was profoundly sobering. Why had she survived when so many had perished? She must have some sort of guardian angel enveloping her, keeping her safe. A guardian angel who had protected Douglas too. In return, she vowed she would live life to the full, give something back. Her hospital would be her legacy. She had the tools now to make it the place of excellence she had always hoped it could be.

But she was also leaving something behind. During the ocean crossing, she needed to mourn the loss of Douglas McLennan, as if he had died; to wallow in those feelings of emptiness. That way, when she stepped back on American soil, it would be as a woman reborn. Tennyson's words came to mind: *'Tis better to have loved and lost, than never to have loved at all.*

Oh, how she loved him. Her nighttime thoughts were filled with memories of his green eyes, his firm mouth. During the day, she would sometimes have a question she wanted to ask him and feel again the sharp stab of his absence. But they could never be together, and she would forge a life alone, giving everything to the hospital.

The cold began to creep its way under her furs and into her bones. Reluctantly, she left the starlit sky and retreated back inside. This part of her life was over. She needed to prepare for the next to begin.

PART THREE

FORTY-EIGHT

There was a foot of snow on the roofs of the harbor buildings in Boston, but a path had been shoveled away along the pier, leaving beige slush. Phoebe took it carefully, Adeline close behind. Peering between the buildings, the clock on the Old State House said it was just after noon.

Phoebe heard a man call her name and looked up, startled. Thaddeus, of all people, stood by the family coach, wearing a tall, black hat and a thick overcoat. She picked her way over the ice toward him.

"Thaddeus. Dear brother."

They put their cheeks together in a mock kiss.

He nodded to Adeline. "Mrs. Hale."

"What are you doing here?" Phoebe asked.

"Meeting you."

She took a step back. "Oh?"

"Thought I'd drive you home."

"You've been *waiting*?"

"You know the office is nearby. I told the harbormaster to let me know when your ship docked."

She studied his face. "That's unusually kind. Has something happened?"

"What?" Thaddeus tutted. "No. Well, clearly things happen when you've been away for a couple of months—"

"Seven weeks," said Adeline.

"What is it, Thaddeus? What's wrong?"

"Nothing's wrong."

Phoebe raised an eyebrow.

"Bloody hell! Let's get you into the carriage." He opened the door.

"Whoa! What about Mrs. Hale?"

"She can hire a carriage home, can't she?"

Phoebe was appalled. She now had a much better idea about whether a public cab could be afforded by a working woman. "Why don't we drop her off?"

"I really don't have time to traipse all over Boston. Look." He scratched around an inside pocket and produced a five-dollar note. "This should more than cover it, Mrs. Hale."

Phoebe's jaw dropped.

"Thank you, Mr. Van Bergen," said Adeline, her eyes narrowing. "I can manage by myself."

Phoebe's toes curled with embarrassment. She glared at her brother. "And what about our things? Our luggage?"

Thaddeus rolled his eyes. "Your maid can deal with that, surely."

"I don't have a maid."

"Sure you do. You—"

"Thaddeus. I do not have a lady's maid." Phoebe enunciated each word. "It's just the two of us. And Mrs. Hale traveled as my companion, *not* my servant."

Thaddeus glared at the two women and muttered something under his breath. If Phoebe had been hoping for an affectionate homecoming, it had turned bad-tempered in about two minutes. So much for a new beginning in Boston.

Phoebe hailed the steward she had come to rely on during the voyage and arranged for him to send their luggage to the two addresses.

Thaddeus opened his mouth to intervene, but thought better of it. "I'll wait for you in the carriage," he yelled over his shoulder.

Phoebe apologized profusely to Adeline for her brother's behavior, and they said their goodbyes, promising to meet as soon as they had each recovered from the long Atlantic crossing.

"So, Thaddeus, what's the problem?" Phoebe asked, as soon as they were sitting opposite each other in the carriage.

"No problem. It's just that we've moved house."

Phoebe jerked her head up. "You and Florence have left?"

"We *all* have. We've moved out of Louisburg Square."

Phoebe was flabbergasted. *All.* That meant her as well. "Moved out? Where..."

"Back Bay."

"Back Bay!" So not even the same neighborhood she had grown up in. "I thought you liked being close to the politicians at the State House."

Thaddeus grimaced. "Back Bay is plenty near enough. And most all of the legislators live there anyway. Most of the cream of Boston society too. Or they will do, once the construction work is completed."

Her anger was building alongside her shock. "Which is why Florence wanted to move there, no doubt."

"Look, Pheebs, you know we have to live in the manner expected of us. As the Van Bergens."

"Mother and Father's house was one of the most delightful on all of Beacon Hill," she replied indignantly.

"It was pokey and old-fashioned, and you know it."

"And home." Phoebe glared at Thaddeus, feeling completely powerless.

"We have taken a magnificent mansion. I daresay even you will be impressed when you see it. Right on the corner of Dartmouth and Commonwealth."

Phoebe blinked at him. "I've just arranged for my luggage to be sent to Beacon Hill." She knew it was hardly the most important thing, but she was finding this news hard to comprehend.

"Someone will send it on. Lots of things keep on getting delivered there."

As the carriage rattled on, Phoebe's thoughts turned to the most important thing in her life now: the new hospital. It was being built in the West End, near enough to walk from Beacon Hill when the weather was fair. Now she would be shackled by constantly asking Thaddeus for the carriage. She ground her teeth and clutched her bag harder. A solution began to form in her mind which could suit all of them.

"Say, why don't I carry on living at Louisburg Square. Let's face it, Florence would be much happier without me at the dinner table."

"Can't be done," said Thaddeus, shaking his head.

"I'd be perfectly able to manage—"

"Can't be done. We've sold it."

"Sold! I've only been gone—"

"Seven weeks. Mrs. Hale said."

His sarcastic tone was getting under Phoebe's skin. "You can't have—"

"Got a very good offer on it."

"But we don't *need* the money!" Phoebe shouted and then saw a flicker of something uncertain in Thaddeus's eyes. "Do we?" She leaned forward. "*Do* we, Thaddeus?" she asked more forcefully.

He vaguely waved a hand. "You know how volatile railroad stock can be. It's wise to be careful. Take a good deal when it's offered."

"But not volatile enough to stop you buying a new mansion," she grumbled, sitting back again. "What about all my things?"

"They've been packed up for you. Honestly, Pheebs, you've got a much nicer room in the new place. Much bigger."

As if a bigger room was going to make everything all right.

The carriage rolled past Boston Common, instead of taking the familiar route up Beacon Hill.

"What about all of Lex's belongings? You know, his things from childhood? His books?"

"Florence had them all boxed up too. They'll be in storage until he and Ginny decide where to live."

Phoebe was dumbstruck by this high-handed behavior. "And what about Mother's things?"

"Such as?"

She could slap his supercilious face. "Such as her pictures. Her embroidery. Her collection of Delft pottery."

"Florence has incorporated the best stuff into the new house. You'll be amazed when you see it."

Amazed. Possibly. Phoebe could think of a good few other words.

They drove slowly along wide Commonwealth Avenue, the driver taking it steady in the icy conditions. Snow was piled up on the sidewalk making a lumpy wall, dirty brown at the bottom, then layers of different shades, until the top layer of clean white snow cleared by city workers today.

They rolled past trees bare of leaves, past rows of tall villas, none of them more than twenty years old, with even newer ones as they trundled further from the old heart of the city. There were gaps like knocked-out teeth between buildings, waiting for an investor, or the skeletons of buildings where work had stopped for the winter.

Eventually, they pulled up at an enormous villa occupying a corner plot. Made of the red brick so familiar in Boston, it was on a larger scale to the house she had grown up in. There was a heaviness to the design. The sidewalk level was made of stone, with the basement windows seemingly cut in half, giving the servants who worked below very little light, she imagined. Above, the windows were tall and wide. There was one bay window made of angular sides, unlike the smooth curve of Louisburg Square.

Phoebe got down from the carriage and there was a twinge around her heart. As with Fairview, this building was drawing on

European architectural styles. And Douglas? He lived in the original.

Douglas. She was still thinking of him all the time, wishing she could share an experience or ask his advice. He would encourage her to see the house move as a new adventure. Perhaps she should be grateful for another break with the past—a Boston past that included Hector. She simply had to be stoical about the fact that the past also included the man she loved.

Florence met them in the expansive hallway, under a chandelier which glowed with tiny gaslights. She was wearing an ivory silk dress of high fashion.

Florence opened her arms. "Welcome, Phoebe, dearest. Welcome to the new Van Bergen home." She actually spun round and let out a satisfied sigh, as if she had built the place herself. "Wonderful, isn't it? Let me show you—" Florence was already moving toward double doors leading from the hall.

Phoebe's limbs felt heavy and she really could do with skipping the guided tour. "Florence, my dear. Perhaps I could see it later?"

"Nonsense. Come and have a look, while Merriman arranges for your bags to go up."

"I haven't got them yet." She threw a sideways look at Thaddeus. "I asked a steward to send them to Louisburg Square."

"Nothing to wait for then."

Florence did not even give Phoebe time to remove her coat before setting off. She traipsed after her through reception rooms, a formal dining room with curved conservatory, a music room where Phoebe briefly ran her fingers over the piano, relieved it had been brought to the new home. Then up a huge, ornate staircase to a billiard room, a library, and up to the third floor where Florence opened a door with a flourish.

"And *this* is your room."

It faced south so would get plenty of light. Thaddeus was right:

it was much larger than her old one. The furniture was new and fashionable. But. But it wasn't home.

Even though she was exhausted, Phoebe dragged herself to dinner because she didn't want to show weakness in front of Florence or her brother. She chose one of her most flamboyant dresses from those in a closet the size of Adeline's bedroom. Phoebe already found she needed a lady's maid to get her dressed—how long had *that* resolution lasted? She noticed she had lost weight over recent weeks. Florence would be jealous that Phoebe could pull her corset narrower. The flowing bustle behind served to emphasize her slim waist. She asked the maid to tower her hair above her head, adding to her height, and finished the effect with some carefully chosen pearls from her mother's collection.

The dining room sparkled from gilt and looking glasses. Phoebe took her seat and was relieved it was only the three of them for dinner.

Florence chattered away, updating her on the gossip. Thaddeus rarely spoke, seeming preoccupied—but then, he'd never been loquacious at the dinner table. Not a single question was asked about her trip. Not one. It was as if she'd been away in Manchester by the Sea for the past weeks, not the other side of the Atlantic. Phoebe kicked herself for expecting anything different.

The lack of interest had the benefit that she did not have to conceal anything, not even that she had almost lost her life in a railroad disaster. She didn't have to tell them about Douglas and how much time they had spent together. Didn't have to conceal that she thought about him hourly.

"And Hector, he's engaged," Florence said with a curl of her lip, as she carefully cut her veal.

"Hector?" Phoebe had barely been listening.

"Sure. Engaged."

"Who to?"

"Miss Horowitz." Florence popped a small piece of veal in her mouth.

Phoebe frowned, trying to place her.

"You know. The Horowitzes. Lived out Cambridge way..."

Phoebe shook her head.

Florence lowered her voice. "Jewish. Quite a surprise. She'll convert, of course."

Now Phoebe recalled them: generous patrons of the new art gallery. "Hector will have met her through his father's bank, I daresay."

Florence waved her fork. "Hmm. You let that one slip through your fingers, Phoebe."

Phoebe glanced at Thaddeus and there was another of those shadows crossing his face. She wondered how much he knew about the true nature of his college friend. Douglas had implied a good deal.

"We'll be hosting far more society events here," Florence continued enthusiastically. "Which is lucky for you. We don't want you ending up an old maid."

Phoebe blinked at Florence, who had already rattled on to her next subject.

They reached their dessert course when there was a knock at the door.

Thaddeus checked his watch. "That'll be Cutler. I said to meet me here, rather than the office."

Phoebe put her head to one side as she looked at him.

"A business associate," Thaddeus explained.

"Why not ask him to join us here, darling," said Florence, putting her hand on Thaddeus's arm. "He can have some of this delicious trifle."

Thaddeus looked doubtful but grunted. Phoebe guessed he could tell his wife was not to be gainsaid in this mood. He nodded to Merriman.

Phoebe suppressed a sigh. She was not in the mood for one of Thaddeus's associates tonight.

Mr. Cutler was shown in. When he removed his hat, his hair was gray, even though his beard retained streaks of dark brown, and Phoebe reckoned he was in his sixties. He was of average height, average build. Average. Except for an intensity in the eyes. They swept the room and absorbed every detail.

They were introduced. Phoebe was relieved he was old, otherwise he might think she was on display for the marriage market, being dressed in her finery. But then, a few of her contemporaries had married men in their sixties.

He thanked Florence for inviting him to join what was clearly a family supper. Florence reassured him, and he sat opposite Phoebe.

She recognized a Southern accent. "Where are you from, Mr. Cutler?"

"Hmm. All over. I've lived in most parts of the States."

"I meant, originally."

"Originally? The South. As I'm sure you can tell, Miss. Alabama way."

Phoebe said no more; she had a sense she had offended him.

"And you are an associate of my husband?" asked Florence.

"Might call me something of a fixer."

Phoebe noticed Thaddeus slide a finger inside and around his starched collar. He was nervous; and Thaddeus was never nervous.

"I hear you have been traveling, Miss Van Bergen," said Mr. Cutler.

She was so surprised at being addressed, she almost spluttered, even more so that he knew something of her.

"England, I believe?"

Goodness, Thaddeus must have said something.

"Scotland. Mostly." This was the first time someone had shown interest.

"Never been. What was it like?" Cutler asked.

Life-changing? She could hardly say that out loud. What did a man like him want to hear?

"Dreich, mostly. Their word for bleak weather."

Cutler chuckled. He fumbled with his spoon, dropping it with a clatter, and Phoebe noticed his hand was damaged, with two fingers missing. Her heart went out to him, but she didn't say anything.

He caught her looking. "Old railroad injury," he said quietly to her. "Used to be more—what shall I say?—one of the workers. Rather than one of you gilded folks."

Phoebe smiled at him conspiratorially.

Thaddeus fidgeted and took the first opportunity to usher Mr. Cutler into the library for cigars and spirits—and to discuss whatever "fixing" was on Thaddeus's mind.

Phoebe knew Florence would soon be bored of her company and went to her room as soon as she was able, ready to sleep for a week, as long as people would leave her alone. In Britain she had begun to feel homesick, but now she wasn't sure she even had a home.

FORTY-NINE

All it took was one day's rest for Phoebe to be itching to get back to the hospital. She knew it would be hard with memories of Douglas at every turn, but she had to overcome her regrets. She was welcomed back warmly, and was heartened that staff and patients seemed pleased to see her. The President of the Board met her for lunch and updated her, although she could tell they had been treading water, waiting for her and Adeline to return.

Adeline was fired up with ideas from the symposium. Phoebe decided Adeline should take over the day-to-day running of the hospital, so she could spend all her time on plans for the new one. She needed someone she could rely on, now Douglas was no longer there.

Her office looked like a war room. She attached floorplans and elevations to the walls, folders and files were neatly stacked with their spines clearly labeled. She hosted meeting after meeting: the architect, the master builder, the accountant who would raise his eyebrows with every new requirement and grumble that the sick women would never want to go home, such would be the luxury of the wards. Phoebe knew this was hyperbole and prayed no rumors of profligacy reached her brother's ears.

Phoebe spent time in the cramped wards and spoke at length

to the doctors. Sometimes she would find herself gazing out of the window, wishing Douglas were part of the team. He had so much more imagination, more *vision* than the remaining doctors. She fretted that a women's hospital attracted less prestige and thus less able medics. Still, this was countered by the quality of female staff. There were few opportunities for clever, capable women in Boston. Phoebe would look at Adeline, and knew she could have been running the city, had she been born a man. Adeline had already made contact with a leading doctor at the Madison Avenue women's hospital in New York with a view to luring him to Boston.

The meetings with the city fathers were the trickiest and Phoebe made a point of hosting them in the dining rooms of the smartest hotels in order to flatter their sense of importance. The new hospital required the demolition of a number of buildings in the West End, near North Station. The structures were old and mostly derelict, and she knew she was doing the city a favor by buying up land and knocking down slums. Nevertheless, the mayor acted as if it were prime property she was removing. She brought her architect so he could talk about water supply and sewerage, clean air and coal deliveries. She was familiar with every detail, but the mayor needed assurance from a man.

Gradually, the legal agreements were put in place, written carefully by Briggs, the Van Bergen family lawyer. The demolition work began. Florence was appalled that Phoebe spent so much time at the building site and would come home having to brush dust off her hat and coat. But Phoebe couldn't stay away: she was *so* excited it was happening, at last. She longed to be able to share progress with Douglas. One night, she impulsively started to write him before screwing up the piece of paper in anger. How could she be so weak? He had made it clear he did not want to continue any contact.

The rubble was carted away and the footings began. The builders set up a little ceremony with a silver trowel so Phoebe could put mortar on one of the bricks and hammer it in place. Even though none of the family turned up, the workmen cheered and she had never been so proud. If only Douglas could have seen her.

As the months passed, she began to get used to that ache of loneliness in her chest, but her frustration with living in Back Bay grew. It was too far to walk to the site in the West End, even now the warmer weather of spring had melted all the snow. As she had feared, she battled daily for use of the carriage.

Finally, she could bear it no longer.

"I'm going to find somewhere to lease on Beacon Hill," Phoebe declared over dinner.

Florence looked at her as if she had said she was going to join the Amish. "Why would you even *say* that?"

"It doesn't work, me living here. Beacon Hill feels like home."

"But it's changed so much over recent years. It's filling up with artists and artisans." There was such distaste in Florence's tone.

"I know. That's why I like it."

Florence looked appalled. "But you can't live among those— what's the word for it?—*Bohemian* types."

"Why not?"

Thaddeus rolled his eyes. "The Van Bergens belong here. Beacon Hill might have been the right place in Father's time, but the elite are here now."

"But the hospital is going to take more of my time. It will help to be closer."

Thaddeus threw his napkin at the table. "You can't go making decisions based on a *hobby*."

Phoebe felt like Thaddeus had slapped her on the face.

"You need to get married," he continued, his face reddening. "And then you'll live wherever your husband tells you to."

Phoebe was too shocked to speak.

Florence put her head to one side. "You do *want* to be married, don't you, Phoebe? You haven't become one of those awful *progressive* women, have you?"

"Sure, I want to be married," Phoebe said, blinking back tears. "It's just..."

"Just what?"

What could she say? That there were thousands of miles between her and the only man she wanted as a husband? That anyone else would be second-best and she was done with making compromises.

"Oh, for goodness' sake, Pheebs," said Thaddeus, picking up his fork again. "You're not holding out for *love*, are you?"

The sarcasm dripped off him and Phoebe glanced at Florence, fearful she was hurt by such cruel words. If she had, Florence did a fine job of hiding it.

Thaddeus chewed his mouthful of beef, speaking before it was swallowed. "You're not going to Beacon Hill and that's that. I'm not signing the lease for you."

She looked at the food on her plate and had lost her appetite. "You're not my only brother, you know."

"I'm the only one *here*."

Phoebe thought about Thaddeus's words all evening. She wrote to Lex, laying out her needs, estimating the cost of setting up her own household—how many servants she would require, what her annual outgoings might be. She begged his approval and, with Briggs as a second trustee, that he grant her independence.

In the morning, she took the letter to the Van Bergen offices herself, knowing there was a regular packet of correspondence sent to the railroad construction team in Canada.

Phoebe had to wait longer than a month for the reply, but it was more than she had dared hope for: Lex was on his way back to Boston with Ginny. She was with child and he wanted her to have the best possible care. He would sort out leasing a place for Phoebe as soon as he got back.

Phoebe crushed the letter to her chest and leaped up in delight, searching the mansion until she found Florence.

Florence took the news with polite interest and Phoebe felt a pang of sympathy for her sister-in-law. She wondered if she was being insensitive: Ginny was returning to have a Van Bergen child, when Florence, after many years of marriage, had failed to produced one.

In early May, as the abundant leaves of the elm trees shaded the promenade on Commonwealth Avenue, Lex and Ginny arrived, throwing the whole household into uproar. Lex strode from room to room, admiring the size, the quality of the building materials. Phoebe followed Ginny and Florence into the parlor, a thousand questions on her lips.

Florence spoke first. "And when is the longed-for event?"

"The end of June, I think," said Ginny.

Phoebe threw Ginny an appraising look. Her experience at the hospital had given her some skills in these matters and she thought Ginny looked further along. "And how are you feeling?"

"Can't say it's been easy. There were a couple of months when I couldn't keep anything down." She glanced at Florence. "Sorry, you might not want to know..."

"Well, you look like you've made up for it since," said Florence. "You've put on some weight around the face."

Phoebe raised an eyebrow and was about to admonish Florence, when she looked closer and saw Florence was right. Ginny did seem fuller around the chin and her cheeks were pink. "And what about now? Are you feeling better?"

"Sure. Except for this darn headache that never seems to go away." Ginny rubbed at her temples and tried to give a weak smile of reassurance.

"Would you like to see one of our doctors at the Women's Hospital?"

"That's one of the main reasons for coming back. Lex says he wants the very best treatment for me."

"I'll talk to Mrs. Hale about an appointment. To be honest, I suggest you make sure she's there as well. Storer and Minot both have their skills, but I trust Mrs. Hale's judgment the most."

. . .

Lex was good as his word about giving Phoebe her freedom, and the very next day accompanied her to Beacon Hill to see a place available to lease near the top of Mount Vernon Street. It was a pretty double-fronted house, side-on to the road, with a front door and a porch that opened onto a small yard planted with flowers and shrubs.

They were given a tour and Phoebe pronounced it perfect.

"Do you not think it a little large for you?" asked Lex. "You'll be rattling around like a marble in a tinderbox."

"I was thinking of asking Mrs. Hale if she'd like to join me, as my companion. We got on famously during our trip to England and Scotland."

"Excellent. Although Ginny is going to miss your company."

Phoebe caught a glance, and an unvoiced understanding about Florence passed between them. "Ginny can come visit any time she wants, and I'll be with you in Back Bay so often, you'll be sick of me."

The lease was signed the following day and Phoebe made arrangements to move into her new home immediately.

That evening, she passed the door to the library and heard her brothers arguing. Phoebe was pinned to the spot. Thaddeus was berating Lex for authorizing the lease and sufficient funds for her new household.

"You had no right, Alexander. You haven't even looked at the latest finances for the business, yet you're *throwing* money around."

"Are you saying Phoebe can't have her own life?"

Phoebe took a deep breath and straightened her shoulders. She should be part of a conversation about her future. She opened the door. Thaddeus flashed her a shifty look and threw himself into a chair. Lex pushed his hands in his pockets and leaned back against a sideboard, crossing one ankle over the other.

Phoebe calmly took an armchair near the fireplace. "Do please continue. As you can imagine, I'm very interested in this conversation."

Thaddeus grunted.

"What's going on, Thaddeus?" asked Lex.

"We need to be careful about these unnecessary expenditures."

Lex folded his arms. "Are you saying we can't afford it?"

"No. Not exactly."

"Not exactly!"

Thaddeus shifted in his seat. "There's been a lot of expenditure lately."

"I can see that," said Lex. "This place is pretty extravagant. But you're saying nothing for Phoebe? You know it will be better all round for her to be independent."

Thaddeus gestured to the ornately carved bookcases. "We need this place to make sure people continue to have confidence in us. Investors, I mean."

"Are investors losing confidence?" Phoebe asked.

Thaddeus got up to fill his whiskey glass and Phoebe thought he looked distinctly uncomfortable. "We've had one or two hiccups. It doesn't help that Alexander is going more over budget with every mile he builds. That most recent bridge was twice the expected cost."

"We can't skimp on these things. You heard about the bridge that collapsed in Scotland?"

Phoebe gasped and covered her reaction with a cough.

Thaddeus didn't seem to notice. "Sure," he said, returning to his seat. "We're in the railroad business. Bad news spreads."

Lex raised an eyebrow at Phoebe. "You heard of it?"

Phoebe affected a shrug but was sure the color of her complexion had changed. "Of course. It happened when I was in Scotland."

Lex returned his attention to his twin. "That's what confidence is about, Thaddeus. Building a railroad people can trust."

Thaddeus took a mouthful of bourbon. "There are competitors out there all the time. Ready to stab us in the back, if we don't stab them first."

"Is that really how we want to conduct Van Bergen business?"

"Damn you, Alexander. Don't be so bloody naïve." He slammed down his glass and marched from the room.

"Sorry about that, Phoebe." Lex pushed himself away from the sideboard. "Looks like I'm going to be in the office tomorrow, finding out what's going on."

"You don't think... you don't think the hospital funding is at risk?" Phoebe was bringing this round to her particular concern, not thinking about the whole family, but she couldn't stop herself.

"No, Phoebe. I doubt it'll come to that. Lots of your money is protected in a trust. But remember to play nice with the other rich families. Guess you never know when you might need their help."

FIFTY

Phoebe moved into the Mount Vernon house within the week and the new surroundings began to ease the pain around her heart. She was getting on with her life, no longer living in the past thinking of what-ifs and if-onlys about Douglas. She brought all her things that had remained in storage, as well as some furniture and decorative pieces from her childhood home. Florence was right that some of it was heavy and dark, but Phoebe treasured the connection with earlier Van Bergens.

Adeline was delighted to move into her own suite of rooms. They engaged Mrs. Washington to cook for them, a former slave from Virginia, as well as a parlormaid, lady's maid, and a couple of manservants. They ate in a corner room with windows on two sides overlooking the street and yard. Phoebe enjoyed the bustle of Beacon Hill again, a place where horses were constantly going up and down the street, where vendors made deliveries, and artisans invited people into their homes to be persuaded to buy objets d'art.

"I examined your sister-in-law today," said Adeline over dinner.

"Ginny? She said she'd seen Dr. Minot and he was very reassuring."

"Yes, I was there at the time."

"I was relieved, because that headache was clearly getting Ginny down."

Adeline grimaced.

"What?" asked Phoebe, her senses immediately on full alert.

Adeline swallowed her food. "I wasn't happy with Dr. Minot's assessment, so I went to see Mrs. Van Bergen in Back Bay. Thing is, it's twins."

"No!"

"I suggested it to Dr. Minot earlier, but he didn't agree. He just ummed and ahhed. But I'm sure."

Phoebe trusted Adeline's judgment. "Lex and Thaddeus are twins. Do you think it runs in the family?"

Adeline shrugged. "Perhaps. But I have other concerns. You've seen mothers at the hospital have convulsions?"

"Yes, once or twice. It's very frightening."

"There are things a good midwife looks out for that warn us it might happen. Not just headaches. Mrs. Van Bergen has been seeing lights, like stars. And you noticed a puffiness in her face?"

"I did."

"That can be a sign, along with similar swelling of the hands and feet."

"Oh my goodness. Is this... serious? Could she lose her life?"

Adeline spoke quietly. "It's rare. But it's possible. It's called 'puerperal eclampsia.'"

Phoebe frowned; the term was familiar. "Wasn't that what Douglas's lecture was about? In Edinburgh?"

Before Adeline could answer, Phoebe was pulling open the drawer in the sideboard.

"I keep all my notebooks here," she said, flipping through the pages. "Yes, here! *The Treatment of Puerperal Eclampsia by Chloral.* He said... trichloroethanal"—Phoebe had to try twice to get the right pronunciation—"is an aldehyde that reacts with water to form chloral hydrate." She looked up at Adeline, hoping she would have a better understanding of these substances. "My notes say it can be used in small doses as a sedative for eclampsia. Look, here. I've written, *laudanum drops seem to make convulsions less likely, but carefully administered chloral should reduce the reliance on the compound later.*"

Adeline leaned her chin on her hand, narrowing her eyes in thought. "I'll check my notes from the lecture as well."

"Whatever Douglas recommended, we should try. Ginny's... well, she's the closest I have to a sister." Phoebe put her hand to her chest, steadying herself from the thought of something dreadful happening to dearest Ginny.

Adeline nodded. "And it's a better option than what Dr. Minot would recommend if I raise it with him."

"Which is?"

"Blood-letting." Adeline grimaced. "I've never seen that make any difference." She tapped her fingers against her lips. "I'm going to write that New York obstetrician from Madison Avenue again. He seems more forward-thinking."

The next few weeks were filled with anxiety. There was nothing Phoebe could do to help, so she packed her days with meetings with her architect and bookkeeper.

On a stuffy Friday evening in mid-June, Phoebe came home to find a short note had been delivered.

Mrs. Hale and the doctor here. Decided to induce Ginny. Could do with your calm presence. Going crazy waiting. — Lex

"Neither of us will be here for dinner," Phoebe shouted to Mrs. Washington as she flew up the stairs. "I've got to go straight over to Back Bay. Mrs. Van Bergen has gone into labor." She paused on the staircase. "Say, when did that note arrive?"

"'Bout five o'clock, Miss Phoebe."

That should be fine: only an hour ago, even though she'd been induced.

In her room, she pulled out a leather bag for her overnight things. Her maid came in to help her pack, but Phoebe shooed her way. She treaded more carefully going back down the winding staircase, lugging her bag. Throwing it to the floor by the door, she groaned. She needed a quicker way to get to Back Bay than walking. She called Simpson, their general manservant.

"Say, could you go next door and beg—I mean absolutely *beg*—for their horse? I need to ride over to Back Bay."

"I'll do what I can, Miss."

"And don't come back without it," she called after him.

Simpson raised a hand as he hurried off.

Mrs. Washington laid a plate of food on the table. "It'll take some time to saddle up, Missy, so you might as well get something wholesome inside you. Could be a long night ahead."

She didn't want to eat; she wanted to be with her brother and Ginny, but Mrs. Washington was right about this, as she was about most things.

Simpson secured the bag behind the saddle and helped Phoebe up. She was a competent rider but not expert like Lex, who seemed born to be in a saddle, rather than run a railroad empire. She picked her way carefully over the cobbled streets, down the steep hill, and skirted the Common before making her way up Commonwealth Avenue, which was busy even at seven in the evening.

She found a stableboy at the back of the Van Bergen mansion, who saw to the horse, and went in through the tradesman's door, much to the surprise of Merriman, who still quietly kept the Van Bergen household rolling. Inside, all the rooms were glowing. A maid took her to the reception room at the front of the house, where Lex was striding back and forth. He saw her and crossed the room in a moment.

"I'm so glad you're here," he said, grasping her hands.

"Sorry it took so long. I didn't get your note until I got home. How is everything?"

Lex went to stand behind his chair, pushing a hand through his hair. "The doctor arrived this afternoon."

"Oh, please tell me, not Dr. Minot. He's a decent doctor, but I wouldn't trust him with Ginny—"

"No, no. It's..." He paused and Phoebe saw discomfort flash across his face. "Well, the doctor Mrs. Hale said was best. She's here too. The doctor said it would be safest to induce Ginny now."

Phoebe nodded. Ginny hadn't had a convulsion over recent weeks, but the headaches and eye problems had continued and been joined recently by a sharp pain, just below the ribs.

"The doctor's brought some sort of special equipment for Ginny to breathe from, to help the pain."

"D'you mean chloroform?"

"That's the word. I was worried it might poison her, but Mrs. Hale said it would help."

Phoebe felt a glow of pride deep inside. Adeline had learned so much in Edinburgh and been busy making contacts with medical experts in different states since their return. It looked like the one from New York had responded to her call. She loved that Adeline was stepping up and making these decisions.

"And now? Have they said how things are?"

"Fine. Everything's fine," said Lex, gripping the back of the chair so hard his knuckles whitened. "Or, at least, that's what they say. Every time I ask. Which must be every ten minutes."

"Does Mrs. Hale say it's fine?"

Lex nodded.

"Then there's no reason to think it won't be." She untied the ribbon at her throat and pulled off her hat. "Where's Florence?"

"Gone to stay with a friend. Said she couldn't bear the noise."

"Thaddeus with her?"

Lex shook his head. "Union Club."

Phoebe unbuttoned her coat. "Probably for the best. Now. Have you eaten?"

"They keep putting bits of food in front of me, like a cat who's hidden under a bed and has to be lured out with tidbits." Phoebe laughed. "But I don't feel like eating."

It was understandable. She tried to hide it, but Phoebe's stomach was screwed up in anxiety about Ginny. She glanced around the magnificent room, with its tall windows in the bay that looked out over the Avenue, partly hidden by great sweeping drapes in dark blue damask. The wallpaper had birds hiding among branches. There was a medley of plates of food on the table.

She needed to do something to encourage Lex, so picked up a sausage wrapped in bacon and popped it in her mouth. "Hmm, Lex. You should try these. They're delicious."

He waved a hand and threw himself into the chair. "Maybe later."

Phoebe could see she had her work cut out, keeping Lex distracted for the next few hours. She pulled a chair closer to his, worrying that dragging the chair might damage the glowing parquet floor.

"When did you last see Ginny?" Phoebe asked.

"Some hours back. She looked exhausted. Flushed and sweaty."

"I'm not surprised. It's hard work."

Lex dragged himself to the table and nibbled at one of the sausages. "As long as no one's experimenting on Ginny with that contraption. I told Mrs. Hale to get the best possible care. No expense spared."

Phoebe tapped each hand on the arms of her chair. "And I'm sure she's done that. Honestly, Lex, chloroform has been used by some doctors for years. Progressive ones no longer believe the Bible ordains women should experience pain in childbirth." Phoebe slipped off her shoes. "If you'd just waited six months, you could have used my brand-new hospital."

Lex huffed a laugh as he dropped the half-eaten sausage and tried a chicken leg instead. "Is it that close to being finished?"

"It's what the master builder says."

"Phht! When can you ever trust a builder to keep his word?"

Phoebe grinned. "That's why I spend so much time at the site. Making sure it opens on schedule."

She needed to distract him, to get Lex thinking about something that had nothing to do with hospitals or medicine. She asked for a retelling of the story of how he had met Ginny. Then she wanted to know about Canada, what his work involved, what the landscape was like, how Ginny was taking to the different environment.

The grandfather clock in the hall continued to chime as midnight came and went. At last, in the small hours, a maid scurried in. Lex leaped to his feet.

"Mrs. Van Bergen—she's well?" His scratchy voice betrayed his fears.

"Very well," said the maid.

Lex's mouth broke into a grin from ear to ear. Phoebe had never seen her brother so elated. She released a huge sigh of relief, saying a silent prayer of gratitude that all was well.

"And the babies? What have we got?" he asked as he straightened his clothing after lounging so long in the chair.

"A boy and a girl. Mrs. Hale says you can come up and see them."

"Oh, thank God!" He dashed to the door. "Come on, Phoebe."

She waved her hand. "You should have some time, just you and your new family."

"You sure?"

"Absolutely." She smiled. "I'll be up soon."

She peered at the ornate clock on the mantelpiece: it was half past four in the morning. She could have a short nap and then go up and see dear Ginny and her new niece and nephew. She settled onto the sofa and put her feet up on the fabric. A boy and a girl. Typical of Lex to get everything so perfect and she couldn't be more delighted for him.

FIFTY-ONE

The sound of birdsong woke Phoebe. Her neck felt like it had been in an instrument of torture and it took a moment to work out she was sleeping on a sofa in the reception room at Back Bay. She smiled as she remembered: Ginny was safe. The babies were delivered. All was well.

Someone had draped a blanket over her: probably one of the maids. Her shoes were neatly paired beside a chair and her jacket hung over the back.

Phoebe slid her feet to the floor and dragged herself upright. She walked to the bay window and looped one of the drapes over its ornate hook. The sky was streaked with pink, glowing as if the sun was proudly showing off the dawn for the first time. A single morning star twinkled. It was going to be a God-given, beautiful day.

The grandfather clock sounded and Phoebe paused to count the chimes. It was only half past five, an hour since Lex had gone upstairs to meet his new family. She remembered resting her head on the sofa to catch a few minutes' sleep. Maybe it would be the right time for her to go up to see them all now. Her insides fizzed as she pictured the scene upstairs.

She caught sight of herself in the looking glass over the fireplace, and snorted. Her hair looked like a bird's nest and her white blouse was crumpled. She pulled the remaining pins and shook her hair loose.

Hearing footsteps in the hall, she recognized Merriman's voice talking to someone. The poor old butler had probably been up all night. There was a man's voice: this might be the doctor from New York. Phoebe hurried in her stockinged feet into the hall, not wanting to miss her moment to thank him by putting on her shoes.

Merriman was showing the man out, holding the front door open. He was wearing a coat and carrying a black leather medicinal bag.

Phoebe cried out. "Doctor, is everything—"

The doctor paused but didn't turn. He seemed to be waiting for something.

Phoebe also stood motionless. Everything about the man's outline was burned into her brain. His stance was so familiar it made her heart leap.

But it didn't make any sense.

"Douglas?" She whispered the name, feeling foolish, because it *couldn't* be him.

Slowly, he turned to her. Their eyes locked as they stared at each other. His face was in shadow and Phoebe struggled to interpret his features.

She wished there was something nearby to steady herself against as her legs felt weak.

"I don't understand... You came back. Have you moved to Boston? Without telling me?"

Douglas stepped away from the door and into the hall. She could finally see his features. His jaw glowed with dark-blond stubble and his hair was untidy. He was so close, she could smell his cologne. He swallowed. "No. Alexander telegrammed me."

"Where?"

"Scotland."

She squeezed two fingers to the bridge of her nose as she tried to work this out. "You have come all the way from Scotland? Just to tend Ginny? Are you... are you staying?"

He looked out of the open door again. "Partly to tend Mrs. Van Bergen. I don't know about staying yet. It depends."

Phoebe's throat was parched dry. "What on?"

He turned his head back to meet her gaze, and spoke in a whisper. "On you."

There was someone on the grand staircase behind Phoebe, a rustling of skirts, a gentle clearing of the throat. Douglas looked up at the person and pushed back his hair with his fingers. He looked worn out.

Phoebe glanced round: it was Adeline, one hand on the banister, standing still as she watched them both.

Merriman coughed and broke the spell.

Douglas shifted his medical bag to his other hand. "I didn't expect you to be here." He nodded once to the staircase. "Mrs. Hale said you both lived in Beacon Hill."

"I do. But Lex..." She ran out of the words. It wasn't *her* who had to explain her presence in the Van Bergen mansion.

"Aye. I should have realized." A muscle ticked in his jaw. He turned to go and then looked at her over his shoulder. "I'll be back later to look in on Mrs. Van Bergen. Might we talk then?"

All Phoebe could do was nod. She could no longer trust herself to speak.

Douglas hurried through the doorway and Merriman shut the door behind him, before discreetly disappearing through the staff door.

Phoebe was still standing in the middle of the huge, ornate entrance hall. She turned to the staircase.

"Adeline?"

"I can explain," she said sheepishly.

"You damn well better." Her nostrils flared.

Adeline hurried down the remaining stairs, pausing on the final step, using the wooden newel post as a support. "After I examined Mrs. Van Bergen, I told your brother I was concerned. He asked who the best doctor was and I said Douglas McLennan, because that's the truth, and you know it. We both know it. Mr. Van Bergen said, fine, send a message to him. I, of course, said it wasn't possible because he's in Edinburgh. Mr. Van Bergen just shrugged, you know, in that way he has, and said, 'If he's the best, then Ginny needs him. I'll send a cable.'"

Phoebe puffed out air through her nose as she pictured Lex. He was single-minded when it came to Ginny. But she was still furious with Adeline. "Why didn't you tell me about this?"

Adeline's eyes softened. "Because I didn't know what he'd say. The idea of him coming all this way seemed crazy. And, dearest Phoebe, I didn't want to open old wounds."

"Old wounds?"

Adeline stepped down to the polished floor and wrung her hands together. "You were heartbroken when we left Scotland. I could see that. But I've also seen you start to recover. Anyway, before the end of the day, Mr. Van Bergen had a cable back from McLennan saying he'd come—but not to say a word to you."

Phoebe's legs felt like the bones were dissolving and she would collapse any moment. She backed away until she leaned on the marble-topped table beside the wall. "Not tell me? Why?"

Adeline stepped closer. "I can only guess at that. You will have to ask him yourself. He only arrived yesterday afternoon and we haven't had time to talk about anything other than the twins' delivery." She shook her head. "It has put me in a very awkward position over the past fortnight and I didn't like hiding it from you."

Phoebe put her palms to her cheeks. "To travel all this way, to attend the labor of a woman he barely knows—it's extraordinary!"

One side of Adeline's mouth raised in a smile and she raised an eyebrow. "Oh, Phoebe! He didn't come here to tend Mrs. Van Bergen. He came because he knows she's precious to you. He's come for you."

The room started spinning and Phoebe clutched the edge of the marble with one hand. "But what about..." She put her other hand on the top of her head, trying to work through everything in her mind. "And Joan? What about...?"

"Whatever you need to know," said Adeline firmly, "you'll have to ask him."

Phoebe looked at the closed front door, picturing where he had stood just minutes before. The man she thought she would never see again.

Her heart beat so hard, she could feel the blood pumping in her neck. He had asked to visit her later. There was no way she could wait until later in the day for him to return. She would explode before then.

Phoebe rushed back to the reception room and sat to pull on her shoes. She went to the mirror and began to tidy her hair before throwing the pins on the mantelpiece. For goodness' sake, what did it matter what her hair looked like? Every minute, he was walking further away. Adeline handed her the fitted jacket to go over her blouse and she tugged it on.

She dashed to the hall, pulled back the heavy bolt on the door, dragged the oak door open, and rushed down the steps to the sidewalk.

FIFTY-TWO

Douglas had almost tripped down the steps in his eagerness to get away. He'd adjusted his bag and set off down the long avenue to the Common.

Dammit. Dammit! That wasn't how he'd planned it at all.

He had pictured their first meeting in his head. He would have a bath, shave, change into fresh clothes, then go to the Beacon Hill address Mrs. Hale had given him. There he would explain everything to Phoebe and, depending on whether she understood his actions, ask if she would accept, or even just *consider*, his proposal of marriage. And if she said no, he would be on the first steamer out of Boston. That was the plan.

What he hadn't expected was to be struck dumb by her voice calling his name.

Or turning to look at her, to be so mesmerized, he forgot basic good manners, let alone any prepared speeches. She had looked... luminous. Her loose dark hair had formed a halo around her face. Her gray eyes were limpid, fixing him to the spot, even though his heart was telling him to rush forward and hold her, to crush her lips under his.

He began to wonder if this had been complete madness. She

had shown no joy in seeing him—only shock. Would she want a man who had married before and was now breaking a promise by proposing a second time? That was what he needed to explain, but he hated the idea of doing it in that gaudy Van Bergen mansion, with disapproving looks from her family, and servants back and forth.

The sun had risen and it was going to be a sweltering day. Sparrows twittered in the elm trees, pleased to have freedom before the city came to life and this boulevard filled with carts bringing stone and workers to build the smart new properties.

He heard a noise behind him: someone calling. It was none of his business; he lowered his head and pushed on.

"Douglas! Wait!" The words were louder, and he knew that voice.

He paused and turned. *Phoebe.* A rush of sensations hit him so hard, he felt nauseous.

She picked up her skirts to run faster down the sidewalk. Her hair flowed free and her unbuttoned jacket rippled.

"Douglas!"

He took long strides toward her. She stopped about ten feet from him and leaned on a railing with one hand, breathing hard to recover her breath.

"I need to know." She stood and fanned her face with her hand. "What did you mean about staying, when you said it depends on me?"

He wanted to blow on her pink cheeks to cool them but curled his fingers more firmly around the handle to his medical bag. "I think you know *exactly* what I mean."

"Do you mean... do you mean it depends on me giving you your job back?"

He breathed out through his nose. "No, Phoebe. I'm not here for the job." He shook his head and stared at her. "I'm here for you. That's... if you'll have me, once I've explained."

She closed her eyes and spun away from him, burying her

fingers in her scalp, letting out a sound as if his words had stabbed her. "But you said there is too much in my past."

He lowered his brows. "Too much in *your* past?"

"When I left Taybrae Hall. That morning, you said, '*We both know we can never be together.*'" She turned back and there were tears in her eyes. "Douglas, you are the one man who knows everything about me. Who knows what happened... with Hector."

He took a step back and dropped his bag to the ground. "That's nae what I meant at all. Did you think... Did you think I didn't want you because of the *miscarriage?*"

"Surely you wouldn't want to marry a woman who—"

He stepped forward and grasped her hands. "That means nothing to me. *Nothing.* I promise you. You were the victim of an evil man. But you were, and remain, the most perfect woman in the world." He shook his head, hating that she had thought this the reason for his reticence. He had so much to explain, and fast. "I meant there was too much in *my* past."

She stared at him. "You mean Joan."

"Aye. Joan."

The tears had subsided but left her gray eyes sparkling. "And yet you're here. Something must have changed."

He looked around, uncomfortable that they were standing on the street within sight of the Van Bergen mansion.

He let go of her hands and gestured toward the Common. "Could we perhaps..."

She nodded and they fell into a slow step beside each other, Phoebe with her hands behind her back. He held his case on the side furthest away from her.

"It was the telegram from your brother. It came when I was staying with my aunt in Belgrave Crescent. To be honest, I thought it high-handed and entitled; typical of a Van Bergen. I tried to resist the idea of being commanded back here. I ken it would be painful for both of us. But he was asking me to help the woman you think of as a sister. I could never deny helping someone you care about. My first intention, though, was to do what I could without you knowing and leave."

They crossed an empty road and continued slowly down the next block.

"Isla was there when the telegram arrived. She could see I was in torment. So she told me about your carriage journey back to Edinburgh, that you asked about Joan and she had not spared any of the details. I thought you would condemn me for my actions. But Isla said you didn't pull away in horror. She said you were kind and understanding. More than that, she said you cared for me. I mean, *truly* cared."

Phoebe turned to him to speak, but Douglas briefly put up his hand. "Please let me finish. I have been trying to find the words for some time. You see, until then I was still captured by this idea that I had to live out my days as a widower. As some sort of penance. Isla asked how I would feel had it been Joan alive and something had befallen me. I thought about it, and of course I wouldn't have wanted her to live in widow's weeds. I'd want her to have a full life, to find happiness elsewhere. And Isla, she said that would be the same for Joan. She'd want me to fall in love again."

He stopped next to a sandstone wall protecting the front yard of a grand house. He turned, his gaze swiftly flowing over her.

"And, God knows, Phoebe! I have fallen so deeply in love with you, it touches every atom in my body. Every nerve is alive to you." The words were spoken before he could stop them. There was no point holding back now. "I decided that once Mrs. Van Bergen was safe, I would seek you out, to find out. Could you love me? Could you see a life with me?"

Phoebe stood before him, her eyes blazing. His heart raced, as he knew his future depended on what she said next.

She took a slow step forward, close enough to lift both hands to his cheeks. She held his gaze. "Of course I love you," she whispered. "How could you ever doubt it? I love your unfamiliar accent. I love how other doctors infuriate you. I love the way you fight for every sick woman you treat. I love that you have to count the beats when you dance. I love... you."

She raised herself on her tiptoes, closed her eyes, and kissed him gently on the lips. It was as if his body was flooded with honey. He ran his tongue lightly over her lower lip, her breath mingling with his.

He pulled back and dropped his case once more, putting both hands on her waist and turning her until her back was against the wall. He stared down, drinking in every feature, her skin glowing in the dawn light, her dark eyelashes curling at her cheek, her pink mouth with that tiny notch in the upper lip. He had remembered every part, but she was even more captivating because she was flesh and blood, heat and movement.

"You are so... touchable," he growled.

He slipped his arms further around her waist until she stood close enough for him to feel the rapid rise and fall of her chest. He stared at her mouth and kissed her once more, passionately, his eyes closed. Heat shot through him, making his skin feel feverish. Still holding her against him, he threaded one hand through her long, loose hair, like a skein of silk.

She raised her hands to the back of his neck, kissing him with an urgency that matched his, and let out a gentle moan that told him she had longed for this as much as he had.

Finally, he pulled back, resting his forehead on hers, gathering his breath. A clattering cart disturbed them, a man whistling and yelling some sort of encouragement.

She giggled. It was the most wonderful sound he had ever heard.

"Not sure if this is seemly behavior," she said, a line of perfect white teeth biting her bottom lip.

"Not sure I care," he replied, but pushed himself away from where he was guarding her, uncertain what to do next.

Phoebe turned toward the Van Bergen mansion. "I should get back. I haven't even seen Ginny and the babies yet."

"Perhaps. But they were all sleeping deeply when I slipped

out. Later might be better." He was reluctant to let her go, but it was also the truth.

She straightened the blouse beneath her jacket and looked him over. "You must be exhausted yourself. Adeline said you have only just arrived."

"I assure you I've never felt better."

She laughed. "Did anyone fix you breakfast?"

He shrugged, thinking food no longer mattered. She loved him. She loved him as he loved her.

She pulled the front of his coat together with each hand. "Look, why don't I fix you breakfast at my place."

He snorted. "You can make breakfast?"

"No," she replied, a beautiful smile curving her lips. "But I have a wonderful cook." She turned and started walking toward the Common. "I've taken my own place back in Beacon Hill."

He picked up his bag and fell into step beside her. "Aye, Adeline said. That's very... brave."

They sauntered as if this moment in the dawn light would last longer if they took it slow. He slipped her hand in his, and as her fingers closed tight, the swelling in his chest made him think he might float, not walk.

They crossed the road to enter the Common. The sun was fully up and the morning dew was evaporating from the grass. Noises grew as Boston stretched itself into life. A man trotted by on a horse.

Phoebe slapped both cheeks with her palms. "Oh, fiddlesticks!"

"Phoebe?"

"I forgot the horse!"

"The *horse*?"

"I rode it there last night. I've left the horse in Thaddeus's stables."

Douglas burst out laughing and pulled her close once more. "I'm sure we can sort it later."

"But it's my neighbor's horse."

"Then I'll have to sweet-talk your neighbor for you."

He threaded her hand through his arm as they made their way up the narrow streets of Beacon Hill, over the undulating cobbled sidewalks.

Phoebe stopped in front of a tall house with its own small garden.

"D'you like it?" she asked, raising one eyebrow to him and biting her lip.

"Aye, it's braw."

She grinned. "I'm assuming that's good. Only leased at the moment. But, well, you know."

The front door was open and at last he let her go from his side. He could smell bread baking.

"Mrs. Washington," she called. "I've brought a friend home for breakfast."

"That's fine, Miss Phoebe," a voice hollered from the kitchen. "I only just made some for me an' Simpson."

Mrs. Washington bustled through to the entrance hall and looked him up and down.

"Hadn't thought the friend would be a gentleman. Mighty early to come visiting, mister."

"Dr. McLennan has been attending the confinement of my sister-in-law. He arrived in Boston yesterday and hasn't slept since. I thought we could give him breakfast."

He followed Phoebe into the small but well-proportioned room and she urged him to sit at the circular table.

Mrs. Washington carried through two plates laden with eggs, bacon, Boston beans and bread. She set them down. "So, how's the folks in Back Bay?"

"All perfectly healthy," said Phoebe. "A girl and a boy."

"Twins," said Mrs. Washington. "Just like Mrs. Hale said. And where you staying, Dr. McLennan?"

"Mr. Van Bergen arranged a hotel for me."

Mrs. Washington looked at him skeptically. "If you don't mind me sayin', doctor, you look tuckered out. I'm gonna get the maid to fix up the bed in the guest room. If you been up all night, you gonna crash soon, Dr. McLennan, mark my words. And then you'll need to sleep before going back to your hotel."

Phoebe called after the retreating Mrs. Washington. "Oh, and Mrs. Washington. We need to sort out fetching next door's horse."

EPILOGUE

Despite Phoebe's fears that no one would come, people were gathering for the opening of the new hospital.

"Don't worry, folk will be there," Adeline had tried to reassure her an hour earlier.

Phoebe felt sure she'd forgotten something but couldn't think what it was. She'd decided the speeches should take place in the garden of a nearby church and fretted that maybe she should have found a place indoors, what with the cold October air. At least the food was under a pavilion, she'd seen to that. Mrs. Washington had been proud to take charge of the arrangements.

A huddle of Boston Brahmin arrived in full plumage: extended bustles, swirls of fringed fabric, multicolored feathers flapping from extravagant hats.

Phoebe hurried to welcome them. "Thank you so much for being here. We couldn't have built it without you."

It wasn't entirely true—Phoebe would have used every last cent of her inheritance if needed—but the society ladies smiled and clucked over their own generosity.

She looked up at the building and felt that warm sensation flood over her again. She'd done it: gotten a new women's hospital built, and was about to throw open its doors. She was confident that, with the staff she had recruited, it would be the best hospital on the Eastern Seaboard—as had been her ambition.

She felt a hand at her elbow: it was Dr. Haven, the President of the Board.

"The State Governor wants to talk to you," he said in a low voice.

Dr. Haven steered her over and the governor greeted her as an old friend. Phoebe stiffened: they were nothing more than acquaintances and he had been obstructive many times, but she knew success drew out politicians as surely as sunshine drew out flying ants.

There was a journalist from the *Boston Globe* and the Governor was eager to have his photograph taken. He stood between Phoebe and Dr. Haven, waiting for the flash of magnesium. Phoebe scrunched her lids afterwards, trying to remove the white dots that hovered even with her eyes closed.

She could do with Douglas's calming presence and stood on her toes to look for him, but he must have been collared by someone.

The sound of chatter grew louder as more people arrived.

Lex hurried over. "We've just got here. Quite a crowd!"

"Relieved to see you."

He gave her a quick hug. "It will all go smoothly. Are you making a speech?"

She whipped her head to him. "The Trustees didn't think that was suitable."

"Not suitable," Lex scoffed. "To have the woman who made all this happen say a few words?"

"It's fine. I'm really happier this way. I don't like talking in front of so many folks. Anyway, I begged Douglas to do it instead, as hospital director."

Lex snorted. "Douglas never struck me as someone to enjoy doing speeches, neither."

They were joined by Thaddeus, who made a slight bow.

"Alexander."

Phoebe wished there wasn't so much tension between her brothers these days. It seemed to be getting worse.

Thaddeus turned to her. "Phoebe, I want to say how proud I am of you today."

Phoebe blinked at him. "My. Thank you."

"Mother and Father would have been proud too. It's an enduring way to keep the family name alive."

"I very much hope so." She bit her lip to stop herself confessing that the family name was the least of her motivations.

Thaddeus spotted Mr. Cutler over her shoulder and hurried off.

Phoebe and Lex exchanged a glance. "Maybe he's softening," she said.

"Maybe."

At last, Douglas appeared beside her and leaned in to speak in her ear. "I think it's time to take our seats on the dais."

It took a while to weave their way through the guests. As Adeline tried to encourage people to sit, Lex had gone to stand at the back, next to Ginny and another woman. Each of the women was holding a baby and were swaying side to side to keep the infants pacified.

"Who's that?" Douglas asked.

"Where?"

"Standing next to Ginny."

"That's her younger sister. Marie-Louise," she said. "She's here from the Midwest."

Douglas nodded. "Doesn't look too happy to be here."

Phoebe looked more closely. It was true: although Mary Lou stood out from the crowd like her older sister, there was something about how she raised her chin, and how her eyes narrowed as she observed all that was taking place. "She's changed a lot since I last saw her. Really become a woman."

Douglas put out his hand to steady Phoebe as she went up the steps. They exchanged a look and a smile, and she didn't care who saw how happy they were.

Everyone was seated and Dr. Haven started the proceedings. First, he asked the Governor to speak, then one of their congressmen. Phoebe wondered if women would have given birth before these speeches were over.

"Dr. McLennan," said the president, once the congressman had sat. "I invite you to say a few words, as Director of the Van Bergen Women's Hospital."

Phoebe watched him rise and take his place at the lectern, as a light autumn breeze rippled his hair. Her chest rose with pride that he was being acknowledged in the role he had surely been born for. He took a sheet of paper from his jacket pocket. She knew what he was going to say, having heard him practice the day before, and again this morning.

His deep Scottish voice poured into her and warmed her from inside. Instead of listening to the words, she watched his movements as he changed weight from one leg to the other, clenched and released the lectern.

Her mind drifted to their time in Dundee. She had never told anyone in Boston about what had happened there. It felt like a secret protected by the distance of an ocean. They spoke of it sometimes, though, the two of them, in quiet times or late at night. Nearly losing their lives was not an experience to forget.

She had pondered many times why they had survived. Looking up at Douglas now, and at the brand-new hospital building behind him, she began to wonder if there was some higher purpose, if they had been saved for this meaningful work.

Her hands closed into fists. All the lives that had been lost were not meaningless. She could not believe she and Douglas were somehow more special than everyone else. Each and every life was precious.

But the truth was, they *had* been rescued from that freezing water. Douglas's bravery and strength had saved them both. She gave thanks daily and was determined that every day she would show her gratitude by trying to make the world a better place. That was what this hospital had become—the manifestation of her gratitude for Douglas's life and her own.

People applauded with the end of the speeches and the president led the way off the stage to the front of the building. The guests all followed.

The entrance to the hospital was wide, with double doors sheltered under a large porch. The top was an arch of sandstone with the name carved: THE VAN BERGEN WOMEN'S HOSPITAL. A red ribbon extended across the entrance, guarded by Adeline wielding scissors.

Dr. Haven put up his hand for silence.

"And now," he said in a voice loud enough to carry across the street, "I call upon Mrs. McLennan to cut the ribbon and be the first to enter."

Mrs. McLennan. She still felt a frisson of delight when addressed in that way and wondered if the thrill would ever lessen. Having almost lost each other, they had been determined to marry as quickly as possible, once Douglas returned to Boston. At the moment, Adeline still lived with them on Beacon Hill, but had started the search for somewhere closer to the hospital. One day, Phoebe hoped there would be the children Douglas said would complete their family.

Phoebe took the scissors and deftly sliced the ribbon. There was a cheer and laughter. She pushed the doors open, then paused to turn back, extending her hand to her husband, whose eyes shone with love, and she entered the new building with him by her side.

A LETTER FROM THE AUTHOR

Dear Reader,

Thank you so much for reading *An Ocean of Stars*. Phoebe Van Bergen was introduced in *Under A Gilded Sky,* and I hope you enjoyed finding out her story.

If you would like to join other readers in keeping in touch, here are two options. Sign up here to read about my new releases:

www.stormpublishing.co/imogen-martin

Or pop over to my website and sign up to my monthly newsletter. You'll get giveaways, advance news on books, quirky historical insights, and behind-the-scenes as an author:

https://imogenmartinauthor.com

Or do both! I look forward to meeting you.

Your email address will never be shared and you can unsubscribe at any time.

If you enjoyed this book and could spare a few moments to leave a review, that would be hugely appreciated. Even a short review can make all the difference in helping other readers discover my book for the first time, and every single review helps. Thank you so much.

I have been fascinated by the United States all my life. When I was a teenager, I took a Greyhound bus from San Francisco to New York. Over those three days of staring out of the window at the majestic mountains and endless flat plains, stories wound themselves into my head: tales of brooding, charismatic men captivated by independent women. My research trip to Boston was vital for this book. You'll find out more if you sign up to the newsletter.

Many of the incidents in *An Ocean of Stars* draw on events that really happened, and I write about them in my newsletter. Sadly, however, the symposium on women's health is fictional.

If you want to make contact, the best place is my Facebook page or the feedback page on my website. I love hearing from readers. I can also be found on other social media platforms. Come and say hello.

Thank you again for being part of this amazing journey with me, and I hope you'll stay in touch—I have so many more stories and ideas with which to entertain you.

Imogen

instagram.com/imogenmartinauthor

facebook.com/ImogenMartin.Author

bookbub.com/profile/imogen-martin

amazon.com/stores/Imogen-Martin/author/B0CCZ258S6

ACKNOWLEDGMENTS

I continue to be grateful every day to have an editor as wonderful as Vicky Blunden. She knows exactly what is needed to make a book shine. Thank you for your support and everything you do.

I feel so lucky to have Storm as my publisher. Led by Oliver Rhodes, the company truly puts the author at the heart of the business, while constantly innovating to find new readers. Thank you to Jade Craddock and Maddy Newquist for editorial input and to Elke Desanghere for marketing. A big thank you to Jo McGill and her legal-eagle eyes for my errors.

Getting the historical details right is important to me. For this book, I took a wonderful trip to Boston, doing a deep dive into its history, walking the streets and taking the train out to Manchester by the Sea.

My deepest thanks go to Karin Downs, who met me for lunch in Harvard. A warmer, kinder woman you couldn't hope to meet. She introduced me to Mount Auburn Cemetery, gave me valuable insights into the city, as well as women's health. I'm hoping no one was put off their food as we discussed various diseases that might afflict my female patients.

Thank you to the tour guide at Massachusetts State House who took the time to show me images of the building from its original construction—although I'm disappointed that the ornate halls and staircases were built after the date of this book, so I could only use the Doric Hall.

Thank you to Liz Weisblatt, who took me round Nichols House Museum, Beacon Hill, which is the model for Phoebe's home. I learned so much about interiors and what life was like on Beacon Hill in the nineteenth century.

I am very grateful to John McPeake, who has sailed for Northern Ireland, and smoothed out all the errors I'd made in the sailing race scene. He even drew me a diagram. Any remaining mistakes are my own.

My mother was increasingly frail as I was writing this book, and died before it was complete. Unlike Phoebe's relationship with her dying mother, I was close to Mum and am forever grateful for the love and support she gave me throughout my life. I miss her dearly.

This book is dedicated to David, the youngest of my three brothers. I've still got the biography of Andrew Carnegie he loaned me, that kicked off many of the ideas for my books. David is unfailingly kind, supportive, wise and optimistic. We had fun wandering through his home city of Edinburgh, choosing which houses my characters should live in. Thank you, David, for being at my side throughout my life.

And to all the Edinburgh Martins—memories of those festivals, birthdays, and Hogmanays will be with me forever, and I look forward to many more with you.